WHEN WILD FLOWERS BLOOM

ASHLEY MANLEY

WILDFLOWER
BOOKS
LLC

Identifiers:

ISBN: 979-8-9899682-4-4 (eBook) | 979-8-9899682-5-1 (paperback)

Book Cover by Elise Stamm, Blue Heron Graphic Design

First edition: September 2024 | Wildflower Books LLC

To the ones doing it scared, this is for you.

A note from Ashley

Dear Reader,

Out of all the amazing books in this world, thank you so much for choosing mine to read. I hope you fall in love with Birdie and her band of misfits as much as I did while writing about them.

Please know, Birdie's story is not an easy one; there are sensitive topics woven into these pages along with glimmers of hope and times of humor. I do write with explicit language and open door scenes of intimacy. If you are not a fan of spicier romance, you can easily skip chapters 26 and 34 and the end of chapter 36.

Thanks for being here.

xo, Ashley

One

I NEVER EXPECTED THE last year of my life to start this way, but here I am. Buck naked and so nervous I want to puke.

Dropping my head side to side, I attempt to stretch the anxiety-induced tension out of my neck. I'm screwed, and not in the way I want to be.

My reflection stares back at me from the sticky note-lined mirror—I can't do this.

A one-night stand? Whose bright idea was this anyway?

Oh yeah—mine.

Hands trembling, I pull my long blonde hair to one side, eyes pinging from the sticky notes back to my body. Tattoos, scars, muscles, fragility. Strong yet broken, the paradox of my life.

"Okay, Birthday Girl, let's repeat why we're doing this," I say to myself, plucking the note titled *Reasons to Follow Through* from the mirror. I point a finger into the air, like a sort of charismatic leader, feigning conviction as I read it. "Because this day is likely marking the beginning of the end. Because one last night will help strengthen us for battle. Because though we are royally fucked, we can still fuck." My face twists hearing my voice say the last statement. I've never once called sex *fucking*. I'm not some kind of barbarian.

But maybe that's who Tonight Me is. Someone who's vulgar about sex, especially the casual and unattached variety, drinks alcohol, and doesn't give a shit about rules. Or lists. Or consequences. Tonight Me doesn't have a care in the world. Tonight Me is just a girl who celebrates her birthday with a good lay.

The thought tightens my throat, and again I study each of the lists, my body, and overall ridiculous situation.

I'm doing this.

Taking my go-to blue dress off the hanger, I pull it over my head until it slips down my body. I rub my hands down my hips, accentuated by the navy fabric, and adjust the thin straps on my shoulders that show off the arms that have spent too many hours in the gym. Hours that have all prepared me for this very moment. This year.

I smooth fabric across my chest, convincing myself that instead of boyish, my flat chest makes me look athletic. Approachable. I scrunch my nose—*are chest size and approachability even connected?*

I grab a pair of underwear from a drawer before putting them back, deciding that no, Tonight Me is a commando kind of girl. I try not to let myself be disturbed by this.

I could call the whole thing off; it's not like anyone knows my plan. Instead, I give my reflection a small smile, find the sticky note that says, *42% of women meet one-night stand partners in bars* (a statistic I found on the internet) and let a fresh batch of determination take hold of me. Pulling another note from the mirror—the most important one—I skim it for the hundredth time and drop it into my purse.

With one last deep breath, I force myself out of my house, into my minivan, and down the five miles of road to the highest rated bar in town: Libby's Outpost.

I've driven by it daily for years but have never once stopped. Turns out, someone who doesn't drink alcohol or have any kind of social life has no actual reason to go into a bar.

In the parking lot I pause, staring at the neon beer signs with one last deep breath that propels me toward the entrance.

A little voice inside helps me fortify myself with positive affirmations as I open the door. *You can do this*, it says as I nudge through the crowd.

When I slide onto the stool, the voice tells me, *You look like a million bucks in that blue dress.*

I force myself to believe it. This dress will be the magical vessel that shows off my most desirable parts and hides everything I lack while guiding me to the man who will satisfy my needs for a night.

With a jolt of feigned confidence, I flip my blonde, windblown mess of a mane over my shoulder, my unspoken, *Look at me, boys.*

Of course, I have no idea if there are any acceptable *boys* in this place because it's so dark and crowded, but internet statistics from a random poll are on my side. This will work.

I hope.

The bartender, a pretty woman who looks to be late thirties with dark hair and red lips, wears a plain black tank top that shows off her lean build and olive skin. She drops a coaster in front of me with a smile. "Whatcha drinkin' tonight?" she asks.

Other than occasional glasses of red wine with dinner, everything I know about alcohol comes from my dad's dusty bottle of scotch and movies.

"Two fingers," I say, firm, taking the movie route.

She tilts her head to the side, eyebrows pinched. "Two fingers..." –she pauses and cocks her head—"of what?"

Shit.

"Umm...do you have anything organic?"

When I smile, she frowns. *Right.*

My eyes dart around the wall of bottles behind her for something that screams woman on a mission without artificial dyes. Something strong that will burn my throat and the doubts of everything I'm about to do.

Bingo!

"Triple sec," I say with confidence at the same time an explosion of clacks come from balls colliding at a pool table behind me, making me jump.

"You want two fingers...of triple sec?" Her red lips press in a tight line.

I nod and look down the length of the bar to see if I'm forgetting something. Garnishes. *Right.*

"And an olive. And orange wedge!" I point my finger at her like a gun with an unspoken *and don't you forget it.*

"Two fingers of triple sec…with an olive and orange wedge. Got it." She gives me one last lingering look before turning away and grabbing a bottle.

"That's an interesting order," a man says from a stool next to me.

I turn my head to look at him. His dark hair, long enough to tuck behind his ears, frames a handsome face with a square jaw. He has a beard, thick yet trimmed, and a toothpick bobbing on his lips. The corners of his dark brown eyes crinkle when they meet mine. He's wearing a black T-shirt—plain—that pulls across his shoulders and chest.

In a different life, I would touch him to see if looks this good are real, but lucky for him, I'm in this life and not wasting my time.

I flick him an uninterested smile as I pull a blue sticky note out of my purse and alternate between skimming it and scanning the crowd.

"I've never seen you in here before," he says, taking a pull of his beer.

I shift on my stool as the bartender sets my drink down.

"Aren't you observant."

Translation: *Leave me alone.*

He doesn't. "Do you live here?"

I look at him. "I'm from..." My gaze drops to the mountainous label on the beer in his hand, reminding me I'm someone else tonight. Someone free. "The Rockies." Aiming for mysterious, I miss with awkward. "I'm here visiting family."

Both he and the bartender are silent as their eyes ping from me to each other to the drink in front of me.

I pretend not to notice.

I down the liquid in my glass in a single gulp and suck the orange wedge like I've seen on TV. I eat the olive next, smacking my lips and following with a loud sigh that I hope masks my disgust. It's gross, like orange juice syrup mixed with salad dressing, but I don't show that. I smile. Tonight Me likes it.

The bartender's eyes widen like a cartoon character. "Okay," she drawls, dragging out the word with a sort of skepticism that I ignore. Smiling, she reaches across the bar. "I'm Libby, the owner, by the way." She lifts her chin toward the man next to me. "This is Bo."

Some of the tension dissolves from my shoulders, no doubt from the hard alcohol, as I shake her hand. "I'm..." I pause, panicking slightly. Tonight Me is someone who does everything different. Has a different name even. *Yes!* "Pam. Yes, Pam." I clear my throat. "Beesly. That's it. Pam Beesly." My only idea for a fake name is the secretary from *The Office,* and it makes me want to punch myself in the face.

"Well, *Pam Beesly,* nice to have you here...from the Rockies," she says.

She drops my hand, giving Bo another knowing look before walking away to help another customer.

"I guess you *are* from around here?" I ask, turning to look at Bo.

He has a casual, easy way about him. Maybe he's faking it like me, or maybe he's lucky enough to have the kind of life where happiness comes as easy as breathing. Either way, it suits him. Either way, Real Me feels like a gigantic bruise being pushed on when I notice.

"Guilty as charged," he says, lifting his bottle. "Why are you here alone if you're visiting family?"

"It's my birthday," I say with a grin.

His forearms drop to the bar, his chin pulls back, and a crease forms between his eyebrows. "Where is everyone else?"

I'm about twelve seconds into my lies and already confused.

"Sleeping." I clear my throat, glancing at the clock to see it's only seven o'clock. "We had an early party because of the time change between the Rockies—where I live—and here in North Carolina where I'm visiting family." Every word feels like trying to fit a round peg into a square hole. I realize that math makes absolutely zero sense, so I add, "We partied all day and drank alcohol, so now they are tired. I just needed a break. Alone." I pause, then, "To celebrate myself."

"Ah," he says, eyes narrowing slightly as he looks at me, removing the ridiculous toothpick balancing on his bottom lip. "Well, happy birthday, Pam Beesly," he says before taking another pull of his beer. "How do you plan on celebrating yourself?"

I smile. "With fine spirits and a one-night stand, of course."

Bo chokes on the drink in his mouth.

I laugh, waving a hand toward him. "Don't worry, you don't meet the criteria," I say, pressing the sticky note smoothly on the bar top.

His face is a mismatched landscape of amusement and curiosity as he looks down at it.

"What's this?" he asks, leaning toward me to read it better. When he's in my space, he smells like so many good fresh things—clean, crisp, evergreen. Winter in summer. A mountain breeze.

"My list," I say like it's obvious, leaning away slightly from him and his scent. "For finding the right candidate."

He rubs a hand across his bearded chin when he leans back. "So to recap," he starts, amusement spreading more with each slow spoken word. "You are here from the Rockies, alone for your birthday, are going to have a one-night stand, and made a list, on a sticky note, of qualifications?"

My spine straightens defiantly, as if my skeleton is offended by the way he says it. *Like I'm ridiculous.*

"Yes," I say defensively, glancing back at my list.

Another scan of the crowd. There are a few couples tangled up in dark corners, but plenty of men who seem unattached. It's a small town; Bo probably knows everyone here.

"You know," I say, turning to look at him. "You could help me."

"Help you?" The laugh that comes with the question is a deep, rumbly sound I feel in my own chest.

"Yes. You probably know everyone here!" I gesture to the people around the room. "And I have no clue where to start."

There's a playfulness in his eyes as he looks at the small blue piece of paper and back to me.

"Explain the list and then I'll help you. *Maybe*," he says, bringing the bottle back up to his smiling lips. The look on his face is cunning. Like this is a sort of game.

"Done," I say, happy to share my well-thought-out bullet points. "One, on a scale of one to ten, I want a seven—max. I'm sure that's the opposite of what some women want, but I'm looking for mediocre looks here. Attractive enough to hold my interest, but not so good-looking I feel like I'm staring at the sun. Eight and up?" I solemnly shake my head. "Hard no. I'll just end up thinking about the hotness later, and it negates the purpose. Tonight is it."

He stares. I continue.

"Two is straightforward. Single. No weird loopholes; they have to be unattached. Not because I'm looking for a future, but because I wouldn't do that."

He nods, something flashing in his eyes as his jaw tics. "Of course."

"Three, mid-level charming. Same as one. I don't want to cringe at the experience, but I can't think of the things he says later. Funny, not too funny. Attentive, not too attentive." I pause, a silent *got it?* and he nods again. "Four, he needs to live alone. I'm not doing some weird walk of shame by a mom sitting at a kitchen table reading her newspaper."

"I can see how that would be awkward," he says with a smirk.

"And five," I pause, considering what I've written. "Age. Between thirty and forty-five." I look at him. "I don't know, I'm thirty-seven today—would it be weird if he was thirty? Is it creepy of me to prey on the young?"

This time he laughs, and for the first time I notice his perfect white teeth. "Prey? Thirty is still a grown man, Pam Beesly."

I like the way my fake name sounds on his lips.

"How old are you?" I ask.

"Thirty-five," he says.

I shift in my stool. "So would that feel weird? I mean, you being younger than me, if I were to come up and suggest, you know..."

"I think *weird* is the last way it would feel."

Before I can even think about what he's implying, Libby grabs my empty glass.

"Another drink?" she asks with a smile.

When my mouth opens, it's Bo's voice I hear. "Libby, Pam Beesly here wants our help to find a one-night stand in this crowd."

Her eyes go saucer-sized as her smile morphs to a gaping O.

I square my shoulders and lift my chin—again—the only move I know that tells everyone to take me seriously. "I do. And I would like another drink. A beer...in a bottle...without rocks." I toss my hair over my shoulders and rest my forearms on the bar.

I know I'm doing terribly; I can tell by the way everything I say feels backward in my mouth and all the staring. When she puts a bottle of beer in front of me, I simply take a sip and try not to react to the weird, bready taste.

Libby looks at my list, eyebrows pinched, as I will the beer down my throat. "What's this?"

"Her list for finding the right man," Bo tells her before I can respond, a smile curling half his mouth.

I stay silent as she leans over the bar and twists her neck so she can read it. When she's done, she looks at me, nose scrunched. "Sounds like you're looking for a dud."

My chin jerks back in offense. "No!" My eyes flick to the list then back to her. "Not a dud, just someone…without risk. Easy."

She snorts, resting her forearms on the bar and cocking her head to the side. "A.K.A. A dud."

When I look at Bo, his eyebrows raise as he takes another sip from his bottle. Like he agrees with her. Which irritates me.

"Tha—"

"If this wasn't a one-night stand," Libby says, cutting me off, "what would you have on this list? Like if you were looking for something…not easy."

I hesitate. I've never once in my adult life let myself think of this. A sort of dream man who would make me swoon. Those dreams died long ago when I was a ten-year-old standing at a gravesite.

Still, I hear myself clear my throat and say, "Patient." As soon as the word is out, Libby stills mid-wipe of the rag and looks at me like she wasn't expecting it. "And adores his family. And accepting of people. Has a career he loves," I pause, thinking of my own parents. "He would make things people love maybe…" My voice trails off as I allow myself to get lost in a fictitious image that will never be real.

Libby's "Wow," makes me blink out of my fantasy land, reminding me I'm in a bar, not looking for a happily ever after. I'm here for an orgasm, not a wedding band. When I look at her, she has a look on her face. Like she knows something I don't. "Hear that, Bo?" She pegs him with the same look she was just giving me. "Sounds an awful lot like someone I know."

His chin dips, eyes narrow. When he says, "Libby," she waves a dismissive hand through the air but locks her eyes on mine.

"Like someone who builds houses?" she asks me.

"Um, I guess." I mirror her position, forearms on the bar. "But I'm not sure what that has to do with anything. I don't need a builder for what I'm about to do."

Bo shifts next to me. This time, when he says Libby's name, there's a stern tone that wasn't there before. Palms facing him, she rolls her eyes muttering, "Have it your way," with a shake of her head. Then she's gone, down the bar pouring a drink.

I turn to Bo, ignoring whatever it was that just happened. "So what do you think?"

"Tell me something you like," he says, ignoring my question.

"What does *that* have to do with anything?"

He shrugs. "Tell me something you like so I know who a good match would be."

"Fine." I pause, thinking of my favorite things. "Lists," I say, straightening my spine at the way his eyebrows pinch. "I like lists because they give me control in the chaos."

There's a seriousness to the way he looks at me that makes me feel exposed, so I quickly add, "And country music." Then I fully deflect with, "Tell me something *you* like."

"Sitting at this bar with you." It comes out of his mouth so easily I roll my eyes. I don't have time for his…whatever it is.

I point to my list. "Are you going to help me do this or not?"

"Have you ever had a one-night stand before?" he asks.

"Maybe…"

"Do you usually drink two fingers of triple sec?"

He's trying to shatter my lies, and it makes my blood boil. "Why does that matter?" I demand.

He stares at me as a George Strait song starts to play through the speakers. My plan—and heart—cracks with every familiar lyric. The normally comforting sound of his voice becomes a cruel mockery of my life.

My forehead drops to the bar, eyes screwed shut, and I hear myself groan, "I can't do this."

Bo's stillness lets me know he's uncomfortable, not that I blame him. Nobody comes to a bar to sit next to this kind of crazy, even I know that.

The silence that follows lasts years.

"Why don't I meet these sticky note criteria?" There's a playfulness in his rusty voice that I can hear even with my eyes closed.

Somehow, I lift my head off the bar, stitch myself back together, and look at him.

"All this"—I gesture from his head down the length of his torso—"is way more than a seven, my friend."

He laughs with a shake of his head and bobble of his toothpick, but even in the neon, I swear the peaks of his cheeks turn the slightest shade of pink. For the first time, I notice his dimples, visible despite the scruff of his beard.

I force another sip of my beer and swallow the gag before it comes out of my mouth.

"What about him?" he asks, pointing to a guy shooting pool.

I scoff. "Maybe a six, but that gold chain takes him down to a four."

He laughs softly, then repeats, "Him?" tilting his head across the bar to a man who smiles with all his too-big teeth when our eyes meet.

I fight to keep the laugh in my mouth. "You know, it's the beret and fully unbuttoned shirt that makes it hard to say if he's a one or a twelve."

He laughs, hair falling across his face, toothpick bobbling on his lips.

I don't know if Bo knows that I need this or if it's just who he is, but it's what we spend the next hour doing. I don't drink any more of my beer and he doesn't order another one as he asks me to rank every man in the bar.

Just like that, I'm a stranger in a foreign land, and he's a local on a barstool. When we get bored of my ranking, we talk about nothing important. I don't tell him about my family, about my fate, and I don't ask about his. Every answer I give him is more truth than lie, but never fully me. It's easy and fun, and for one night in my whole exhausting life it doesn't feel like a battle to the death.

I forget about my rules and plans, and I soak the ease of him in like a dry sponge absorbing water from a swimming pool—entirely and with excess.

"What's with the toothpick?" I ask as it rolls across his lips. Mesmerizing.

He pulls it out and looks at it, as if he's forgotten it was there. "Gives me something to do with my mouth." Then he gives this smile that starts out small before slowly curving into something big. Dangerous, even. Without pulling his eyes off mine, he snaps the toothpick in half and drops it into the mouth of the empty bottle in front of him.

Either his words or his smile or the unexpected snapping of wood heats my chest. My neck. Some place low in my belly.

I shift on my stool. "What would be on your list?" I ask, driving the conversation away from his unnerving mouth. "If you were in the same position as me, I mean."

He blows out a small breath, looking away from me and spinning the empty beer bottle in front of him. "I don't think what I need can fit on a sticky note."

"Why?"

He hesitates, still spinning the empty beer bottle in a way that's hypnotizing to watch. When I don't think he's going to answer, he says, "Because sometimes life is messy."

Then we're quiet. As much as I want to ask what he means by that, I know what it feels like to not want to talk about it too. What it's like to have a mess.

Finally, "I have to go," and I hate the words as soon as I say them. Maybe it's him or maybe it's because it's just not everything else, but I don't care. I don't want it to end. I want to be Pam Beesly at a bar with a man named Bo forever.

"I'll walk you out," he responds. And when he stands, I notice how tall he is, how much space he takes up, and how he can wear a pair of blue jeans like it's a high-paying job.

I say goodbye to Libby, who gives me a genuine smile and an easy, "Come see me again if you're ever in town." She says it like she means it—like maybe we could be real friends—and it makes my chest ache.

Outside, we're in the empty parking lot around the back of the building lit only by a streetlight. Muffled sounds of music come in waves from the front of the bar when the door randomly opens and closes.

Bo crosses his arms over his chest and leans on my minivan with a smirk, light flickering in his eyes like two slivers of the moon. "Nice ride."

I shake my head with a small laugh. "It's for work." Then I remember, "My dad's work, I mean."

I notice how alone we are as much as I notice my urge to touch the strands of hair that tumble across his forehead. To want his beard beneath my fingertips. Between them.

"When do you go back to the Rockies, Pam Beesly?" he asks.

"Tomorrow morning," I say, leaning against the minivan as a small smirk tugs at his lips.

"I can't let you go without telling you…" His pause has the power to make me stop breathing. "Nobody drinks triple sec straight."

I snort out a laugh. "That explains the taste."

I look him over one last time. From the lines and angles of his face in the night to the casual ease of his body leaning against my minivan. In a different life…in a different life.

My façade is already faltering, the Cinderella effect of the night starting to fade. I'm thinking of tomorrow's workday, what I'll have for breakfast, how the alcohol is damaging me, and what time I'll go to yoga to try to undo it all. My mind is loud, cluttered, and makes my eyes burn.

I lift my chin toward him, a million different things I want to say bouncing through me. I debate asking him if he wants to go back to my place, but Pam Beesly doesn't have a place here. This is the end, and I want to cry because it's *always* the goddamn end.

"So Bo—" I don't know what I'm going to say next, but it doesn't matter. He unfolds his arms, steps forward, and presses his palms against the minivan on either side of me. A capturing.

It's his pause.

My slight nod.

Then impact.

His mouth is on mine and my body goes limp while simultaneously being shocked to life by a jolt of electricity from the way it feels to have his skin touch mine.

As fast as his mouth touches me, it pulls away. And—*what the hell?* That's nowhere near enough.

Eyes flicking between mine, he must see that I want more, because a wicked grin spreads across his face as he—*slowly*—leans toward me.

When his lips find mine again—bliss.

His tongue, rubbing against my lips—melting me—retreats away when I open my mouth. He's teasing me. I can feel his smile when I too eagerly use my own to reach for his. I can't help it. I want him. *This.* Desperately. And he knows it. He pushes his body up against mine and he's already half-hard, sending a fresh shot of want blazing through me like a brushfire.

His mouth moves across my jaw and down my neck, tongue swirling against my bare skin. He grips my hips so tightly I might bruise. And yet, I don't care.

The way he feels and tastes is like everything else about him—a mountain breeze.

When he pulls away, I'm breathless. The smolder in his eyes matches how the inside of my entire body feels.

Compared to his quiet, my panting sounds like a hurricane.

Don't let him go, the little voice inside me whispers.

So I don't.

Just this once.

Instead of getting in the driver's seat, I match the heat in his gaze, pulling the handle to the back door. When it slides open, I wrap one hand around his neck, and we fall inside the back of the van together.

Two

His body, too big for the space.

My laugh.

His smile.

My legs.

His lap.

Hungry mouths.

Bitten-off noises.

Hands on my hips.

Fingers in his hair.

Bunched dress around my waist.

A touch between my thighs.

His breathy, "Are you sure about this Pam Beesly?"

My desperate, "I've never wanted anything more."

His belt.

The

single

condom

in

my

purse.

My cry when he fills me.

His smile against my skin.

My sadness when it ends.

My eyes fly open in the darkness of my bedroom as a new bout of pressure starts to build within me. The real-life minivan porn won't stop replaying in my mind and a very real part of me doesn't want it to.

In my limited experience, even in a minivan, it was the best sex of my life.

Fighting sleep all night, I crawl out of bed at four o'clock in the morning, resigned to the fact that this is how today is going to be: exhausting and exhausted.

A sleepless night and a distracted morning are my consequences for breaking my own damn rules. Ninety minutes of power yoga, a large omelet with pasture-raised eggs, and making lists for my day do nothing to stop the cruelty of feeling every way Bo touched me—I touched him—over and over again.

My plan of having sex with a stranger to help prepare me for the year ahead has completely backfired. I'm not prepared; I'm a train wreck.

Every single minute that has ticked by on the clock from then until now has left me a little angrier than the last for getting dealt such a shitty hand.

In a different life...I shake my head, not even letting myself go down that rabbit hole. *Again.*

Sam—a grouchy Vietnam veteran—is my Wednesday morning client. I usually show up with library books and breakfast from the local bakery for him, but today, nothing. I'm empty handed, and he notices, glaring at me like I killed a litter of puppies as I step into his living room.

I go through my usual list of chores—laundry, dishes, cleaning the floors—but I'm operating on autopilot. I fold his towels and feel Bo's rough hands. I do the dishes and feel his tongue on my skin. No matter how many times I shake my head, I can't shake *him.*

For once, I'm happy Sam repeats the same stories from Vietnam every week. Usually, I engage, but today it's just nods and hummed responses. The plus side of being so clearly distracted is that his normally grumpy personality is extremely easy to deal with. Every, *"Do you hear what I'm saying, Bonnie?"* I casually respond to with, *"Yep, and that's still not my name, Sam."*

The hours either drag on or fly by at warp speed. It's miserable.

Finally, at 3:55 P.M., I park in the gravel driveway of my afternoon appointment, and my exhale could fill a hot air balloon. I just want to get through this meeting, crawl into bed, and forget what I did and how vast the feeling of either wishing it didn't happen or could happen again is.

I lean toward the windshield of my minivan and study the small cabin that's tucked in the side of the hill. The summer flowers—yellows, pinks, reds, and purples—that explode on the bushes around the porch that's dotted with wind chimes and rocking chairs create the perfect balance of chaos and charm. It belongs in a fairytale more than rural North Carolina.

I double-check my reflection in the rearview mirror. Honey-colored hair in a bun, fitted white tank top with slouchy jeans, sandals, and a pair of dangly leather earrings. Somehow, my brown eyes look bright, not bloodshot from sleep deprivation like I'd expect. I look put together—the lie I'm selling the world today.

The appointment was scheduled just last week, but with the events of last night, my mind resembles applesauce. I barely remember a single detail about the woman I'm about to meet. I thumb through the file quickly to get my head on straight. Veda Monroe, seventy-nine years old, lives alone, has severe arthritis, help with daily chores requested by her grandson, Daniel Monroe. Skimming the rest, I close the file and shove it in my tote bag that's already overflowing with papers and binders. I've been running my senior companion business for years, and these first meetings are either welcomed with open arms or stopped by a brick wall.

Another deep breath and I'm out of my van, crossing the bright green yard, noting a silver sedan and cherry-red Jeep in the driveway, and climbing the steps of the large wraparound porch. The door swings open at the same time I raise my hand to knock.

There, with the same stunned eyes as mine, stands Bo.

Seconds or minutes or hours later, a woman—who I assume to be Veda Monroe—fills the doorway next to him. If the world wasn't spinning out of control, I would have noticed her mismatched beaded earrings, pink linen shirt, and white hair pinned in a braided bun. I would marvel about how she barely has a line on her seventy-nine-year-old face and be envious of the kind of beauty she has that the years don't dent.

I can't register any of that, at least not in a way that lets my mouth move. Instead, there's only staring. Me at Bo, Bo at me.

Silence stretches like saltwater taffy across the doorway, until Veda's voice hurtles me back to earth.

"You must be the babysitter," she says, tone knotting amusement with annoyance.

My mouth opens and closes so many times without saying anything that I feel like a fish.

"Birdie." My voice rivals that of a pubescent boy with strep throat when I finally speak. I force my trembling hand out. "Hawkins. Birdie Hawkins. Not a babysitter unless you have a baby." My laugh is a weak *ha ha ha*.

She eyes me with skepticism before reaching her own hand out. I don't look, but I can feel the way her fingers twist in one direction under her papery skin, no doubt from the arthritis.

"Veda," she says. "And this is my grandson, Daniel, but everyone calls him Bo." She drops her hand from mine and cuts her eyes to him.

Somehow we shake hands, Bo and me, and the familiar roughness of his skin is sandpaper against my own. While I'm completely dumbfounded, there's amusement that lifts his lips. Lips that also have a toothpick pinched between them. "Nice to meet you, *Birdie*," he says with an emphasis that wraps around my spine. When I try to pull my hand away, his grip tightens. "You look like someone I've met before." After all my efforts to stay alive in this life, this is where I've come to die.

"Does she?" Veda asks, eyeing me with a shrug. "Either way, come on in. Let's get this over with."

I yank my hand free of his and decide to never look at him ever again. This is a disaster.

Veda leads us into an eclectically cozy living space that smells like damp earth and lilac candle. The candle instantly makes me cringe, because carcinogens, but the damp earthy smell confuses my senses. It could be an indoor herb garden as much as a harboring of black mold. Wonderful or awful. Delicious or deadly.

Like Bo's presence.

They sit quietly on floral upholstered chairs next to each other while I nervously take several binders full of papers, a notebook, and assortments of pens out of my canvas tote bag and spread them across the coffee table.

"Your home is amazing," I manage to say through a mouth of cotton balls while sorting everything out into neat piles, relearning how to breathe.

Bookshelves covered with colorful pieces of pottery border the room like a hug with arms made of marbled blue pots and earthy red bowls. Even though they all look different, it's evident the artist is the same.

The response they give is a mystery because the words are such a mushy sound in my ears around the loudness of my heart pounding. If I say something back, it's a hum that means nothing.

Veda nods with narrowed eyes as she looks from me to the stacks in front of me. Bo just looks like he's on the brink of a laugh, and that might be worse than the initial staring.

"This looks like more than it is," I say, putting my shaky hands on my hips. "But I like to bring all the options of ways our days can look together so I can be most helpful to you. I have some sample schedules, lists of things I do at other clients' homes, etcetera."

Veda stares at me blankly, blinking.

"And I like to take notes on likes, dislikes, medications, any diet aversions. I'm happy to cook…" My voice trails off as I look through the open space of the combined living room and kitchen, spotting a box of vanilla wafer cookies on her kitchen table. Processed food, that means I'll be bringing groceries. *Noted.*

I take a breath and smile again, clapping my hands together as I lower myself to sit on the purple velvet couch across from them. "Where would you like to start?"

Then we sit in a room of silence, blinking and breathing, that goes on for an eternity. I don't look at Bo, but I know he's staring at me while Veda stares at the table of papers and sticky notes.

"How about I get us some tea?" she finally asks. "Then we can go through all of this."

I swallow my anxiety. There's no doubt the tea isn't organic based on the box of cookies. After the beer I had last night, and that disgusting triple sec, I can't just put whatever I want in my body. I might as well drink a glass of melted down metals straight!

Her eyes narrow in my pause, turning almost into two little slits that have me squirming. Her beautiful face is now carved to a near point—a hungry hawk assessing its prey.

"Tea sounds great." My voice is shaky. "I can get it, if you'd like."

She's already standing. "I'm slowing down, not dead!" she snaps with a glare before walking out of the room.

When I hear her banging around in the kitchen, the weight of being alone in this weird-smelling room with Bo nearly pulls me through the wide-planked wooden floor beneath my feet.

"Birdie, huh?" he asks, tongue in cheek.

I close my eyes and take a deep inhale before blowing it out, letting myself look at him. In this moment, I'm living two separate lives. One of them paradise, the other hell, and I don't know how to tell them apart. *He's here!* At the same time. *He's. Here.*

In the light of day, Bo looks the same as he did in the neon lights of last night but amplified. His eyes that were dark last night are now brown with flecks of gold, one with a freckle beneath. His hair and beard are longer than I thought—almost like they need a trim—but somehow, they suit him. While his T-shirt clings to his chest for dear life, much like I did last night, the arms I had considered toned are now clearly muscular. Skin covered cords reaching down to his hands. Hands with knuckles which I now see are covered in faded pink and white scars.

"Please, Bo." My plea is barely above a whisper. "Don't."

His jaw tenses, toothpick still on his lips, as he stares at me in a way that strips me bare. As if he knows I have the kind of life where I need to pretend to be someone else but can't talk about it.

Then Veda's back, saving me with a glass of iced tea I don't want to drink. When it's in my hands, I look around the table I've covered with papers for space to set the glass, but it doesn't exist. I settle on just holding it while repeatedly crossing and uncrossing my legs.

It's like when Bo opened the front door a thick poisonous fog rolled out that's paralyzed my ability to speak or think in complete sentences.

We are sitting around the coffee table covered in all my papers and lists and plans, and for the life of me, I've got no words.

"Well, Bo this is your big idea, why don't you ask what you want to ask," Veda huffs, cradling a glass of iced tea that rattles softly as her hand trembles and her twisted fingers work to maintain a grip on it.

He looks at her. "Gran, you act like I'm putting you in prison." His eyes flick to me. "I can't be here as much as I want—I try to stop by in the evenings after work, and I see her on the weekends, but I know there's a lot to do around here and she needs help"—his eyes cut back to her—"even if she won't admit it."

She huffs again, and he shakes his head before looking back at me.

"Why don't you tell us about yourself," he says from his relaxed posture on the chair across from me. He's the epitome of cool, wearing scuffed up work boots, faded jeans, and a plain T-shirt.

His legs spread wide as he sits back and one arm drapes over the back of the chair.

He's not touching me, not even close, but he might as well be sitting on my lap and tying a plastic bag around my head with how suffocating he is.

I sit up straight, clear my throat, and feign composure. "Well, I started Forever Fun seven years ago after nearly eight years working for the park district as the senior events coordinator. I loved my job but wanted more one-on-one time with the people I was working with. I have regular clients I visit, and sometimes we go on group day trips." I hand them each a stapled packet of papers from the table without making eye contact. "Here's a list of references if you'd like to call any of them, and some sample schedules I have with my other clients. I know you requested three days a week—another client I had just relocated, so I have Mondays, Tuesdays, and Thursdays available." I pause, swallowing through the dryness of my throat, then continue. "I'm prompt, hardworking, and fun to be around. I have no problem helping with housework or playing games. I like to cook, and use all organic ingredients, and I'm happy to clean—with nontoxic products of course." The only person who laughs is me. "I drive a minivan." My voice cracks when Bo poorly covers a smile that shows his dimples. "...for ease of entry." Heat crawls up my neck as soon as the words leave my mouth. "So I can take you on errands or any kinds of doctor's appointments as needed. And I'm first-aid and CPR certified." After stumbling through my resume, I smile.

The only sound is Bo flipping through the papers too fast to be reading anything.

"Bah!" Veda huffs. "Bo, I don't need this." There's desperation in her voice as she looks at him, tossing her papers on the other stacks. "I can make my own junk food, run my own errands, and clean with my own toxic chemicals!" Her palms and twisted fingers raise in outrage.

Tension knits Bo's forehead when he looks at her, turmoil in his eyes. "Gran, please." Then to me, "But she has a point. I read all that on your website before I submitted the application. Maybe not about the minivan…" He tilts his head slightly, lips twitching. "But who are *you*? If I'm trusting someone to come here three days a week and deal with this battle-ax, I need more than that. I mean, you could be Pam Beesly from the Rockies for all I know." He leans forward in his seat and props his elbows on his knees, a smile curling his lips.

My cheeks heat—again—at the reference. I clear my throat. "Of course. Right. Well, what would you like to know?"

"Why aren't you drinking the tea?" Veda shouts before Bo can ask anything.

Ugh. I forgot about the tea. I cringe, eyeing the glass of amber-colored toxins with a wedge of lemon on the rim in my hands. I have to drink it. It won't be the end of the world. I'll take some activated charcoal when I get home to purge the poison from my body, and it doesn't have to be a big deal. My body will never know the difference. At least, this is what I tell myself as I take the first sip.

I hate how good it is.

They watch me, and before I know it, I drink it all.

"Delicious," I say, forcing a toothy smile.

Bo snorts out a laugh before asking, "What do you do in your free time?"

I open my mouth to answer but Veda cuts in again. "Are you married?"

What does that have to do with anything?

"No..."

"Kids?" she demands.

"No." My eyes narrow.

"How old are you?"

I scoff. "Thirty-seven, but I don't see why—"

"Hobbies?" she barks.

"I go to the gym and—"

"What do you do for fun?"

"I—"

This time it's Bo interrupting with, "Are you dating anyone?"

What?

"Are *you* dating anyone?" I shoot back.

I don't know what they want to accomplish with their interrogation, but I'm close to snapping from the irrelevance of it all, the weird smell, and how good Bo looks in the light of day.

Finally, he's quiet, leaning back into the chair, taking up too much space and grating on my last nerve.

"Ha!" Veda bursts out. "Bo's married," she says like it's funny, sliding her gaze from me to him.

My jaw drops along with my stomach and the empty glass that I've been holding in my hands.

What?

The glass doesn't break, but the ice spills, and I fumble to pick it up from the floor. Every cube shoots from my trembling fingers like a frozen missile as I try to grab them.

Married. Married? Married!

I hear Bo say, "Gran, we're here to talk about Birdie, not me."

When I work up the nerve to look at him, it's with pure hatred, my own eyes turning into slits. *Married.* I want to puke or lie down or puke *and* lie down.

In yet another long stretchy silence, a switch flips. I don't care. I can't. It was never going anywhere, and the fact that he has no moral compass just makes it easier for me to accept.

I refuse to let this be the thing that stops me. I'm here for Veda, not him. He's an inconvenience; she's my priority. I will get through this meeting then let myself freak the hell out about my potential role in destroying a marriage later.

"Congratulations, Bo, that's great," I say, voice even. When I turn to Veda, lost confidence found, I square my shoulders. "Veda, why don't you tell me what you're looking for. I'm happy to do whatever you need. Your *married* grandson here might have set this up, but I'm here for *you*. That's my whole purpose, really. As I'm sure you've gathered, my personal life isn't very exciting." I give a weightless self-deprecating laugh. "But I love what I do, and I'd like to think the people I work with enjoy having me around."

Her sharpened features soften slightly, and she waves her hand as if erasing my words. "What are the tattoos on your chest?"

My throat pinches. I glance down and see my shirt has shifted and green tendrils of ink are peeking out of the neckline. I tug at the straps before looking at her.

"Wildflowers," I say.

"Why?"

"Because I like them."

"Do they cover your whole chest?"

"Yes."

Her eyes drop to my chest again before returning to my face. She notices.

"Why?"

I swallow hard but don't look away from her and definitely do not look at Bo, who is still as a statue on his chair. Last night I managed to keep his hands distracted in other ways—he never once touched my chest. But now, in this shirt and this proximity, there might as well be a spotlight shining on me.

"Because even ugly things can be beautiful."

Then, stretchy silence.

Finally, she nods.

"Fine."

"Fine?" Bo asks, seemingly stunned as he turns to look at her, taking the stupid toothpick out of his mouth.

"You heard me, Bo, don't make me repeat myself," Veda says sharply, glaring at him.

I stifle a laugh. Despite her age, adorable home, and declining use of her hands, the woman keeps everyone on their toes with the way her mood switches directions like a boomerang.

She turns to me. "I'll see you tomorrow. I eat breakfast at eight if you want to join."

"Sounds great," I respond, relieved, stacking up the papers that nobody cared to look at.

"And Birdie?" Veda says. "No more of this." She gestures at all my unappreciated materials on the table. "The other old farts might like that, but not me. Just show up in clothes you don't mind getting dirty."

I nod and pack up my things in silence. I don't look at Bo, not as he intensely stares at me or when Veda sends him to get something for her from one of the shelves. I only hurry to get out of there as fast as possible.

After a quick and cheery, "Bye, Veda, see you in the morning!" I'm out the door, taking my first full breath and scrambling to my minivan.

In the driver's seat, the key is too big for the ignition. Like something in the weird-smelling house made it swell to the point of uselessness. I'm stabbing at the side of the steering wheel mani-acally and to no avail.

I hear the front door open and close, the deep, "Birdie wait!" but I just keep stabbing my key and not going anywhere.

Then Bo is at the driver's window pressing palms on either side of it looking at me with an unreadable expression.

"It's not what you think," he says, key finally clicking into place.

The engine starts at the same time my head turns to face him.

"You have no idea what I think!" I snap, shifting the gear into reverse.

He doesn't move from his position. "You lied about your name. Where you lived!" he argues.

The laugh that bubbles out of my mouth is a frozen sound devoid of humor.

"I'm not even going to explain how that compares to what you *did*."

He opens his mouth like he's going to say something, but when our gazes clash he stops.

"I'll make it easy for you. Bo, are you married?" I ask, calm.

He pushes off from the door and rubs a hand down the side of his face. "Yes, but—"

I cut him off. "Did you fuck me in the back of this van last night?" I demand, stunned at how effortlessly the question rolls off my tongue.

His eyes widen.

"Birdie, it's not wha—"

I cut him off with a glare. "It's exactly what I think, Bo."

I back up slowly, throw it in drive, and leave him standing in the middle of the driveway.

Three

THE MOUNTAINS OF NORTH Carolina are a dream in June. With the windows down as I drive, the colors of twilight seem everlasting on the horizon. I imagine every word spoken today blowing out to live the rest of their lives in the velvety green hills and valleys around me.

I grew up in the next town over, Rocky Ridge, but now Laurel Hills is home. It's small, with a little downtown and a handful of restaurants and shops, but no matter where you stand—mountains. Less than an hour to the busy city of Asheville, it feels like another world.

I park outside of my small white house on the edge of town and let out a long full breath that holds the weight of my disastrous day.

On the steps of my porch sits Huck—an eight-year-old foster kid who lives next door with a couple I've always just known as Miss Alice and Mr. Steve. They've had foster kids rotating in and out for the years I've lived here, but Huck is the first one that I've gotten close to. Since the day he moved in nine months ago, we've been friends.

"Hey, Huck," I say as I sit next to him.

"Hey, Birdie," he says, a little too loudly.

"How was your day?"

"How was your day?" he parrots.

Right.

I smile. "What I meant to say was, I wonder how Huck's day was."

He looks at me. "Huck had a good day. I made this robot out of Legos." He holds up a colorful blocky creation. "And sometimes a female praying mantis will eat her mate."

I widen my eyes dramatically. "Well, it sounds like a praying mantis can have a day worse than I had."

"Birdie had a bad day." He frowns.

"Birdie had a bad day," I say with an exhale, looking at the bubblegum sky.

A bark followed by a whimper and the excited tapping of claws comes from the other side of the door behind us.

"George Strait is barking," Huck says.

"I wonder if Huck would like to walk George Strait with me." I tilt my head toward the door with a smile.

"Huck would," he says without making eye contact.

When I open the door, the goldendoodle pounces out of the house and licks Huck on the face. He lets out a rare, loud laugh. It would sound awkward and out of place coming from any other kid, but with Huck it's liquid gold.

It's our near-nightly routine. Me coming home, Huck waiting for me, and the walk that always follows.

With the dog on a leash, we fall into step together on the sidewalk, Huck careful to avoid every crack.

When he and I walk the dog, sometimes we talk, sometimes we don't—he decides. I like the company; he doesn't always want the conversation.

"Huck wonders why George Strait is named that," he says after we walk quietly for a few minutes.

"George Strait was my mom's favorite singer," I reply. Like they always do, the words teleport me to a time where "I Just Want to Dance with You" plays on a CD in the living room, and my dad twirls my mom around for no reason other than she loves it.

The dog barks at a squirrel and pops the memory.

"Huck wonders why Birdie had a bad day." He looks up at me as we stop at some trees where George Strait sniffs and marks his territory.

"Hmm," I say, thinking of how Veda and Bo sent bulldozers barreling over my life in the last twenty-four hours. I have no idea how to explain any of that to a kid. "I had a bad day because some people don't understand me."

"Some people don't understand me too."

I look down at him and try to remember who I was at eight. I wasn't who I am now, that's for damn sure. I was an ordinary kid who had a mom who wore floral wrap dresses and spun around the kitchen to country music while she baked cookies. I didn't know about troubles or what it meant to be misunderstood. Now, at thirty-seven, my life is so different—*I'm* so different—and I can't imagine grappling with these same feelings at his age.

His tiny shoulders carry a heavy weight, one I desperately wish I could lift for him.

I reach my hand out to him. "At least we have each other."

He eyes my hand, like he isn't sure if he's going to take it—but today he does. "And George Strait."

"And George Strait."

"The praying mantis can turn its head 180 degrees," he says, jumping over another crack.

"That's impressive. I wonder what else Huck can tell me about them."

"Some praying mantises can eat hummingbirds."

My eyes widen as I look down at him. "Why on earth would they do that?"

"Why on earth would they do that?" he repeats as we stop at a small field in the neighborhood, taking the dog off the leash to throw a ball to him.

I let out a breath, frustrated with myself for being so distracted I can't speak right. Smiling, I try again. "I wonder why a praying mantis would eat a poor little hummingbird."

He laughs. "Because they're hungry, Birdie."

I throw a ball the dog chases. "I guess you're right, but that's such a sad thought. I wonder what else you know about them."

And for the rest of the walk, he tells me more than I want to know about the insect. For those few minutes, despite the unusual topic of conversation, we have each other.

Lying in bed, I fight sleep. Again.

Trying to name the mix of emotions that sit on my chest is like trying to pluck a single grain of sand out of a mud puddle.

Furious that Bo lied to me.

Annoyed by how him opening the door had the power it did.

Devastated that even if the first two things weren't true, my life wouldn't allow for anything different. Time wouldn't allow for anything different.

Nauseous over how much his touch still lives on my skin like a phantom limb.

Humiliated about, well, everything.

I suck my cheeks in as I stare at the dark ceiling. *Tomorrow will be better.*

I grab my phone off my nightstand, typing *Daniel "Bo" Monroe* into the search bar. I need to see his wife. Just a picture so I can visualize the woman whose marriage I just tainted, whether she knows it or not. For what? So I can feel even worse? I don't even know the answer to that.

The top result is for a cabin building business, Monroe Cabins. I click on the link, ending up on a website that features a picture of him in a hard hat standing next to a cabin. He's a builder. I squeeze my eyes shut, thinking of Libby's question. *Like someone who builds houses?* It's almost as if she wanted this to happen. Even if he was married? What woman would do that?

I shove the thoughts away, clicking one of the icons that links to a social media page. All professional photos of finished and in-progress cabins, no hint at his personal life or wife.

I click to make one larger, examining the details. The mountains are filled with cabins, but his are unique in that they also look modern. Like you could walk in and see animal heads mounted on the walls as much as abstract art. My thumb scrolls across the pictures, the wood of the logs combine with industrial metal finishes to create a sort of architectural art.

Swiping to the next one, I clumsily hit the heart icon in the corner. I flinch with an audible, "No!" as I drop the phone like a hot potato. If he runs this account, he'll see my name. He'll know I was looking.

Before my phone makes it to the nightstand, it vibrates with a text.

Unknown number: *A little bird told me you see something you like.*

Shit.

Me: *It was an accident. How did you get this number?*

Bo: *You accidentally ended up on my business page and liked a photo from 8 months ago at 9:30 at night?*

My body is so hot I feel like a hog on a spit over a fire. I don't respond. I can't. How the hell can I defend myself?

Three dots appear and disappear before finally:

Bo: *Gran gave me your number so you could reach me if you have any questions.*

No.

Me: *I don't.*

Minutes pass in a silence that's only broken up by the sound of the ceiling fan spinning above me.

Bo: *That house you liked is one of my favorites—I could show you sometime.*

The emotion that's been stewing isn't muddled at all, it's a crystal-clear vibration of rage.

Me: *You should probably show your wife.*

I turn off my phone, put it on my nightstand, and let Bo steal another night of my sleep without permission.

Four

VEDA'S KITCHEN TABLE HAS a chipped coat of red paint on it and a lilac candle burning in the middle. I sit across from her quietly as she eats a bagel, watching me watch her. Bite, chew, swallow, repeat. Her fingers are tangled as she works to pick up the smaller final pieces, but the firm expression on her face doesn't falter. Like the efforts of her body are wholly separate from her emotions.

Finally, when it feels like we might be slipping into a staring contest, I speak.

"Listen, Veda, yesterday was...yesterday." I shake my head and laugh under my breath. "I really can be helpful with whatever you need me to do while I'm here. Is there anything you'd like for me to take care of to make things easier for you? I know that arthritis can be a bear sometimes, I've worked with several people that have dealt with it." My eyes drift from her to the candle. My urge to blow it out becoming so powerful it's like a second person living beneath my skin.

She studies me as she takes a sip of her orange juice then dabs her mouth with a napkin.

"Tell me about what happened." She nods toward my chest.

I'm wearing a loose-fitting T-shirt and cut-off jean shorts today, but it's clear she knows what she saw.

It's not something I'd usually discuss with a client so early on, yet something tells me if Veda and I are going to have any kind of chance at getting along, I must do this.

I fight the impulse to look away from her. "I had a prophylactic bilateral mastectomy when I was twenty-five."

"English, please," she says curtly.

I snort a laugh. "I preventatively had my breasts removed."

Her slight nod signals me to go on.

"My grandmother, Birdie Rose, died when she was thirty-seven from breast cancer. My mother, also Birdie Rose, died from the same cancer also when she was thirty-seven. When I was eighteen, I took the money I was given for my high school graduation and paid to have genetic testing done. I'm positive for the BRCA1 genetic mutation." I swallow hard, letting a long silence hang that is synonymous with this house before the rest of the words take form in my mouth. "There's roughly a 65 percent chance I will get breast cancer—so"—I shrug—"I got rid of them."

Veda leans back in her chair as she looks at me.

"All the women are named Birdie Rose?" she asks.

"I guess they were hoping it would finally stick." It's morbid, but I laugh.

"Your ovaries?"

"Hmm," I hum, slightly surprised she knows to ask. "I considered having them removed—I'm at a higher risk for ovarian cancer, among a litany of others, and there's a 50 percent chance I'll pass the gene on to any child, so I won't have kids—but the side effects of the surgery can be severe for someone my age. Maybe someday, but for now, I'm cautious."

She nods.

Of all the topics of my condition, my decision not to have children is the most difficult for me to talk about. My breasts are gone, that's fine, but babies... It was painful in my twenties to imagine, but at thirty, the devastation reached a fever pitch that I wasn't sure I'd survive.

"Why didn't you get implants? Seems to be what most people do, especially at your age," she asks before taking a sip of coffee, her bent fingers trembling around the mug.

I pick at a fleck of paint on the table. "They do, but after reading about them I didn't want the risks that they come with. I'll never have a normal life—I know that—and I figured whether I had boobs or not didn't make a difference to the outcome."

Her eyes narrow. "What makes you say that?"

"You're asking a lot of questions for someone I don't know much about," I say, propping my elbows on the table and giving her a light smile.

"Well, if it turns out you're as enjoyable to be around as you say you are, maybe I'll share more." Her lips lift slightly before she takes another shaky sip of her coffee.

I clear my throat. "Fine." This time I don't look at her. I stare at the warm morning light that dapples through the kitchen window and dances across the wood floor. "I watched my dad carry his grief right along with me when I lost my mom. I decided then, in those dark days of standing and crying at her grave then watching him cry much longer than that, I never wanted to cause that. To ultimately hurt someone in a way that's bottomless." The steady feeling of my heartbeat brings me back to my body, and I blink through the burn in my eyes. I force a smile then add, "And now that I'm thirty-seven"—I blow out a breath—"who knows how much time there is, if family history is any indication..." My voice trails off with all the grim words of my fate. "Anyway, my focus is staying healthy—alive—without the added worry of ruining someone else."

"Is your dad still around?" she asks, unreadable expression on her face.

The mention of my dad makes me smile. "He is. He lives in Rocky Ridge."

She sets her mug down. The coldness on her face melts away like an icicle in the sun. With her hair pinned back in a tight bun that showcases colorful earrings dangling from her ears and her cream-colored linen overalls and bright blue shirt, she looks...nice. Beautifully nice. There are lines on her face, but they are soft in a way that suit her. Define her almost.

"You don't like the candle," she says, making me realize I've been looking at the purple toxic wax in a jar. Again. Probably frowning.

I shift uncomfortably in my seat, not wanting to offend her. "It's not that. I'm just very...conscientious of what's in my environment. I like how it smells, it's just the ingredients..." *Could kill me.* I don't say it, but she must know, because in an instant *puff!* she blows it out.

It might be the single nicest thing a near-stranger has ever done for me in my life, and for the second time today, I blink back tears that I rarely let myself cry.

When she slides her chair away from the table she smiles again. "I want to show you something."

In the middle of Veda's sunroom, everything falls into place. Racks of pottery in various stages of completion line shelves on one of the walls. Buckets and canisters of glazes labeled with a Crayola-like palette fill a rack along with hand tools. In the middle of the room is a large table next to a potter's wheel and stool.

The wet, earthy smell is at its most powerful as we stand in the warmth of the sunbathed room.

"You're a potter," I say, circling in place to take in all the details.

"I'm a potter," she replies. "Or, was." She holds up her hands to showcase her crooked arthritic fingers and gives a regretful smile. "The body doesn't always agree with the mind. I still dabble on my good days, but stubborn fingers make for reluctant clay."

"Hmm," I hum softly. Agreeing and aching for her all at once. "You've made beautiful things."

"And I wouldn't change a thing knowing I can't anymore." She raises her eyebrows at me, like that's supposed to mean something.

Like everything else in the eclectic cabin, the room just feels like *home*. There are mismatched curtains framing windows and colorful blankets draped over chairs. Every detail looks handmade, but not in a half-assed kind of way like a mom who got drunk while scrolling the internet would do. Each item screams careful skill and thoughtful dedication. It's amazingly juxtaposed.

"Bo built this house and surprised me with this space—designed it all on his own so I'd have somewhere to work with lots of light." She studies me as I look around.

"He's talented," I say flatly.

"You don't like him," she replies without heat.

"Something like that."

She gives a small laugh. "His dad, my son, died in a car crash when Bo was six. His mom, too young and free to be a mother alone, left him on my doorstep. It's been us ever since."

"I'm sorry to hear that." I let my fingers gently trace circles on the metal top of the potter's wheel.

She sighs. "Well, you know as well as we do about tragedy and how we manage after. Nobody knows what the fuck they're doing."

Her severe *fuck* makes me pause.

She laughs.

"Do you have a better way of saying it?" Her beaded earrings swing as she moves, and despite the sadness of what she's just told me, she smiles.

Then we're quiet as we stand in the middle of her studio sun-room and it's as if silence is an important part of our conversation. Like when I'm with Huck, we talk even when we don't.

"I met Bo before yesterday. I didn't know he was married." The confession tumbles out of my mouth, clunky and awkward. "Why did you tell me?"

"I'm not blind," she says, raising her eyebrows. "I know my grandson is handsome, I just don't know if his good looks are enough to make a woman go mute on my front porch." She drops her chin until she's looking at me from the top of her eyes.

I busy myself by studying a canister of glaze.

"I told you because I wanted to see how you'd react." My eyes widen and meet hers. I don't need to know her long to not be the least bit surprised at the slight smirk on her lips. If she wasn't seventy-nine and a client, I might consider her a complete bitch. Might even say it. She stares at me, smug, like she knows what I'm thinking before she continues. "Either way, yes, he's married. Mandy. She's a lot like his mother was..." Her voice trails off, as if there's more to the story. When she doesn't go on, I don't press her. Regardless of how many unanswered questions I have, it just doesn't matter.

I am the same age as my mother was when she died and her mother before—my fate is sealed. Men, married or otherwise, have no place in my life.

I decided long ago I would never get married, never have kids, but now that I'm racing a clock, any sort of relationship, no matter how casual, is just as cruel for everyone involved.

I clear my throat, put the glaze back on the shelf, and look at her. "So what should we do today? We didn't get very far on that yesterday."

Her smile deepens the soft lines on her face as she stiffly wiggles her fingers and her blue eyes twinkle. "You have two good hands, Birdie," she starts. "Today I'm going to teach you to use them."

Five

There's still clay under my fingernails when I drive up my dad's driveway with George Strait whining excitedly from the passenger seat. He knows a steak bone is in his near future the minute he sees the familiar face and overzealous wave with a glove-covered hand.

I barely have my door open when the dog bounces over my lap, sprints across the yard, and pounces on my dad with an obnoxious bark.

When I'm out of the van, walking across the yard, it's the familiar scene of home: the house I grew up in, the shop I did homework in, the man who helped me do it all.

"Hey, Little Bird," he says as I lean into his hug, inhaling his token scent of sawdust and soap. When I pull away, the smell of smoke from the preheating charcoal grill on the porch fills the air.

"Hi, Dad."

He squeezes my shoulder when I look at him with a smile. At sixty-three, my dad's a handsome man. Distinguished. A full head of hair in various shades of grey. Soft-spoken and laidback with a welcoming sort of presence. I remember as a kid most of my friends worried about the way their parents would react when they got in trouble, but I could never relate. My dad always just handled things in stride, his voice never elevating, even when he was furious.

"Come see what I'm working on," he says, holding open his shop door for me, easy smile on his face.

My eyes immediately go to the familiar Little Bird Furniture sign that hangs on the wall. What started as a hobby when I was a kid morphed into a full-time profession after my mom died. Now, Greg Hawkins's tables are some of the most sought after in the southeast.

In the middle of his worktable lays a large, asymmetrical cross-section slab of wood. The edges are rough with pieces of bark clinging to it, but the rings are clear and the coloring a deep shade of brown. There are holes and indentions along the surface, making it almost look like a huge puzzle piece made of wood. Then I notice cracks—big ones. The slab is broken.

My eyebrows lift. "A busted cookie slab, Dad? I've seen you make something more impressive than this," I tease.

He laughs, blowing the dust off an empty mason jar and pouring himself his after-work glass of scotch.

"I was so excited for this one. You can see why—look how big it is. And the coloring?" He whistles in admiration. "It's walnut. Got delivered earlier this week. When I unwrapped it"—he takes a sip of his drink and lets out a sigh—"cracked into three pieces." He shakes his head.

I drag my hand across the surface of it, the familiar roughness of the wood coarse beneath my clay-covered fingers. "What are you going to do with it now?"

"That's the exciting part," he says, looking down at the same broken piece of wood as me. "In Japan, they do something with pottery called *kintsugi*." He pauses, his way of letting me tell him if I know what he's talking about, but I stay silent, my way of saying I don't.

Another sip of scotch and he continues. "Kintsugi is the art of repairing broken pottery. The pieces are glued together in a special way, often with gold, that showcases the cracks and breaks instead of hiding them."

"The broken becomes art," I say.

"The broken becomes art," he says.

There's a comfortable silence as we look at it, imagining our own version of what that might look like.

"You putting this thing back together with gold, old man?" I ask with a grin.

He laughs. "Hardly! I'm thinking a deep turquoise epoxy with gold leaf mixed in for the cracks and a dark stain on the wood."

"Not concrete?" I tease.

He shudders. "Don't remind me."

A couple years ago, my dad built a custom countertop, but instead of his usual epoxy to fill in the cracks, the man wanted concrete. He fought with sanding, rebar, and the sheer weight of it for months, vowing never again once it was done.

I look at the cracked slab. "It'll be great, Dad."

He grins, draping his arm around my shoulder as we leave the workshop and walk across the yard. "What's new with you, Little Bird?"

I sigh, knowing there's not enough scotch in the bottle for the long version, the true one. Instead, I go with, "I have a new client—a potter. She taught me to make a bowl today."

He tucks his chin in surprise. "*You*?"

I laugh at his tone. Me doing anything creative is a shock; it's not how my brain works.

"Yes, *me*. You aren't the only one who can make things in this family. As soon as we fire it you can put it on display and tell people your seven-year-old daughter made it."

"Tell me about it," he says.

Then I do.

I tell him about Veda teaching me to wedge the clay. *This gets the air bubbles out,* she told me as I repeated a motion she compared to kneading dough. Then I formed it into a ball and pushed my thumb into the pliable, gritty center. *Now pinch,* she'd said. I did, placing my thumb in the center and the rest of my fingers on the outer surface. Gentle pinch, slight pull, slight rotation, repeat. Over and over until some kind of hybrid bowl-mug was sitting in my palm.

You're a natural, she said with a smile.

It looks like a child made it! I laughed, glancing up at the woman that I couldn't quite figure out.

Well, children make things without fear—that's a compliment.

On my dad's front porch in rocking chairs, country music floats through the screen door while George Strait chomps happily on a bone.

"Little Bird, your momma's eyes are distracted tonight," my dad says, looking at me as we rock quietly.

He always calls them that. The eyes I always think look like boring almonds too big for my face had fit hers perfectly, and it's a compliment that I never tire of hearing.

"Hmm," I respond, letting my head drop back in the chair.

My dad lets the silence hang gently between us until I break it.

"I'm thirty-seven," I say. A short sentence summarizing endless suffering.

He sighs, heavy, reaching his hand over to find mine, giving it a tight squeeze. "That you are."

His silence is my safety net. The place he'll catch me if I fall.

"I'm scared, Dad." A boulder lodges in my throat as my eyes burn with the confession. *Scared* feels like too small a word. I'm terrified. Thirty-seven sounds so old when you're young, but now that I'm here, it doesn't seem that old at all. It seems like nothing. A speck. Barely a beginning.

"If you would have known how it was all going to end with Mom, would you have done it differently?"

"God no, Birdie!" he says it so quickly—so adamantly—it startles my heart to a stop.

He smiles. "Everything in this whole world ends—we forget about that during a tragedy. Maybe it's our way of making our misery feel special to us, but it's another lie we tell ourselves. It's all ending. Me, you, the trees growing all around us." His pause prepares me for something profound. "My time with your mom was too short, but I suspect any amount of time with her would have been. I got some of it though, and I got you. Some is better than none, Birdie. Don't you forget that."

He looks at me until he's sure I hear what he's saying and pats my knee. When "I Just Want to Dance with You" starts to play, my body is so conditioned to our Thursday night routine I don't even have to think about what comes next. I stand and so does he. Hand in hand, one arm draped over his shoulder and his palm in the middle of my back, my dad and I dance to one song just like him and my mom used to do, smiles on both of our faces as we shuffle around the porch to the voice of George Strait.

When I load the dog in the van, my dad gives me a tight hug. "You know more than your mom and grandma did, doctors know more. And you've had the surgery. This year will be different for you."

When he pulls away, his smile looks almost forced, like even he doesn't believe what he's saying. Like he's saying it to comfort himself as much as me. I just nod. "Love you, Dad, thanks for dinner."

"Love you too, Little Bird."

After a too-long bath and a nightly skincare routine that involves a jade stone, jojoba oil, and red-light therapy, I drop my towel to the floor and stare into the mirror. My chest, besides the fact it looks nothing like it's supposed to, is an unexpected work of art. Every shade of the rainbow lives on my skin.

I had known when I scheduled my mastectomy that I'd get tattoos to cover the scars. It wasn't until a summer day driving by a field of wildflowers that I decided what I wanted. It had been a bad day, but the flowers still bloomed. Beauty when life felt anything but.

I took a dozen packets of wildflower seeds to the tattoo artist, Seth, for design ideas. I asked him to draw something that would cover everything from armpit to armpit with every color under the sun. It took multiple visits and hours with the needle poking in and out of my flesh, but once it was finished I felt a completeness that I didn't know was missing. Closure almost. Acceptance.

I trace the colorful petals with my finger. The bumpy unevenness and scars left in the wreckage of my surgery now hidden by petals, leaves, stems, and tendrils that dance across my skin. Other than Seth, my doctor, and George Strait, not another living being has seen my chest in its entirety.

Even the men I've been with—despite the recent lack of tradi-tional sex—haven't seen me completely bare. Always in a tank top or lacy bralette. None of them ever argued or pushed for anything different. Like they didn't want to see what I looked like as much as I didn't want to see their faces if they did.

Tonight, I'm at peace with it. Some nights, it's not so easy. Some nights I look at my reflection and cry and scream, but not tonight. Tonight I'm okay. Like it could be so much worse than this.

I wrap the towel back around me at the same time my phone dings.

Bo: *Gran put me in my place today because I made you mad. She already likes you more than me.*

I read it—twice—but don't respond.

Bo: *I'm going to call you.*

I drop the phone like it's a bomb about to detonate when it immediately starts ringing, Bo's name flashing on the screen.

When the ringing stops:

Bo: *I'm going to call again.*

Again, it rings, and I stare at it on the counter, biting my lip, trying to imagine what he has to say to me. Again, I don't answer.

Then:

Bo: *Pam Beesly, last time. Please answer.*

Then the ring. Once, twice, and on the third time, I push accept without speaking.

"Birdie?" His deep voice echoes through my tile-covered bath-room and I stare at the phone like he might pop through the screen.

He clears his throat. "Okay, this is nice and weird of you, but I guess it's progress." I can hear the smile in his voice through the speaker before his tone turns serious. I can't help but wonder if there's a toothpick dancing on his lips.

"I didn't tell you I was married because it's not a real marriage. Not really. Not anymore. Mandy and I were together a long time and got married because it's a small town and that's what people expected. Hell, maybe at some point it's what we both wanted. Seven years ago it started crumbling, six years ago she took off to Nashville to chase her dream of being a singer and we—*I* haven't talked to *her* since. I've filed for divorce, tried to figure out how to get her to sign, but I'm stuck. So technically, I'm married, but that's it. I don't wear a ring, I don't talk to her, I don't see her, and I don't love her, at least not in the way a man should love his wife."

He pauses. I'm silent, holding my breath.

"You there?" he asks.

I exhale. "Yes."

"If I thought I was ever going to see you again, I wouldn't have done what I did."

"Gee, thanks," I say, not bothering to hide my offense.

He puffs out a small laugh. "I don't mean it like that. I mean, whatever reasons you had for wanting one night, I had my own. And I guess you being you and—I got carried away or caught up in the moment and..."

His voice trails off, letting all the unspoken words hang between us.

"Okay," I finally say.

"Okay," he echoes.

In the quiet, my heart tries to pound out of my chest.

"Gran showed me the mug you made. It's very cute." I can hear the amusement in his voice.

I snort. "It's a bowl, asshole."

"Well, it's a cute bowl."

I shake my head, but smile.

"Good night, Bo."

"'Night, Birdie."

Then I hang up, get into bed, and dream about broken things being glued back together with gold.

Six

FRIDAY IS MY DESSERT. The sweet spot at the end of every week.

My mornings are spent with a woman named Mabel, and in the evenings, I indulge in all my favorite self-care rituals.

Mabel is seventy-five and the sauciest woman I've ever met. Maybe even insane.

To look at her is like looking at something that doesn't make sense but somehow works. Like a piece of wild abstract art that turns into something depth-filled after enough study.

There's her hair, which she still dyes a vibrant color best described as Merlot—her bright white roots always *just* showing. Then there's jewelry. Loads of it, gaudy and gold, which hang from her neck, ears, and wrap around her fingers. Her lipstick wouldn't be so bad, even in the bright red shade called Sinful, but it always puts a streak across her front teeth that she never seems to notice. Even her obnoxious animal-print leggings that would be dubbed tacky by most people suit her. And, of course, she's also obsessed with trashy romance novels starring Scottish men.

Oh, and Mabel is a former nun.

I'm not much of a reader, but each month she picks a book for me to read so on Fridays we can discuss. Two years into this unofficial book club and I've learned way more about Mabel's preferences in the bedroom than I ever cared to know. She swears the reason she left the convent was because she couldn't handle the rules, but the more I read these books with her, the more I'm convinced that there was only one rule she didn't like: celibacy. Mabel is just plain horny.

This month, we are reading *Kilted Love.*

"What did you think about the fellatio?" she asks as we sit on her plastic-covered couch, books in hand.

"Hmm..." I look at the kilted, shirtless man on the cover, recalling the scene she is referencing, not wanting to discuss *fellatio* with Mabel. *Again.*

She holds up the book and points at the half-dressed man on the cover. "I bet that Gavyn looked like a snack standing only in his tunic, making any woman hungry. I don't blame the lass for letting him squirt her in the back of the throat." When she fans herself with her book, I pretend to get a phone call and walk out of the room, giving her two minutes to calm down.

"Let's go on an adventure, Birdie dear," she says when I return.

"Where to?" I ask.

She looks around her small house, thoughtful. "A nursery. I think I'd like to get a plant. Jungle the place up a little." She wiggles her ring-covered fingers.

I do a quick search that leads us to a nursery on the outskirts of Asheville. The website says it has the best selection of exotic plants. Once Mabel heard the word *exotic*, there was no talking her out of it. I didn't have the heart to tell her I wasn't saying *erotic*.

Armed with her walker she doesn't need but uses sometimes in case "the spirit moves her," a small notebook and pen she always keeps tucked in the waist of her leggings to "take notes," and a fresh coat of lipstick, Mabel takes off toward the succulent section—emphasizing *suck* when she says the word. I leave her to it, stopping under a sign that says carnivorous plants, instantly thinking of Huck.

A little girl stands next to me staring at the same plants with about forty glittery butterfly clips in her hair.

She looks at me, eyes big and blue. "Do you know anything about a penis flytrap?"

I laugh, looking down at her. "I think you mean *Venus* flytrap. And a little." I kneel next to her so I'm at her eye level, looking at the bug-eating plant she's holding. "My friend Huck told me that they have little hairs on them to let them know when a bug is walking around so they can eat it." I snap my fingers together like a clam.

Her eyes widen.

"Will it bite my finger?" she asks, breath smelling like peanut butter.

"You know, I just don't know, maybe we should find out." I put my finger on the tiny hairs of the plant. When it pinches down, I wiggle my finger around gently, pulling it out to reveal it's intact.

"Phew!" she says.

"Right?" I pause dramatically. "I was worried there for a minute."

"Which one are you buying?" she asks.

"I think this one." I hold up a bushy plant with little pitchers all over it. "It's called a pitcher plant and there's sweet, sticky stuff that traps the bugs before they die at the bottom of these pitchers. I'm giving it to my friend Huck." I tell her with a smile.

A man's voice calls, "Lucy?" and she spins around, plant in hand, and takes off running.

"Daddy!" she squeals "Look what I found! And this lady showed me it won't even bite my finger!"

Laughing, I turn around.

And there, with the same stunned eyes as mine, stands Bo.

"Bo," I whisper, hoarse.

"Birdie," he says, cool.

I look down at Lucy. "You have a daughter."

I'm 99 percent sure I say that out loud because he says, "I have a daughter."

"Do you know her, Daddy?" Lucy asks.

"I do, she's a friend of Gran's," he says, giving her a genuine smile and rubbing the only spot on her head not covered in clips.

Pulling my boneless body back together, I reach my hand out to her. "I'm Birdie."

"I'm Lucy!" She shakes my hand with too much enthusiasm.

"How old are you?"

"Seven." She smiles, showcasing her tiny-toothed smile and missing front teeth.

Seven. Looking at Lucy is like looking at a dream stolen, and it has me blinking.

She tells Bo something about her plant, but I'm not sure what. My ears, eyes, and internal organs have all turned to some kind of sludge.

It's only once Mabel's, "Hubba, hubba. What have we here?" registers in my ears that I can function again.

Her walker scrapes against the concrete floor of the nursery as she gives Bo a red-toothed grin while she circles him like a shark.

"Mabel, this is Bo and his beautiful daughter, Lucy," I say.

She eyes Bo like he's the highlander of all her wildest fantasies.

"Mabel, it's nice to meet you," he says, reaching out his hand with a handsome smile that carves dimples into his face.

When she takes it, she looks at me. "Birdie, you've been keeping secrets from me," she murmurs, holding his hand for much longer than necessary. "We might need to read some of that lumberjack erotica I was telling you about." Her eyes slice back to Bo and she bites the air.

His lips press into a line—he's either terrified or amused—and I squeeze my eyes shut. This woman—no filter or shame.

"On that note," I say with a slight laugh. "Mabel and I have to get going." I hold up my plant. "Lucy it was nice mee—"

"We're going for ice cream next door if you want to come with us." Her little voice cuts me off as she tugs Bo's hand, begging. "Please, Daddy!"

My eyes meet his. There are a million and one reasons why I do *not* want to do this.

Mabel doesn't care or wait. "I love ice cream, lead the way, dollface."

The decision is made.

Bo smiles, but it almost looks forced. Like he's as unsure about this as I am. If he's thinking what I'm thinking, then we're both thinking: that night in the minivan ruined my life.

Lucy's walk-skip stride and Mabel's scraping walker lead us to the registers, out the doors, and across the parking lot to the ice cream shop. The door opens, greeting us with the aromas of waffle cones, coffee, and too many sweet things to name.

While everyone is distracted looking at the menu on the wall, I pull it up online and find they have a raspberry sorbet with minimal ingredients. Juice, sugar, and water. It's as close to perfect as a dessert can get for me.

At the register, Mabel, Bo, and I all pull out our wallets.

"Mabel, please, my treat," Bo offers.

"Bo y—" Before I can finish, Mabel is in full force.

"I have no problem paying for a Mountain Man like you." When she wiggles her eyebrows, I giye Bo a look that says, *don't bother.* He listens, slipping his wallet into his back pocket.

"Well, I have no problem eating an ice cream bought for me by a woman like *you*," he says, giving her a wink that earns him yet another saucy look from her.

Treats in hand, we find a picnic table outside. I'm quiet as Mabel tells Lucy mostly PG-version stories of her life. But when she starts with, "One time I was in Scotland, and I met a man..." I cut her off.

"Lucy, why don't you tell us something about you," I say, shooting Mabel a warning look that she scoffs at.

Once Lucy starts talking, she never stops. She tells us about every kid who was in her first-grade class and who she hopes she is with in second grade. When Bo gets ice cream on his beard, she tells us about how he always gets spaghetti noodles in it too. When she notices the tattoo at the neckline of my shirt, she tells us that her dad has tattoos on his back. I hide the fact my mouth waters at this visual, but it earns a sensual, "Ooh la la!" and lengthy wink from Mabel.

"Lucy Goosey, you can't tell these ladies all my secrets," he says to her, giving her a playful nudge before taking a lick of his ice cream that makes her giggle.

"Speaking of secrets," Mabel says, white sheen of vanilla covering her lips as she pulls her notebook and pen out of her waistband. "Would you say you prefer top or bottom, Bo?"

Oh my God!

My jaw nearly hits the picnic table.

"Mabel!" I hiss, but she ignores me, eyes staying locked on Bo.

Instead of shying away, he grins, props his elbows on the table, tucked hair falling in front of his ears, and his brown eyes dance.

"Well now, Mabel," he says coyly. "I'd have to say that depends on the circumstances." His eyes cut to mine before he adds, "And the space available."

My face lights on fire as Mabel says, "Flexible, I like it," and writes something down in her notebook. Why she needs this information I'll never understand, and God knows I'll never ask, but she scribbles with the intensity of a reporter at a White House press conference.

"Top or bottom what?" Lucy asks between licks of her ice cream.

"Bunk beds," Bo says, his gaze staying on mine a beat longer before looking back at her.

"Daddy's always on top," she says, matter-of-fact.

I can't help it, I laugh. We all do. Because what is even happening here?

By the time ice cream is over, I realize it was fun. Really fun.

I secure Mabel and her walker in the minivan while Bo straps Lucy into her booster seat.

Lucy is screaming invitations for me to come over and play, and Mabel is shouting her home address for Bo to make a house call. We slam the doors on both of them.

"Sorry about that," I tell him as we stand between our vehicles.

His, "I'm not," comes with a cheeky grin.

"You have a kid," I say.

"And you have a nymphomaniac," he replies, nodding toward where Mabel is staring lewdly through the windows.

"That I do." I laugh.

"Do you want to join us for dinner?" he asks, leaning on the side of his cherry-red Jeep. "It would be rude not to extend the invite Lucy so graciously keeps screaming."

As if scripted, Lucy's muffled shout comes from the other side of the door.

"I can't date you, Bo," I tell him with a lift of my chin.

His laugh surprises me. "In case you haven't noticed, I can't date you either."

My eyebrows pinch and he reads my confusion.

"Birdie, I have a kid. And wife..." He shakes his head. "But you seem like you can use a friend."

I scoff, not bothering to hide my offense. "What the hell is *that* supposed to mean?"

"For starters, you told Gran and I you don't have a social life. And you spent your birthday alone at a bar pretending to be someone else." My chin pulls back, mouth gaping, but he doesn't stop. "You need help."

"Hel—"

"Gran told me about your situation," he says, cutting me off. "Your surgery. And decisions. And what this year means to you..."

My face heats, and I don't know if it's anger or embarrassment or both. "And?" My arms cross over my chest.

"And you seem to be someone who wants to stay alive but doesn't know how to live. Alive but not living. Not really."

Alive but not living? Is he right? No... *No.*

Again, I scoff, because he doesn't know me. I'm living. Alive *and* living.

"Just because you spent one night with me doesn't mean you know me, Bo. I'll have you know the reason I can't have dinner with you is because I have plans. Which, I'm guessing shocks you since you apparently think I'm some kind of lonely loser with no life."

He laughs. "I didn't call you a loser." I try to ignore the fact he leaves out the lonely part. "What kind of plans does Pam Beesly from the Rockies have on a Friday night?"

"I go grocery shopping on Friday nights, thank you very much."

"Grocery shopping?" he asks incredulously.

"Hey!" I say, voice rising slightly. "Don't knock it 'til you try it. There's hardly anyone there, and you can read all the labels without worrying about being in someone's way. Then I go home and prep everything for the next week. There's satisfaction in filling glass containers with the perfect amount of sliced bell peppers in a well-organized fridge, I'll have you know."

His eyebrows pinch, voice lowering, "You really spend Friday nights buying groceries?"

"And meal prepping," I add. "And then I have a self-care night. I go for a long walk with my dog and soak in a bath, sometimes I watch a nature documentary with David Attenborough's relaxing voice. It's a whole magical thing."

I give him a look, my wordless, *See how much I'm living?*

He shakes his head, hair falling into his face, but his eyes are smiling.

"Okay, Birdie, if you say so."

"I do," I say firmly, opening the driver's door to the minivan. "And you don't have a toothpick in your mouth today."

He grins, eyebrows raised. "I'm unpredictable like that."

With that, he's circling his Jeep, opening the driver's door as I drop into the seat of the minivan before I can say anything else.

It's only after I'm driving away that I let myself wonder what it would be like to have dinner with them.

Seven

After dropping off Mabel and her plant—a very phallic-looking cactus—I walk the dog with Huck, take a spin class at the gym, and finally walk through the doors of the grocery store where the relief is instant.

There's soft music playing over the speakers, like the DJ designed the playlist just for me, and combined with the emptiness of the aisles, the calm that washes over me rivals that of someone on an actual vacation.

I wave to my regular cashier, Monica. Her black hair is in its usual dreadlocks, but today they are tied up with a bright pink headband which pops against her dark brown skin. "Right on time, Birdie!" she calls with a smile as I grab my cart.

"I'm nothing if not prompt," I say to her with a laugh.

I always start in produce, where I'm free to examine every item I put in my cart with scrutiny and at my leisure.

I'm interrupted mid-prod of a bag of oranges with, "Fancy seeing you here."

I close my eyes, knowing before I see. *Bo.*

I don't look at him when I ask, "What are you doing here?"

I hear the smile I refuse to look at when he responds, "Well, I'm either here because I enjoy grocery shopping on Friday nights or because you enjoy grocery shopping on Friday nights."

"You know, I knew you were a closet Friday night grocery shopper from the moment I met you."

Then, because I can't not, I look at him, and damn him for looking so good in a Monroe Cabins T-shirt and blue jeans, leaning effortlessly on the handle of an empty cart. His crooked smile and toothpick somehow add to his appeal. His hair, usually loose and tucked behind his ears, is pushed back, showing off the angles of his face more than usual. Even in the harsh lighting of the grocery store, Bo is a damn treat.

My yoga pants, sweaty cropped top, and unkempt ponytail might as well be garbage bags next to him.

After letting myself drink him in long enough that even Mabel would be proud, I drop the bag of oranges I've been holding in my cart and start walking away.

To the surprise of no one, he follows.

"How can I help you?" I ask, investigating an onion.

"I told you I want to help you."

I scoff. "Self-centered much? In case you haven't noticed, what I need help with gets billions of dollars of funding each year, and they still can't figure it out. I don't think you have the cure for cancer, Bo." I shoot him a look as I put two onions in my cart and move to the next bin.

"That's not what I mean."

I ignore him, irritated he's here, in my Friday night ritual, on my holy ground.

He stays too close as I work my way through every vegetable. Watching. Hovering.

Finally, it unnerves me just enough I stop pushing my cart, turning to face him.

"Since you won't leave me alone, I'm listening."

His smile is smug and annoying as hell. He holds up his hand and stuck to one finger is a pink piece of paper. No, a stack of pink papers. *Sticky notes?*

My eyes narrow, but damn him, I'm curious.

"I made a list," he says, proud.

"Of?" I ask, stretching my neck from side to side but doing nothing to squelch my anxiety and impatience over whatever it is he's doing.

"Of how to help you really live." When he beams, I want to punch him in the face.

"You know what?" I start pushing my cart away from him, heading toward the dairy section. "No. I'm *living*, Bo. This is absurd. And offensive."

He follows, his own cart rolling right beside mine, ignoring me. "If you're *living*, why are you here alone on a Friday night?"

"Why are *you* here alone on a Friday night?" I respond.

"Because I dropped Lucy off at her cousin's house so I could come find *you*."

I hate his answer with every fiber of my being.

"Bo, I get it, I'm alone. I'm easy to take pity on because of my family history and the fact I'm likely to drop dead any minute. But this"—I wiggle my finger between us—"isn't happening."

"I already told you it wasn't," he says, tilting his head just enough some of the pushed back hair falls toward his face. His lips pinch, stilling the toothpick as if trying to hide a smile.

I blow out a frustrated breath.

I weigh my options, mentally making my own lists. On one hand, I could do whatever he has on those notes—*live,* or die, depending on what they say—and spend time with him, which in turn could lead to some kind of friendship and him watching me die. On the other hand, I could ignore him, continue living my life the way I am, and die alone.

And while the latter is the tidier and more straightforward of the two, it sounds depressing as hell and makes a sour taste fill my mouth.

I'm living...*am I living?*

I pull out my phone.

"What are you doing?"

I glare at him. "I'm seeing if you're right." I angle the screen toward him so he can see *What does it mean to feel alive?* typed in the search bar.

He laughs in disbelief, rubbing a hand across his bearded jaw. "You're looking it up?!"

I pin him with a look that I really hope conveys, *Fuck off* before reading the answer aloud:

"Feeling and being alive requires a deep psychological and physical meeting of needs. A sense of unity within, often a heightened experience of senses and awareness. When in a state of aliveness, there's a deep-rooted sense of joy along with an indescribable feeling of freedom. To be alive means to have a passion for living."

I pause, considering this, and scoff. Then feel slightly attacked.

Are my needs physically and psychologically met? Hmm...

Do I feel a sense of unity and experience all senses? Well...

Deep-rooted sense of joy? Feeling of freedom? Even I'm not this delusional; I know the answer is no. No, no, no.

When I look at him again, he's smug. Again. Like he knows exactly what I'm thinking.

"Why do you want to do this?" I ask, skimming the words on my screen again.

He shrugs. "Maybe selfishly it's a reason to be around you even though I know I can't have you."

I attempt to translate what that means, but everything jumbles together. He is the least of my concerns in this moment, as the internet, in its infinite wisdom and source of definitions, called me dead even though that's the opposite of what I want. What I've been working for.

Finally, I say, "Fine."

When he grins, I hold out my hand. "But let me read the list."

"Uh-uh." He shakes his head, scraping his knuckles under his chin before shoving the sticky notes in the pocket of his jeans.

"That's part of it. It's a surprise." When my nostrils flare he adds, "But I promise you won't get hurt."

I shake my head, push my cart another two steps, then stop.

Again, I ask, "Why are you doing this?"

His response is instant. "Because I know how it feels to not have a say in how your life happens."

I squint at him, but when he doesn't say more neither do I.

The way he looks at me has an intensity—a hopefulness that I can't explain. For the first time, part of me wonders if he needs this as much as he thinks I do.

I swallow, my body vibrating with too many things. Fear? Excitement? Anxiety? It's hard to pinpoint one.

In the year that will likely be my last, can I do this? With him?

I like my life. I think.

I study him. His toothpick rolling effortlessly across his lips and his brown eyes sparkling with green and gold flecks that look like two gemstones on his face.

Then, like I'm not so terrified I might pass out, I push my cart again, saying over my shoulder, "I need bread if you're going to follow me."

I'm not looking at him, but I know he's smiling. I feel it.

The sound of the wheels of his cart screakily rolling across the floor confirms what I predict.

"Tell me about the cabins you build," I say, stopping my cart in front of a rack of bread. "How'd you start?"

"Lincoln Logs on Gran's floor," he says, strolling to an easy stop as he leans on the handle of his cart. "I got a degree in architecture from NC State, but it was always cabins for me. My parents lived in a cabin, and then growing up making them with toys—I guess they kind of felt like home for me. I worked for another builder for a while before finally going out on my own right after Lucy was born."

"The ones I saw online are beautiful," I say, grabbing a loaf of bread off a shelf before cringing at the ingredient list and putting it back. "Is that why your hands look like you've been in a fight with barbed wire?" I ask, eyeing his scar-covered fingers draped over the handle of his cart.

He chuckles, making a fist with one of his hands to examine the faded lines that are slashed across them. "Most of these are from logs." He pauses, smile wide. "A select few are from bad teenage decisions."

I laugh under my breath, ponytail whipping across my back as I shake my head and start pushing my cart again.

"How did you start doing what you do?" he asks, watching me read labels, cringe at ingredients, and put food back on the shelf.

"Not as fun as Lincoln Logs," I smile. "I know there's a good chance I'll never get to be old, so I figured it would be a great way to live my life. Experience a chapter I might not get to otherwise. It was either that or be a teacher, but since I got to be a kid, old people it is."

His nod is subtle as I read another label and groan. "God, I hate buying bread. Whatever happened to flour, water, and salt?"

"You know, I'm always wondering that," he deadpans.

I shoot him a look.

"Tell me about your wife," I say.

"Hmm…" His cheeks fill with air before deflating. "I don't really know what there is to tell. She never wanted kids; I always imagined she'd outgrow that. She got pregnant and we fell apart." His words hit my sternum like a wrecking ball, but I must hide it well because he continues. "Then she went to Nashville or wherever she is." He shrugs, as if it's just that simple.

I clear my throat, staring at the back of a bottle of juice I can't focus on. "Do you miss her?"

His response is immediate. "For Lucy."

I put aloe juice in my cart, earning a look from him that makes me chuckle despite the shock of his words.

He clears his throat. "You know, you had a look on your face when you met her. Like you'd seen a ghost."

The blood drains from my face in such a rush it makes me dizzy. Nauseous almost. I've stopped in the middle of the aisle and can't make myself move as he leans on his cart next to me, waiting. Waiting for something I've never said out loud to anyone else.

"I've always wanted kids," I say, half-truthing it.

"And?"

My mouth is dry, like it's filled with sand. I'm not ready to tell him—or anyone.

"And I can't have them." I don't look at him as I say it, and his pause makes me think he wants to ask more. Instead, he picks up a box of cookies.

When he sees me eyeing them, he shrugs and defensively says, "They're organic."

I click my tongue with a shake of my head. "Oh, Bo, you have so much to learn."

Then, leaving my least favorite topic in the aisle of overly processed sweets, we walk around the nearly empty grocery store. As I shop, he asks me about every item I buy. *Why did you pick that one? What are you going to do with that? What does that even taste like?* And my personal favorite, *What do you have against red dye 40?*

He's quizzing me in the cereal aisle and a voice interrupts the music over the speaker. "Good evening, shoppers, just a friendly reminder, we will be closing in ten minutes."

Bo responds with a loud, "Boo!"

At the register, Monica has a knowing smile on her face as she talks to us. "Birdie, I didn't know you had a boyfriend. You need to bring this man around more often!"

Before I can correct her, Bo says, "Monica, I keep telling her the same thing."

I roll my eyes at them both, but I'm also smiling as we walk out of the automatic doors together and put the groceries in my trunk.

He leans against his Jeep that's parked in the next space as I do the same against the minivan. Then it's the looking: me at him, him at me.

"Bo." I say his name because the silence is charged. Heavy.

He smiles one of his slow-to-grow smiles, arms crossed over his chest. "Birdie."

I shake my head and roll my eyes.

"Now what? When do we start this Birdie Comes to Life school?"

He laughs softly, but the pause that follows—the way his eyes search mine—makes me want to rip out of my own skin. Anxious.

I open my mouth at the same time he unfolds his arms, pushes off the side of his Jeep with a familiar step that puts him in front of me, pressing one palm on the minivan by my head. He leans in close—so close his Bo Mountain Breeze consumes my senses and makes my knees buckle. When I imagine sliding the door of the minivan open, I clench my hands into fists at my side.

"You're too pretty to be spending your Friday nights alone at grocery stores," he says, voice low. Between his tone, what he says, and the way his beard barely scrapes against my skin, I stop breathing. Unsure of what he's doing or what's coming next. What I want to come next.

A quick move of his free hand and his palm settles at the base of my throat then slides up the side of my neck where two fingers stop and press gently to the spot just beneath my jaw.

I suck in a breath, my own heart pounding against his fingers. I press into the balls of my feet, pushing my back firmly against the van.

"What are you doing?" I ask with a whisper, not pulling my eyes off his. The truth is, I don't care. Standing here with him looking at me with fingers pressed against my pulse point is more than physical, it's intimate. Like him feeling my beating heart is him feeling a me I've yet to meet.

"I'm feeling you come alive," he says, leaning forward slightly. A move that makes my lips part.

When his eyes drop to my mouth, they linger, then close, tight. As if the moment is a log being sawed in half, his jaw clenches at the same time his hand pulls away.

The instant he does, my breath rushes out of me in a gust, and I bring my own hands to my neck. As if trying to replicate a touch I never will.

We stand, staring at each other, inches between us, but there's something crackling in the space. An exchange happening of something I can't place.

Without a word, I slip into the driver's seat of the van, my pulse pounding in my ears, and blow out another shaky breath as I buckle my seatbelt.

What just happened?

When I roll my window down, he takes it as an invitation to press a palm to either side of the opening, the sinewy lines of his arms on full display, and rounds his back slightly until his eyes meet mine.

"I can't be with you, Bo," I say, mustering every ounce of forced gumption.

"I can't be with you either."

"Then you can't touch me like that again." I shake my head "It's confusing and..." *Feels too good*. "If we're going to do this little list of yours, it has to be as friends."

He nods. "I know." He looks away from me, studying something across the parking lot before looking back, and when his eyes meet mine again, he pushes to a stand.

"'Night, Birdie," he says.

"'Night, Bo."

As I drive away, all I can think is: What did I just agree to?

Eight

Saturday greets me with an hour at the gym followed by running errands, one specifically for Veda after some research I do on arthritis, and the showdown I'm now having with Huck in my kitchen.

"C'mon, Huck, just try it," I say as he stares at the ceiling with his mouth clamped shut.

"Please," I beg, dragging the word out. "I made it red, just for you."

He looks at the loaf of bread, eyes nearly closed with his skeptical squint.

When Huck and I first started spending time together, his food aversions drove me crazy. He showed up on my porch with an orange sports drink, orange lollipop, and a can of spray cheese. I nearly collapsed as every horrible ingredient and potential side effect he was holding raced through my mind.

My disgusted, *Why don't you just do a line of arsenic off the counter?!* Was met with his, *Why don't you just do a line of arsenic off the counter?!*

Now, after many deep breaths and months of getting to know him, I've learned to accommodate him in ways that don't involve any frustrated shouting.

Huck's current food color of preference is red, and while I understand that Miss Alice is doing the best she can, the red sports drink he shows up with today promptly ends up in the trash.

Today's spread features strawberries, homemade bread I dyed using beet-based food coloring, a smoothie made with strawberries and raspberries, and meatballs in marinara sauce.

So far, he's tried zero of them.

"I wonder if Huck would like to give a meatball to George Strait," I say, switching tactics.

The slightest smile ghosts his lips.

"I wonder if Huck would like to give a meatball to George Strait *and* eat a meatball at the same time."

Without warning, he pops one into his mouth while simultaneously dropping one on the floor for the dog. As George Strait laps his up, Huck chews, then smiles.

"Huck likes the meatballs," he says loudly, grabbing another one for him and the dog.

I laugh as they eat every single one out of the casserole dish.

The rest of the foods aren't as popular. The strawberries are too mushy; he spits those out. The smoothie is too cold; he screams after one sip. The bread he flat out refuses.

One out of four is better than nothing.

In the living room, we play Connect 4, his favorite game, about seven hundred times.

Finally bored of playing, we spend the rest of our time together watching a documentary about bugs.

Just before dinner, I walk him home, Miss Alice greeting us at the door.

"Hi, Huck! Please go get ready for dinner," she says, smiling at him.

He gives me a high-five and a loud, "Bye, Birdie!" before running inside.

"Birdie, if you have a minute," Miss Alice says, stepping onto the porch next to me, concern etched on her round, rosy face.

"Sure. Everything okay?"

She nods, one of her curly white-blonde hairs falling in her face.

"I don't know if Huck has mentioned it, but we've been meeting with potential families for adoption this summer."

What?

My mouth opens as I shake my head. "He didn't tell me."

"Just as well, none of them want him." The way she says it is a punch to the gut. Like he's a used car sitting in a lot with too many miles on the engine. "The behaviors and the food..." She shakes her head with a sad smile. "It's a lot for someone to take on, you know?"

I nod, even though, no, I don't *know*.

"Why are you telling me this?" I ask.

"You're around him so much, I just want you to be aware in case you notice his moods changing from it. I don't know how much longer I'll be able to keep him here."

She must see the shocked expression on my face because she follows up quickly, "It's Steve, my husband, he had a heart attack."

My eyes widen, earning another quick response. "He's fine, Birdie, nothing major, but he needs calm, quiet. We might be reaching the end of our time as being foster parents." Then another sad smile.

Miss Alice and Mr. Steve never had kids, I never asked why, but they've spent the last twenty-five years taking in foster kids, never officially adopting any of them. I assume they are in their late fifties or early sixties now, and that ship has probably sailed for them.

"I'm sorry to hear about all this, Miss Alice," I say, trying to register what she's saying. "Of course, I'll tell you if I notice anything, but please let me know if I can help. I'm happy to take him more for you, I'd hate to see him go."

I can't imagine it. I've only known him nine months, but it's hard for me to picture coming home and not finding him on my doorstep. Who will walk George Strait with me? Who will I make new foods for on Saturdays?

She nods, stepping inside. "I will. And you should know, Birdie—he adores you."

Hours later, in my own kitchen with my own plate of dinner—wild-caught salmon and sweet potatoes—I can't stop thinking about what Miss Alice said. *None of them want him.* I hate it for him. Hate *them* for it. I want to call them all, tell them how great he is even though he's different, and then wish them good luck finding a better kid.

Even worse, I wish there was something I could do about it. I can't change Mr. Steve's heart, nor do I blame them for wanting to have a house without kids. Obviously, I can't adopt him. I'm unmarried and likely to leave him an orphan again. I couldn't do that to him.

Like with everything else, I'm helpless.

Holding a mug of chamomile tea, I cozy into the couch with a heavy sigh, and turn on the TV, smiling when I land on *The Office*.

As if there's a hidden camera watching me, my phone dings with a text from Bo.

Bo: *What are you doing?*

Me: *You'll never believe it—watching The Office.*

Bo: *Planning your next alter ego?*

I laugh.

Bo: *What are you doing tomorrow? Gran's watching Lucy and I want to take you somewhere.*

Me: *The gym and whatever Mabel is forcing me to read.*

Bo: *This will be better. Wear whatever you wear to the gym. Send me your address and I'll pick you up at 9. We'll find something to check off your list.*

I pause, terrified. Terrified of someone else being in control and of me not having a clue what is about to happen. Terrified I won't bring something I need or will be forced to drink some kind of toxic chemicals.

No, that's crazy, he wouldn't do that.

Would he do that?

Somehow, my fingers type, *Fine. Where are we going?*

Bo: *To church.*

Nine

My mom was devoutly religious, a southern Baptist through and through. We went to church every Sunday. When she died, we buried the habit right along with her body. My dad has always believed religion happens outside of a building, saying, *"God would never box himself in with four walls."*

I always agreed.

For whatever reason, I agree to go with Bo to his athletic-wear version of church without any questions. As promised, he shows up at nine, and I meet him outside in my yoga pants, T-shirt, and tennis shoes while carrying a large hat and a contingency bag. He's so aggressively handsome in a ball cap, slightly fitted joggers, and T-shirt my neck flushes from the sight of him alone.

"Birdie," he says with a lift of his lips—free of the usual toothpick today.

"Bo," I reply, smiling despite myself.

He hands me a pink sticky note with *Break Routine* written across it.

When I look at him, he grins. "Today's task."

Before I can question it, we're standing at his Jeep, and my eyes widen.

"Where are the rest of the pieces of your car?" I demand, balking at the missing doors and roof.

His eyebrows pinch. "I took them off. It's gorgeous out."

"Is it safe to drive around without doors?" I ask, strained.

His laugh dies when he realizes I'm serious. He clears his throat. "Umm, yeah, it's safe, Birdie. They sell the Jeep so it can be driven like this."

I nod slowly. Then, "What if it rains?"

We both look up at the clear blue sky, and he looks at me like he's not sure how to answer my question.

I look from him to the Jeep with all its missing components, to the sky, back to him. Tension creeps in my shoulders, taking its hold on me. I stretch my neck. Consider my options. Stay or go. Go or stay.

"Fine," I relent, putting my bag on the floor, get into the seat, and hope I don't blow away on the highway.

When he's in his seat, he glances over at me, then the bag, as he starts to back out of my driveway. "What's all that?"

"Contingency items."

He raises his eyebrows.

"You were all cryptic and I didn't know what I'd need. I have grass-fed beef sticks if I need a snack, nontoxic bug spray, my sandals with a copper grounding plug if I want different shoes—oh!" I lift the large straw hat. "I didn't know if we would be in the sun…"

His eyes widen. "Not really, but a little. The hat seems a bit…large." His teeth work over his bottom lip as though he's physically fighting a smile from showing. "I have sunscreen."

I scoff. "Do you know what they put in that stuff?"

At the question, he puffs out a laugh but doesn't respond.

I take in the Jeep as he starts to drive—it's very him. Casual. Fun. In the cup holder, there are toothpicks wrapped individually in clear plastic sleeves, a couple Lincoln Logs, butterfly clips, and three princess Band-Aids.

I pick one up; he notices. "For boo-boos," he says with a small smile.

I nod, putting it back into the cup holder along with the rest of his Bo paraphernalia. Relics of life. Pieces of him.

Then, as if we've said all we need to say, we ride in silence as he drives us out of town and toward the mountains, the warm wind from all directions blowing our hair around.

When he parks at a trailhead, I wait for a *Gotcha!* that never comes.

"A trail?" I ask, unbuckling.

"Mhm." He grabs a backpack from the back seat and two water bottles. "I hike to church; didn't I mention that?" he asks with mock confusion.

I climb out of my doorless seat and look around. "Like Machu Picchu?"

He laughs, says, "Something like that," then tilts his head toward the trail, already walking.

I assess the situation. There are trees, but I can see on the trail there's light shining through. Before leaving the Jeep—and my bag of stuff that can't be locked in so I'm sure will be stolen—I grab my hat, securing it with the strings beneath my chin.

We're quiet as we start. Finding a rhythm both with each other and the roots and rocks of the trail beneath the soles of our shoes. Big trees and boulders line the path on both sides. The smell is fresh, but also distinct. The color green if it had a scent. A nuanced combination of soil, leaves, and elevated air.

When we stop for water, Bo watches me with an uncomfortable intensity as I drink from one of the bottles, cicadas loudly buzzing in the summer air.

I wipe my mouth with the back of my hand, self-conscious.

"What?" I demand, dropping my water bottle into the backpack.

"That hat is ridiculous," he says.

"So is skin cancer," I deadpan.

He makes a sound that's softer than a laugh as we start to walk again.

After a bird sings a song for so long in the distance I wonder how its lungs have the capacity for such work, he says, "Why did you come into Libby's the way you did?"

My mouth clamps shut, eyes glued to the ground.

"This is called sharing, Birdie. It's what *friends* do."

I pin him with a look but relent when I realize there's nowhere for me to go to avoid this conversation.

"Fine." I sigh heavily, looking anywhere but at him as I walk. "My thirty-seventh birthday has been a looming date on the calendar since my mom died. I know myself well enough to know that no matter what I've done to prepare for it, I'll never stop believing it's the year I'll get cancer. The year I'll die. So I told myself, fuck it, if this is the beginning of the end, for just once, I'm doing something that I never do."

He huffs a laugh. "A one-night stand?"

"Sex." The word pops out of my mouth like a jack-in-the-box and his step falters on the trail next to me.

"You don't have *sex*?" If he's trying to mask his shock, he fails. "*Ever*?"

I laugh through my exhale. "Not actual sex, no. At thirty I..." I shake my head—he doesn't need to hear *that*. "Anyway, it doesn't matter why. I don't want to have kids. I don't want to pass this burden"—I gesture toward my chest—"onto another generation. The best way to avoid that and keep everyone around me safe is to just...not." I shrug. I may not love my reality, but I have come to accept it. Since most people don't understand it, staying alone is always the easier option.

The thing is, I actually like sex—evident by what I recklessly did in the back of my minivan with a stranger, I *really* like it—but it's not worth the risk. So I figure out ways to stay...pleased...without it. The few men I've casually dated are happy with that—until they aren't. And now, with my age, even casual dating is off the table.

We cross a shallow rocky creek when he says, "There's birth control."

I scoff. "Filled with synthetic chemicals and hormones that will wreak havoc on my body? Pass."

"Condoms? You..." His voice trails off with the unspoken *used one with me.*

"They fail," I argue sharply.

"Everything has a risk, Birdie. Hell, even this hike could be where it ends!" When he laughs incredulously, something inside me snaps.

The rage triggered with those words is as intense as it is instant, and it stops my legs in the middle of the trail.

"You know what—people that say shit like that have no clue what risk is." His eyes flash with regret, but it's too late. I can't control the anger in my voice any more than the words that come with it. "I went to a doctor once who told me genetics loads the gun, but lifestyle pulls the trigger. Well guess what, Bo? The gun is pointed at my head and it's fully loaded!" I realize I'm yelling but don't seem to care because I keep going. "Don't you dare tell me about risks. If history is any indication, there's a chance I won't live to see my next birthday. When you think every cold—every ache—is cancer coming to kill you, come talk to me about risk. This hike is the *least* of my goddamn concerns."

Before he can respond, I'm at a near jog up the trail trying to get away from him.

"Birdie, I'm sorry—*wait!*—I didn't mean it like that." There's a plea in his voice that tugs at me as he hurries beside me, but I don't give in.

The trail gets steep, my breath wheezing like a broken harmonica, but I can't shake him, and he doesn't slow down.

His mouth is on a constant replay of, "Stop, Birdie! I want to talk about this."

Trying to keep my oversized hat on my head as I work to out-hike him, I can barely breathe.

When a branch snags my hat, anger zips through me. Worse is knowing that I'm not even mad at him, I'm pissed at whoever it is that deals out gene pools.

I want to scream, roar even. I'm jealous of every wild animal that gets to come loudly unhinged without being judged.

When the thick trees we've been walking under fade to a rocky ledge, we reach the summit. We're standing on a cliff that overlooks the lush Blue Ridge Mountains as far as the eye can see. It's so beautiful I feel it in my fingertips, eyelids, and between every rib.

The peaks closest to us are bright green, but as the lines move into the distance, curving and lifting from the earth, they turn to a blueish purple before completely blurring into the sky at the horizon line.

I've seen these mountains a thousand times, but for some reason the emotion that has no place to go makes my chest so tight my skin might rip. Desperate. Restless. Even the forever-reaching valleys around us aren't big enough to hold everything I have bottled up.

I stop fighting it. Mouth open, head back, eyes closed, I yell—scream. The visceral call comes from my belly, lungs, throat, and mouth. My hat slips off my head, hanging by the cord around my neck to the middle of my back. My toes curl in my shoes and my fists clench at my side.

It's simple—a long, loud, *ahh!*—but says everything I don't know how to. It's cathartic, and I need it so badly I do it again.

Somewhere in that next primal yell, Bo's hands are cupped around his mouth, and he joins me with a howl that turns my yell to a laugh.

The echo of our calls bounces off the trees, mountaintops, and into the deepest parts of my soul.

When the last whispers of us are gone, it's serenely quiet. A calm after a storm.

I blink back a tear before it can roll down my cheek.

"Tell me something you like," he says.

I smile, not pulling my eyes off the mountains. "This view… You?"

"You," he says, sliding my hat up from where it hangs down my back to the top of my head again.

I snort a laugh.

"I ruined church," I say, staring at the bigness around us.

He bumps his shoulder against mine. "Not even close, Pam Beesly."

"So I told you more about me than I'm sure you cared to know. If we are going to be friends, I assume you need to tell me something about you," I say, staring out the windshield as we drive out of the mountains.

He chuckles, wind blowing his hair in twenty-seven directions as one hand casually drapes over the steering wheel. "What do you want to know?"

I consider this. What *do* I want to know?

"Why are you called Bo?"

"Ah, that's a good story. My grandad always wanted a dog—that he wanted to name Bo—but Gran said the dog hair would get in her clay. As you can imagine, she got her way with that." He grins. "When I came along, I got the name." He shakes his head, hair whipping across his face. "Old man never did get a dog."

When he shrugs, I laugh. "Named after the dog that never was. I like it."

"What else?" he asks, shifting in his seat, running a hand through his hair and glancing over at me. His brown eyes look almost gold as the sun shines through the open roof of the Jeep.

"Do you date?" I ask. "Women, I mean. Other women."

Again, he laughs, but there's a more serious undertow when he answers. "I tried to, a couple of times. It's complicated. I have a wife, and there's a guilt associated with that even though I don't want to be with her. Even though she left me and Lucy. Especially Lucy. Most women don't want to date a man who's legally married. I'm bound to another woman, it's hard to see a future in that." He shakes his head. "And then there's Lucy, my priority."

With both hands now on the steering wheel, he twists his fingers around it. "I just don't know how it fits."

As we pull up to my house, I stay silent, considering his situation. How strange it must be. I'll never have a spouse, but he has one that essentially doesn't exist. I'll never know love, but in some ways, neither will he. At least not anymore.

When he parks in my driveway, Huck's waiting on my porch. I smile and wave at him through the open doorway of the Jeep, and he mirrors me from where he sits. He's wearing a shirt with grasshoppers on it today.

"Who's that?" Bo asks as I climb out of his Jeep with my oversized hat in one hand, bag that didn't get stolen in the other.

"Huck. My neighbor. And *friend*," I say, my emphasis trying to prove a point. "Do you want to meet him?"

His answer is in the form of him sliding out of the driver's seat and rounding the front of the vehicle.

"Birdie! Birdie!" Huck's too-loud voice calls as he hops from the step and runs toward me, a blocky smile, more rectangular than curved, plastered on his face. The sight of it makes me grin.

When Huck gives me a high-five, Bo is standing next to me.

"Huck wonders where Birdie's been!" he shouts.

I smile. "I went hiking with my friend Bo today."

Bo and Huck study each other like they are trying to solve a riddle.

"Hi, Huck," Bo says.

Huck shakes his head, mouth clamped shut.

"I wonder if Huck could tell Bo something about insects," I say, trying to break the ice between them.

His eyes light up. "Grasshoppers were alive before dinosaurs."

"They must be really old!" Bo says with such an obnoxiously terrible old man impression it makes Huck bark out a laugh.

"I wonder if Huck would like to walk George Strait with me."

He nods, and I hand him my key. "Let him out, please."

He doesn't hesitate before taking the key and sprinting toward the door.

"George Strait?" Bo asks, eyes still on Huck.

"It's my dog," I tell him. "He was my mom's favorite singer."

We watch as he opens the door and the dog storms out, licking Huck in the face before bouncing down the steps.

"He's autistic," I say. "The speech patterns, that's part of it. He doesn't like questions."

"You're good with him." The observation unknowingly lashes a million cuts across my heart.

A bouncing, barking George Strait pounces toward me when Huck says loudly, "Huck wonders if Bo is coming on a walk with us."

Bo glances at me before kneeling next to him. "I would love that, but I have to go home right now." He pauses. "But Bo wonders"—his eyes flick to mine, as if asking if he's doing it right and I nod—"if Huck and Birdie would like to have dinner with Bo sometime." They both look up at me.

What?

I swallow hard, concurrently wanting to say *Yes!* and *Absolutely not*.

"I will have to think about it." *For a long time.* "And ask Miss Alice if Huck's allowed."

Bo leans closer to Huck and loudly whispers, "That means yes, Huck."

At this, Huck laughs.

Then, like he didn't just make my heart expand to the point of pressing against bone, Bo gets in his Jeep, flicks a casual two-finger wave and grin in my direction, and drives away.

Ten

WHEN I GET TO Veda's house Monday morning, my, "Knock! Knock!" call as I open the unlocked front door is met with her, "Back here!" from the sunroom along with a steady humming noise.

In the sunroom, the wet clay spinning in the middle of the potter's wheel is being pulled into a cylinder by two large hands.

Bo.

The stool seems too small and his body too big as he rounds over the wheel like some kind of giant. His eyes lift to mine with a playful look, dark hair falling from behind his ears into his eyes, clay still spinning. The sight of him sends a million butterflies fluttering from my belly to my throat.

"Bo." I say his name like it's a complete concept.

"Birdie," he says with a smirk, toothpick perched in the corner of his mouth, before returning his attention back to the clay.

There's a short silence interrupted by Veda's, "Well isn't anyone going to acknowledge me?" which makes me snort a laugh.

"Sorry. Good morning, Veda," I say with a cheeky grin, holding up the bag I'm carrying. "I brought you something."

I look at Bo again, watching as he moves his fingers slightly and turns the straight walls of the cylinder into something curvy. Sexy, somehow.

"I didn't know you knew how to do this," I say to him.

He looks up at me. "Nowhere near as good as you." He nods toward my misshapen pinch pot sitting on a shelf while the clay still spins between his hands.

"Ass."

"Isn't he though?" Veda laughs softly.

Redirecting my attention to her, I pull a pair of puffy purple gloves out of the bag.

"I did some research, and nothing is guaranteed, or overnight of course, but I read these might help with your hands. They heat up and help with pain relief and mobility." I take out a box of tea. "And this tea supposedly alleviates the inflammation."

The only sound is the hum of the wheel spinning while she looks at them. Quietly.

I keep talking because I don't know what else to do in her silence. "It might take a few months, the reviews I read said six months for some people, but I thought maybe it was worth a shot…" Her expression is unreadable as she looks at them and I wonder if I've overstepped.

"Don't be stubborn, Gran," Bo calls from the wheel.

He shakes her from whatever she's been thinking. "Of course. Thank you, Birdie, I was just imagining how ridiculous I'm going to look with those gloves on." She smiles, but I swear it's either sad or forced, or both.

"Damn!" Bo's cry makes both our heads turn to look at him. The former vase is now a mangled blob. "Another one bites the dust," he says with a grin, standing up.

He washes his hands in the sink, dries them, and gives Veda a hug and peck on the cheek. "Love you, Gran, I'm off to work." Then, lifting his chin toward me, "Walk me out, Birdie?"

It's only once we're outside that I realize I didn't hesitate to follow him.

"You here to brag about your pottery skills?" I ask, hands on my hips and eyebrow raised.

"That was just a bonus." He smiles, leans against his Jeep, and crosses his arms. "I just wanted to see you."

"Liar," I say, fidgeting with a button on my shirt, noticing for the first time he's holding a Lincoln Log in his hand. "Looks like you came to get your toys." I point at his hand.

He chuckles. "Ah, I did need this." His small smile bleeds into a wide grin as he taps the Lincoln Log against my bicep. "But I meant it when I asked you, and Huck if he's allowed, to come to dinner."

All I can ask is, "Why?"

He turns toward the Jeep—doors off, of course—and steps up into the driver's seat. "Because I like *The Office*, why else, Pam Beesly?"

I snort out a laugh.

"I'm serious, Bo."

"Me too," he says with a twitch of his lips that makes his toothpick bobble. "I'm helping you, remember? If you want to live, it means getting out and doing things. With people. Without lists."

"Oh really? Because last time I checked, you're the one making a list for me."

He grins as he pulls the seatbelt across his chest. "I meant without *your* lists."

My eyes narrow. "Bo, I don't need your help. I *like* lists." God that sounds pathetic. "And I do things...I went hiking with you. And Huck and I eat new foods on Saturdays..." Again, pathetic.

He raises his eyebrows as if I've proven every point he's been trying to make.

I sigh. "Fine. Maybe."

"See, that's not so bad." His voice is teasing before turning serious. "But I'm also here to ask about Gran."

My chin pulls back. "Veda? Why? Is something wrong?"

He shrugs. "She says no, but something seems...off. Different. I can't explain it really. It isn't just one thing—I don't know." He shakes his head, blowing out a slight breath. "I'm probably overly worried. It's part of the reason I wanted to have someone here, to keep an eye on her because I can't."

I nod, considering what he's asking.

"Obviously I'm here to keep an eye on her, Bo. And I'll help however I can, but you need to know, if she has something going on, that's between her and her doctors and you. I can't be involved if she doesn't want me to be."

Despite the seriousness of my tone, he laughs as he turns the key in the ignition. "Birdie, leave it to you to bring rules and regulations into this conversation."

I roll my eyes, hands on my hips. "I'm serious, Bo."

"Yeah, yeah." He shifts the gear and the Jeep starts to slowly roll backward. "Let's find something to mark off that list this week."

Before I can respond, he lifts two fingers off the steering wheel at me in a wave before he drives away.

"My grandson likes you," Veda says as soon as I walk through the door.

I scoff. "I do *not* think so."

"Do you know how many times he's come over at eight in the morning to throw a vase on that wheel?" Her eyes narrow. "One! This morning!"

Tension from what she's implying makes my shoulders creep toward my ears, and I drop my head toward my shoulder to ward it off.

"Coincidence," I say, quickly diverting with, "What's on the agenda today?"

She huffs. "Ignore me! Fine! What do I know? I'm just the old lady with crooked hands!" Then said hands are waving above her head.

"I *am* ignoring you. What do you want to do? I can clean?"

"Have it your way," she sighs, looking around the sunroom. "I want to teach you to glaze, so we'll work on that. Then maybe I'll show you how to throw on the wheel if you want. And it's nice out, so we can go work in the garden." I nod in agreement, loving how that whole day sounds. "And then, when I let you put these ridiculous gloves on me, we'll talk about my grandson."

Before I can respond, she shoves a canister of glaze in my hands.

Frustration sticks to me like superglue on fingertips all day. Annoying. Inescapable. Obvious.

Veda starts things off easy with the glaze. It's just painting, but for some reason those three coats on my small bowl feel like I'm trying to recreate the *Mona Lisa*. There are thumbprints and brush hairs and puddles. I want to throw it against the wall.

Behind the wheel, all hell breaks loose. Veda doesn't yell, which might have been easier, instead she guides me with a singsong cadence to her voice that peaks with every last word, frustrating me to the point of grinding my teeth.

When the lump of clay floats all over the spinning wheel, her, "You've used too much water," song makes my nostrils flare. "Your elbows aren't tucked," is sang on a loop along with, "You aren't applying equal amounts of pressure with both hands."

It's after she asks, "Are you even trying?" that I pull my foot off the pedal and glare from the blob of clay to her.

"I can't do this," I snap.

She scoffs. "Of course you can. You aren't listening to the clay, Birdie."

I use my clay-caked hand to cup my ear.

"I listened—it said I should quit."

Another scoff. "You're *fighting* it."

Of course I'm fighting it—this glorified piece of mud is fucking annoying.

"Start the wheel." I push the pedal, reluctantly. "Now, hold the clay like I showed you."

I do as she says, making a tight C-shape with my palm and fingers before wrapping it around the wet spinning ball.

"Now, take your other hand and chop down on the center."

Again, I follow her directions.

"Now, close your eyes," she says softly.

My eyes narrow, silently asking, *How the hell is that going to work?*

Her eyes dance with a knowing response of, *Your eyes open isn't getting you anywhere.*

On a heavy sigh, I close my eyes.

"Now, feel the clay."

She pauses as my hands mold to the wet grit of the moving lump.

"If you start to get frustrated—feel the clay. If you start to get distracted—feel the clay."

So I do.

Spinning beneath my hands, when it gets too wide, I pull with my outside hand. As it gets too tall, I push with the outer edge of the hand on top. Back and forth, back and forth, until my hands find a rhythm with the spinning of the clay.

When I open my eyes, she's smiling, and so am I.

"Now that that's over, let's turn this thing into something, shall we?"

After I successfully make a small bowl, we eat lunch, weed her garden, and start our last hour of the day together in the kitchen. Veda sits at the table, hands wrapped in the puffy warming gloves I bought, quietly watching as I do dishes.

"Let's get this over with," I say without looking at her.

"Bo likes you."

The *here we go again* groan her words provoke is instant and irritated.

"You have to listen to me talk because I'm paying you and I'm incapacitated with these stupid hot boxing gloves, so you listen," she says sharply. "*And* you like him."

I open my mouth to defend myself, but the look she gives me stops me cold.

"You like him, and I know what you said—about the testing and your family history and you being some kind of oracle predicting your own death." At these words, I glare at her, because—what the hell? Through clenched teeth, my *Veda* goes unheard. As much as I want to remind her that the two greatest indicators of my genetic predisposition died at the same age as me, nothing suppresses her drive to keep going. "But we're all dying, Birdie. Today, tomorrow, the day after that. We will all say goodbye or get said goodbye to. You can't outrun it by forcing your aloneness on everyone. That's a damn goodbye all in itself! Worse, even—a goodbye before hello." Then, with her hands shoved in big purple puffs on the table, she's quiet.

I feel more than naked standing in her kitchen as we look at each other. Like my clothes, skin, and bones have been ripped away to reveal whatever it means to be human, and this woman sees it. *Me*. My aloneness.

"Veda," I start, through gritted teeth. "We're friends. As an oracle"—I scowl at her—"I know I can't get involved with him because of what will likely happen, but did it ever occur to you it's not what he wants?" I raise my eyebrows. "He doesn't want anything more because of Mandy. So even if you were right, you aren't, not really. There's nothing here. He says he wants to help me—apparently everyone thinks I'm some kind of loser that can't manage my life—but I'm fine. And he's nice. That's all this is."

She scoffs. "Well, he's as stupid as you are."

I glare at her, *again*, with words that I'll regret starting to form in my throat before I shove them down.

"I'm going to put the towels away," I mutter, grabbing the laundry basket and walking out of the kitchen and down the short hall to the bathroom.

At the sink, I splash water on my face and smack my hands against the counter so hard the medicine cabinet door swings open from the vibration of it.

I take a deep breath, trying to level out my frustration, and splash water on my face again.

I lift my chin, face-to-face with the open medicine cabinet, and freeze.

Pills.

Lots of them.

I shouldn't, but I pull the door fully open and pick up one of the many opaque orange bottles, *Veda Monroe* written on it, before putting it back. Then I pick up another. And another. I don't recognize the names of anything, but there are at least a dozen different prescriptions lined up in front of me.

I close the door quietly, my heart pounding in my ears.

Something is wrong. Does arthritis need this much medication? I don't think so. Does Bo know about all these? He just asked if something was wrong; surely he would have mentioned this much medicine.

I put the towels away, schooling my expression before walking back to the kitchen.

She's waiting, hands now out of the gloves.

"How about some tea?" she asks, like we didn't just almost get into a catfight. Like there isn't a cabinet full of mystery medication just waiting down the hall.

"Okay," I say with a forced smile, grabbing the box I brought.

Silence is our conversation for the rest of the day.

Eleven

"Bonnie, did I ever tell you about the Donut Dollies in ' Nam?" Sam asks. His voice is a loud gruff sound as I organize his piles of mail on the coffee table, cane leaning on his lap.

In all my time spent with Sam, he's told me so much about Vietnam sometimes I swear I was there with him. The Donut Dollies might be the first topic I don't recognize.

I smile at him as I drop a piece of junk mail in the trash and shout-say, "I don't think so, Sam, and my name is Birdie!" Sam refuses to wear the hearing aids his kids keep buying him; therefore, my throat is usually exhausted at the end of every Wednesday.

"Bah!" He swats an annoyed hand through the air, as if batting my name away. "Either way, you ain't got no tits!"

I can't help it, I laugh. Out of every client I have, Sam is the biggest pain in my ass. I was offended the first time he told me how disappointed he was in my chest, but now it's just part of our banter. He tells me I'm flat-chested, I tell him he's a grump.

"Tell me about the Donut Dollies!" I say loudly, opening an electric bill, highlighting the due date.

He squints at me from his chair, rolling his cane between his hands. "First of all, they had tits, and nice ones." He shoots me a glacial look, as if I need to be taking notes on how to grow *tits*.

"Noted!" I roll my eyes. "What else?"

With a sigh, the grumpy old man's face softens to an expression that's almost wistful. Sam's eyes look into the distance at a place that doesn't exist anymore.

"'Nam was a hot hellhole, I've told you that much, I know. It was miserable. Even on days where your friends weren't dying or you weren't worried about dying yourself, it was still miserable. It didn't take much time there until home seemed like a fairy tale. The way kids imagine Neverland is how you start to picture home. Unreachable. Mythical." He startles me by sending his cane slamming onto the top of the coffee table and scattering the stacks of mail with a loud *thwack!* "Get that photo album for me over there on that shelf!" he barks. I glare at him and all my scattered papers before doing as he says.

His old, spotted hands tremble slightly as he flips to the page he's looking for. "Here we are." His finger taps heavy on a photo.

A group of men—kids really—leaning against a military-style vehicle with a canvas roof, somehow smiling despite every horrible thing Sam has shared with me. They are bare-faced, bare-chested babies with crooked smiles and a pain rooted beneath their ribs that the photos don't capture.

He flips the page again. "That's me." He smiles.

Young Sam in the photo is handsome, wearing what I imagine would be an army-green hat if it were in color and a white T-shirt. His arm is draped around a girl with her hair in two dark braids and a patch-adorned dress. She's smiling. She looks like the girl next door.

"Is that a Donut Dollie?" I ask, leaning down to look closer at the photo.

He nods.

"They'd come to camp and play games with us, give us snacks, sometimes Kool-Aid or coffee. Why we needed coffee in that hot hellhole I'll never know, but we drank it anyway because they smiled at us when they poured it. They were a taste of home when life was anything but."

Then he's quiet, staring at the album, no doubt thinking about that time of his life that words will never accurately describe. I've heard his stories every Wednesday for nearly two years, and I still can't wrap my brain around what it must have been like to be there, fighting that war in those conditions. Looking at the photos, I know now he kissed his youthful innocence goodbye in that jungle.

He flips the page again, and a photo of him grinning and covered in shaving cream, fills the page. He chuckles.

"Is this the day you learned to shave?" I tease in a voice loud enough he catches my tone.

Another chuckle, another wistful look. "They had us play a game this day. I'd just lost my best friend, Mac. He died right in front of me." I'd heard the story of how Mac died before, some kind of explosion, while Sam watched the whole thing happen, unable to stop it. "Anyway, the Dollies came right after that, and they wanted to play this game with shaving cream. They blindfolded us and we sprayed each other all over the place. We laughed, really laughed. For a split second, I forgot Mac was gone."

He slams the album shut and drops it onto the table with a thud where the once organized mail is now scattered. "They were the best worst days of my life," he says with a heavy sigh. "I hated it all, but I'd do it all again. It's confusing to anyone who wasn't there."

"Thank you for telling me about them!" I tell him, realizing I mean it. I'm honored to know his story.

I look from him to around his house, now seeing it differently after this story. He has albums on shelves and pictures of him on the walls. A soldier. Father. Husband. Friend.

Artifacts of a life, no matter how hard, well-lived.

Then I look back to Sam—skin spots, thin hair, bulbous nose.

If I somehow lived through this year, and the next, and the ones after that so I could be his age, what would be on my walls? What stories might I tell? Do I actually have any? Standing in the midst of the richness of the life he's lived, a life so full he surrounds himself with pieces of it and retells the stories of it every week, mine is inadequate. Bland.

For some reason, the thought puts my singularity under a magnifying glass.

Bo was right. I'm alive but not living. I feel that truth on a cellular level.

He squints at me, and I prepare for a barked-out order that usually comes with it, but instead, rolling his cane between his hands, his voice is calm. "The Veterans of Blue Ridge is hosting a fundraising event in a few Saturdays. There will be a band and dancing and some of my friends from 'Nam. My kids are busy, so I'm wondering if you might take me."

My chin jerks back in shock. He's never asked to do anything like this. *Ever.*

"I'd love that, Sam. It's a date!"

"Bah!" The grump in his voice returns with another swat through the air. "If I'm going on a date, it's with someone with better tits than yours."

When I laugh, I swear he smiles through his frown.

Twelve

I watch Veda's mannerisms under a microscope, hoping for something that lends to an opening of conversation about the medication, but I can't find one. No cough, no unexplained winces of pain, just arthritic hands.

"Why are you staring at me like that?" she snaps as I wedge the clay.

"I'm not staring," I lie. "I'm wondering if you ever smile."

When she surprises me by laughing, I do the same, sarcasm our currency.

I make another bowl on the wheel, this one with less frustration, and the original pinch pot I made is done in the kiln. It's hideous, covered in a color that resembles actual shit, but I give it to my dad anyway when we have dinner that night. Like the good dad he is, he beams at it.

"Little Bird, you are an artist!" he says proudly with a lift of his scotch-filled mason jar.

"That's one word for it," I say with a smile.

Bo texts me about dinner every single night; I ignore him. After him asking about Veda's health then me finding the medication, I can't talk to him. Not yet. Possibly not ever.

Then, Mabel.

After we play rummy and have Scottish smut book club, Mabel spends our entire time talking about Bo and her curiosity over what kind of marks his beard would leave on different areas of her skin. When *her* fantasies make it hard for *me* to think straight, I let her watch *Fifty Shades of Grey*, which shuts her up long enough for me to clean and make her meals for the weekend.

All the while, she writes God knows what in her little notebook.

After walking the dog with Huck and spending an hour at the gym, I cross the parking lot of the grocery store. Relaxed before I even make it to the doors.

I wave at Monica as I walk in, turning then stopping mid-step as I approach the carts. There, with a stupid smirk, toothpick, and playful fire in his eyes, stands Bo.

I school my expression, passing him like my heart didn't skip a beat at the sight of him, and grab a cart. "Grocery shopping on a Friday night again, Bo?" I ask without meeting his eyes, pulling a cart from the line and pointing in the direction of the produce. "Might give people the idea you need a life."

"Birdie, good to see you too." Amusement leaks into his voice as he follows me.

I stop at the bin of potatoes, picking one up and rolling it in my hands. "Is this one of your little list items?"

He snorts. "No. You've been ignoring me, and I need…" He grabs a random fruit from a nearby basket, tilting his head slightly to read the label. "A dragon fruit."

He holds up the spikey pink ball with a proud grin.

I bite back a smile, putting two potatoes in a bag and setting it in my cart. "I'm sure you do."

"Does it bother you that I'm here?"

I look at him. I want to say yes. Pulling my head side to side to combat the tightness that's creeping across my shoulders and up my neck from his presence alone, I want to tell him to leave me alone. Instead, I hear myself say, "No."

After a silence of us pushing carts around the produce bins, I ask, "Do you remember your parents?"

His chin pulls back, eyes widening slightly.

I shrug.

"If you're going to keep showing up here, I might as well get to know you."

With a slight smile. "Fair." Then, "And a little. I was just a kid when my dad died, but I remember random things—one year cutting a Christmas tree down with him, another year a birthday party with my mom and him hanging a piñata." He shrugs. "Almost every good memory I have from my childhood is with Gran. My grandad taught me to fish, but when he died, Gran kept taking me. Things like that. Who knows where I'd be without her. Not just me—Lucy. She's filled in my gaps since Mandy left."

I avoid his gaze as I compare two blocks of cheese.

"Do you remember your mom?"

I nod and smile easily. "I do; I was ten when she died. I have great memories—some fading a bit—of her. Dancing, baking. She always had freshly cut flowers in a vase."

I allow myself one breath of imagining how different life would be if she were still here before shaking the thought and putting one block of cheese in my cart, one back on the shelf.

"Have you ever been in love?" he asks.

I snort a laugh, neither hesitating nor acknowledging the hole it opens in my chest. "No."

I glance over at him as I stop in front of the yogurt. He's married; I don't need to ask if he's been in love.

"That's kind of sad, isn't it?" he asks.

I raise my eyebrows. "Asks the man who lets his love life be controlled by a wife who ran away? Gee, I don't know."

His jaw clenches, making me wonder if I've overstepped before deciding I don't care.

"What's your greatest regret?"

His words bring me to a stop. A loaded question I'm not sure I can answer.

The thought of answering it feels impossible, yet somehow my mouth says, "I got pregnant when I was thirty."

In the middle of an aisle, he's next to me, throat moving slowly when he swallows as he waits for me to continue.

"I was dating a guy for a while, but somehow it wasn't that serious. We used protection, a condom every time, and it worked until it didn't. As much as I wanted kids, I already knew I didn't want to give my problems to someone else, so when I was one day late on my period, I took a test. Pregnant. I broke up with the guy and cried for twenty-four straight hours." I blow out a shaky breath, pulling my shoulders back slightly. "Then I found a place that could help me. I went and sat in the parking lot and stared at that building for hours every single day." As I say the words, I'm instantly teleported back to a time seven years ago.

I'd just started my business, and for the first time felt like maybe, even if my life would never look like I hoped, it could still be good. Meaningful. Then the test, the pregnancy, and the decision that followed shattered that delusion. I can still see what I was wearing that day: leggings with two small holes in the knee and a mustard-yellow flannel shirt with brown lace-up boots. It was cold and grey outside, and the November rain pounded angrily on the windows. I had to reheat my coffee three times that morning. It's funny, the things we remember about the days we want to forget.

"You put the baby up for adoption," he says softly.

I almost laugh at how naïve he is when I look at him—how badly I wish it were that simple.

"I had an abortion." Four words and I'm hollow.

His sharp inhale sends shame shooting to every corner of my body, but I don't cry. I can't about this. I mourned the baby I'd never have for so many hours—weeks—in the aftermath of my decision. I'd negotiated with myself then that I wouldn't let this be the rest of my life: me crying about things I can't change, no matter how tragic. I know myself well enough to know that once I let the tears fall, they'll never stop. Not for this, not for anything.

I blink my gaze away, studying boxes of something I don't care about. I let the confession hang between us as a gentle song by Jewel starts to play over the speakers. The moment is mismatched. Soft music and hard truths.

"And that's when everything changed. *I* changed. I stopped having sex, stopped putting any effort into forging real relationships, and became hyper focused on the things I can control. How I felt in that clinic wasn't worth what I was doing with people I didn't care that much about. I didn't even agree with abortion until it was my turn to have this potential little person get scraped out of me. Funny how we're able to bend our beliefs when we need them to suit us, right?" My laugh is borderline cold and anything but funny. "It was the hardest decision of my life. I'm not saying I'd change it, but I think of it. Constantly. It's not a regret of my choice, more a regret that I had to make the choice. And Lucy..." I shake my head, as if trying to shake away my own reality. "She's the same age my baby would have been. That first time I saw her, when you told me it looked like I'd seen a ghost. It felt like it. Like looking at a life not realized, I guess."

Taking a deep breath—one filled with both relief and regret—I close my eyes and it's like I'm standing in the middle of a tornado, everything around me spinning out of control trying to rip me apart. His sharp inhale, his speechlessness—I know this will be where whatever this is ends. The man who begged his wife to have a child will never want to be friends with the woman who willingly eliminated one.

And yet, when his big warm hand cups my cheek, it surprises me almost as much as the fact that I lean against it. He's not running out of the store like his life depends on it; he's staying. It pulls a relieved exhale from me that I didn't know I was keeping in. His palm on my face is the singular thing that keeps me upright.

There's a lot I don't know about Bo. A novel's worth of quirks and stories and habits I'll never have the privilege to learn. But in this grocery store with all my broken pieces being brought to light, I'm certain that he's a man who knows how to hold space unlike anyone I've ever met. An allowance, no matter how messy.

When I open my eyes, it's our familiar staring: me at Bo, Bo at me.

"Birdie," he says, voice low. "No one person was made to carry so much alone."

"What's your greatest regret?" I ask, my face still leaning into his palm.

He laughs softly. "Letting the wife who ran away control my love life."

Whatever I open my mouth to say is swallowed by the rattle of metal colliding and a woman's voice. "Excuse me, can I squeeze by y'all?" She looks apologetic when she asks, clearly aware that I'm having some kind of episode.

Then I notice—my Grocery Store Confessional is taking up the entire aisle.

I move my cart to the side with a loud rattle to give her space. "Absolutely, I'm so sorry."

She smiles and pushes her cart by us, and I turn back to Bo.

"Have you noticed I'm complicated?" I say, attempting to lighten the mood.

"You know, until you brought it up, I hadn't," he says easily, grabbing a jar of peanut butter from the shelf.

I shake my head, nose scrunched. "Do you even consider what kind of oils that's made with?"

He grins. "Of course not, that's what I have you for."

And like I didn't just rip open an old wound and nearly bleed out in front of him, he spends the next half hour quizzing me on ingredients as we walk through the grocery store.

In the parking lot, bags loaded into the back of my minivan, Bo leans against his Jeep parked in the space beside me as I open my driver's side door and lean in the doorway.

"Can George Strait and I come to church with you on Sunday?" I ask.

He gives me one of his slow-to-grow smiles. "I thought you'd never ask."

I smile, nod, and drop into the driver's seat, window rolled down.

"And Birdie?" he says as I start the ignition. "Wear a bathing suit."

Thirteen

GEORGE STRAIT AND I meet Bo at a trailhead Sunday morning, and he's waiting in swim shorts, a T-shirt with the sleeves cut off, and a backpack.

"Hi," I say, tugging the leash to keep the dog from pouncing on him.

"Hi," he says with a slight lift of his lips, void of a toothpick today. He squats down next to the slobbering goldendoodle to give him an ear scrub and high pitched, "Hey, buddy! There's a good boy!" before standing and flicking his eyes back to me amusedly. "Nice hat."

I am, as usual, in my wide-brimmed straw hat, shorts, and cropped T-shirt. But today, per his request, black bathing suit ties peek out at the neckline.

"I brought this for you." He pulls a blue ball cap out of his bag and tosses it to me, Monroe Cabins written on the front in scripty font.

I shoot him a look that makes him laugh. "You can't keep hiking in that ridiculous thing."

"Why not?" I demand.

"Because it's huge and you're constantly stuck in branches."

He's not wrong. The hat is a pain in my ass. I consider wearing it anyway to prove a point, but his simple hat offering—with his last name written on it that excites me way more than it should—is the obvious far better option.

"Fine," I mumble, tossing my straw hat into the van and putting the one with his name on my head. I know he likes it because he smiles, which makes me smile.

Without another word, we're on the trail, the familiar roots and rocks under my feet. This time, instead of being surrounded by thick woods, we hug the bank of a river on one side the entire time. We find a rhythm easily in the silence and he takes the dog's leash like it's something he's always done. I fall into step behind him, and the soothing sound of the water rushing around rocks becomes our soundtrack.

"How did you start this?" I ask. "Hiking to church?"

He doesn't slow down, just looks over his shoulder slightly as he continues up the trail. "I've always loved it out here, but like most things in life, I didn't do great at making it a priority. When Mandy left, Gran wanted time with Lucy, so she started taking her on Sundays. Most people go to church at that time, which has never been my thing—but out here?" He shakes his head, and I hear the happiness in his voice when he continues. "Out here, I feel it. My head is clear, worries dissolve, and I know what's important."

He lifts the hand not holding a leash in a half-shrug. "Maybe it's God or maybe it's just disconnecting in a world that feels the need to constantly plug us in, whatever it is, it's my sacred spot—holy ground, whatever you want to call it."

"Do you ever bring Lucy?" I ask, stepping over a large protruding root.

He shakes his head.

"I never bring anyone."

Maybe it's his conviction about what he's said—how sure he is out here, regardless of how different. Or maybe it's because he's welcomed *me* into this space for some unknown reason, but it's beautiful. Special. A gift to be here *with* him.

"You still back there?" He stops, facing me, making me realize I've been quiet.

"Sorry," I say. "That's amazing. I love that you do this."

"Looks like *we* do this," he says with a smug raise of his eyebrows before turning around.

The laugh I make is a soft *pah!* and it's the only noise either of us make besides our footsteps. I don't think about cancer or dying. I don't think about how I told Bo my hardest truth in the grocery store. I don't think about Huck getting adopted. It's just a steady stream of *roots and rocks, roots and rocks* that floats through my brain along with the rustle of the water next to us.

It's as though I've stepped into a meditation app and my mind has never been so calm. Clear.

When he says, "We're here," it startles me. I have no idea how long we've been walking or where *here* even is. We've been going up at a slight incline, but it hasn't been steep, and now I see the river that we've been next to has been replaced by a slick-covered stack of smooth gigantic rocks. Boulders. Whatever's bigger than a boulder. They're huge and cascade down a gentle slope.

The water is glossy, and if the rocks weren't there it might be a waterfall we were looking at instead.

"It's beautiful," I say, mesmerized by the movement and the way the light shimmers off every wet inch of stone.

"Wait 'til you feel it," he responds, making my head whip toward him.

His arms lift, elbows bend, and he tugs at the neckline of his shirt between his shoulder blades, yanking it overhead. There's a shit-eating grin on his face when his head pops out from the cotton.

Bo is shirtless and I can't help it, I blatantly gawk. The sight of him—his muscles and tattoos that I very much see now—makes my mouth drop. An outline of mountains covers the space between his shoulders where the muscles of his neck melt into the muscles of his back in shades of grey ink with silhouettes of trees dotting the slopes.

When he turns around, it does nothing to stop my staring. Defined chest, subtle abs that lead to—a T-shirt hits my face at the same time Bo says, "Earth to Birdie," stopping my thoughts from going any further in that direction.

George Strait plops at my feet and I shake my head too many times with rapid blinking. "Sorry...swimming?" I ask, looking back at the water-covered rocks. "Hardly looks deep enough."

He points to the base of the rocks. "Down there it is."

My chin pulls back when I see the pool that he's talking about. "Then why are we up here?"

"We are going to slide down these rocks"—he glides a finger through the air—"and land in there." His hand does this splashing kind of motion that translates to exploding or being obliterated.

He smiles when I frown. "Uh, that's a hard no. Is this even legal? Or regulated?" The pitch of my voice increases with every syllable.

"I knew you'd ask, so I looked it up, and there isn't a single recorded injury or death from doing this." He has the nerve to look proud when he recites this information.

I scoff. "*Recorded?!* People get hurt all the time and don't call the authorities!" This is absolute insanity and *not* happening.

"Birdie—"

"Don't *Birdie* me," I snap. "*You* slide down this death trap and I'll meet you at the bottom."

I reach for the dog's leash and Bo grabs my hand, my gaze lifting to his in a way that I can't control. Like our eyeballs are opposite ends of magnets that have to point at each other because laws of nature say so.

"Birdie." His voice lowers and takes on a softness as he looks at me. "If I thought you'd get hurt, I wouldn't bring you here. But I've been coming since I was a kid, you'll be fine. I'll be with you the whole time." He drops my hand, bends down to his backpack, and pulls out a sticky note. When he hands it to me, I see the words *do something scary.*

My heart pulsates with a swift and constant *ba-dum!* at every surface point of my body. I look from him to the rock-slab slide, to the pool at the bottom, back to him. I stretch my neck side to side...repeatedly. In seconds, *I can't do this* turns to *Can I do this?* then *I can do this* until, finally, *I want to do this.*

It's a truth I'm not prepared for.

"If this is how I die, Bo," I say, jerking my hand from his and throwing the cap off my head. I toe my shoes off before peeling down my shorts, revealing a simple black bikini bottom. "I'm going to haunt your ass for the rest of your life."

"Deal. But you aren't going to die."

His smile is giddy, like a kid on Christmas morning, and he kicks his own shoes off then ties the dog to a tree.

Then my shirt is off, exposing the high-necked bikini top I'm wearing. I allow myself one deep breath of being self-conscious before turning and facing the water.

His eyes rake over me, approving. One side of his mouth hooks into a smirk. "Nice suit."

I roll my eyes. "Let's get this over with."

He leads the way, down a short rocky ledge then across to the top center of the highest slab. The water, barely deep enough to cover my toes, rushes across our feet and slips down the rocks. It's so cold I wince, and goose bumps shoot up my legs.

I gasp. "Jesus! This is freezing!"

"That's part of the fun, Pam Beesly." His tone implies this shouldn't terrify my heart to a point of pounding at a different rhythm.

We sit, ass to frigid rock, hand in hand. The water is so cold as it flows around my hips my skin hurts to numbness.

I look at him; he nods.

"Bo, I don't thi—"

I'm too late. He scoots himself forward just enough to hit the first slope, gravity taking him down the same way the water is, pulling me along with him.

We're sliding—fast. One drop. Two.

My fingernails dig into his hands, breeze licking at my skin, rock bumping underneath me. When I scream, it's only for it to be swallowed by the water.

It's an awful, heart-stopping, breath-stealing temperature that shoots a numbing pain from the roots of my teeth to the tips of my fingernails. My entire body feels like a brain freeze.

Our heads pop out of the water at the same time and my, "Holy shit, that's cold!" mixes with his deep, throaty, "Ahhhh!"

He smiles, droplets of water that are one degree shy of becoming icicles hanging on his beard. The desire to touch it—him—is visceral.

As if he can read my mind, he squeezes my hand that I'd forgotten he's holding.

Treading water, inches away from each other, and instantly I forget the cold or the pounding of my heart from the adrenaline over what we just did.

"Now what?" I ask, breathless from the cold, or him, or both.

"Let's do it again," he says, squeezing my hand again.

I respond with an instant smile and nod.

Like two overgrown children, we climb back up the trail and slide down the rocks again. And again.

Fourteen

June fades into July and my life falls into a routine that is just different enough to make me notice it. I go to the same classes at the gym, see my same clients during the day, and walk the dog with Huck every evening, but now Bo is waiting for me at the grocery store on Friday nights and invites me to church with him on Sunday mornings.

For the first time in my life, there are people besides my dad waiting for me at the end of the day, and it warms me as completely as facing palms to a hot fire on a cold day. I still can't commit to dinner with him; for whatever reason, that seems like a bigger deal. Like saying yes to a meal at his house means saying yes to something else—something I can't name but know I can't do.

Smiling toward the late July sun—finally warm enough to be considered hot—I cross Veda's yard.

My "Knock! Knock!" call at her door I usually give when I push it open three mornings a week dies on my lips. The door is locked.

For the first time in nearly two months of working here, I have to use the key she gave me. When I get inside, "Veda?"

Standing in her living room, every light is still off at eight o'clock and the coffee pot is empty.

"Veda?" Her name echoes around the colorful details of her quiet house. I walk back to the sunroom.

Empty.

"Veda?"

I walk down the short hallway—she isn't in the bathroom, but her bedroom door is closed. I knock gently.

"Yes, in here," her muffled voice calls, prompting me to push it open slowly.

Despite the fact the lights are still off, the bedroom glows from the morning light pouring through the sheer white curtains. She's sitting on the edge of her bed in a powder blue nightgown massaging her hands. Her bright white hair is wild around her face. She looks like a sleepy version of her. Angelic.

"Hey," I say softly, walking in. "Everything okay?"

Her eyes narrow. "Can't a woman sleep in every now and then?"

I squint at her, trying to understand what she isn't saying, and sit on the bed next to her.

We sit in a heavy silence. Looking at her, there's nothing obviously wrong other than the fact she slept later than usual, but I know by the way she sits—lets me sit—there's something.

"I wasn't snooping, but I saw the medicine," I finally say. "A few weeks ago."

She nods subtly but doesn't say anything.

"Do you want to talk about it?"

This time, she smiles and looks at me sideways.

"Getting old is a real son of a bitch." She pats my knee. "How about some breakfast?"

I force a smile back, knowing better than to push for anything more.

"If I'm making breakfast, you're wearing the gloves while I cook," I say, nudging her gently before standing up.

"Birdie," she calls as I'm walking toward door, making me pause. "Don't mention this to Bo, please."

I want to argue, but the look on her face tells me I won't win. Instead, I just nod, trying not to think about what I'm promising as I walk to the kitchen and start making her coffee.

Huck is waiting on my porch when I get home but there's no blocky smile. He doesn't even look at me when I drop onto the step next to him. He looks how I feel.

"I wonder what the strongest insect in the world is," I say, staring at the sky.

"Rhinoceros beetle," he says flatly.

The dog whimpers from behind the door. "I wonder if we should walk the dog."

He doesn't answer, just stands up and waits.

George Strait on a leash, we start walking, in silence.

"I found out today my friend is sick, and I don't know how to help her," I tell him.

Huck hops over four cracks in the sidewalk. Finally, "I found out today that I can't keep living with Miss Alice."

Whatever is happening with Veda vanishes from my mind with that sentence. I've known it was coming, but somehow, hearing it come out of Huck's mouth crushes down on me like a rockslide.

I've watched movies where something tragic happens and adults hide their emotions from their kids. I'm not a parent; I don't know anything about how to raise a child or why that's what people do, but at that moment, I don't care. A sheen of moisture covers my eyes, and I don't try to hide it.

I reach my hand out toward his, and today he takes it.

"Huck wonders if I could live with Birdie," he says, looking up at me.

The tears that well in my eyes fall in one drop then two as I look at him. I desperately wish it was easy as just saying yes.

"I don't think I'd make a very good mom," I say, looking at the dog as he sniffs around the tree.

Huck steps over another crack. "I think so."

He's a kid. He doesn't know what he's saying. He has no clue I'd just be a temporary fix that would need to be replaced later. He needs two good parents, not one with a foot in the grave.

I don't say any of that. Instead, "I always thought the leafcutter ant was the strongest bug in the world."

He barks out a laugh. "No, Birdie!"

With that simple statement, the rest of the world doesn't exist.

At his house, Miss Alice greets us at the door, sending Huck in to get ready for dinner.

"Huck told me about him having to leave," I say.

She smiles sadly. "It's just too much. With Steve. We're getting old, Birdie!" She laughs softly. "And with his condition, it's more work than we can handle."

I almost tell her if having rules govern your life and eating specific foods is a condition, I need a doctor and a diagnosis, but instead I just nod.

"I wish I could do something..."

She stares at me, twisting the dishtowel in her hands, seemingly trying to choose her next words carefully.

"You know, I've never asked how you're so beautiful, young, and single. It's none of my business, but you clearly like kids. If you ever wanted to adopt him, I'd speak for you. In the court, I mean. About how you are with him, how much he loves you..."

Adopt Huck?

"Miss Alice, that's so nice of you but..." My pulse rams behind my eyeballs and I don't have the energy to explain why I can't be the one to take him. After everything today, it's a conversation I don't have the mental bandwidth for. "I'm not married. Isn't that kind of part of it?"

She chuckles. "Goodness, no! This is modern America, Birdie! Sometimes I think they *prefer* one parent." I use the time it takes her to open the door and step inside to imagine the life she's describing—Huck living with me...as my *son*. It's farfetched. Silly even.

Before Miss Alice closes the door she adds, "Just think about it."

Fifteen

"It's August, Birdie. What say we read some lumberjack erotica?"

Here we go.

I cut my eyes to Mabel as I fold laundry. "Do I have a choice?"

She *tsks* me, passing a copy of *Wood of Love*.

It is, in fact, about a lumberjack. I want to light it on fire more than I want to read it, but the striking resemblance the guy on the cover has to Bo makes me both laugh and tingle enough between my legs for me to put my copy in my bag without arguing.

I may never touch Bo again, but I have no doubt that reading this book and imagining it's about him might be the next best thing. Naturally, I don't share this with Mabel who looks at me like she's picturing the very same things I am.

"Birdie, I bet you could get that bearded boy toy of yours to pose shirtless for a photo. We could compare him to our new main character, Aaron," she says, batting her overly mascaraed eyelashes with a sinful smile that showcases her red-stained teeth.

I look at her, this former nun of a woman, and realize how envious I am by how freely she speaks about sex. Maybe it's because I've never had close girlfriends or maybe it's because it's Bo and his looks are so good it seems greedy *not* to talk about them, but I don't ignore her inappropriate topic of conversation like I usually do. Today, I feed into it. I want to fantasize and giggle with her about what it would be like the way I imagine other women would. *Normal* women.

Folding a cheetah print pair of leggings, a smile covers my face along with a heat on my cheeks. "You know, sometimes when we hike Bo takes his shirt off."

"Heaven on a hot dog!" Mabel yells, fanning herself with her hand, dropping back onto the couch dramatically before bouncing back upright and hopping to her feet. "Hold that thought, Birdie dear, I need a gin and tonic for this one."

She's across the small room and grabbing a bottle of liquor from a glass cabinet before I can blink. I laugh in disbelief. "It's nine in the morning, Mabel!"

"Bah! If you're about to tell me about that man without a shirt on, I don't care what time it is."

While Mabel has a cocktail, I explain every detail about his muscles—the way they slope and curve down the length of his torso—and the tattoos that add to their appeal.

Then, when I think I'm done, my most unexpected confession of all: "I had sex with Bo in the minivan." As soon as the words are out my eyes widen in shock.

She gasps. "Mary Magdalene patron saint of orgasms, pray for us sinners!"

My face is so hot I wonder if my skin is going to melt off my skull, but the swearing she does under her breath—and the fact she pulls her notebook and pen out of her waistband—keeps the giddy smile plastered on my face.

"Birdie, why aren't you spending every night in bed with that man?" she asks as she takes a long slurpy sip of her cocktail. "If I were forty years younger, I'd be permanently stuck to his throbbing member!"

I snort. "It's more complicated than that."

"Life's complicated!" she shouts in disbelief and sets her cocktail on her glass-top coffee table. Her eyes look past me, as though she's watching something a thousand miles away, and her voice lowers. "You know I was a nun and left the convent. What you don't know is why I left. I fell in love, hard, with the groundskeeper, a man named Paul. It was the real kind of love that chews you up and spits you out. Every breath I took around him was a gasp, just like one of our books." She smiles, her love for him clear as day all these years later. "He wanted to marry me, and I wanted to marry him. But then I just thought, what if I'm supposed to be a nun again? In my mind, I'd left God for this man—God, Birdie! I got indecisive and couldn't commit. It was a damned if I do, damned if I don't in my mind. I grappled back and forth with this until he didn't want to wait anymore..." Her voice trails off, gaze still somewhere faraway and long ago.

"What happened?"

"Ahh, well, that's a story for another day. But he was it for me. My great love story that ended too soon. I had lots of sex—good sex too—but there was never another him." She smiles, sad yet fond, and blinks rapidly, as though she's bringing herself back to her body.

"Would you change it? If you could?"

"Of course, I would!" she cries without hesitation, picking up her cocktail again. "Hindsight is a soul-sucking whore like that."

Her words make me laugh, but there's no heat behind them. She might feel regret for how parts of her story went, but the woman in front of me is also smiling.

It's stupid, but I've gotten used to grocery shopping with Bo. I've always thought my Friday night routine was relaxing, but he's somehow made it fun *and* relaxing. Every week for the last month, he's outside the store, waiting for me, same question on his lips of, *What's on the list for us tonight, Birdie?* before leaning on a cart and strolling beside me—toothpick tickling his lips—while I read labels.

I don't just look forward to seeing him, I expect it.

When I walk up to the doors tonight and he's not there, there's an uninvited sinking feeling in my belly. I check my phone, no messages. I look around the parking lot to the spot where he always parks, no Jeep.

I wave to Monica and grab a cart, but instead of pushing it to the produce section, I sit on the bench just inside the doors. The bench, usually reserved for old men waiting on wives to shop or cashiers on break to scroll their phones while they drink a Mountain Dew, becomes the place I wait for Bo.

Ten minutes. Twenty. Thirty minutes pass.

Every time the automatic doors slide open, it's not him walking in.

I sit on the bench next to my empty cart for an hour before I accept it—he's not coming.

The worst part is, I can't even get mad. I didn't invite him to meet me here; I just assumed he would keep showing up. Aside from our hikes, we don't really do anything else together. Sometimes he stops by Veda's, but that's obviously for her and not me. Why I expect him to spend every Friday night for the rest of his life grocery shopping with me almost has the absurdity to make me laugh. Or cry. Or both.

When I stand up, I look toward the produce section and can't make myself go to it. Like my sacred space will make me feel worse instead of better tonight.

With a disappointed slump, I push the cart back to the designated area, give Monica a sad smile, and walk out of the store.

The whole drive home, for the first time in my life, I feel how alone I am. It's like Bo showing up amplified everything that's not.

That will never be. Whether I die this year or not—there's nobody to share it with.

As I pull up to my house, I see the Jeep parked at the curb before the shape of the man standing illuminated in the porch light.

Bo.

Shoulders wracked with tension, I open my door and make the short walk across my yard. All I can think is: what is he doing here?

"You forgot your groceries," he says with an easy roll of his toothpick when I'm next to him.

I dig in my purse, looking for my keys with manic punches, refusing to look at him.

"What are you doing here?" I sound angry and, for the life of me, I don't know why.

"Well, I stopped by the grocery store—where you were sitting on a bench seemingly waiting for someone—before I came here to wait for you."

The. Nerve. Of. This. Ass. Hole.

"One, that's weird. And two, I wasn't," I snap, lifting my eyes to his defiantly as he takes a step toward me. Then I add, "My foot hurt so I didn't feel like walking around the store." Followed by, "And I needed to rest it."

His gaze flicks down to my foot and his lips twitch again before his eyes return to mine. "I'll tell you what I think, Birdie. I think you were waiting for me. I think you like spending time with me and realized maybe doing everything alone—even your beloved grocery shopping—isn't as fun."

Bastard.

I scoff. "You're delusional. Your grocery commentary is mediocre at best, and the food you buy makes my skin crawl."

I fumble to get the door unlocked, pushing it open.

He leans close to my ear, whispering, "You're a liar, Pam Beesly."

The scrape of his beard on my skin and the depth of his voice is some kind of potent combination that makes my eyes close.

My "Fine," barely makes it out of my mouth as I step inside the house. If Bo wasn't so damn close to me, he would have never heard it. "I was waiting for you." I pause before saying with only slightly more conviction, "Because you need guidance with your food choices."

He vibrates with a laugh then faces me again, standing up straight. "Such a little liar."

He's got me. There's nothing else to say. I was waiting for him because I like being around him. It's a truth that I can't grasp.

George Strait circles us excitedly, whimpering with maniacal tail wags, before retreating back to his dog bed. On instinct, I walk into the kitchen and flick on the lights, only to remember I don't have any groceries to put away.

Without an invitation, Bo follows me.

I face him, hands on my hips, ignoring the way his hair is pushed back and how I seem to very much appreciate that look. "Well, you're here with my full attention. How can I help you?"

"Don't I get a tour?" He leans a hip on the counter, letting his eyes dance around the kitchen and connected living room before landing back on me.

"Ha!" I bark. "No. You'll get a tour when you don't show up after doing some kind of weird psychological experiment on me."

He smiles, like this isn't unnerving—like him being in my house after making me wait for him on a bench isn't at all annoying—and pulls a sticky note from his pocket, waving it through the air.

I scoff. "Are you kidding me? After all this, you want to do something for your little list?"

"What are you thinking about right now?" he asks, ignoring me.

"Hmm...I'm thinking about the irritating man in my house, the fact I need a shower, and wondering if I have the parmesan cheese I need for Huck's meatballs tomorrow."

"Perfect." He hands me the sticky note.

Be fully present.

I hold up my arms. "Be present? Done. I'm here, aren't I?"

"Not if you're thinking about tomorrow's meatballs and parmesan cheese," he teases, plucking the toothpick out of his mouth and tossing it in the trash can beside the refrigerator.

I roll my eyes. *Of course he makes it look effortless.*

Before I can argue, he takes three quick steps to the doorway and turns off the light. The glow from a small lamp in the connecting living room and the moonlight filtering in through the windows are all that light the space.

It's one small move—a flipping of plastic and the connection of wires—but it shifts the energy of the entire house.

Standing in the dark, my defenses strip away. Like all the effort I've put into ignoring whatever I feel for him vanished with the light.

When he's standing in front of me, I realize I'm holding my breath.

"What do you see?" he asks, voice low.

"Umm. You, I guess. I see you." My gaze goes over his shoulder. "And the lamp." I drop my head side to side. "Are we done?"

He ignores me. "What about me? Tell me more. Being present means you are tuned into the moment, your senses. In the dark, you have to work harder. You can't just glance then let your mind wander off to meatballs."

He smirks. I sigh.

Hesitate.

Clear my throat.

"Okay," I begin. "I see your hair, the way it's pushed back tonight instead of tucked behind your ears."

He nods, and I shift my weight from one leg to the other, a sort of thickness filling the air and seeping into my lungs.

"I see the line of your jaw and point of your chin." As if my words are somehow connected to his tissues, his jaw clenches. "And the way that, even with your beard, your dimples show with a slightest of smiles." I pause, realizing he's not smiling, and I've just said something I don't see now, that I just see. All the time. "In the dark, your eyes look almost black except for where the light hits them slightly—there they look some shade of gold." The right side of his face is bathed in the moonlight pouring through the window. "And you have one freckle below the corner of the right one."

"What else?" he asks, voice low. Rusty as an old nail.

My eyes drop from his face, and he swallows. "I see you swallow. It's slow, like it's a struggle." He repeats the motion, and I wonder if it's on purpose. "And I see the way your shoulders slope before slipping to the muscles of your arms. The way your T-shirt wraps around them."

Somehow, just describing him, my chest tightens.

"Your turn," I say, trying to buy myself recovery time.

He shakes his head.

"This isn't about me, Birdie."

"It is if you're in my kitchen. Your turn."

A nod.

Slow swallow.

"I see the way your hair is wild because you've been at the gym. Curled pieces against your forehead the color of honey when the light hits it. And your eyes, that look almost like coffee, are always moving, assessing. You have eyelashes that probably make other women jealous."

For the first time, I'm thankful for the dark, because heat shoots across my chest and up my face. But I'm still. A statue. Wondering if he can hear the pounding of my heart.

"I see the way your lips are shaped like a heart when they close. And the inviting slope of your neck to your shoulder. How your shirt always seems to pull to one side, close to falling down your shoulder but never quite doing it. Like it wants to be touched."

I nod—I think.

"Your turn again." His voice is so coarse it creates friction in my veins. "What do you hear?"

I close my eyes. Breathe as deep as my lungs will let me.

Listening.

"My heart...that's it. I only hear my heart."

The quiet pause that follows lasts three heartbeats.

"Keep your eyes closed," he says, his voice coarser than a whisper.

I do as he says, flinching slightly when something touches my neck. It's light and cool. Gentle. Soft, but not cloth. Something delicate.

Whatever it is moves across my neck.

Down my arm.

Across my fingers.

When it touches my hip, he slows. Even through my yoga pants, chills wash across me.

He drags it down the outer line of my leg, stopping inches above my knee before pulling it across the front, then up the inside of my thigh.

Slowly.

Up.

Up.

Stop.

Less than an inch away from the spot where a pressure is building, he's still.

My pulse in my ears and the rapid rising and falling of my chest is how I imagine a skydiver reacts before they throw themselves out of an airplane.

"Bo?" I whisper, eyes still closed.

He doesn't answer, but I hear his breathing. Shallow as mine.

Four heartbeats later, he's moving again, making the ache between my legs turn almost unbearable as he drags the object across my pubic bone—skimming. A teasing drive-by that makes my thighs flinch. One thought crosses my mind: I would let him do very naughty things to me with whatever it is he's holding. Without regret.

Then it's gone, slipping down my other thigh, across my leg, retreating up the hip.

At my belly, he stops. He's barely touching me yet I'm throbbing. Everywhere. A fiery torch in human form.

The way my body is buzzing, if Bo just put his hands on me—once—I have no doubt I'd melt into some kind of screaming orgasmic puddle on my kitchen floor in the matter of seconds.

Instead...up.

Sternum.

Throat.

Against my will, my head drops back.

He drags it along my jaw, across my lips. The sweetness of it dances up to my nose. *A flower.* A flower in Bo's hands has become some erotic magic stick that nearly scorches the clothes right off me.

By the time he finishes, he's closer to me, heat radiating.

"What do you feel?" His voice comes out like molasses, dripping to every corner of me.

"You."

When I open my eyes, he's there. Looking at me. Close. The rising and falling of his chest matches mine. What's in me is in him; I see it. Feel it.

He sets the flower he'd pulled from a vase down on the counter—a zinnia that I'll never look at quite the same—not taking his eyes off mine.

We're inches apart standing in my kitchen, staring at each other in the dark. Half hidden by shadows.

"What are you thinking about?" he asks.

"You," I whisper. Instant.

He doesn't move.

"What are we doing, Bo?" I ask, not moving.

He licks his lips. "I don't know."

"I might die."

"And I have a wife."

Looking at Bo, I think of Mabel and the things she missed out on with Paul. Her *hindsight is a soul-sucking whore.* I know what we both have to lose, but in this moment, all I want him to do is this.

"Bo—" My next words are stolen by the sound of George Strait barking. I blink, twice, and shake my head out of whatever trance I've been standing in. The dog that somehow moves like a silent ninja is standing at my feet, wagging his tail. Pissing my vagina right off.

I laugh under my breath, scrubbing my hand across the top of his head. When my eyes find Bo again, he's backed away from me far enough to turn on the light, causing both of us to blink to adjust to the brightness.

He smiles at me, but it doesn't meet his eyes as he lingers in the doorway of the kitchen. "I should go."

I don't want him to, but I nod, walking him to the door then onto the porch.

I stop at the top of the steps; he stops at the bottom.

Then.

"If the offer still stands, I think I'd like to come over for dinner."

Sixteen

I've already sweated through my underwear. Twice.

Every item of clothing I own sits in a pile on my bed as I try on another outfit. And another.

Why I'm so nervous about dinner makes no sense, yet here I am, freaking out.

Finally, a winner: long floral skirt and cream-colored linen shirt with strappy sandals. I quickly braid my hair to the side, showcasing the big feathery earrings that dangle from my ears.

After texting every concern I have about food—for both me and Huck—I told Bo I'd just bring my own cooler. When he said we were having pizza, I nearly canceled the whole thing and offered to cook instead.

He told me to relax, and I did. Sort of.

When I stood on my porch last night and said I wanted to come for dinner, I thought I'd have time. His version of time and mine are very different. I expected a week; he gave me twenty-four hours.

"What's the big deal? You have to eat dinner every day, don't you?" He said it like I haven't planned my meals for the next month. Like I wasn't nearly having a stroke in front of him.

Yet, here I am, cooler in tow as I meet Huck out at the minivan. The sight of him makes me give an audible *aww!*

He's wearing a blue checkered button-down shirt with a red bow tie, and his hair is combed to one side. It's so adorable—he's so proud—my heart squeezes as I open the van door for him as Miss Alice waves at us from the porch.

"Huck wonders what Bo's house is going to be like!" he shouts from the back seat.

"Me too. It's probably a tent," I joke, making him laugh as we drive.

When we get there, I'm both incredibly surprised and not surprised at all. Bo lives in the cabin I accidentally liked on his social media page. It's a poetic sort of irony as we stand outside of it, windows glowing in the middle of the patch of woods as the sun just starts to set. Like Veda's house, I don't even need to go inside to know the stacked-up logs create a space that feels like home. Bo built something people both love and share love in. Where life happens.

Lucy meets us first, bouncing down the steps in a yellow dress, running to us at a full sprint. "Birdie!" She hugs me and it's all arms, butterfly clips, and giggles before she pulls back and stares at Huck.

"I like your bow tie," she says to him.

He grips my hand and steps behind me, quiet. I kneel down next to him. "Huck, this is my friend, Lucy. I think she has a Venus flytrap plant somewhere."

Lucy nods. "I do!" She beams. "Do you want to see it, Huck?"

Before I can interfere, "Do you want to see it, Huck?" pops out of his mouth.

Lucy giggles and puts a hand over her mouth. "Sorry, I forgot. What I meant was…I wonder if you want to see my Venus flytrap."

Bo told her.

Then I see him, walking over to us, and I simply stare. Apparently, I find explaining to your kid how to handle people who are different extremely attractive, because all I want to do is shove my tongue down his throat the moment he's next to me.

Huck squeezes my hand, reminding me we aren't alone, and I give him a nod. He looks at Lucy and smiles. She starts running with a shrill, "This way!" and he follows.

Then it's just me, Bo, and my cooler facing his cabin.

"It looks better in the pictures," I say, picking up the cooler, which he immediately takes from me.

"Photoshop can do wonders these days." He looks at me, letting his eyes wander from my head to my toes without care as he rolls a toothpick across his lips. "And you're beautiful."

The thank you I say is a flustered mumble as we climb the steps of the porch.

He sets the cooler down outside the front door and looks at me. Gentle yet serious. "I'm leaving this out here, but if you want any of it, I'll come get it and I won't be upset."

I nod. He means it. If I run out here and pull all of my food out and heat it on his stove while they eat pizza, he won't be mad. The relief that knowledge gives me is a freeing gift I'm not sure he knows the value of.

He opens the door, we step inside, and I see three things at once.

One, the house is gorgeous. It's all exposed wood and black iron and windows. The walls are mostly bare, showing off the logs they're made of, but there are also pictures hanging too. Lucy. Veda and her late husband. Cabins he's built. Snapshots, nothing fancy. He has exactly one plant in the space, and it sits in a pot that his gran made. Artwork that Lucy has made covers the fridge.

As if it wasn't already obvious, it confirms that Bo is as sentimental as they come.

Two, the large island countertop is made of two slabs of irregular wood with a center filling, known as a river. But it's not just any river—which is usually epoxy—it's concrete. I know the counter as well as my own face. I run my fingertips across it, familiarity tingling my skin. My dad made it, and I spent many of our Thursday night dinners standing around it in his shop as he talked me through the steps.

This means, without a doubt, Bo knows my dad. He's been to the home I grew up in and the shop my dad and I figured out how to be a different kind of family in after my mom died. I don't know if I believe in fate, but for some reason—this feels like it. Like Bo having this piece of me in his house means every list, rule, and safeguard in the world couldn't have prevented me from meeting him.

It's not the sheer beauty of the house, nor the fact Bo owns something my dad made that steals the breath right out of my lungs: it's number three. The food. All the ingredients are lined up on one counter, labels facing toward us. There are four balls of dough, all colored red, and bowls of shredded cheese—organic and pasture-raised per the label that's next to them—all dyed the same color. Red cheese, red dough. Marinara sauce simmers on the stove sending the smell of tomatoes and garlic swirling through the air.

Bo could be next to me as much as in a rocket ship heading to the moon; the food is the only thing I see. Hand to my mouth, I walk around the counter and read every label. They are brands I usually buy, that he's watched me buy in our hours in the grocery store. Even more, the coloring, with natural dye, is for Huck.

He bought food he never would have and colored it a ridiculous color so we would be comfortable in *his* house.

Standing in Bo's kitchen is like watching my life change and I'm gobsmacked by it.

Finally, my eyes find his, and I can barely swallow.

"Does it pass the Birdie ingredient inspection?" he asks, hands shoved in the front pockets of his jeans.

There are a million and one things I want to say. *Thank you! Veda raised you right! This is the nicest thing anyone has ever done for me! Mabel is going to die when she hears this!* But all I can make my mouth say is, "Your wife is a damn fool."

A laugh bursts out of him at the same time he bumps my shoulder with his. "Her loss is your gain, I guess." And, though he says the words in my ear, they spread through my body and imbed themselves in my bones. Fossilizing himself into me.

When the kids come downstairs, we roll the dough. Huck won't touch it, but he likes using the rolling pin. Then come the toppings and putting them in the oven. Lucy sings the whole time, and Huck laughs. Bo and I drink a glass of wine—one he drove all the way to Asheville to get because it's organic.

His thoughtfulness is a boundless thing, and every single detail he's included feels like him reaching a hand into my chest and plucking another sliver of my heart out that will forever belong to him.

I've never had a meal like this planned for me before. Every guy I've dated simply bought bags of salad that were really just hunks of iceberg lettuce and called it health food. Hell, even the grass-fed steak my dad feeds me on Thursday nights come from a butcher I order from.

When dinner is over and the kids sit at the table playing Connect 4, it's a sort of comfortable feeling I've never known as Bo and I sit together on the couch and watch them.

"Thank you for this. Again. And again." I stretch my legs across his lap. With his dark hair tucked behind his ears, worn Monroe Cabins T-shirt clinging to his chest, and bare feet sticking out from the bottom of his jeans as they prop up on his coffee table, it's such an easy scene it almost hurts. A temporary glimpse of something beautiful that can't be mine. A life for people who have more time.

He slides a hand under my skirt and squeezes my calf, saying, "Bet you wish you would have said yes sooner," with a grin.

"Ha!" I lift my wineglass to my lips, saying over the rim, "Joke's on you! Why do you think I let you come grocery shopping with me? You never would have known how to do this."

"All this time I thought I was the only one using psychological warfare tactics." Another squeeze on my calf then he runs his palm along my shin. What he's doing isn't even remotely sexual, but the heat from it slinks right up my legs and hits between my thighs where it simmers. Lingers. Thoughts catapulting to my near flowergasm from last night, raising my body temperature by degrees.

Get your shit together, Birdie.

From the table, Huck shouts, "You won!" at Lucy, and I snort out a laugh as the sound pulls me from the lewd desires dancing in my mind. His smile is a permanent rectangle above his now crooked red bow tie. He's so damn happy.

"Have you thought about adopting him?" Bo asks.

I set my wineglass on the coffee table, filling my cheeks with air before blowing them out slowly.

"Miss Alice, his foster mom, brought that up. She's trying to find another home for him—her husband is sick." I pause, imagining all the *what ifs*. "I don't know how to be a mom. Look at all you had to do to make dinner for me—" I laugh with a dramatic gesture toward the entire Whole Foods worth of ingredients in his kitchen. "How would I be good at raising someone else?" I pause, more *what ifs* dancing around my brain. "And because of my situation, I wouldn't do it unless I had someone that I could put in my will to take him when I die."

I don't miss the way his breath stills and eyes widen. I've spent my life talking about death—my grandma's, my mom's, mine—I forget everyone isn't as blasé about the subject. I don't want to die, but I've also accepted there's a good chance I will, likely sooner than later.

"Anyway, I don't have a lot of people in my life. My dad, but he's in his sixties and I wouldn't want to put that burden on him..." I drop my head back on the armrest of the couch and stare at the exposed beams that line the ceiling overhead.

He shrugs, not looking away from the kids. "Gran took me in when she wasn't that much younger. She figured it out."

The mention of Veda tenses my whole body. I won't be able to lie to him if he directly asks me how she's doing—my plan is to avoid talking about her at all costs. The second she told me not to tell Bo about the medication, it started eating away at me like a slow-growing parasite.

"And Libby helped me. A lot." He turns to look at me, clearly oblivious to my internal struggle, rough palm sliding up and down my shin. "People have a tendency to show up if you let them."

I consider arguing, reminding him that I don't have all these people like he does, but looking at him—his genuine sincerity and belief in what he's saying—I stay silent. Instead, I drag my legs off him and busy my mouth by taking a final sip of my wine. He'll never understand; he has people, I don't.

"Either way," I say, dropping my head side to side. "I don't know if my dad would want to, and I wouldn't want to ask anyone else."

He looks at me—really looks at me—and when he opens his mouth to say something, I stand, guilt over Veda clinging to me like a bad habit.

"Mind if I take a picture of that live edge river top and send it to my dad?" I ask, diverting the direction of the entire conversation.

His eyebrows pinch as he stands slowly. "Live edge river top?" He laughs, pulling the toothpick out of his mouth. "How the hell do you know that phrase?"

Right.

"My dad got into woodworking as a hobby when I was younger." I shrug. "Guess some of it stuck."

Staring at my ceiling fan, I replay the best dinner of my life in my head, over and over. I thanked Bo at least a dozen times, but it still doesn't seem like a big enough word for what he did. When we said goodbye, I was awkward. Like we were leaving something unfinished. Mostly because he stood—casual—toothpick rolling across his slightly smirked lips while I loaded Huck in the minivan.

As the kids yelled back and forth at each other through the closed window, all I wanted to do was touch him. Run my fingers through his beard and let his hands rest on my hips. But he didn't make a move to get any closer, and neither did I. I opened my door, gave him some kind of rigid wave, and drove away. My stomach flip-flopping in my belly the entire drive.

Grabbing my phone, I send a quick, *Thank you. Again.*

Bo: *You're welcome. Again.*

Me: *Are you free Thursday night? I want to take you and Lucy somewhere for dinner.*

Bo: *Depends. Are you coming with me to church tomorrow morning?*

Teeth scraping my bottom lip, I smile at my phone.

Me: *Pick me up on the way?*

Bo: *Always. And I want to tell you something, but I know you'll just argue if I say it in person...*

Three dots appear and disappear and my heart pounds like a jackhammer in the silence.

Bo: *If you want to adopt Huck, I'll take him if anything happens to you. I'm not going to bring it up again, because I don't plan on letting anything happen to you, I just want you to know. I'll be here. For you. And him.*

I can't breathe. Every inch of skin on my body shrinks around my bones.

Then, like he's a damn clairvoyant and knows my brain stopped working with his offer, *Night, Birdie*, is the last message he sends.

The next morning at church, he doesn't bring it up. Neither do I.

Seventeen

Bo doesn't know where we're going when I pick them up. I'm a woman of so few surprises, and this is something I can give him that nobody else can, and I want that. It's embarrassing how desperately I want it.

When we turn into my dad's driveway and the white wooden house and metal-sided shop come into view, Bo recognizes them. Anyone that orders a custom piece in the area comes here to iron out details; he's probably been here at least once.

He scrubs a hand across his beard and laughs a disbelieving sound. "Your dad is Greg Hawkins."

George Strait barks from the back of the van when he sees my dad's waving arm, and Lucy giggles from the noise.

I tap my chin thoughtfully. "Did I forget to mention that?"

"No wonder you're throwing around phrases like *live edge river slab*. Little liar," he teases, poking me in the side with his finger.

When Lucy and the dog tumble out of the back of the van, Bo's smile nearly cracks his face in half before he wraps a hand around the back of my neck and presses his lips to mine. It's not passionate, not long. It's not a kiss that's supposed to lead to something else. There's no tongue, no hands cupping my face—it's almost chaste. His lips are on mine just as fast as they pull away. A peck.

He doesn't kiss me for sex. His kiss is what I imagine happening at the beginning of the day over a cup of coffee before he asks, *How did you sleep last night?* As though I'm familiar—loved, even. Like he's so happy he couldn't not and keeping it to himself would go against every instinct of what it means to be alive.

I know that's not what Bo is thinking as I look into his dark smiling eyes, I know that, but I can't stop *myself* from imagining it. With him. What would it be like if he kissed me over coffee in the warm morning light or when he signed a contract for a new cabin because he just couldn't not?

As often as I've replayed the ways we touched each other that first night we met, this simple kiss of his changes me the way the sunrise changes the horizon—drastically.

He pulls away from me, still smiling, and opens the door while I sit like an idiot with my mouth hanging open. I know I should tell him to stop whatever that was, but I can't. I'm greedy to know him, greedy for his skin to be against mine in any way I can have it. Someday it will hurt. Someday this all might be a bit like Sam's Best Worst Day stories from Vietnam. But right now? Right now, these are just the *best* days, and I can't let myself let that go.

He has a wife, and I might only have a few good months left in me, but as true as those two things are, I care less about them with every day that passes.

Through the windshield, I watch Bo give my dad the kind of hug that's half handshake, half pat on the back and I can tell he's introducing Lucy because my dad kneels down to shake her hand. My heart stutters. Seeing my dad with Lucy is a glimpse of something that I've stolen from him. The grandchild he'll never have because my decision took it once, and my shitty genes will take it forever.

He stands, smiles at me, and resumes his too enthusiastic wave overhead.

It's his familiar hug, smell of wood chips and soap, and easy, "Hey, Little Bird!" when I join them.

"Hi, Dad." I smile, leaning into him. "I see you've met Bo and Lucy."

"Lucy, I welcome with open arms," he says, looking down at her fondly. "But this guy?" He nods toward Bo then brings a hand to his chest in mock pain. "Too many bad memories, Birdie. How dare you after what that concrete did to me!"

We're laughing as we walk into the workshop, busted cookie slab still on the table. The cracks that made it broken before are now filled with turquoise epoxy mixed with gold. It still needs to be sealed, but it's stunning.

"Dad!" I gasp. "It's amazing."

He reaches toward his shelf for a mason jar, but today grabs two, blowing off the dust and pouring a scotch for both him and Bo.

"What are you doing with this piece, Greg?" Bo asks, taking a sip, circling the slab.

My dad drinks from his own glass with a satisfied *ahh!* before answering.

"Don't know yet. It's not what I planned so I'll need to find someone who likes a different kind of beauty. The unexpected kind. The kind that takes bravery to love." He eyes me, then Bo, like that's supposed to mean something, and we fall into a silence that's either extremely comfortable or completely uncomfortable. I seem to be the only one that notices because they look at the slab and sip their drinks calmly while I can't stand still. In my thirty-seven years on this planet, I've never once brought a boy home—my dad knows this means something. He probably knows what it means more than I do.

It's Lucy's high-pitched giggle and the dog's playful bark from outside that finally cuts the quiet.

"You better feed us old man," I say. "That dog wants a bone."

Dinner has its own kind of energy, different than when it's just Dad and me. Bo and he talk about all things woodworking, lumber, and building, laughing occasionally when one of them tells a story that's shocking by the other's standards. Lucy sits next to me on one side and tells me all about a summer camp she went to at a dance studio.

When she says, "My dad tells me to be humble, but I'm pretty sure I was the best one there," I can't help but laugh.

Bo's hand rests on my leg just above my knee, squeezing it every so often, as if reminding me he exists. Little does he know, I'll never be able to scrub that fact from my mind, body, or soul. Every time his grip tightens, my eyes meet his, and no matter where he is in the conversation with my dad, his lips pull slightly to one side in an almost-smirk, one of his toothpicks dancing in the movement.

When our after-dinner routine leads us to the front porch, it's the three of us in rocking chairs, the dog chewing a bone, and Lucy chasing lightning bugs.

"So, Bo," my dad says in his slow easy voice, the slightest hint of playfulness. "What are your intentions with my daughter?"

If there were a drink in my mouth, I'd spit it. Instead, my eyes bug out with an exasperated, "Dad!"

Bo chuckles, unfazed, and reaches over to my lap and grabs my hand in his. "Well, Greg, I'm trying not to fall in love with her, but she's making that damn difficult."

My head snaps to face him and I try to yank my hand away. His grip only tightens. He smiles. *Smiles!*

"That she does," my dad says, lifting his glass to his lips, giving me a smirk.

I yank my hand free and raise my palms toward them both as I stand. "You know what? No, Bo, that's not funny. And, Dad, seriously? That's how you defend my honor?!"

Hands on my hips, the heat in my words cools instantly when the song that floats through the screen door shifts to the familiar George Strait tune. My dad sets his glass down and grabs my hand, grinning as he stands.

He wants to dance. After that. With Bo just sitting here.

As though my dad can hear my thoughts, he says, "Bo," –takes my hand in his—"Birdie and I have a George Strait dance every Thursday. It's tradition, right, Little Bird?"

I'm annoyed, with both of them, but I hear myself say, "Yep!" as my dad starts twirling me around the porch. My annoyance fades to contentment in a matter of seconds from the familiarity of it all. When he spins me, I'm mid-laugh when Bo and Lucy start dancing right next to us. She's hugging his legs, standing on his toes, and he's smiling as he looks down at her, fingers tickling her hair. My heart swells so much there isn't enough room for a full breath to get into my lungs.

"Your momma's eyes are happy tonight, Birdie," my dad says as we dance. "He's a good one."

"He is," I say softly, looking over my dad's shoulder to Bo. Our gazes collide and hold. There's an intensity in the way he looks at me. Like it might be generating an actual temperature that could burn anything that comes between our line of sight on each other.

When the song stops, my dad hugs me. "Do it scared, Little Bird," he whispers in my ear. "Some time will always be better than none." Just like he always does, my dad sees me and all the worry I carry around with me like a suitcase that's permanently fused to my hand.

What if I get sick? is all I can think. Only I'm not just thinking it, I say it out loud because my dad's arm is around my shoulder, squeezing it, as we watch Bo run around with Lucy and the dog in the yard. "Then you'll have someone to fight with you, Birdie. Just like your mom did."

Lucy is asleep when I park in front of Bo's house. When he lifts her out, her eyes stay closed as he carries her inside to her bed. I wait on his porch, unable to stand still.

Do it scared. My dad's words could be my life slogan.

When Bo's back outside with me, his Bo-ness is intoxicating. Casual T-shirt, jeans, tousled hair, dark eyes—under the warm glow of the porch light, everything about him has a sexier texture.

Then his hands are on my hips, and my breathing stops.

"What are we doing, Bo?" My eyes search his, praying to find some kind of answer revealed in the way he looks at me.

He shrugs. "Living."

Living. He's right. I know it down to my marrow. Down to whatever marrow is made out of. The way he makes me feel—makes me want to feel.

I swallow. Scared, but alive. "If I get sick?"

"I'll be here."

"And Mandy?"

He sighs. "And Mandy."

I close my eyes, blowing out a breath, not knowing what his response means but somehow understanding it. Because, just as much as I'm destined to die of cancer, he's married.

He lifts his palm to the side of my neck, fingers resting lightly on my skin as his thumb brushes my earlobe, tilting my chin toward him.

"I want to kiss you," he says, his rusty voice crawling all over my skin. Under it.

"I think I want that too," I whisper, sliding my hands around his waist, pressing my fingers into his back.

Then, he does.

Lips to lips, tongue to tongue, scrape of his beard against the smoothness of my skin. The way Bo kisses me melts my bones.

My hands move from his waist, up the length of his torso, and press into his chest.

When his mouth leaves mine, it's to nip a trail down the column of my neck that sends heat firing through me.

Pulling away, his forehead drops to mine.

His breathy, "I want you to come inside," meets my nervous, "I'm not ready."

He smiles.

"I'll wait."

I smile.

"Okay."

No arguing, no telling him not to ask again. The okay I give him is the best I have.

"Okay," he says, smiling, pulling his forehead away from mine. "Can I see you Saturday?"

"Actually, I have a date."

"Oh really, Pam Beesly?" The way he raises his eyebrows tells me he only half-believes me.

"I do. With one of my clients. At the Veterans of Blue Ridge. There's a fundraiser with music and Vietnam vets. I might find my once in a lifetime love there," I say with a grin.

He ghosts one last kiss on my lips. "Maybe you will."

Eighteen

"I wonder what Huck thought about Bo," I say, popping a meatball into my mouth.

Huck grins and drops a meatball on the floor for the dog before eating one himself. "He's nice, Birdie. I think he likes me."

I snort. "Of course he likes you, Huck, I wonder why you would say that."

Another meatball plops to the floor, and George Strait eagerly licks it up.

"Some of the kids at school don't like me," he says with a matter-of-fact tone that squeezes at me. "Miss Alice gets frustrated when I don't eat the right food."

I sigh, looking at him. "You don't worry about that, Huck. People get frustrated with me all the time. They think the food I eat is complicated or my lists are silly!" I could talk this kid's ear off about all the ways I annoy people. "Some people will get you, some people won't—that happens forever and to everyone, even when you feel like it's just you."

He's quiet, as though he's trying to hear the words I've said twice.

He picks up a Lego creation off the table and fidgets with it in his hands.

"Huck wonders what happens when I leave Miss Alice's house." There's a tinge of sadness in his words and my mind instantly goes to Bo's offer—to take him if I do, after I'm gone.

I believe him—he would. After seeing his effort with the pizza, I know he understands him, but the worry I can't shake is if it would be a burden on him. Would he resent me for the rest of his life because he got a kid he never planned for who's so different? On one hand, even if he did resent me, I'd be dead, so maybe that argument doesn't matter. No—I still don't want to be responsible for his unhappiness, even from the grave.

"You'll end up somewhere great, kiddo, I just know it."

I push the pan of meatballs closer to him and he smiles slightly before taking one for himself and one for the dog.

"Huck wishes he could live with Birdie," he says with a full mouth, "and Bo and Lucy."

With this, I'm speechless. I don't know how to even respond. On one hand, it's a reality that doesn't exist. A pretend world. But on the other, I can imagine it. Us—and Bo and Lucy—living a good life...*together*. It's a jarring realization that nearly takes my breath away. Not just the image of it—a fabricated portrait in my mind—but the notion that I would want it. Almost long for it.

"Me too." Because I really do.

"Some termites mate for life," he says, shifting the focus of the entire conversation. "And they have millions and millions of babies."

I scrunch my nose. "That sounds like a lot of meatballs."

He laughs loudly, marinara sauce staining the skin around his mouth.

When we finish our lunch, we spend the rest of the day watching videos about termites.

Nineteen

THE VETERANS OF BLUE Ridge is a faded, tan-painted block building on the edge of downtown Laurel Hills.

Sam is dapper in a pair of dress slacks, shined shoes, white button-down shirt, and more cologne than usual. On top of his round bald head is a faded black cap with the words Vietnam Veteran stitched in gold. Shuffling across the parking lot, he uses his cane in one hand while I hook an arm through his other.

"We'll be the talk of the town walking into this shindig together!" I shout-say to him with a teasing smile.

He winces then shouts, "Don't yell, dammit, you'll blow my eardrums out!" He points to his ear—he's wearing his hearing aids. I don't bother hiding my grin.

"Must be a special group if you actually want to hear them," I say.

His eyes flick down to my outfit. A cream-colored sleeveless shirt that stops just above the waistband of a long red skirt. I pulled my hair up into a high bun, and, in the spirit of patriotism, gold stars dot my ears.

He grumbles something when he looks back to my face, no doubt about my *tits*, but his usual scowl is in a straight line. Sam is basically smiling.

We walk by the sign that says "Welcome to the public! We support our Vets!" as I push open the doors. Sam's usually somewhat stooped posture straightens, as if he's proud, and he steps inside with a swagger that isn't usually there. Chin lifted, shoulders back, it's still grouchy Sam next to me, but he's also the baby-faced soldier in his photos.

I start to pull my arm out of his, thinking maybe he'd like to make this entry on his own, but when my forearm starts sliding by his, his elbow pinches it to his side as we walk. He wants me there.

Inside the block building is an open space filled with round tables surrounded by metal folding chairs. There's a drop ceiling with watermarks, but there are also strings of bulbed lights that give it a playful, modern feel. In the corner is a stage with a guitar, drums, and a couple of microphones with tattered speakers on either side. Band members laugh as they plug in cords.

A few folks call, "Sam!" and raise their drinks to him as we walk by. In response, he nods, slightly pinching the rim of his hat toward them. He's beaming.

There's a small bar, a dozen people that look like Sam at different phases of life—hats embroidered, showcasing their own spots in history—laughing with beers in hand. At the tables are the oldest of the veterans—canes, walkers, and the occasional wheelchair tucked under the edges. Most of the men have round bellies, and the women beside them have white hair and bright lips.

The only way I know how to describe the scene is inspiring. Because though it looks like a building that needs work, the people that fill it do not. They are men and women like Sam, stories filled with Best Worst Days that lived to talk about them. Just *lived*. They came back from wherever they were sent and somehow found camaraderie on the other side. Twin flames, soul mates, other halves, whatever the right word is. Their chapters of hard truths didn't define the rest of their lives. The symphony of voices and random bursts of laughter form a sort of triumphant anthem that covers my arms in goose bumps.

"What are we just standing here for, Bonnie? Let's go find the boys!" Sam tugs my arm, pulling me from my thoughts.

I smile, not bothering to correct him. "Let's do it."

When the music starts to play, Sam has a beer, and we're at a table with his friends. When he introduces me, he says, "This is Birdie, she's the best I could do." I'm so stunned at the fact he knows my name that I ignore the rest of the introduction. Everyone around the table laughs and says an assortment of, "We won't tell anyone if you kick the cane out from under him," or, "You must have drawn the short straw," and my favorite, "We all ignore Sam," when they shake my hand.

When they catch up with each other, I'm not part of the conversation but can't stop smiling or get enough of hearing them talk to each other.

In a small patch of worn linoleum flooring, people start to dance to the classic rock covers the band plays. Due to their age and declining mobility, there aren't big wiggles of hips or bending of knees—dancing takes on more of a shuffle—but they twist, shoulder shimmy, and snap fingers softly with smiles on their faces, lips singing every lyric.

Sam's knee bounces as his toe and cane tap to the beat next to me.

"Do you want to dance, Sam?" I ask him.

He answers by way of a facial metamorphosis: scowl turns to flat line turns to grin.

"Do I ever!" he shouts.

The way he jumps from his chair with his cane is like a spring that's been trapped in a small box finally set free.

We shimmy and twist and shuffle like everyone else on the dance floor. One song turns into two into five. Sam never stops smiling. This grouchy asshole of a man is the happiest I've ever seen him as we dance to a cover band and sweat drips down my back.

Somehow, a circle of dancing bodies forms around us. In the spirit of putting on a show, I take Sam's cane and he dances without it for a few seconds—his hands in loose fists overhead as he shuffles, his friends all clapping and cheering.

Finally, when I'm thirsty and Sam's legs are tired, we walk back to our table, breathless.

"That was fun," I say, smiling.

"That's what it's all about," he replies. "I'd go to war a hundred times knowing that nights like this were waiting on the other side."

His grey eyes are dancing as he says it; he means it. All his Best Worst Days were worth it.

He takes the last sip of his beer and sets his empty plastic cup on the table.

"I'll get you another beer," I offer, standing up. "I need a gallon of water anyway."

I don't miss his, "It's about time you do something useful," as I walk away.

When I look over my shoulder at him, he's smiling.

At the bar, I order water and a beer and wait while the busy bartender hustles around.

"I have to admit," a deep voice says into my ear, "I didn't know Pam Beesly had moves like that." The familiar scraping of a beard against my skin shoots chills across my neck and awareness to every corner of my body. I don't have to look, but I do.

There stands Bo.

Twenty

I'VE ACCEPTED MY BODY does this thing where all breathing, heart beating, and logical thinking stops at the first moment of Bo recognition. I know now to expect an ache to touch him or be touched by him. I know that, for just a few seconds, my bones will go soft, and I will have to fight to stand upright. I've stopped stopping myself from noticing the way lines crinkle around his dark brown eyes with his slow-to-grow smile, the way his hair is tousled to accidental perfection, and how he wears a beard and T-shirt—tonight with a flannel over it—like I've never known possible. I know his smell, that damn Bo Mountain Breeze, will go into my nose then infiltrate my body like an infectious disease at first contact, making my mouth water.

And that toothpick that rolls across his lips that I once found ridiculous, briefly becomes the object of my intense jealousy for the audacity it has to be so close to his mouth.

I fought all those things the first times we saw each other, but now, I just let it happen. I accept that he has the power to do this—to ruin me. Like a traveler seeking refuge from a storm, I've learned to just wait it out until I can breathe again.

"What are you doing here?" I ask, almost dizzy from the shock of him.

He leans casually against the bar next to me. "You told me you might find your once in a lifetime love tonight, I needed to see who he was."

I tuck my chin down to my shoulder, looking away to hide my smile.

"Any luck?" he asks.

The bartender sets the drinks on the bar, and I drop cash down before picking them up.

"Not yet, but the night's young." I raise my eyes to his. "Do you want to meet my date?"

"Lead the way," he says, and picks up his own beer from the bar, following me through the crowd.

At the table, we sit. It's introductions. There are, "I knew your grandfather, Bo" comments and him thanking them each for their service. He's so damn thoughtful it hurts. I want him to say something stupid, be arrogant, show me something undesirable, but it's impossible. My dad was right; he *is* a good one.

Then, one of them says, "You married that Greer girl, didn't you Bo?" and I remember *that*.

Because yes, Bo has a wife.

Somehow, despite how big of a deal him being married is, I keep it shoved out of my mind. Between our hikes and grocery shopping and dinners together, she's gone, and it's been simply a legal matter. Like a pending date for traffic court. At least, that's what I tell myself.

Bo clears his throat, toothpick moving slowly from the left to right side of his mouth as if he's trying to figure out how to answer him. "I did."

"Where's she these days? You two still together?" the man asks.

I pull my head to one side, breathing through the question. Because yes, technically, they are still together, I realize.

"She's in Nashville I think, but I'm not really sure." He shifts in his seat several times.

Then Sam, who has been watching me the entire time Bo has been talking, says, "I went to Nashville once. That whole damn city is too loud if you ask me." The man formerly known in my mind as grouchy Sam winks at me.

The music shifts to a slow song, a cover of "Unchained Melody," and a handful of couples move to the dance floor, shuffle-swaying as they cling to each other. I turn to Sam. "Should we show them how it's done?"

His eyes bounce from me to Bo as he rolls his cane between his hands. "Bah!" He lifts one hand from his cane and swats it through the air. "You'll ruin my reputation."

"Not mine," Bo says.

Before I object—before I say anything—he stands, grabs my hand, and pulls me toward the small dance floor.

His fingers from both hands splay across the small of my back and mine interlace behind his neck. Every part of our bodies is touching but all I can think about is a wife he has that I don't know.

"You're upset," he says softly, his words mingling with the moody lines of the song. Our sway falls into the beats of the music and our eyes lock.

"You're married."

"I am."

"And even if I didn't spend my days trying to outrun the cancer that I know is chasing me, you'd still be married."

"I would."

"And I don't know what the hell to do with that," I snap.

He nods; I look away. Staring at the other couples, some over twice my age, that somehow figured out how to make it. I'm jealous of them. So jealous it makes a sour taste fill my mouth.

"Maybe we were stupid to think this could be anything more." When I say the words I know make logical sense, my insides twist at the same time his muscles tense beneath my hands.

The way his body reacts tells me I'm right, even though I don't want to be.

The song ends, and I pull away. "I have to get Sam home."

I don't wait for his answer.

I gather Sam, say quick goodbyes to the table, and get into the minivan. Bo doesn't chase me or try to stop me.

My jaw is clenched so tightly as I start to drive, I physically prevent a single tear from falling.

"I was married to my first wife when I fell in love with my second," Sam says in the quiet of the drive.

My hands wring around the steering wheel, annoyed by how perceptive he is.

"She was dying, and I couldn't leave her," he continues.

Stopped at a red light, I glance over at him. "I'm sorry to hear that."

He barks out a loud, "Ha!" then smiles. "My first wife was a pain in my ass. Complained about everything. Nag, nag, nag. She had some kind of heart condition. Bonnie was her name."

"Bonnie? Really?" My voice drips with sarcasm. The name he always calls me is that of a dead wife that he apparently loathed. *Swell.*

He grins as the light turns green.

"Anyway, Bonnie was sick, and Margaret was the nurse. I loved her from the moment I saw her. Even though Bonnie was the bane of my existence in the end, she gave me children I loved, and we had good years before we didn't. I couldn't leave her—wouldn't," he says, looking out the passenger window.

"What happened?" I ask, blinker clicking as I turn. "With you and Margaret, I mean?"

"Well, she took care of Bonnie like she was supposed to." He pauses. "And she waited. Her faith in me was stronger than her worry over what we should or shouldn't do. How it would look. She waited. Bonnie was gone within six months, and I married Margaret three months after that. We had twenty-seven beautiful years together before she passed."

Then it's silence that stretches the rest of the drive and as I help him into his house.

"Birdie," he calls as I start to leave. "Even without the tits, you're more of a Margaret than a Bonnie."

I smile. "Sam, I think that's the nicest thing you've ever said to me."

His old hand bats through the air and the grumble returns to his voice. "Don't get used to it."

I snort a laugh. Sam has gone from being a royal pain in my ass to one of my favorite people on the planet in the matter of hours.

After I drop him off, the drive home and my crawl into bed is filled with the loudest quiet I've ever known.

I'm in a war I don't understand with myself.

Bo.

Bo *and* myself.

When my phone vibrates it's a simple, *Church tomorrow?*, and my reply of *Yes* happens so fast it's instinct—habit.

The only way to possibly respond.

Twenty-one

CHURCH IS QUIET. WHEN Bo picks me up, it's a hushed, "Hey," we exchange followed by a drive into the mountains with each of us looking out our respective missing doors.

We hike—silence.

We reach the summit—silence.

George Strait spends too much time sniffing another dog's butt on the trail—silence.

The roots and rocks under my feet I've come to consider my weekly therapy do nothing to smother the argument my brain is having with itself.

Bo is married vs. He isn't *with* her.

I'll probably die vs. I might not get sick.

Tragic ending vs. Happily ever after.

Don't let him go vs. Tell him goodbye.

If there ever is a time to yell my feelings off the edge of a cliff, it's today, but somewhere on the trail when I catch him smirking when he looks at me, the silence switches from being a way to organize my thoughts to some sort of stubborn refusal to be the one to talk first.

Even with the smirk, his silence lets me know he's in his head as much as I am. Maybe he's brought me here to tell me his goodbye. Maybe that will break my heart but also fix this whole mess.

When he parks at my house, I stare out the doorless Jeep. Huck, my steadfast visitor, sits on my porch waiting.

"Is this our first fight?" Bo asks.

"Second," I say, turning to look at him. "Our first fight was the *first* time your wife came up."

His laugh comes in the form of a puff of air through his lips, and our eyes lock as I rest the side of my head on the headrest.

Looking at him look at me, I feel his pull. Like he's another sun with its own gravity, able to will everything toward him by just simply existing—even the words I don't want to say.

"I'm scared I'm going to fall in love with you." The power of him rips the truth right out of my throat and sets it free like a million dandelion seeds in a summer breeze.

He mirrors my posture, head tilting against his own headrest.

"I'm scared I'm already in love with you."

"I'm scared you won't want me because of the sex."

"I'm scared I don't care about the sex."

"I'm scared you're married."

"Me too."

Then we're quiet, sitting in our own seats, looking at each other. Knowing without saying it, something is happening.

"Birdie!" Huck's call pulls my head in the opposite direction and the dog starts to whine from the back seat. There, blocky smile in place, his face fills the open space beside me.

"Hey, Huck!" I say with a grin.

"Hi, Bo!" he shouts.

Bo lifts his chin and smiles. "Huck."

George Strait clambers to my lap from the back seat and jumps through the opening and onto Huck who immediately forgets about me and starts chasing the dog around the yard.

I turn back to Bo. "Did you mean what you said about adopting him?"

He nods. "I did."

"Okay."

"Okay," he says as I get out of the Jeep and turn to face him from the open passenger doorway.

"Now what?" I ask. "I don't know what any of this means."

His easy smile covers his face, dimples carving his cheeks when he says, "I want to take you out next weekend. Friday?"

Grocery night?! I know he sees my struggle because he laughs. "Yes, *grocery night*. There's something that only happens on Fridays. And it's for the list."

I shake my head with a snort. "The list? Haven't you accomplished your goals with that?"

He shrugs. "I need a reason to keep seeing you. Friday?"

My nod is met by his toothpick-holding smirk.

"And, Birdie?" He lifts his chin. "Lucy is staying with her cousins overnight."

Like everything else he's just said, I have no idea what I'm supposed to do with it as I watch him drive away.

Twenty-two

"You've lost weight," I say, crossing my arms and leaning against the doorway.

Veda flicks her fingers through the air. "It's probably all that healthy stuff you're making me eat," she says dismissively, lifting a mug to her lips at the kitchen table.

I thought I noticed it a couple weeks ago, but now in our third month together, the same shirt she wore the first day I met her is noticeably baggier. Veda is thinner.

"Veda," I say with a pleading breath. "Just tell me what's going on." Our eyes meet and hers narrow at me. "*Please*," I beg.

Other than me finding the pills and her sleeping in one morning, her weight loss is the only sign there's something off.

We look at each other with a steadfast kind of resilience. I want to know what's happening as much as she doesn't want to tell me.

"Birdie, I'll be eighty in two months, of course I lost weight—that's a lot of years to be carrying these bones around!"

She smiles as if she's said something funny, but I see it for the lie it is.

She stands up, pushing her chair from the table. "Either way, we have stuff to load in the kiln," she tells me as she walks down the hall, me trailing on her heels.

"Veda, ple—"

"And I want to teach you some hand-building techniques," she says over me. "I realized last week when you left with six bowls I haven't taught you how to do anything other than throw—can you believe that?" She steps into the sunroom.

"Veda!" I shout, making her hear me.

She stops.

"Veda," I repeat, this time softly to her back. "What is going on?"

Her shoulders droop. She turns to face me, slow.

"Birdie," she starts, narrowing her eyes just slightly. "I've lived a good life and I'm getting older. That's all it is. It's the natural ebb and flow of it all." She smiles—really this time—and her mismatched beaded earrings jingle when she takes a step. "Now wedge some clay, let's make something strange today."

I know she's deflecting. I open my mouth to explain I could find some way to help if she would just tell me. The look in her eyes stops me. It's not angry or sad, isn't the scary hawk-like glare she gave me the first day I met her—it's desperate. She doesn't want to talk about it. Being a girl with no mom from a young age to a woman with no kids, husband, or breasts at an adult age, it's a look I understand well. Some things are more manageable when you lug them alone.

"Fine," I say. Then without another word, I cut a chunk of clay, wedging it out like she tells me to.

There are things I like about making something out of clay on the wheel—the steadiness of the spinning, the predictability over certain movements on the outcome. The precise steps that are required. It's soothing. Now that I've got the hang of it, I can even say it's reliable. Tangible steps with a clear goal.

This technique Veda teaches me today is something else. Something unlike me entirely: it's wild. Veda and I sit rolling coils—long ropes of clay—for hours, lining them on top of one another. She shows me how to connect them with wet clay and shallow cuts, a technique she calls scratch and slip, and how to lay them in different shapes. Instead of perfect symmetry and lines that make sense, this style of pottery is sheer chaos. It is everything I'm not, but for some reason, I love it.

"I want to adopt my neighbor, Huck," I say, rolling one of the coils like a snail. "But I'm scared that if I die, he'll be an orphan and have to start all over in foster care."

She hums in understanding next to me, slowly—shakily—using her palms to press down on her clay.

"And Bo said I could put in my will that he would take him if I died. Which"—a breath rushes out of me in a gust—"is incredible to even offer." Then I face her. "I guess I'm just wondering if he means it. Or if you think he would resent me? Or regret it?"

Her smile drips with pride. "He means it, Birdie. If Bo says something, he means it."

I believe her.

Then we fall into a comfortable silence, stacking coils in various shapes and patterns until we have two wonky vases in front of us that have so many holes they will never hold water.

I laugh when I look at them. "Do these look like they are supposed to?"

"They aren't supposed to look like anything, Birdie—that's the beauty of it."

I agree. It feels like beauty even though they look absurd.

"How'd you find pottery?" I ask, filling a bucket up with clean water in the sink.

"I was always artistic, loved painting—watercolor mostly—so I went to art school. I'd never done anything with clay, almost dropped the class after the first day, but there was a cute boy, so I stayed." She smiles, though it isn't for me. "And I fell in love—with him and the clay."

I wipe the table down with a big sponge, the dry clay turning to muddy streaks across the top. "What happened?"

Her smile widens across her timeless face. "The boy, Daniel, didn't have an artistic bone in his body, but I sat next to him and helped him. I didn't have experience with the medium, but I was better than him!" She chuckles. "As I taught him, we fell in love between those shelves of art supplies. He took the class on a dare—his friends apparently never believed he'd stick with it. Right before finals he leaned over and whispered, 'Veda, I would have hated this class if I didn't fall in love with you.'" Her eyes are wet, but her smile stays.

"Then we got married. I became an art teacher; he went to work for the city. We had Daniel and a good life. I taught art for nearly thirty years before I became a potter full time."

I wrap our vases in plastic bags as I think of it all. A younger Bo-like kid in a college class he has no business being in. I smile at the image.

Then an idea.

"You know, Veda," I start. "We're due for a Forever Fun field trip. Since you've assured me there's nothing wrong with you"—I pause, shooting her a look that silently says, *but I don't believe you*, before continuing—"would you be up for hosting it here? Sometime this fall? I'll clean everything up and take care of everything, I would just need you to tell them what to do—teach them. Something like this would be great with the coils, or like, those little monster sculptures kids make?" I laugh. "There are only two of them right now."

"When are you thinking?" she asks, considering it as she washes her hands at the big utility sink.

"Anytime really. Usually, I do something three or four times a year, but we haven't done anything since spring. If you aren't up for it now, we can wait until December or—"

"Not December," she says quickly. "How about September or early October? It will be nice out. The fall colors will inspire us," she adds.

I smile. "I love that. *They'll* love that. Thank you."

Mabel, Sam, and Veda—all together with clay on their hands. It has the making of a sitcom episode written all over it.

"Gran?" a voice calls from the front of the house along with the sound of the opening and closing of the door.

"Back here!"

In a few booted steps, Bo steps into the sunroom.

I look at him as I put the last of the tools in their bins and bite my bottom lip to hide the smile that happens because it can't not when he's around.

"Birdie," he says with a smile just big enough for his dimples to show through his beard.

He's wearing his usual blue jeans, but instead of a T-shirt, he's in a tucked-in blue button-down with the sleeves rolled up.

My, "Hi," comes in a breathy whoosh that lets me know I like this look on him *very* much.

"Birdie, stop staring at him," Veda says, making my face flush as she narrows her eyes at me before softening her face toward him. "Why are you all dressed up?"

He walks over to where she's standing at the sink and gives her a hug and peck on the cheek.

"Meetings." He looks at the table. "What did you girls make today?"

I point at the plastic wrapped vases. "Things that won't hold water."

He chuckles. "I like it."

"What are you doing here?" Veda asks, rinsing the sponges.

"Just saying hi. I'm heading to get Lucy...and I needed some of these." He grabs two Lincoln Logs from a basket I've never noticed and waves them around with a grin before doing a double take of Veda. "Is Birdie feeding you, Gran? You look like you've lost weight."

When she turns around, I raise my eyebrows knowingly toward her, and her face morphs to a point in response. Our wordless battle begins.

"You know, Bo," I say, holding her gaze. "I thought the same thing."

She doesn't shy away, eyes turning into little slits. "If Birdie would cook something edible, maybe I would—"

"Okay, okay," Bo laughs, cutting her off, kissing her on the cheek. "I get the point. Birdie's food is too healthy. Just don't go withering away on me."

While his voice is playful, Veda and I stand in a stubborn staring contest.

My *I know something is going on with you* meets her *I'm not telling you a damn thing*.

Finally, when my eyes start to burn from not blinking, I relent, and damn her for the smug look on her face when I do.

"I should get going," I say, looking at Bo as I start out of the sunroom.

"I'll walk you out," he says, walking out ahead of me. "Gran, I'll be right back."

"Veda," I say sweetly. She smiles so innocently I almost laugh. "See you Monday."

With one last look at her, I grab my purse and walk the short distance to the front porch where Bo is waiting.

"She might be the death of me," I say with a laugh mixed with a sigh as we walk across the yard to my van.

He chuckles. "She's harmless." His eyes squint. "I think."

I shake my head.

"What are you doing with random Lincoln Logs all the time?" I ask, eyeing the aged brown miniature logs in his hand.

"Building cabins, of course." A toothpick dances in his mouth as he grins.

I laugh under my breath as I open the door of the van. "Probably helps with material costs." I give him one last look, feeling my tongue swell in my mouth at how damn good he looks before pulling my eyes away. "Huck's probably waiting."

He rounds his back, leaning on the frame of the door when I pull it closed.

"The only eight-year-old I've ever been jealous of."

Putting the key in the ignition, I shake my head at how smooth he is then shift the gear to reverse.

"See you tomorrow night?" he asks, pulling away from the van.

"See you tomorrow night." I back up a few inches then push the brakes. Heart pounding, I add, "I'm going to try to adopt Huck."

His slow-to-grow smile is wide. "I think you should."

I just nod, looking back through the windshield at the gravity of those words, before giving him a wave and driving away.

When I get home, instead of walking the dog with Huck, I visit Miss Alice and start the application process to adopt him.

Twenty-three

HAVING NO BREASTS MAKES getting dressed up a special kind of surprise party. It's either awful—puffs of chest fabric showcasing everything that's missing. Or it's amazing—there's never a worry about filling something out too much. There is no pressure to show cleavage because there is none. At the same time—there is no cleavage.

Usually, I don't spend much time dwelling on this. Over the decade since I had my mastectomy I've learned how to dress my different body. The question I have getting ready for whatever my non-grocery shopping Friday night is: hide my chest or embrace it?

I'm wearing blue jeans—fitted and high waisted. I don't have my chest working in my favor, but all my hours spent trying to outrun cancer on stationary bikes, treadmills, and elliptical machines have done wonders for my ass. My body is far from perfect, but it's lean and strong.

The shirt is where I'm stuck. The puffy peasant top I'm wearing has me looking like an actual peasant. *No.* I yank it off with a sigh.

Standing in a lacey tank top, my version of a bra, and jeans, I stare at myself. The top is black, fitted, sexy by most standards. With scalloped edges, it dips low on my chest, between where most women would have breasts. Instead of cleavage, creamy white and soft pink petals of a tattooed mountain laurel peek out of the dark lace. When I ordered it online, the girls in the photos had worn it as a shirt and I was jealously scandalized at the thought. Now, as different as I look from the busty models that pulled it off with sex appeal to spare, I'm feminine. As close to sexy as I've felt in twelve years.

I tug at the straps, exhaling at my reflection, thinking of Bo's last words, *Lucy is staying with her cousins overnight.*

What did that mean? Mabel told me it meant we were going to *hump like rabbits*, her exact words this morning. I laughed, but she doesn't know that I don't have sex. She'd be devastated with that revelation.

Now, it's all I can think about. Would he want to do other things? Would that be enough? Would he want to see my chest? Would I be able to show him?

My skin starts to tighten around my skeleton the same time Bo knocks on the door, pulling me from my spiraling thoughts that are quickly turning into anxiety. I stretch my neck side to side, willing myself to relax. His timing makes the decision of what to wear. Big earrings, big hair, and a little shirt are who I am tonight.

With one last look at my reflection and a long deep breath, I go meet my date.

"Seriously?" I look through the windshield and frown at the familiar neon sign. "I skipped my Friday night ritual for Libby's?"

He looks at me like he's offended. "They have the best triple sec in town. I thought you'd be happy."

I roll my eyes. "Funny."

He gets out, circles the Jeep at a jog, and opens the door for me before I'm even unbuckled. Standing there, it's like I'm seeing him for the first time all over again.

When I opened the door at my house and saw him, my heart stuttered. He looks the same as he always does in jeans, fitted T-shirt, face that makes me want to confess all my sins, and body that makes me want to commit new ones—but something is different. Like this date is a step across a threshold and there's no turning back.

When his eyes burned a path down my body as I stood in the doorway, I squirmed, panicked, and acted like I had forgotten my sweater. Which is why I'm now wearing a granny cardigan over my once-sexy outfit.

"Where's your toothpick?" I ask him as we walk across the parking lot.

He shrugs, salacious smile curling his lips as he opens the door. "I thought I'd keep my mouth available tonight."

My chest tightens, eyes widen, but before I can say anything, his hand is on the small of my back, guiding me inside.

It's crowded—way busier than the last time we were here. Music comes from big speakers, and bodies are everywhere. It's loud and lively—a vibe. Without hesitating, his hand slips from my back to my hand, leading me across the room to the bar. Libby's there, pouring liquor from a bottle, red lips smiling. "Pam Beesly from the Rockies!" she cries happily.

The dim lighting of the bar is a blessed thing for hiding the mortified blush that I know has swallowed my face. "Believe it or not, that's not actually my name." I laugh through my humility. "It's Birdie."

Her smile somehow widens.

"Birdie suits you," she says, nodding toward my chest. "Nice ink."

I don't know why, but I look at Bo with the comment. His lips pull to one side in a half smile, and he squeezes my hand.

"So what are y'all drinking tonight? Beer, Bo?"

He nods. "You know it. Birdie? Water?" He looks at me.

I know alcohol is bad for the body—I read a study once that connected even just occasional drinking with an increased risk of cancer. I also know Bo doesn't care whether I drink or not. I know all of these things, but for whatever reason, I answer with, "I'd like a cocktail." Then to Libby, "Not triple sec with an olive."

She laughs. "Okay, well Bo has already told me you don't really drink, so what kind of flavor do you want? Do you like cranberry juice? Or pineapple?"

I look at him—*he's told her about me?*

He nods, like he's taken up residency in my brain. Which he has.

"Either of those are fine."

Another smile, then she's scooping ice and pouring vodka and cranberry juice—that's surprisingly organic. *Who knew?*

"Alright ladies and gentlemen," a theatrical voice says over the speaker. "Starting us off tonight are Meghan and Taylor, who will be singing some Cyndi Lauper." A small pocket of applause is followed by a couple random *wooo!* calls from the crowd as the music starts and the girls giggle into microphones.

My eyes widen. "Karaoke?" There's no hiding the shock in my voice.

Bo grins, dropping my hand to take our drinks from Libby. "Isn't it so much better than looking at lettuce?"

"Do you sing?" I ask, cringing at the terrible voices singing and cackling "Girls Just Wanna Have Fun" through the speakers.

"Nope." He chuckles, eyes crinkling as he takes a sip of his beer. "Bet I can get *you* up there though."

I pin him with a look. "Don't even think about it."

Lifting the straw of my drink to my lips, anxiety creeps into my shoulders. I take a sip. It's not strong, but strong enough for me to notice the foreign warmth of the alcohol slide down my throat and into my belly with the first taste.

Bo's hand lands on the small of my back, draining every ounce of tension out of my muscles with his touch.

We don't sit on stools; we lean at the end of the bar where it meets the wall at the edge of the crowd. Even though the air is cool outside, here with all the bodies, I'm hot. Once I finally start to sweat, I reluctantly shed my sweater. I might as well be naked in my ridiculous maybe-shirt, hugging the sweater in front of me.

Bo sees, because of course he does; it's in his DNA to see people as much as cancer is in mine. He takes my sweater and purse—my props for hiding myself—and gives them to Libby to keep behind the bar.

I wrap my arms around myself, instantly exposed. Like I'm baring my secrets to a room filled with strangers.

He slips his hands between where my arms are pinched to my ribs, prying me away from myself. He drags his palms down my arms until his hands catch my wrists and encircle them. Leaning in, close enough his beard scratches my face and for me to hear his voice over the bad singing and shouts of the crowd. "Wildflowers don't hide when they bloom, Birdie."

His words echo through me like a yell in a valley, stealing my voice. My breath. My ability to do anything but stare at him and try to stay standing through the free fall that's happening within me. Bo looks at me like I look at every colorful petal my eyes have ever seen—with an awestruck wonder.

The spell of the moment is broken by a too-loud, too-sharp note from the stage, followed by what seems to be a friend of Bo's walking up to us. As Bo slips into a catch-up conversation, I step aside, sipping my cocktail, waiting for my heart to return to a normal rhythm in my chest.

"How's your drink?" Libby calls from over my shoulder.

I turn toward her, smiling. "Surprisingly better than the one I had last time I was here."

She laughs.

"You set the bar low with that one."

"I'm sorry I lied. I'm...complicated," I say, facing her across the bar.

She nods, her smile turning from playful to understanding. "Aren't we all?" She shrugs. "And Bo explained. I get it."

"You two are close. It's nice. How'd you meet?" I ask, taking another sip of my drink.

Her smile falters as her eyes flick to where Bo's talking with his friends. "He married my sister."

I choke on my drink in a way that turns into a hacking cough.

She winces. "Sorry. Figured the only way to do it was to rip the Band-Aid off. She's a hot mess and doesn't deserve him, so this"—she wiggles a finger between us—"doesn't have to be weird."

I just nod, because—what the hell? His invisible wife is wrapped around everything like an invasive vine.

Bo walks up next to me, draping an arm around my shoulder. "What'd I miss?" he asks casually.

Before either one of us can answer, the DJ's theatrical voice cuts the moment with, "Next up, we have Birdie Hawkins. Birdie, come on down."

My stomach drops to the floor along with my jaw. Bo leans down, beard scraping across my cheek, and whispers a rusty, "Told ya," into my ear.

When I glare at him, he waves a sticky note in front of my face that says, *Surprise yourself.*

"*Bo, n—*"

"She's right here!" he shouts. Then it's a kiss on the cheek and pat on my ass before he nudges me toward the stage.

Twenty-four

MICROPHONE IN HAND AND computer screen with music notes taunting me, I now know I hate Bo.

He and Libby are side by side at the edge of the crowd, smiling like this is some kind of twisted dream come true. Everyone else in the bar is staring at me in my not-really-even-a-shirt shirt.

I look like a prostitute, and I can't do this.

"Now the song is a surprise to everyone, even little Birdie here," the overzealous DJ says with his slicked back hair and obnoxious sequined shirt from his table in the corner.

The music starts. A fiddle riff that anyone born in the last forty years can recognize if they listen to country music. I groan and drop my head. It's Shania Twain's "Man! I Feel like a Woman,"and Bo is an asshole.

When my eyes meet his, he winks. *Winks!*

The electric guitar starts to play, and the beat of my heart matches its sporadic rhythm. When the first words flash on the screen, my cracked voice only gets half of them out. I wince. Then a break, more lyrics. I sing-say more of them. The ball bouncing over the lyrics on the screen is moving fast—too fast.

I stumble through verse after verse, until the chorus, which of course I know, because I know country music. Someone cheers for me. Then I sing every word—horribly of course—but I'm smiling.

There's a shimmy I somehow make which causes a group of girls to scream—a bachelorette party, as indicated by a sash that says *Bride to Be!*

The bachelorette and all her friends storm the small stage to stand next to me—we're arm in arm singing horribly into one microphone. Their faces mirror mine—we're smiling. Laughing at how bad we are. This is an alternate universe because we're—*I'm*—singing and smiling in front of a room full of people.

By the final, "Man! I Feel like a Woman" we belt out, we all do a thing with our hips where we bump into each other, and we laugh. *Laugh!*

These women are singing and dancing and laughing with me and Shania Twain while I wear a scrap of fabric, and I have never felt so free in my whole life.

It's over; there's clapping. Some guy cups his hands and yells, "Encore!" and I laugh—*again.*

The bachelorette and her friends hug me, drunkenly inviting me to the wedding.

When they loudly scream, "I love you, Birdie!"—the only volume they seem to operate at—I hug them back.

I don't know what this is, but I love it.

All the while, I still hate Bo.

I hate him the entire time I walk off the little stage, through the cackling crowd and right over to him.

I hate him when I put my hands on my hips, square my shoulders to him and say, "Bo, you're a goddamn asshole, and you're going to pay for this."

I especially hate him when he looks at my glaring, drops his head back, and laughs before putting his hands on my face and pulling me in for a kiss so hot that I don't think I'll ever come up for air. In front of everyone. In front of everyone, he kisses me in a way that assaults every single one of my senses with his mouth and his hands and his all-consuming Bo Mountain Breeze until the crowd is clapping and howling.

The DJ over the speaker says, "She's *really* going to feel like a woman tonight, folks. Next up, we have Toby singing 'Friends in Low Places.' Toby, come on up."

When we pull apart, I'm breathless. He's smiling.

He holds my face just inches from his. "You were amazing."

"I hate you," is all I can say back, but there's a smile that pulls at my lips.

"Tell me something you like," he says, soft.

"Murder," I say. "You?"

"You," he says, and this time, I don't laugh. Because his smile drops; he's serious.

He nods toward the door, and the mood shifts from playful to something else. Because I don't know what's on the other side of the door, but it sure as hell isn't a crowd of people and bad karaoke.

I don't resist. A flower bending in his Bo Mountain Breeze, moving however he wants me to. Leaning and swaying at his will with no regard for my own.

Libby must see what's happening better than me, because she comes around the bar, giving me my purse and sweater, and hugs me goodbye. It's not an awkward hug; it's real. When she wraps her slender arms around me, it's a tight squeeze, like she's imprinting herself in my life, giving me a glimpse of something sweet. A friend I didn't know I needed.

"I hope I didn't scare you off," she says, looking me in the eyes. "Mandy is my sister, but her choices aren't mine. Bo is family to me, and that boy is in love with you."

I suck in a breath, eyes cutting to him where he's saying goodbye to his friends. "That's not what this is, Libby. And he's married, and I'm...you know, Pam Beesly complicated." I laugh softly.

She rolls her eyes. "And also, an idiot. Do you see the way he looks at you?" She shakes her head. "He came by earlier with bottles of organic juice in case you wanted something other than water. That's not what he does—that's not what any man does! And Mandy..." Her voice trails off with the pain in her eyes. "They might be married on paper, but that girl's gone. She left him, left Lucy, left all of us. She chased dreams bigger than all of us."

I get it then, she doesn't hurt for Bo, she just hurts. Libby lost her sister.

I hug her again.

"I don't have any friends," I blurt out, laughing at my own awkwardness. "If you ever want to go to yoga or something…" My voice trails off with my own insecurity.

She squeezes my arms before dropping her hands by her side. "I'd love that." She gives me one more smile before retreating behind the bar and lifting her chin in goodbye toward Bo.

He grabs my hand, pulls me close, and leads me toward the door and whatever comes next.

Twenty-five

Bo is in my house and using up all the oxygen. My breathing is so shallow standing in my living room facing him, I'm pretty sure air is just coming into my nose and shooting back out with no real purpose. George Strait pants next to me before lying down on his dog bed and it's oddly comforting. Like Bo's effect is universal.

"So," I say between faux breaths, "now that I've *invited* you here, I can give you the tour?" I don't think I meant to ask as much as offer, but the flexion of my voice makes it a question so I go with it.

"Lead the way," he says easily, crouching down to pet the dog who is now sprawled out on a big pillow on the floor.

"So, you can see, we are standing in the living room, and I have a Greg Hawkins original coffee table," I say with mock formality, relaxing just a little. My style is clean and modern—cream-colored walls, neutral tones everywhere, and a couple house plants. As someone who perpetually errs on the side of anxious, I designed the space with my nervous system in mind. The table my dad made for me is a honey-stained wood and sits asymmetrically next to my tan couch. Other than the recent addition of my colorful bowls and mugs, it's the most unique thing in my house.

For some reason, as I watch him look around, I become hyper-aware that while his house has pictures hanging on the walls, mine are bare. Other than one photo of my dad and I from my college graduation that sits on a shelf, nothing. Someone walking in here might think it's a short-term rental property more than my home of nearly a decade.

We move to the attached kitchen, equally tidy, neutrally col-ored, and as obviously void of humanity as the living room. White cabinets, white backsplash, butcher block counters, essential oil diffuser puffing the scent of vanilla into the air. The only pops of color are a vase Veda gave me that has flowers in it and my calendar wall that has sticky notes and highlighted dates.

Bo instantly goes to the calendar, giving me a look of, *Seriously?*

I snort, standing across the room from him. "Guess you didn't see this last time. Did you expect anything different?"

He vibrates with a laugh. "This looks like a command center for an entire country."

"Does not," I argue, stepping next to him and admiring my own organization. "Look." I point to a list. "You can see what I'm eating for dinner three weeks from now and what class I'll be taking at the gym. Isn't that satisfying?"

He blinks with disbelief at me before looking back at the calendar and points to a date at the end of September where I've written *Forever Fun Clay School*. "What's this?"

"Gran offered to teach the other oldies a clay lesson," I say with a smile.

He laughs on an exhale, then his tone turns serious. "How does she seem?"

A pit forms in my stomach with the question. I can't lie to him, but I also can't break Veda's word. "Hmm..." I pause, noticing my hands are shaking and gluing them to my hips, clearing my throat before I add, "Like she's almost eighty and annoyed by my food."

He nods silently.

"Why do you ask?"

He shrugs. "Just wondering. She *is* almost eighty—I worry." His gaze finds mine. "I'm glad she has you there. She loves you."

Guilt bleeds into every vein with what he says, and I blink my eyes away. I tell myself I'm not lying, but it feels like I am. I don't even know what's wrong with Veda, so really, I'm not actually keeping anything from him. Just speculations. Concerns. A feeling I can't name. Whatever she's hiding from me, I'm also hiding from him. The second she told me not to tell Bo, my bed was made. Not just ethically, but legally, I can't tell him whatever she shares.

"If Veda loves me, I'd hate to see how she'd yell at me if she didn't like me," I say, attempting to pull myself from my thoughts.

He chuckles softly, fingers interlacing with mine as he takes a step. "This calendar is riveting, but show me the rest of your house."

Happy for the change of subject, I lead the way.

There are only three other rooms in my house: a hall bathroom, a guest bedroom, and the master bedroom. The first two are easy, but when I open the door to my bedroom, it's a flirt with disaster. A danger zone. Four walls that suck the moisture from my mouth.

He didn't show me his bedroom, so I have no idea what to show him of mine.

"So this is my bedroom," I say, shaky, stalled out at the doorway and not daring to step inside.

He drops my hand and walks in without me. Like everything else, it's in shades of cream and tan with a plant in the corner. Instead of a bright lamp, there's a soft red-orange glow of two salt lamps.

Seeing him next to my bed makes me want to march over to him, shove his broad shoulders, and watch him drop onto my mattress. Instead, I stay in the doorway, gripping the doorframe as though I physically need to keep myself from moving.

His fingertips graze across my blanket; both my throat and thighs pinch shut.

"What's this?" he asks, lifting a book off my nightstand.

My cheeks heat instantly. *Mabel's lumberjack book.*

This is enough to make me move. *Fast.*

I rush over to him and reach for it. "It's Mabel's!" I shout, trying to snatch it out of his hand. He pinches his fingers around it, amused look on his face as he waves it over my head. "Bo, I'm serious. It's nothing—"

"If it's nothing, why does it matter if I look?" he teases.

My face is hot—my entire body is hot—I think I might die from overheating. *He can't look in there.* I'm frustrated and flustered, trying to grab it from him while he reaches it higher, just out of my reach.

"Bo!" I shout, jumping with a swipe of my arm through the air only to bounce off his broadness empty-handed.

Asshole.

"Birdie," he coos, twisting me until he has me pinned to his side with one arm as he holds the book in his other. "*Wood of Love?*" he asks, reading the title, clicking a sound with his tongue as I writhe under his arm until I break free with a grunt.

"Fine!" I bite out. "Just get this over with so I can go die." I sit on the bed, cross my arms, and wait for death.

"I'm going to read it to you," he says, smug smile on his lips.

My voice comes out something between a groan, a yell, and a whimper. "Bo! No!"

"Ah yes," he says, dropping onto the bed, laying back with one arm bent behind his head, the other holding the book, as his ankles cross. "I see our main character is named Aaron." His eyes dramatically look somewhere in the distance, repeating, "*Aaron,*" in a breathy voice.

"I hate you." I drop my face to my hands as he thumbs through the pages.

"Let's find the good stu—" He pauses, looking over the top of the book toward me. "I see you've highlighted your favorite passages here, Birdie." He whistles, raising his eyebrows. "I'm shocked that, '*naked, his legs were like oak trees, but what was between them*

was a sequoia' didn't make your highlight standards." He continues, trying to suppress a smile as I beg him to stop. "Ahh! There
are quite a lot of things that Aaron does that y—" He stops.

Shit.

I can't have sex with Bo again, I know that, but that doesn't
mean that I haven't thought about it. *A lot.*

His weight shifts the bed next to me—he's sitting up. I can't look
at him. Even if he has some kind of feelings for me like Libby says,
other than fourteen-year-old girls, who really does this? Perverts,
that's who!

"Birdie." The throaty way he says my name—the familiar scrape
of his beard against my cheek, rustiness of his voice, and warmth
of his breath—makes me physically ache. Like a cat's tongue being
dragged all over me inside and out. "Tell me."

I shake my head quickly.

"Please," he begs.

I turn my head slightly until my mouth is at his ear.

My trembling, "Fine," is a sultry sound I don't recognize.

"I highlight the...stuff..."

Another shallow breath.

"...and I changed Aaron's name to Bo..."

I squeeze my eyes shut, barely getting air in my lungs,
then—quietly—add, "Because I imagine it's you."

My head gets fuzzy, like I might be about to slip into a coma. I'm
so lightheaded, and he's so still, it's unbearable. I've freaked him
out—of course I did. What kind of degenerate do I have to be to
even do that? Even worse, as mortified as I am at the confession,

I'm extremely turned on. Like something deep inside my body is thrilled that he knows.

Because I'm a pervert.

"I'm sorry," I say. "It's just, you know, I don't really have sex, and then with you—" I turn my head more so I can apologize to his face. I may be depraved, but I'm not a coward. His eyes are dark, the low light of the room making him glow. "I know it's weird, and—and—and," I stutter, heat incinerating my body with every word, "—and creepy or gross or—"

He cuts me off with a kiss. Fast. By the time his tongue finds mine, he's pulling away.

"Birdie," he says, so close I can feel his breath on my skin, "if I had my way, I'd be ripping your clothes off right now and fucking you until you couldn't walk for a month. *Weird* is the last word I would use to describe how I feel about you thinking of me when you *touch* yourself."

Fire zips from the back of my eyes to the deepest part of my belly and explodes with a throb. I have never—*ever*—had anyone say *anything* like that to me. *Ever.*

"I want to read this to you." He pauses, swallows—slow and audibly—and I wonder if he feels the same thickness in his throat as I do in mine. "And I want you to show me what you do."

No.

NO!

I cannot do that. I won't.

"Bo, I don't think..." My voice trails off as he reaches into his pocket, pulling out another sticky note.

He hands it to me. I read it. *Do something because it feels good.*

I look at him, my body seized with panic.

I take a shaky inhale.

Then.

"Okay."

Twenty-six

WEARING ONLY A PAIR of boy short underwear and a lacy shirt formerly known as a bra, I stand in the warm glow of my bedroom, shaking. Every way I imagine this ends with me humiliated. Yet here we are, staring. Me at Bo, Bo at me.

I am every bit of the descriptive words that are used in Mabel's books. Heaving, heavy, achy, starved.

The book, dog-eared and closed on the bed, seems way too small to be able to make me feel all these big things.

Bo stands next to me, fully clothed, and runs his knuckles lightly down my arm. A wave of chills wash over me like a mountain waterfall.

When he drags his hand back up, his fingers trace the thin strap of my top, making my throat close at the proximity of his hand to my chest.

"Birdie," he says, kissing my shoulder in some way that makes fiery desire rush down my arm and out of my fingertips. He tugs the strap gently. "Can we take this off?"

Panic replaces desire immediately. For twelve years, I've been covered—protected. This isn't about hiding my nakedness; this is about hiding my brokenness. The ugly cracks that define my life: past, present, and future.

A shaky breath.

A—slow—lifting of my eyes to his.

"Please," he says, clearly reading my hesitation.

Another shaky breath.

Then, a nod.

I don't want him to see, but a very real part of me wants to know that *someone* has seen. Someone that I've chosen in this life to, just once, see all of me, even the ugly, before I die.

He stands in front of me, eyes laser focused on mine, and slips his fingers under the lacey hem at my waist before lifting it.

Slowly.

A peeling.

My arms raise, he pulls the fabric across my skin, and the shirt is over my head. On the floor.

The moment the air touches my skin—panic. My arms snap across my chest, hands covering the spot where breasts should be. I'm not sad, but a single tear falls down my cheek as my entire body turns into my own pounding heart.

Hand to cheek, he thumbs the tear away, lightly kisses my lips, and his eyes search mine. They move like he's reading the lines to a secret text that nobody else knows about, and I've told him something important without saying a single word.

His gaze holds a question, his worry, so I nod. Because, *Yes, I'm okay.*

Gently, he pulls my arms down to my sides. I close my eyes, not able to look at him while he looks at me—all of me—and force myself to breathe.

His fingers, rough and worked, trace the lines of the flowers that cover my chest. I don't have the sensitivity of my breasts like I once did, but in this moment I don't need it. His finger on my skin sends pleasure, want, and need across every cell in my body.

He sits on the bed, pulling my hips so I'm standing—quivering—between his denim-clad legs.

"You're beautiful, Birdie," he whispers.

Fingers gripping into back of my thighs, he leans toward me, mouth landing on my sternum. A trail of kisses, scratchy and warm, drag across my chest. He covers every scar, every dot of ink, with lips and tongue. Somewhere between being so scared I might die and him familiarizing himself with every mark on me, my hands slip around his neck until my fingers tangle into his hair.

My head drops back, and there's a moan that escapes my lips that's as unfamiliar as it is lust-filled.

When his mouth has marked every part of my chest, he moves deliberately.

Wrapping one hand around my hip, he grabs the book with the other.

Stands.

Positions himself so he's behind me, fully pressed against me.

He rounds slightly so his mouth is at my ear. I close my eyes, trying to keep myself standing upright from the intensity of it all.

I hear him work his way to the dog-eared page, and my breath stops. I know what comes next. I've read those pages *many* times.

"*She wondered what he was going to feel like, this stranger named Bo,*" he starts, gravelly voice against my skin, Bo Mountain Breeze making me drunk. "*Would he work her body the way he worked the timber—with rough hands and jaw set—or would it be something different? Wild even? She imagined his hands, no matter how callused, would feel like velvet on her skin. Expensive silk.*"

His hand moves from my hip and drags up the line of my waist, ribs, chest. He stops at my neck, where he slips his fingers into my hair, twisting it around his fist, before kissing the spot where my neck slopes to shoulder. Slow.

Then, "*She'd known men, but never one like this. Seeing him—naked and hard—made her want things she'd never imagined. She wanted him in her mouth, in her body—just in her.*" Bo pauses, and he hardens more against me. "*There was a pressure building, a wetness forming, just by seeing him this way. She couldn't stop it any more than she could stop the way she was looking into his dark eyes.*"

Another pause. Another audible, tension-filled swallow that slides down my own throat.

I lean into him, knowing what comes next will likely cause my bones to disappear.

He continues.

"'*Bo, I want you to use me how you please. Wreck me. Worship me. I don't care which, but I'll take either one,' she said, breathy and desperate.*"

Another pause, but this time he doesn't read. "Which one do you want, Birdie—to be wrecked or worshiped?" he asks.

I nearly choke on my own thoughts. Somehow, I manage a, "Both," and I mean it. Worship or wreck, they seem one and the same in this very moment.

He turns the page, but before he continues, his mouth is on me, tongue swirling circles up and down the side of my neck. I don't know if it's possible, but I'm about to orgasm from the reading and the kissing alone. Like instead of feeling his mouth on my neck, I feel it *there* and another needy moan escapes my lips.

Then his mouth pulls away and my skin tingles where his lips just were as he starts reading again. "*Bo looks at her, eyes somehow going even darker as he drinks in her voluptuous nakedness. 'I'll wreck you then worship you,' he says, growling. Without letting her respond, he hooks an arm around her waist, pulling the softness of her ass against his own hardness and bends her over. Finding her wetness, he growls again, then fills her without warning. They both cry out in pleasure. His first thrust comes slow, a stretching, but the next comes without reservation. And the next. And the next.*"

Bo's own hardness twitches against my lower back, and my body is a powder keg ready to explode. I'm trembling, tense, and so turned on I wonder if this is what death by desire would be like.

The book drops on the floor, and both of his hands grip my hips. Tightly. An undercurrent of restraint in the way he touches me.

"What do you do now?" he asks, voice low and husky.

"I—I—" I can't form words, at least not the honest ones.

He brings a hand to my throat, slowly dragging his fingers down.

Down my chest.

Down my belly.

Down to the waistband of my underwear.

He stops.

"Do you go here?" he whispers.

I nod, but my mouth won't work. Because yep. That's absolutely where I go.

His fingers slide under the waistband, teasing me without touching me exactly where I need it, before sliding out and resting his palm just below my belly button.

"Show me, Birdie," he says.

Pause.

Swallow.

"Please."

It's almost a beg.

I put my trembling hand on top of his, guiding it down again. This time, there's no teasing, his fingers—our fingers—find the spot that's begging for him.

I'm too weak to do anything useful. I realize as he starts to make small circles and well-hitting strokes that I'm just along for the ride. This is all Bo. Melting me. Ruining me.

The release that's been building since the moment he picked me up tonight is about to explode. It scorches me. Everywhere.

"Bo, I..." There's no finishing the sentence. Pleasure rips through me and steals every word and thought. My back arches off the wall he's forming behind me, and a cry escapes my lips. Bo's fingers work me to the point of no return while my entire body shakes and softens with wave after glorious wave.

When it's over, he turns me to face him, a wet noodle in his arms.

With his mouth hovering over mine, he says, "I like that book," and smiles against my lips. Before I can laugh, he kisses me. It's slow, stoking the fire that's already burning.

Again, like some kind of fool, I moan.

I can't ignore how turned on he is against me or the desire I have to pull him into the bed and let him, quote, *fuck me until I can't walk for a month*, my new favorite idea. I want him over me, in me, and showing me what he looks like when he comes undone.

But I know it can't happen.

Instead.

I pull back from the kiss.

Unbutton his jeans.

When he says, "Birdie you don't have to..."

I take the rest of the sentence with another kiss, and a breathy, "Let me."

When he doesn't argue, I slide his jeans down, then his briefs, and drop to my knees.

Twenty-seven

SUNLIGHT SHINES THROUGH MY windows differently on Saturdays. Every other day of the week, it sets in motion what has to get done, but on Saturdays it's an invitation to revel in the warmth and stillness of it. Like inhaling a deep breath of light as golden warmth pours into my bedroom. Dust particles glowing like magical orbs of serenity.

The bed shifts next to me, and I stiffen. *Bo.*

Bo slept in my bed.

Bo turned me into some kind of sex-crazed maniac when he touched me. Which he did—*a lot.*

All night.

Touching.

Kissing.

My face heats, and I'm not sure if it's because I'm actually embarrassed or because it felt *so* good.

I roll to face him. His arms reach overhead at the same time his toes scrape against my legs as he straightens in a stretch with a muffled groan and sleepy smile.

Seeing Bo in ordinary circumstances is a beautiful thing, but him wearing only my white blanket with tousled hair and half-awake eyes is pure sunshine.

"Tell me something you like," he says, notes of sleep still in his voice.

"This," I say, propping up on my elbow.

His brown eyes search mine. "Why?"

"Because of you," slips easily off my tongue, and to my own surprise, I don't look away when I say it. "Tell me something *you* like." I reach my hand over and run my fingers through his beard. It's somehow both coarse and soft, like him.

He grins, catching my wrist with his hand, kissing my palm, and says, "Mabel's books."

I laugh through a groan, dropping my face into a pillow.

The bed vibrates with his laugh, and he rolls closer. One of his hands squeezes my ass as he kisses my shoulder through my hair. Then as if it isn't even happening, he rolls the other way, already getting dressed when I lift my head.

"You're leaving?" I hadn't expected that, but of course he is. He can't stay here forever.

He grins. "Eventually. But I know *you* keep extra toothbrushes, so I'm going to go find one, then I want to make you breakfast." He pauses, tugging his shirt on. "Actually, I *want* to stay in bed with you all day, but I'm *going* to go make you breakfast. Then—"

"Birdie! Birdie!" My screamed name cuts the air, replacing my desire for Bo with an instant shot of panic.

Huck.

Bo's eyes widen as I launch out of bed, throwing on a T-shirt and a pair of sweatpants, and race down the hall. I've never heard Huck scream like this, and every cell in my body knows it means something is wrong.

I open the front door, spotting an unfamiliar car on the street. Miss Alice and another woman stand with Huck on the sidewalk, dragging him toward it.

"Birdie!" he screams again when he sees me. "Birdie! Birdie!" His face is red, eyes wide. Panicked.

"Huck, I need you to calm down," Miss Alice says, trying to soothe him while she tugs his arm.

"What's going on?" I ask, running across the yard. "Huck, are you okay?" I drop to my knees next to him.

"Huck, are you okay?" he mimics. Adrenaline won't let me rephrase myself.

"Miss Alice?" I look at her, desperation in my voice.

"Birdie, Steve had an episode last night, we had to take him to the hospital—it's nothing, they just kept him over night to be monitored—but Huck has to go to another foster home, this is his social worker, Sharon."

"What?" Now *I'm* shouting. "No!" My eyes burn instantly. "No! You can't take him!"

I look at the other woman, Sharon. Desperate. "I started the paperwork to adopt him. My home visit is in a couple weeks, he can stay with me."

She shakes her head. "I'm sorry, it doesn't work like that ma'am. Unless you're a designated foster parent, he can't just stay with you." Despite her sincerity, rage boils in my chest and panic pinches my throat and chest like a vise.

I'm clutching Huck now, so tightly it's as though I'm afraid loosening my grip will make him disappear. "That's bullshit!" I yell at them both. "It's bullshit and you know it."

I look at Huck, cupping my hands on his face, forcing his gaze to mine. "I wonder if Huck wants to live with Birdie."

"Yes," he says, loud, nodding too many times through his tears. "Huck wants to live with Birdie."

I look up at them, still clutching him against my chest. "See! He *wants* to live with me. Doesn't that count for something?" My voice cracks like a dropped piece of pottery.

"It just doesn't work that way," Sharon says softly, hand on my arm.

I snatch it away, jerking to a stand. "Well, it should!" I shout, not caring how crazy I sound or how my words might come back to bite me later.

"Miss, I understand that th—"

"You understand?" I scoff, interrupting her. "Tell me, what does Huck like to talk about?" I demand.

Her eyes widen.

"What color foods does he like?"

She opens her mouth, like she wants to say something, but I don't give her enough time.

"How do the kids treat him at school? What textures does he like? What's his favorite board game?" I pepper her with questions she can't answer all the while Huck's hand is tightly squeezing in my own.

She stares at me like I have three heads, but I don't care. She doesn't know him; how dare she think she knows what's best for him.

"I understand you're upset, but unfortunately that's not the way it works." She's almost sad as she says it.

Before I can argue, I hear Bo's voice. "Birdie?" He jogs up next to us. "What's going on—hey, Huck."

Then everything happens like I'm watching it through a rain-covered windshield.

Miss Alice explains everything to him.

Bo's arms are around me, so tight I can't breathe.

Huck doesn't stop screaming my name.

Not as they drag him down the sidewalk.

Not as they force him into the car.

Not as I shout: *it's going to be okay!*

The social worker says something about the new foster parents.

I tell her to go to hell.

Bo gets an address of someone—I don't know who, all I can hear is Huck's screaming. My screaming.

They close the car doors.

Huck's yells are muffled, not muted.

The social worker starts driving.

I slip out of Bo's arms at a sprint.

"Birdie, stop!"

I don't listen—I run.

She's going slow.

I catch them.

My hand is on the windows on the outside.

I smack it. Twice. Three times. More.

Huck's hand presses against mine on the opposite side of the glass.

"I'll come get you!" I shout.

I keep running; he keeps crying.

"Huck wants to live with Birdie!"

She drives faster.

I slow down.

They're gone.

I stop.

I stare down the empty street.

Bo scoops me up and takes me home.

Twenty-eight

"SHARON GAVE ME THE contact information for his new foster parents, they're only on the other side of town."

My eyes lift to where Bo is leaning against the kitchen counter writing on a piece of paper.

I nod, quietly, before looking back to my now cold scrambled eggs. My mind is stuck on one thought: Huck is gone.

Gone to people who don't know how to make him meatballs or ask him questions. Gone to people who might not own Connect 4.

"Hey." Bo's voice is low; he's next to me, lifting my chin with his knuckles until my eyes meet his. "It's going to be okay."

Again, I nod, trying to swallow the lump in my throat.

He reaches across the counter and pulls the pen and piece of paper he'd been writing on closer to him.

He clicks the pen repeatedly.

"Okay, what else? I wrote down the information Sharon gave me."

Slumped on my stool in an oversized T-shirt, sweatpants, and hair I can see sticking into my peripheral vision like I've been electrocuted, I shrug.

He clicks the pen again, eying me. "Okay," he says, dragging the word out and rolling a toothpick across the length of his mouth. "If I was in your situation, what would you tell me to do?"

Elbows on the counter, I prop my chin in my hands and look at him again. "I'd tell you to make sure you have everything filled out right for the adoption paperwork."

He smiles, nods, and writes it down. "What else?"

"I'd tell you to go to the gym and eat good food because your nervous system will handle the stress of the situation better if you take care of your body."

He snorts a laugh, keeping his eyes glued to the paper, writing. "What else?"

I tilt my head and look at him. Bo in my kitchen, dressed in his same clothes from last night with tousled hair, helping me manage my life. "I'd thank the man who carried me home and helped me write a list on how to keep my shit together."

"You know"—he drops the pen, plucks the toothpick out of his mouth and drops it in the trash can, stepping closer to me—"I'm concerned why a man is carrying me home in this situation."

I laugh.

He drops his forehead to mine and brings a palm to my cheek.

"It's all going to be okay; you know that right? He's at a different house, not gone."

I lean against his palm. Familiar. Comforting.

"I know."

He looks at the clock on the wall; it's almost noon. "I have to go get Lucy from Libby's. Do you want to come with me? Or I can come back here after?"

I shake my head. "No, go. I'm going to go to the gym, eat good food, quadruple check paperwork. I probably need to reach out to Sharon and apologize for acting like a wild banshee."

Another chuckle, another kiss.

"You'll be a great mom, Birdie."

Next to him, I wrap my arms around his waist. My head to his chest, the soft sound of his heartbeat soothes me.

"You know," I say, not pulling my cheek from him. "You're getting pretty good at making these lists."

His body vibrates when he laughs.

"I learned from the best."

"Church tomorrow?" I ask.

"Church tomorrow."

"Birdie! Time for church! We brought a kite!" The squeaky voice is accompanied by a rhythmic tapping on the door.

Pulling on my shoes, I open it, surprised.

"Lucy—hi!" I say, confused, looking up to see Bo crossing the yard.

"Gran doesn't feel good today," she says.

I ignore the undulation of panic that those simple words create and force a smile. "That's too bad."

"I hope you don't mind," Bo says, scrubbing the top of Lucy's head when he's standing beside her. "Gran was tired, and I told Lucy Goosey here we could go to the park."

George Strait barks as if he knows what all this means, and Lucy giggles.

I widen my eyes dramatically and put my hands on my hips. "Well, the dog can't wait to ride with you in the back seat."

Her response is a laugh as the dog licks her in the face.

"You wanna try to load him up, Luce?" Bo asks her. "He's kind of gotten used to the whole back seat, you might have to fight him for it."

Grabbing the leash, she nods, braided pigtails swishing through the air. "Maybe he can sit on my lap!"

Down the steps, across the yard, and at the Jeep, Lucy fails miserably at getting him to cooperate as Bo and I walk slowly toward them.

"You okay today?" he asks.

I smile. "I am. Your lists work miracles, apparently."

He kisses me on the temple. "Good."

After hours at a park—flying kites, swinging on swings, and watching the dog chase ducks—I'm home. As perfect as the day was, all I can think is: I wish Huck was here too.

Twenty-nine

"I HEARD YOU WEREN'T feeling well yesterday," I say over the rim of my Veda-made coffee mug.

She scoffs. "I was tired and Bo overreacted."

"Mm-hmm," I say, eyebrows raised. "I absolutely believe you."

She rolls her eyes before taking a sip of orange juice, hand trembling around the cup.

"I thought I could teach you to make flowers today." She changes the subject.

I only nod.

And while with anyone else it wouldn't be concerning, she's pleasant all day—doesn't snap at me once. Not as she shows me how to make flowers out of clay that I can't seem to make stick together. Not while she's wearing her purple, heated gloves as I do laundry. Not when I feed her a nutritious lunch that she usually calls glorified cardboard.

"Birdie," she says as I'm packing up for the day, "I have a doctor's appointment Thursday I'd like for you to drive me to."

"Of course." My eyes narrow. "Everything alright?"

She gives me the look that says, *Of course not, but I'm not telling you that.*

I sigh. "Right." A brief pause. "Of course I'll take you."

I start to leave when her voice stops me again. "And Birdie?" I look over my shoulder at her. "It probably goes without saying, but don't mention it to Bo."

I nod, hating her just a little bit for asking it of me and hating myself a little more for agreeing to it. Even though I don't know what I'm not telling him, I know I'm not telling him *something*, and it curdles in my gut.

As best as I can, I shove the thoughts—and the guilt that comes along with them—in a box with a lid and put it away somewhere in the back of my mind.

"Sam, I brought muffins!" I call Wednesday morning as I open the door.

"Bah!" He shouts. "Bonnie, I don't need your damn muffins. I'm having a heart attack!"

I look at him, standing in the middle of his living room seemingly fine, and scrunch my nose.

"Are you sure? You look fine."

"Of course you think I look fine—you ain't got no tits!" I don't bother telling him that there is absolutely zero connection between the two. Instead, I drive him to the hospital.

For five straight hours he tells the doctors and nurses: "I got better care from the doctors in 'Nam than this!"

For five straight hours he tells me: "The cots in 'Nam were more comfortable than this damn bed!"

For five straight hours he's convinced he's about to die.

Finally, he's diagnosed with acid reflux, given a bottle of pills, and I take him home.

While most days the experience would send me straight to an asylum, today I'm unfazed.

After several emails with Sharon and Huck's new foster parents, Wednesday afternoons are my newly scheduled day to spend time with him.

I pick him up, his blocky grin a sight for sore eyes. I don't hug him often because he doesn't love to be touched, but today I do. He runs down the sidewalk to me, and when I wrap my arms around him, he hugs me back. His hug gives me the same relief as propping up tired feet after a long day. "I missed you, Birdie!" he says so loudly it cracks my heart.

"I missed you too, kiddo," I reply, smiling as he gets into the van. "We're going to see Bo today."

"I missed Bo!" he shouts, buckling his seatbelt.

When I park at the address Bo sent me, Huck and I both gape out the minivan windows, no doubt for very different reasons. Huck, of course, sees all the heavy machinery and materials around an in-progress cabin being built. But my eyes land on Bo. He's talking to a man, signing something on a clipboard, and pointing at a corner of the property.

He's wearing a T-shirt, ball cap, and jeans, but something about him here makes my mouth physically water. He looks in control. Authoritative. Yummy.

Huck tumbles out of the minivan, screaming, "Bo!" before I can stop him.

Bo smiles at him, waves, and then his eyes hook with mine. It's a smirk, wink, and easy stride as he walks toward us.

He gives Huck a high-five and me a kiss on the temple, just long enough for my body to know he's there and crave more.

"I wonder if Huck would like to wear this hard hat while I show you how cabins are built," he says, resting an orange hat on Huck's beaming eight-year-old head.

"Yes, Bo!" He laughs loudly.

Bo leans in, letting his mouth linger by my ear long enough to say, "I've missed you," before pulling away. I don't know what's wrong with me, but the only thing I want to do is pounce on him like a pogo stick.

Instead, I smile, my face heating, and say, "Show us how it's done, Mr. Monroe."

His toothpick bobbles with his amused smirk, like he's thinking the same thing I am, before taking my hand in his and leading us toward the construction.

It's far from finished—just a short wall framed out around the unfinished floor of the house with one layer of logs stacked onto it.

"The first logs are held in by steel rods," he says, pointing to one. "Then the logs are held together with log fasteners, which are essentially really big screws." He grabs one out of a bucket and hands it to Huck. "I wonder if Huck wants to try."

Huck nods, his enthusiasm at full wattage.

Bo grabs a screw gun, lines the screw up on the end, and shows Huck how to hold it. They find the right spot, then Bo says, "Go for it."

Huck does, pulling the trigger of the tool and yelling happily as the screw starts to spin, chewing its way into the wood.

The whole moment feels like a huge bouquet being put in a vase that's too small. A wildly precious beauty that can't be contained.

When the screw is all the way in, Bo takes us around to see the rest of the house. There's a framed-out space where a future fireplace will go, and pipes coming up from the floors for the bathroom—seeing a space for a future toilet made Huck laugh especially hard. It's nowhere near finished, but walking around the piles of wood and boxes of supplies, my hand in Bo's, I can picture it.

At the site of the future front door, I stop, looking down at the concrete slab we're standing on. In it, locked in place forever, is a Lincoln Log.

My eyes lift to his and he grins.

"Told ya I was building cabins."

I laugh under my breath. "In every one?"

"Every single one." He scrubs his boot over the unmoving toy log. "A little piece of me. Why I'm here."

Huck told me once about a spider—Darwin's bark spider—I remember the name because he said it so many times. It spins the strongest web in the world. Looking at Bo, in his element with a silly log he put into the concrete next to a kid that isn't his, is like having my heart wrapped in its strong web and knowing I'll never get it back. Whether he knows it or not, it belongs to him.

It's a nothing moment. Him smiling and talking us through the details of an unfinished cabin. But it doesn't feel like nothing; it feels like something. *Everything*. It doesn't matter what it is—what it's called or what it means—I know my connection to him is set forever.

"This was amazing," I say to him once Huck is buckled into the minivan.

As he presses a kiss to my lips, he murmurs, "Tell me something you like."

"You. Here," I say into his mouth, smiling. "You?"

"Still Mabel's books." His lips lift slightly as he pulls away. "See you this weekend?"

I bite my lip to hide my smile.

My "Maybe," earns me a knowing smirk from him. Because he knows, when it comes to him, maybe always means yes.

Thirty

Dread sits heavy in my gut as I park the minivan. I had hoped when Veda asked me to drive her to the doctor, it was of the local family variety for a routine checkup, but the fact we are in Asheville staring at the hospital tells me everything I already know. Something is wrong.

"I'm going in with you," I say, opening my door.

She shoots me a glare, which I match. "I won't go in the room with you, but I'm going in," I say, firm, closing my door before she can argue.

Out of the car, I meet her scowl with my own. Our silent battle of wills, finally ending when she blows out a frustrated breath and starts walking toward the hospital.

We cross the parking lot in silence. Summer is getting swallowed up by fall in the beautiful way it does this time of year. If I didn't believe the sky was about to start raining shrapnel on me with whatever's coming next, I might have commented about how nice it is.

Air blows a gust at us as the automatic doors slide open, and we step into the sterile scent of the hospital. A noxious combination of disinfectant and latex gloves, reminding me of the last weeks of my mom being alive. I trudged into that scent every day, telling myself I wouldn't cry when we made it to her room, ultimately breaking down anyway.

"What floor?" I ask once we're in the elevator.

"Eight," she says, gaze on the floor.

Next to the buttons, oncology is written on a directory next to eighth floor.

I push button eight at the same time I realize Veda has cancer.

Everything following the elevator happens in silence and with Veda's diagnosis attached like a shadow in the late afternoon sun: stretched and looming.

We sit in the waiting room, thumbing through home renovation magazines, waiting. Every single page is filled with DIY tips I don't care about.

Veda has cancer.

Bo's text of, *I'm wondering what other kinds of books Mabel has...* sends a gush of guilt, anxiety, and sadness sloshing through me. Instead of responding, I ignore him.

Veda has cancer.

"Veda Monroe," a nurse calls from an open door. The first time for scans, the second time to see the doctor. Both times I look at her, an abysmal pit forming in my stomach at the sound of her name. Both times, she glares at me.

Veda has cancer.

Finally outside, the fresh air replacing the sterile scents of the hospital, there's only the slightest relief. Even the leaves outside, showing the stain of early September yellows, which normally make my heart skip a beat, offer no reprieve. No place to hide from the truth that's stuck to everything.

Veda has cancer.

It's thirty minutes into our hour drive home when she finally breaks the silence. "Last year, I went to talk to my doctor about a cough I couldn't shake," she starts, staring out her window, her hair pinned back in its usual tight bun. "I thought, no big deal, I'll go in there, they'll give me some medication and that will be that." She laughs softly, the jangle of her earrings slicing through the thick quiet. "Of course, it wasn't that easy. They did all their scans and tests and told me a bunch of fancy words that equated to lung cancer. Some kind of slow-growing mumbo jumbo." She waves her hand through the air with a resigned sigh.

I wring my hands around the steering wheel, trying to absorb what she's saying, but say nothing.

"So, they did a little surgery. Cut out all the bad stuff. Told me not to smoke—I've never smoked a day in my life!" She laughs ironically.

My eyes stay glued to the road ahead of us, but I feel her intensely staring at the side of my face before she continues. "The day before you knocked on my door, I had a checkup. The cancer came back. Aggressively."

Then she's quiet, hands in her lap. I swing my eyes briefly from the road to look at her. She's wearing denim overalls over a long-sleeved yellow shirt. She looks just like her, except now—Veda has cancer.

"Treatment?" I already know the answer, but I ask anyway.

I know she shakes her head because of the familiar sound of her earrings. "I told them—and Bo—last time I wouldn't do it if it came back. He fought me, of course, it's what we do for the people we love. The doctor told me even if I put myself through the hell of chemo and everything else that I would probably only be adding a couple months. The medication you found is for managing the symptoms. The pain."

I blink rapidly. "How much time?"

"Six months..." I fortify myself in her pause. "At best."

"Is this why you hired me? Because of my history?" I ask, thinking back to the first time I met her and how her tone shifted when she noticed my tattoos.

"Partly."

My eyes flick from the road to her; hands in her lap, she's as eerily calm as her voice sounds, but her usually timeless face is weathered by lines.

Then we're quiet.

Sometime between when we leave the hospital and when I park in front of her house, the once bright, beautiful sky goes grey—as if it knows her diagnosis—and rain starts to fall in our silence. When I turn the van off, we sit, staring at the droplets that slam onto the windshield.

I've watched clients age for years, but there's always been a kind of bridge between me and the end. There's usually a decline until my services aren't needed because they're bringing hospice in or going to a facility for the final weeks or months. Even though Veda is still sitting in front of me, looking exactly like she did the first day we met less a few pounds, it's different. Like that bridge I've gotten so comfortable with just had a bomb dropped on it and it's been blown to smithereens.

"Do you remember your last days with your mom?" Her voice takes on a harder edge and the question sticks into my chest like a poisoned arrow.

I nod. "Of course."

"Tell me about it," she says firmly, as if she isn't peeling my heart like an orange with her request.

I close my eyes and take a deep breath; my head drops back to the headrest as I let my mind take me to the same place the smell of the hospital had. A memory as vivid as it is devastating. I take one breath before I can talk.

"She spent the last weeks in the hospital. The chemo had made her sick—but the end—the end was worse. She looked like a bag of bones in her hospital gown. Sunken." Rain plops onto the windshield as I sift through my memories. "She slept a lot, not saying much when we visited. My dad stayed most nights in the last days, playing George Strait on a Walkman for her. I was staying with an uncle the night she passed. My dad was lying in her hospital bed with his arms wrapped around her when she went."

I can still picture her, pale, frail, and hoarsely saying, "Hey there, Little Bird," when she could summon the energy to talk during my visits. All the while, my dad stood stoically by, holding my hand while he watched the love of his life slip away, breath by shallow breath.

"I won't do that to Bo, Birdie. Do you hear me?" Her tone is sharp, like she's yelling at me about how to wedge clay more than her own pending death. "Bo will try to save me, and he can't—you know it just as well as I do. He'll ask me to get treatment, and I won't be able to say no, but it's not what I want. This is the end, and he won't accept it. Won't see it for what it is. There are no good goodbyes when you know it's forever."

I nod, numb. Tears for my mom, for Veda, and for what she's asking me to do to Bo well up behind my eyes, but I refuse to let them fall. I swallow them down along with the bile that's rising in my throat.

She reaches her hand over across the open space between our seats and squeezes my leg. "I'm sorry, Birdie."

I look at her, almost laughing. "You're dying and I'm the one being comforted?"

She chuckles. "Well, you fell in love with my grandson, and I'm asking you to lie to him about something he might hate you for.

Me comforting you seems about right." Then she smiles in that knowing way she always does.

I don't even argue. I can't. She's right about all of it.

Because—*Veda has cancer*.

Thirty-one

WHEN I SEE MY dad's too enthusiastic wave through the lightly falling rain, I nearly break. George Strait runs toward him with his normal amount of gumption, but once I'm out of the van, every step takes maximum effort.

I put on a good face for Veda when we finally got into the house after the hospital. I pretended it was just another day and talked about the Forever Fun class she's teaching in two weeks. I spent the drive home in a daze, almost convincing myself that this was all some kind of misunderstanding. Or nightmare. But now, the cold autumn rain slaps my skin, and seeing my dad's familiar face, the truth crushes my chest like a barbell.

My throat burns with all the emotions I try to keep shoved down. I'm so sad. So angry.

"Little Bird, everything okay?" my dad asks, wrapping me in a familiar hug.

I start to say yes, but it's drowned out by a rare sob. Then another. Then another. I bury my face in his chest and let myself weep for the whole damn day. My sobs turn to something on the brink of hyperventilating, I realize it's not just for Veda. It's for Veda *and*.

And everything I never let myself cry for.

My mom.

My abortion.

My genetic mutation.

Bo.

I cry into my dad in the rain for a life I hate. The different life I can never have.

"Shhhh," he hushes, rubbing my back. "Shhhh." Over and over until the well of my tears runs dry in the cool rain.

He walks me inside, flips on the furnace, and gets me a blanket as I sit on the couch.

"Tea?" he asks from the kitchen that opens into the living room.

I sniff, wiping my nose with my sleeve, and nod. He fills a kettle with water and turns the knob on the stove, the familiar *click! click! click!* until the flame catches.

"Veda has cancer. It's spreading. She doesn't have much time left," I say, words distant. Like someone else said them into a glass on the other side of the wall.

My dad's lips droop into a frown. "I'm sor—"

"And she doesn't want me to tell Bo," I say, not letting him finish. A fresh burn builds in my throat, and my own misery leaks down my face.

"She's not going to fight," I stutter through my tears, wiping my nose again. "And she doesn't want Bo to see her the way we saw—" Another loud sob rips out of me, and I bring my hands to my face, jamming my palms into my eyes, trying to press the sadness off me.

My dad sits next to me, tea in hand.

I blow out a calming breath, leveling myself out before I continue. "She doesn't want Bo to see her the way we saw Mom, and she doesn't want him to try and change her mind about treatment."

I take the mug from him, cupping it in both hands, and see sadness fill his eyes.

Then, we're quiet. I don't know how long we sit there, but it's long enough for the dog to push through the doggy door with a muddy stick and chew it into mulch chunks without either of us saying anything about it.

"You can't tell him, Birdie," he finally says.

I already knew that, but a pit forms in my stomach anyway. The only response I give is a heavy sigh.

"You telling him will make her last days worse," he says, giving one of his prolific pauses that means something is coming that I'm not prepared for. "Your mom didn't want to do that last round of treatment."

My mug shakes in my hands with the confession, and I go light-headed. "What?" I whisper, stunned.

"The doctors said it had spread too much; treatment was a last-ditch effort at buying just a little more time. She told me it wouldn't be worth it. It would be bad months on top of bad months. I begged her to try." His voice cracks, eyes glassy. He doesn't look at me, he's looking straight ahead to a shelf, at their wedding picture in a frame. My mom is in a long white dress, a bouquet of wildflowers in her hand, my dad in a suit. Both beaming.

"I thought," he pauses again, swallows hard, then continues. "I thought that miracles happen every day. One more treatment might be where our miracle was waiting. That's what I said to her." He picks his scotch up from the coffee table and takes a sip. "Those last weeks in the hospital—her pain, the weakness." He shakes his head. "I kept thinking, I did this to her." His voice cracks again, and this time it comes with a tear that falls down his face.

I take his hand in mine and lean my head on his shoulder. We sit in puddles of our own grief.

When I finally have the capacity to speak again, it's quiet. Hoarse. "I'm in love with Bo, Dad."

He sighs, heavy, like he's holding every ounce of the weight I'm carrying. "I know you are, Little Bird. You still can't tell him."

I nod, my head still on his shoulder. "What am I supposed to do?"

He pauses, long and weighted. I don't ask, but I wonder if he's thinking about everything he would have changed with Mom. Blaming himself for things that are never anyone's fault though we like to pretend they are.

"You hope he realizes the gift you've given him when the time comes."

Thirty-two

I IGNORE BO.

He calls. He texts. I avoid him.

When I get home from my dad's, his message of, *I haven't talked to you all day. I miss you,* earns a response from me of, *Sorry, crazy day. I'm beat.* It's the most stripped-down version of the truth I can give.

Friday, with Mabel, I force myself through book club and our usual banter, but there's no enthusiasm. I don't even tell her about Bo starring in my very own lumberjack fantasy just a week prior.

He invites me over for dinner that night; I tell him I can't miss yoga.

I do go to yoga, but I spend half of the class in child's pose forcing myself to breathe.

Sunday, I skip church, the first time in our months together, telling him I have to help my dad.

Lying.

Every day that passes the next week makes a brand-new truth crystalize: I have to end it with him.

A lifetime spent trying to make the right choices so I could live just a little bit longer, missing out on big experiences to protect everyone involved. Maintaining order—predictability—so that whatever was coming around the bend would never be a surprise. I'd always be ready.

Yet here I stand in my sweat-soaked gym clothes, staring at my beloved grocery store on Friday night, wrecked. All my rules and order never once prepared me for the plot twist that was actually waiting around the bend.

I love Bo but can't tell him that the woman he looks at like his mother is dying. It's cruel.

I pull a cart out of the line as I walk in, irrationally annoyed by the fact it has a squeaky wheel. Waving feebly to Monica, I head toward the produce.

When I get there, I just stare. Nothing makes sense. Being with Bo, avoiding Bo—both options make me ache.

"You planning on buying anything, or are you just going to stare at those tomatoes all night, Pam Beesly?"

I freeze.

Bo.

He doesn't wait for me to answer before reaching his hand to my face and gripping my cheeks with his thumb and forefinger, squeezing slightly so my lips pout like a fish. He tilts my chin, forcing my eyes to meet his. "Wanna tell me what the hell is going on with you?" he asks, a harshness in his voice that isn't normally there along with a deep crease between his eyebrows.

His dark hair, usually tucked back behind his ears, falls forward over his face. It takes all I have not to brush it to the side.

I sigh through my puckered lips, sadness and panic swirling in my belly. Instantly, my throat clogs, eyes burn, heart fractures.

He must see because his face softens along with his grip on my cheeks.

"Hey," he says, dropping his hand from my face and pulling me into a hug—a touch I didn't know I needed until he gave it. "What happened?"

My nose smooshed against his chest I breathe in his Bo Mountain Breeze. I've missed him—I realize now how much.

I push myself off his chest, lift my chin to face him and swallow back the tears I don't want to cry.

One breath.

Two.

"This isn't working," I say quietly.

His eyebrows pinch. "What isn't?"

Three heartbeats, then: "Us."

He takes a step back. "What? Birdie, what's going on here?"

I shake my head, guilt dragging my gaze to the floor. "It's not fair to you, Bo. If I get sick..." I lift my eyes to his face—etched in confusion—and blink away, focusing on a basket of oranges.

"Birdie, I already said tha—"

"I heard what you said," I snap, squaring my shoulders to him. Damn him for making this harder than it has to be. "And that's part of the problem, you don't listen to me," I lie. Again. Because that's what I do now. The truth is, if anyone has ever listened to me in this life, it's him. "You think I need all these changes—that my life had no meaning before you. Well, you're wrong, Bo. I was just fine and then—then—then—then you show up and think I'm some sad puppy that needs to be rescued. But I'm not. I miss how things were. It was easier, and—and—and I've lost focus on what's important."

When I finally look at him, his jaw is tight, clenching repeatedly. He pulls the toothpick from his mouth and snaps it in half before shoving it into his pocket. After an eternity, he nods slowly, looking around the bins of fruits and vegetables.

"I guess this means you aren't adopting Huck, then, huh?" he finally asks.

My chin pulls back. "Wha—"

"You can't, right? I mean, if I've wrecked your routine too much, then a kid will annihilate it." He looks at me, eyes wide. "Makes sense though. I get it."

"Bo, I—"

"And," he starts, pausing to rub his knuckles under his chin, "I guess this means I won't be seeing you Sundays anymore."

No more church?

"No, I di—"

"Lucy will be disappointed—I think she liked you—but they say kids are resilient, so I guess she'll understand." He gives a knowing nod.

Too knowing.

I glare at him—he's playing me. "What are you trying to do?" I demand.

"Me?" He laughs in disbelief. "What the fuck are *you* trying to do, Birdie?" he asks, voice elevated. "You give me some bullshit spiel about not wanting this, and your lie is written all over your face." He holds his hands out to his side as my nostrils flare.

A woman walks by with wide eyes that I glare at, a casualty of my insanity.

I yank the handle of my cart and start stomping away from him. I'm not doing this.

With him.

I don't need it.

Or him.

"Really, you're just going to walk away?" he asks, following me, making my blood come to a roaring boil in my veins.

Like a delusional fool, I scoff but don't respond, squeaky wheel mocking me as I try to outrun him.

"You know this is insane, right, Birdie?" he presses as I start throwing random items in my cart just to give my hands something to do. Bagels? *Sure.* Cookies? *Why the hell not?* "You're shutting me out for no reason, like I don't mean anything to you—like you don't mean anything to me! I already told you, I don't care about th—"

"Goddammit, Bo!" I stop the cart in the middle of an aisle and look at him, voice borderline shouting. "I'm in love with you."

It's not the whole truth, but it's just as true. I love Bo and it's as wretched as it is wonderful.

His reaction comes in the form of a step, quick hand around the back of my neck, and pull to impact. Bo crushes his mouth to mine and kisses me.

When we stop, it's only because a familiar voice yells, "Oooh-weee! Someone call the fire department 'cuz there's smoke comin' from aisle four." It's Monica, and I can hear the smile on her face.

We laugh into each other's mouths as we pull away. At the end of the aisle, Monica stands behind her register, fanning her face with her hand, toothpaste-commercial-worthy grin on her face. "Y'all get a room!" She cackles before a customer starts unloading groceries in front of her.

"Just so I understand this," Bo says, turning back to me, tucking a rogue hair behind my ear. "You realize you love me, and your reaction is to avoid me and then end it in a grocery store?"

Somehow, despite everything I'm not telling him, I laugh.

"I guess, yes, that sums it up. Why?" I ask, moving from the aisle toward the freezers that line the back of the store. "What would you do differently if you were in love with someone?"

"If I was in love with someone, I would keep texting and calling and showing up at grocery stores when they get skittish, obviously," he says, leaning on the handle of the cart.

I still—the bag of frozen berries I'm holding dangles midair as I look at him.

He whistles smugly, like he knows what he's said but wants to hear me acknowledge it. "So when you love someone, you stalk them?" I ask, slowly lowering the bag into the cart, not giving him the satisfaction of seeing me get all swoony over him. "That's healthy."

The cold air pops out at me as I open a freezer filled with popsicles, and Bo leans next to me, pink sticky note on his finger in front of my face.

"What's this?" I ask, eyes going to his.

"The last one—read it."

I do—repeatedly. Three words that have the power to change the course of my life: *Fall in love.*

I let the freezer door close, swallowing the chill.

"You knew this would happen." I don't have to ask.

He nods, tousled hair falling into his face, dark eyes locked on mine. "For me. From the second I saw you standing on Gran's porch."

"You love me." Another not question.

"I love you," he says, pressing the sticky note to my chest, taking my hands in his, "and you love me."

I simply nod, letting his words wash over me. Bo has a wife and I might die, but we love each other anyway. A flower growing in soil that's too rocky but somehow blooms.

"You know," I say, pulling my hands from his and opening the freezer door again, "your listmaking skills need work."

He laughs as I hand him a box of popsicles. "Really, Pam Beesly? How's that? Seems I got what I wanted."

I shake my head. "Only barely." I lift an eyebrow as I look at him. "Usually if you're trying to win someone over, a proper list needs to tell them how wonderful they are. At length."

Cart moving again, he's next to me.

When I stop to look at the cooler of meat, his hand catches around my wrist, pulling me close to him. Any trace of amusement is gone from his face.

We're close, so close the movement of our bodies when we breathe presses into one another. "I'm in love with you, Birdie," he says, voice lower now. Serious. "If you want the reasons, I can give them to you."

"Bo, I—"

"I'm not done," he cuts me off with a light kiss before continuing. "And you don't get to shut me out because you feel things that are scary; you tell me. And we deal with it. Together. Even if it's hard and ugly. We figure it out and love anyway."

Another pause, another kiss. Everything he says goes into my ears and drips a delightful kind of warmth throughout my whole body like the wax of a candle.

In the middle of the grocery store, I'm speechless.

"I love you because you grocery shop on Fridays, dance with your dad on Thursdays, laugh with Lucy, and take care of Gran the way no one else can." With his final words, a needle pops the bubble of the beautiful dream I'm standing in. Because, yes, I'm taking care of her, but I have no doubt someday he might not see it that way. This reason he's listed for loving me is one he might eventually give for hating me.

But, as if he sees me getting lost in my own head, he gives me another kiss. "I would say I love you because you pulled me in the back of your minivan after drinking triple sec and giving me a fake name, but maybe that's just lust."

I snort. "Well, for a stalker, that's a pretty solid list, but it's not *that* long." The smile that covers my face is huge, giddy, and absolutely ridiculous.

He vibrates with a laugh, an easy, "I can give you one hundred reasons," and another light kiss on my lips.

"You love me," I say, as if trying to manifest my own belief in his words.

"I do."

"Even though there's a good chance I'll die." I offer him an out, my last-ditch effort for us to both walk away from this inevitable disaster.

"There's a great chance you'll die." He's so matter-of-fact. Unfazed.

I slap his chest. "You know what I mean, Bo. There's a great chance I'll die *before* you. Much before you."

"Birdie, I'm not going to live my life thinking about what ifs. My dad died in a car accident and my mom took off, so did my wife. None of them had a genetic mutation that led to their fate. It's just life." He pauses, looks at me. "As much as I can't stay away from you because of Mandy, you can't push me away because of this."

I open my mouth to argue, but he puts a finger over my lips.

"I'm not diminishing your circumstances or how stressful and scary it must be. But I'm telling you, I don't care. I want to be with you. And your groceries. And your lists. I want it all." He pauses, kisses me lightly, then, "Your genetic mutation is mine, Birdie. Let me do this with you."

And this moment is one that I wish I could bottle up. It is the most romantic thing that has ever, will ever, happen in my life.

Sometimes I look at my chest and wish my life was as permanently beautiful as the ink on my skin. Mostly, my life is beautiful the way real North Carolina wildflowers are beautiful—only sometimes. A fleeting blooming just to eventually wilt. But this? This moment in sweaty gym clothes next to Bo who loves me is wholly perfect.

With no way to compete with what he's just told me, "Okay," is all I say.

His slow-to-grow smile is huge, and he rubs his nose against my cheek before repeating, "Okay."

I look at my cart filled with groceries, some that I don't even want. "I need to pay for these."

"You do." He pauses, expression turning wolfish. "Then we're going to take them to your house, put them away in your well-labeled kitchen, and get George Strait."

I raise my eyebrows, crossing my arms over my chest. "Oh really?"

"Birdie, if you think the night I find out the woman I've been chasing for four whole months loves me and is staying anywhere but my bed, you're out of your mind. Lucy is at Libby's. I want you." Then, like we aren't in a grocery store, he squeezes my yoga-pant-covered ass and nips at my neck, pushing the squeaking cart down the aisle.

I don't bother arguing.

He knows just as well as I do—I want him too.

Thirty-three

Bo puts the groceries away while I take a quick shower and pack a bag. I grab clothes, enough for two nights—presumptuously—and start pulling things off my bathroom counter. At the small black notebook I keep in the bathroom, I pause, and anxiety starts to percolate in my belly as I thumb through the pages, filled with numbers.

I haven't told Bo about this, mostly because I'm not sure what it means. What I *want* it to mean.

That's a lie.

I know what I *want* it to mean; I'm just not ready to say it. I don't think, I just grab it, slipping it into my bag along with everything else I'll need before turning the lights off. Whatever I do or don't do with it can be decided later.

Then we're in his Jeep, with the dog, driving to his house. Somehow, I shove Veda's situation out of my mind, because more than I should be sad or guilty, I want this. With Bo.

"So, I'm wondering, now that you're weirdly in love with me or whatever," I say, picking at my cuticles as I look out the window into the dark. "I have a home visit for Huck's adoption in a couple weeks and, if you aren't busy, maybe you'd like to, I don't know, be there for it."

His hand reaches across the center console in the darkness, fingers interlacing with mine. "I'd love to."

I let out an exhale, my thumb rubbing across the slightest raise of a scar across his, and steal a look at him. The lights of the dash illuminate his face and chest. His hair hangs easily around his face, and the angle of his nose and forehead and curve of his lips look like they've been highlighted to perfection. With one hand on the steering wheel, his body casually leans toward me so his other can reach mine. I might not get to love Bo forever, but loving him right in this moment might be the most precious gift I've ever been given.

"I'm glad you love me, Bo," I say. The words a freeing confession. "Me too."

The notebook shakes in my hands as I sit on the edge of Bo's bed in an oversized Smoky Mountain National Park T-shirt. His bedroom—masculine and tasteful—is all exposed logs and dark furniture with a large cowhide rug on the floor. The lights aren't on, but there are four simple beeswax candles lit on his dresser.

I'm terrified. Once I show him, I can't take it back. Well, knowing Bo, I probably *could* take it back, but I know I won't want to.

"I hope that's a notebook from Mabel," he says with a grin as he walks out of the bathroom, pulling his shirt over his head and tossing it into a basket.

The sound from my lips is a nervous gargle of *mhm*.

He sits next to me, slides the notebook out of my hands, and thumbs through it. The numbers mean nothing to him. His eyebrows pinch. "What is all this?"

I clear my throat. "So there's this natural method of birth control where you track certain markers in your cycle," I say, pulse quickening with every word. "And you know I love lists." I laugh softly. He thumbs through the pages again. "Anyway, what I mean is, I guess, that I started tracking everything when we met. Well, that's not true. Of course, knowing me, I've always been tracking my cycle, but I started *really* tracking my cycle in case someday...someday."

I look at him, chewing my lip, wondering how I'm fumbling this so terribly.

He closes the book, eyes searching mine. "What are you saying, Birdie?"

I blow out a long breath. "What we did the other night was great, but I know I need more with you, Bo. I need all of you. I want it. And so, this is my way of offering all of me on Birdie-friendly terms. It's 99 percent effective when followed correctly at preventing pregnancy, and I just thought if you wanted, we could, you know, do *it*."

I squeeze my eyes shut before looking at him. Every morning when I take my temperature and record it, I've wondered how this conversation was going to go if the time ever came to have it. Now it's happening, and I sound like a moron.

"'*Do it?*'" he scrubs a hand across his face, failing to hide his laugh.

"That's not what you're supposed to focus on," I huff. "What I mean is, if you want to have sex, I have a notebook with data-driven dates that I would be comfortable *doing it*. With protection. At least at first. Until I'm less anxious about it." I pause, then, "If you want."

I pull at a thread of my shirt like it's a lifeline, my heart galloping through my chest like a herd of elephants.

Bo reaches across me to put the notebook on the nightstand. When the bare skin of his chest rubs against that of my arm, a tense kind of awareness envelops me.

"Is one of those acceptable dates tonight?" he asks, kissing a trail across my jaw until he reaches my earlobe where he stills, taking it in his mouth, sucking it with a gentle scraping of his teeth.

I shift in my seat, trying to hide how amazing I apparently find having my earlobe sucked on to be. "Umm," I say, voice pinched, him working his mouth on the newly discovered g-spot that's surprisingly attached to my face. "I think so, yes. I mean, sure. Yes." I clear my throat, closing my eyes, adding, "Tonight is a yes. And tomorrow. Not that I'm assuming I'll be here tomorrow. And Sunday..."

He makes some kind of moaning growl with my turned-on ear in his mouth as his hand slides up my thigh and stops, fingers digging into the skin. Close, but not close enough.

He pulls his mouth away from my ear—which, I can be honest with myself, is disappointing.

"Do you want this?" he asks. "You don't have to do this for me, I need you to know that."

He's so serious, so sincere, I want to cry from the gravity of it.

"Bo, I want you. And this. Am I terrified? Yes. But I still want to do it. Scared. With you."

I swallow down the ball of terror in my throat as he smiles.

Before he puts his lips on me again, it's a mumbled, "Thank God."

Thirty-four

The night I met Bo, I was fueled by defiance. The stress intimacy usually causes me didn't exist because it was a planned anomaly. A small wrinkle in the otherwise smooth fabric of my life that I would iron out later.

Tonight, as Bo lifts my shirt over my head in the candlelight of his bedroom, there's no defiance. This isn't an anomaly. I know saying yes to this, with my notebook filled with temperatures and notes, means I'm not saying yes to once. I'm just saying yes.

I'll still never have kids. I won't stop avoiding chemicals and living by my lists. But now, someone on this planet wants to be part of it—me. Entirely. Without changing.

The way he looks at me is the way he kisses me: tender. Like he sees me. Like he loves me.

My hands trace the lines of his chest, down his hard stomach, and unbutton his jeans, sliding them down his legs.

There are countless things I'd like Bo to do to me, but right now, all I do is stare. This man, this beautiful man, is looking at me and my scarred, ink-covered chest, like I'm perfect. It's a truth that I would never have known to believe in if not for him.

He follows my lead. Rough palms on my hips, slipping under the hem of my underwear. As he starts to slide them down my legs, his kiss moves from my mouth to my throat.

To my chest.

To my belly.

Lower.

He slides my last item of clothing down my legs, grips my hips, and pulls me down to sit on the bed as he drops to his knees in front of me. There, he drags me forward until I'm on the edge of the mattress, naked, him kneeling between my legs on the floor.

Our gazes collide, and I know something transcendent is about to happen. Like whatever he's about to do to my body will leave it forever changed. As ruined as one of Mabel's heroines.

"I want to learn every part of you," he says, voice like gravel. He lifts my leg slightly and his mouth finds the inside of my knee.

"I think I'd like that," I reply, weak, as the sensation on my skin goes from being lips to tongue. Bo licks a straight line up the inside of my thigh. A flame to a fuse. Burning.

Up.

Higher.

His hands wrap around the backs of my thighs until his fingertips grip into the tops of my legs, holding me in place as my body starts to struggle to stay still. I know *exactly* where I want that mouth.

My fingers tangle in his hair as he moves his blessed tongue across my skin.

Closer.

"Birdie, I'm going to worship you," he says, dark eyes looking up at me for a split second.

My tongue is too heavy, throat too swollen. There are no words to respond with how much I want that.

So I don't.

Not as he moves to where I need him with his beautiful mouth.

Not when he tastes me like he's savoring it.

Not as he pulls back slightly, close enough I can feel him breathing. *There.*

I expect his touch again, but he doesn't give it; he waits.

Blowing against my skin.

Teasing.

Making my body tighten and struggle with want.

In an exodus of restraint, "Bo, please," slips through my lips. I'm begging and I don't care.

He blows again, grazing me with his mouth. "Tell me what you want, Birdie."

Just the slight vibration of his voice against my skin pulls my hands out of his hair and forces my upper body to drop back onto the bed from the heaviness.

Another blow of his breath, taunt of his mouth. "Say it." Now there's a teasing finger involved, and I swear I wouldn't know my own name if somebody asked me.

"Bo," I choke. "Put your damn mouth on me before I die."

That's all he needs.

With a growl, he licks, working his tongue until it pulls my back off the bed and a permanent whimper from my lips.

He's hungry. Carnivorous, even.

Moving.

There.

Swirling his tongue like some kind of magician.

Over and over and over.

My whimpers turn to curses then to begs. A loop of saying, "God. Bo. Please."

Hands wrapped around my thighs, his fingers grip.

Tighter.

Licking.

Faster.

Close.

Closer.

Gone.

Choppy breaths and curses come out of my mouth as his tongue—slower now—helps me ride out every drop of euphoria.

My legs jerk against his palms, but his grip keeps me in place.

Panting.

His mouth moves.

Up my belly.

Across the ink on my chest.

The column of my throat.

My ear.

My. Ear.

My mouth.

I taste *me* on *him*.

Then before I can take a full breath, he's over me, ripping open a condom with his teeth.

"I love you, Birdie," he whispers, kissing my collarbone before sitting upright. Hard between my legs, he rolls a condom on. "But now I'm going to wreck you."

My just-satisfied body responds to his words like a thirsty traveler at an oasis. Needy.

Again—"I think I might like that," is all I can say. But in truth: I *know* I will.

And there he is.

No hesitating.

Hips driving.

In.

He adjusts himself so his body molds against mine. A melding of our flesh when he fills me completely.

My hips chase his as he pulls back—earning a slight smile from him as he hovers over me—before the refilling.

Again.

And again.

The spot he's hitting with every movement straddles the line of pleasure and pain.

Head back, my fingernails dig into his back.

"God, you feel good," he says, teeth clenched, hair hanging over his face as his dark eyes lock onto mine.

He kisses my neck, now slick with sweat, and slides out of me—slow—causing my hips to chase his until he gives me what I want.

Once.

Twice.

Then.

Three things happen at once: he pulls out completely, hooks an arm around my waist, and flips me to my belly.

He pauses, kisses the space between my shoulder blades, and whispers against my skin. "I love you, but hang the hell on."

When I start to respond, it comes out as a yelp because he's back inside me, making my fists clench the sheets at the same time his hands grip my hips, and he lifts me to fit him.

This time when he drives into me, it's hard. And I scream—loud.

It's good. *He's* good.

I push my palms to the bed, back arching, him moving, barely able to see straight.

Thrusts turn to slams—the wrecking. His promise a fruition.

Grunted curses and moans scattered between kisses are punctuated with his unrestrained movements and a desperate sounding, *Now, Birdie,* from his lips.

With one final drive of his hips and as if my body is completely under his control, *now* it is. With him.

A shaky, sweaty, whimpering impact of pleasure as his fingers grip tighter somehow, last slow movements finishing us both.

Our panting in the dark forms a kind of sexy song I never want to end.

A staccato of breaths and pounding hearts as we crumble onto the mattress.

When I drop to my belly, he's lying next to me, kissing my shoulder. Tender. Both of us working to come down from the highest of highs.

"Tell me something you like," he says as I roll to my back, and his fingers immediately find the lines of my tattoos in the low light.

I laugh under my breath. There are many ways to answer that. His magical tongue that I probably need to tell Mabel about. The way he flipped me over and effortlessly destroyed me. Or, perhaps, the fingertip-shaped bruises that I'm sure will be covering my body when I wake up in the morning.

Instead, I smile. "You molesting my earlobe with your tongue."

He vibrates next to me with his own laugh, finger still tracing the flowers on my chest.

My smile hurts my face as I turn to look at him, barely illuminated by the candlelight. He's goodness embodied. Every single piece of him.

"You?"

"You loving me," he says.

He means it, and that sends a million butterflies fluttering through me.

"I like that too."

Thirty-five

I SIP MY COFFEE on Bo's porch in the morning while George Strait sniffs around the yard at a curious skip. It's foggy. Misty. The way the air gets this time of year in the mountains. The cool greyness of fall completely smothers out the final drops of warm sunshine from summer.

The air is clean, smelling like wet leaves and smoke from a chimney somewhere in the distance.

For the first time in my life, my mind—usually roaring like the rapids of the wildest river of Blue Ridge—is a glass pond.

Sitting in my oversized T-shirt with a blanket over my lap on a porch swing, it's beautiful like the poetic line of a country song. An entire story in a few simple words.

Someone on the outside might say I feel this way because of the sex, but I know it's something else. Something bigger. Like it always is with Bo: more.

He sits next to me, holding a plate of bacon in one hand, mug of coffee in the other. He offers the plate toward me. "Made from humanely raised pigs," he says with a proud grin. "Whatever that means."

I snort out a laugh. "It means they got snuggles," I tell him as I take a crispy piece, devour it, then take one more.

When the dog catches the familiar scent of salty fat, he pounces over to the porch and eats every piece we don't when Bo sets the plate on the ground for him.

"Now what do we do?" I ask, taking a sip of my coffee as Bo wraps an arm around me, pulling me into him. Snug.

"We have to get Lucy from Libby's," he says, rubbing circles along my bicep as he talks. "Then I thought we'd just spend the afternoon here. Make dinner." He pauses, plants a kiss on my temple. Then, with a lower and slightly more carnal tone, "And spend the night replaying what we did last night." He smiles against my skin before pulling away.

I bite my lips between my teeth to hide my smile, but the only thing I think is *We*. Every time he says it, a breeze blows through me, whipping up a pile of fallen leaves in my belly.

"And tomorrow, we'll drop her off at Gran's before church," he says, sipping his coffee.

Gran.

With that, the sweet flitter of leaves within me stills, drops, and is set ablaze by flames of guilt.

Because—Veda has cancer.

Three words sit on the tip of my tongue, slapping against my closed lips. I brave eye contact. He's happy—*so* happy.

"You okay?" he asks, pulling a toothpick from his pocket and slipping it between his lips, eyes narrowing slightly. "You have a funny face."

"Way to give me a complex," I say with a forced smile. "I was just thinking how nice that all sounds." Before he can see my lie for what it is, I blink away, lift my mug to my own lips, and swallow down my unsaid words and guilt with another sip of coffee.

Other than the fact I quasi-hate myself for the one thing I can't tell Bo, it's a perfect day.

When we get to Libby's, she greets me with a hug and a wide, red-lipped smile. She has two boys—six-year-old Jack and nine-year-old George. Her husband, John, a big guy with a wild beard and bright blue eyes, is a police officer with a contagious laugh.

I reach out my hand to shake his, but he looks at it like it's diseased before opening his arms wide and pulling me into a hug. "At last! The famous Birdie who's whipped our boy, Bo!"

Chickens peck around the backyard of their big white house and the boys scream from a pile of wrestling in the grass. Lucy squeals, wrapping her arms around my legs, then Bo's neck, then takes off running with George Strait.

Growing up just me and my dad, it's a chaos of home I've never been privy to. Like a family on TV, scripted to messy perfection.

John hooks an arm around my neck. "Tell me about yourself, Birdie," he says with a friendly kind of gruffness as we walk up the steps of their porch.

I smile. "Hmm…" I want to get this right. Want him to tell Bo how great I am after I leave. "I'm a hell of a singer," I say with a grin.

He booms out a laugh as he pushes the door open. "Lib said the same thing." He pauses, then, "Actually, what she said was, she's a helluva *bad* singer, but still better than Bo."

I raise my eyebrows. "That bad?"

"Birdie, you have no idea," he says solemnly.

"I heard that, asshole!" Bo says, smacking him on the back of the head with a grin as he follows behind us.

And that's our day. Sitting in a kitchen with a family that yells at each other from separate rooms, drinks lunch beers on Saturdays, and hurls insults with the sincerity of compliments.

"I know you don't drink often," Libby says, opening the fridge. "But we picked these up when Bo said you were coming. They don't have alcohol, but I don't know about the taste." She shrugs. "I won't be offended if you hate it."

When she passes me a nonalcoholic can of beer, I'm speechless.

It's just a fake beer, but in my hand, it becomes something precious. A talisman.

I drink one, then two. Because it's good, and being in this loud kitchen with Bo's arm draped around me is too.

John quickly becomes my new favorite person—he's loud and unfiltered, rough around the edges. A human party bus of sorts. He's everything I'm not but has a way of pulling me into the conversation when I'm too quiet.

When Bo tells them, "Birdie here is a sort of George Strait expert," John clings to this like a lifeline.

He peppers me with trivia questions, and I impress everyone by not missing a single one. Not his date of birth. Not his hometown. Not his first ten number one hits. Not the fact he eloped with his high school sweetheart—Norma—in Mexico. My mom loved the King of Country, so by default, I do too.

When he asks, "What would George Strait say on a day like today?"

I pause, grin, then tell him, "'Here for a Good Time,'" which makes him laugh loudly in a way that makes his beard shake. The irony isn't lost on me—I, the person who lives life by lists and calculated decisions, chooses a song that's about life being short and having fun while it lasts—essentially my anti-anthem. But here, it's right. *Good*. Like I *am* here for a good time.

When it's time for goodbye, hours later, Libby hugs me, with a promise of us hanging out together soon, and John puts me in a headlock and scrubs his knuckles across the top of my head like we're frat brothers.

As Lucy talks to the dog in the back seat while we drive, Bo's hand finds mine with a squeeze. Then, like he knows what I'm thinking, says, "They loved you."

And I really think they did.

Maybe because knowing Veda has cancer gives me a different lens to look at her through, but everything about her seems slightly less when we drop Lucy off at her house Sunday morning. Less weight. Less attitude. Less energy. Just *less*.

"You feeling okay?" I ask her when Bo and Lucy are out of earshot.

"Of course, I am," she says with less sharpness. No doubt, a lie. "Just a little tired is all." Then she smiles the kind of smile that everyone gives when they say they are fine that tells how *not* fine they are.

"Are you still good with Thursday? I can cancel if..."

She waves her twisted hand in the air. "Nonsense. If there's some woman like Mabel in this world, I'm not missing my chance to meet her."

Then she smiles, a real one this time, and for a second, I forget—Veda has cancer.

Thirty-six

Bo and I visit a new church. Every Sunday we've gone deep into the mountains, but today he drives us down into the foothills. George Strait, who was gnawing happily on a bone when we left him, stayed behind. With Lucy at Veda's, it's just us, the same as it has been for months, but somehow, with everything that's happened, it's different. Like everything else with him, it's more.

"Why is your backpack so full?" I ask as he hitches the more stuffed than usual bag on his back.

"I brought extra layers in case we get cold." The grin he gives doesn't match his logical explanation, but he's on the trail before I can argue.

It's gorgeous as we start walking. The September air delivers the perfect punch of autumn crisp, and the sky is clear blue. I'm in my usual yoga pants and Monroe Cabins cap with my hair pulled into a ponytail, but today I'm wearing a sweatshirt too. So is Bo. Once we start walking, I warm quickly. When we drove away from the mountains, our lower elevation meant slightly higher temps. I can't imagine needing another layer.

Instead of the usual roots and rocks and steady incline I've become accustomed to, today's trail is flat and mostly packed soil mixed with fallen leaves. The trees around the trail are filled with color. Oaks and maples drip with yellows, oranges, and reds of the new season while the pines hold steadfast to their still mostly green needles. It smells dry and evergreen.

"Why did you pick this trail today?" I ask Bo's overstuffed-back-pack-covered back.

He turns his head to the side, toothpick playing on his lips, saying, "I wanted to show you something," over his shoulder without stopping.

Then, it's our usual comfortable quiet that we have on Sunday mornings. We aren't here to talk. Sometimes, I know we've grown closer when our hikes are over even though we've hardly said a word. Like we get to see something in each other that only reveals itself in our silence.

The trees start to thin. Thinner. Gone.

We are standing in a meadow and it's quiet. Tranquilly so. A deer standing in the middle pops its head up and spots us before half-running, half-leaping away through the most-ly-green-yet-somewhat-yellow tall grass. It's still early, not even ten, and the morning light paints across the field—still wet with the slightest layer of dew—to make it look like a shimmering water-color painting.

"It's beautiful," I say, though it feels like too small a word.

He tilts his head. "It's this way." Instead of following the trail forward, he steps into the grass.

I frown, my eyebrows shooting toward the sky as my voice turns stern. "You left the trail. No."

"I did. C'mon." He doesn't turn to look at me as he takes another step.

I frown again, looking from the perfectly clear trail he's left to the one he's making by smashing down the grass that's higher than his knees.

"Why?" I demand, refusing to budge as I cross my arms. "Is this even legal? Isn't this grass protected ground or something?" If I wasn't sure if I was panicking, the high-pitched sound of my voice lets me know that I am. Other than the time we slid down the rocks, we've never left the marked trail.

He stops walking and turns to face me, smug smirk slanting across his annoyingly handsome face. "I don't see a sign that says we'll go to prison for doing this, and there's something I want to show you that's this way." He tilts his head in the direction he's been walking. The direction *not* on the trail.

I'm bouncing, nervous, weighing my options. Reading my turmoil, he retraces his steps until he's back to me, plucking the toothpick out of his mouth before taking my hand in his.

"Birdie," he coos. "What do you think is going to happen if we walk into this very open, very well-lit, very flat field?"

When he puts it like that...

"My trail guide seems a bit shady," I say dryly. "You left that part out."

He tugs at my hand, slow-to-grow smile curling across his face, then kisses me on the forehead. "Do you trust me?"

I give him an annoyed nod without making eye contact.

"Then you know I wouldn't do anything *shady*."

I can tell he wants to laugh, and I have to bite my cheek to keep from smiling.

"Fine." My gaze meets his where it stays. "Let's go do whatever this stupid thing is before I change my mind."

He smiles, keeping one hand interlaced with mine, and leads me through the field.

In mere minutes, the trail is out of sight, but something far better is in front of us—around us.

The tall grass of the valley has turned into something completely different. A field, yes, but instead of tall grass starting to fade with the onslaught of fall, it's an explosion of color. Blossoms of fiery yellows and fierce oranges, muted only by the occasional faded green blades of the meadow grass mixed in. The field has been set ablaze by a flame of wildflowers.

And it's not just my eyes that experience it—it's as though the field has changed every piece of the atmosphere. The breeze blows cooler against my skin, and the earthy smell that was on the trail has been replaced by something sweet. Ambrosial.

My hands come to my mouth—because *how?*

"What is this?" My eyes move so slowly it's as though I'm trying to commit to memory every single petal covering the field that stretches as far as the eye can see.

"I found it online," he says. "I've never been here, but when I read about it,"—he shrugs—"it looked like you." His smile is warm as sunshine as he takes my hand in his and leads us to the middle, careful not to crush a single stem as he walks. "Someone planted it years ago. One article said some sisters did it to honor their mom, someone else said it was a class from the college doing a project. Either way, it's a mix of only late summer and early fall seeds so it's unexpected. A secret."

I see that now, recognizing several of them as flowers on my own skin. Black-eyed Susans, scarlet honeysuckle, and orange hawkweed. It looks like a postcard—an image that makes people ask, *Is this place real?*

My hand in his, I take it all in. Beauty that has no business being here but is anyway.

When we stop in a small patch of mostly grass, Bo drops his backpack and pulls out a blanket that he spreads across the ground, grin from earlier now something conspiratorial. Then, he pulls out another, and drops it on top of the one already laid out.

His hands rest on my hips when he stands, dark eyes exploding with gold flecks searching mine playfully. "Worth leaving the trail?"

I nod. Because, yes, this is absolutely worth it. "The blanket?" I ask, lifting my chin.

"I realized I've never laid in a field of fall wildflowers, and I thought maybe you haven't either." The tone of his voice implies there's more to it, but I let it slide. Because with all this—my eyes go to the field around us again—it doesn't matter. It doesn't seem real.

He sits on the blanket, stretches out on his back, hands behind his head, and just the sight of him, in all these flowers, makes me do the exact same thing.

We lie on our backs, looking up at the clear blue sky that's framed by the contrasting reds and yellows and oranges that dance around us. They lean and sway in a dreamy slow motion. An ethereal flashback scene from a movie that makes me long for it to last forever.

Fingers interlaced, lying on our backs with colorful petals blowing in the breeze around us, if Bo wasn't already going to be ingrained in me forever, in this moment he is. Pressed into me with the kind of finality of one of his Lincoln Logs in the floor of his cabins. I may never do another thing in my life without this one influencing it. A new gold-star standard which every other moment will be measured against.

"Thank you for this," I say, turning my head to face him, him doing the same. The warm light makes the side of his face glow as hair falls across his face.

"You know," he drawls, tracing a finger down the line of my jaw and neck. "I've also never had sex in a field of fall wildflowers."

I don't bother to hide my smile. "It's incredible. You should try it sometime...should you find yourself in that situation." I roll on my side to face him. "If you have space in your backpack for a condom."

Gripping his hand around my neck, he pulls me close. "One step ahead Pam Beesly, it's in my pocket." Then, his mouth is on mine and I'm so thankful—so burning with need for him—that I almost cry. Because it's a day I can't get pregnant. Because he brought protection. Because we are in the possibly most beautiful place on planet Earth at this very moment.

What starts slow and sweet turns fervent between us. I'm not an exhibitionist, but this. *This*. I just can't say no. Our pants only make it down our legs and the rest of our clothes stay on before he's rolling the condom on and sliding inside of me.

His mouth never leaves mine. He kisses me like he loves me, but he fucks me like he needs me. Fast, hard, and like he's on a mission. Moving like he's losing control.

With the next move of his hips, my back pulls off the ground, and fingers dig into the bare skin of his back under his sweatshirt.

The next, my eyes roll back.

Then a cry.

Deep.

Deeper.

His breathy whisper, "Let me see it, Birdie."

Gone.

Bo sends me to heaven from church with a mix of cries and gasps that dance off the petals and into the wind. A mountain breeze I want to feel forever and always.

Thirty-seven

WHEN I WALK SAM and Mabel into Veda's sunroom, she has spots for them ready with balls of clay, cups of water, sponges, and several wooden pointed tools around the big worktable when we arrive.

"Veda, this is the rest of the gang, Mabel and Sam," I introduce them. "This is Veda."

Sam grumbles about forced arts and crafts while Mabel looks around the room and says, "Lots of uses for the tools in here, Birdie dear." She clicks her tongue and slides a notebook out of her waistband.

I press my lips together in a tight line as Veda's eyebrows pinch. *Here we go.*

Hair pulled back in a neat and tidy bun, Veda stands at the head of the table wearing a flowy blue shirt and pair of black pants with greyish streaks across the legs where she's wiped her clay-covered hands on them.

"Well, Birdie dragged you all here to make something, so let's make the most of it," she says, teasing, which breaks the ice enough to make them laugh.

She holds a small ball of clay in her hands. "I won't mince words, we're all old. Our bodies don't give a damn about what our brains want." She sounds like a cross between a stand-up comedian and an angry school principal. "I've made all these beautiful things"—her hands sweep around the room toward the shelves lined with her bowls and vases—"but my hands have thrown in the towel on all that and I've learned to manage my expectations. You will too. I want you to put whatever you think you should be doing in the garbage can of your mind. We are here with the tools we have, no matter how shaky and weak, to make something beautiful. We're old, not dead, and there's a different measurement of beauty that comes with that."

Her eyes flick to mine before she continues.

"Now I want you to push a finger into the clay, feel it."

Mabel jumps right in, Sam reluctantly following, pushing into the doughy balls in front of them.

Veda guides them through different ways of pinching and pulling, showing them how to form a variety of shapes. I demonstrate with her guidance until I've formed a goofy face on my own ball of clay that makes them chuckle.

"Here are some other ideas." She sets a sculpted bird, elephant, and abstract monster on the table. "But the sky is really the limit. So whatever you love, you can make...in your own way. Whatever you make, I want it to be something that means more than having it look perfect."

"I don't have a creative bone in my body," Sam grumbles.

Veda's hand gives her token swat. "You've survived to grumpy old manhood, that takes some kind of creativity." Eyebrows raised, her words shut him up.

She sets them loose with their balls of clay and combined centuries worth of creativity between them.

They knead, roll, pinch, and push. They talk—laugh. They get to know each other with their fingers in the pliable balls. Sam starts with a story about Vietnam which leads to Mabel telling a story about a Vietnamese man she met one time.

Veda laughs at their stories, a light burning brightly in her eyes. She's happy; they all are. I am.

When Sam starts saying, "I should have made Birdie a pair of t—" I clap my hands, cutting off his unspoken *tits*.

"Let's see what everyone made!" I say, shooting him a glare.

"I made an M16," Sam says, without his usual irritated tone, holding up a clay gun. "It's the gun that kept me alive in 'Nam, bringing me home to everything that was yet to come." He looks at me, and I smile.

Mabel doesn't miss a beat by stealing the moment with a proud declaration: "I made a cock."

True to her word, in her hands—a long clay *cock*.

Her full-wattage smile shows her lipstick-stained teeth, and she wiggles her eyebrows toward Sam.

I snort while Veda gives a stunned, "Wow," and covers her gaping mouth with her hand.

Sam's eyes go saucer sized at the same time he asks, "You some kind of pervert, Mabel?"

She looks at him like he's just given her a compliment and says, "If that's what you're into, Sammy Boy." Then she bares her red teeth at him and bites the air.

"Alrighty then," I say, clapping my hands together—again—interrupting whatever kind of mating ritual Mabel is about to begin. "Veda. Will you show them what to do next while I make lunch?" She nods silently, still stunned from the force that is Mabel.

Sam mutters something about my disgusting health food while Mabel shouts, "I'm starved, dollface!"

I look around at all of them—clay-caked hands and statues—and despite how insane they are, I smile. They're happy—even Veda. *Especially* Veda.

Thirty-eight

VEDA IS IN THE sunroom sitting in a wicker chair when I return from taking everyone else home.

She pulls her chin back, looking at me.

"Your friends are mostly insane, Birdie," she says with a laugh-infused sigh. "That Mabel?" She shakes her head, as if trying to make sense of it. "What was her profession in life?"

I feign seriousness, explaining, "She was a nun until she left in her thirties." As I say it, I realize I don't know what she did after that. I can't believe I've never thought to ask.

Veda almost smiles—like admiration. "Good for her."

Then we're quiet as we clean, because she's right. Because, *good for her.* Mabel is Mabel, but she's also who she wants to be. Unapologetically. It's a gift, when I think about it. A sunflower growing in a field of daisies.

When we're done cleaning, we sit in the two wicker chairs tucked in the corner of the studio.

She looks good today, strong. "How are you feeling?"

"I need your help with something," she says, dodging my question. She digs into her pocket and pulls out a wad of paper.

No.

A rolled paper.

No.

A slender tube with a twist on the end.

"A *joint*?" I ask, stunned.

"My doctor said it might help with some of the pain I'm feeling and with my appetite." She fumbles to roll the joint between her fingertips. "I need you to show me how to do it."

"What?! How would I know what to do?!" My voice raises in pitch. "I've never smoked anything in my life, how the hell would I know that?!"

Her eyes narrow at me as she waves the joint around. "You do all this healthy stuff, I figured you'd know!"

"Me?!" I laugh incredulously. "You're the potter! Isn't that, like, in the job requirement to do drugs?"

Her eyes widen, as if that's a ridiculous stereotype, and she huffs out an annoyed breath. "Fine. You don't know how to do drugs and I don't know how to do drugs, but I want you to show me how to smoke this." She catches my look of *you've got to be kidding me* before saying, "We can look it up on your fancy phone or something."

My eyes slide from the joint in her hand to her face.

"Isn't this bad for you?"

She barks out a laugh. "Birdie, I'm dying of cancer, sweetheart. Who gives a damn?"

It's a valid point.

I look at the joint again. Then her. Then the joint.

"You don't have to do it, just help me light it and show me what to do."

I groan. "Fine." Then add, "But you can never tell Bo I helped you get stoned."

She waves the joint around dismissively. "Bo smoked enough pot in high school to fuel the entire West Coast, but your secret is safe with me."

My eyes widen, and my chin jerks back; again, she laughs.

With another sigh, I pull out my phone, searching *how to smoke marijuana.*

"Is it even in your mouth?"

Her pinched fingers tremble around it as she mumbles something I don't understand through her joint-pursed lips.

"The video said you have to take a long inhale and it will light the end. Are you sucking?" I press the button on the lighter—again—so the flame burns at the end.

Veda makes some blowing motion around the joint before pulling it out of her mouth. "You have to start it Birdie, I can't," she says, shoving the joint toward me.

"Me?" I gasp. "Do you know how harmful that stuff is?"

"Do you?" she demands.

I hate that it's a legitimate question because I have no idea. Picking up my phone again, I type *harmful side effects of marijuana.*

If the government is monitoring me, they will have a field day with this.

"Aha!" I shout, scrolling down my phone as I read the response. "Marijuana is considered relatively safe when used appropriately," I begin, frowning when she laughs and says, "See!"

"Wait—there's more—short-term impaired memory and cognition can occur, slower reaction times, altered judgment." I raise my eyebrows at her like *See?* before continuing, "And! And!" I point my finger into the air, raising my voice with excited conviction. "Prolonged use can irritate the lungs and lead to bronchitis!"

I smile proudly, as if I've said something damning.

Veda rolls her eyes. "Birdie, it's one joint, it won't give you bronchitis." She pauses, narrows her eyes, then, "I'm dying, you can't deny a dying woman her wish."

My nostrils flare. Because of all the things to say, she seems to be forgetting the wish I *am* keeping.

I glare at her. The audacity of this woman. The damn nerve.

She opens her mouth to argue, but before she can, I snatch the joint out of her hand, pinch it between my lips, and flick the lighter on.

Flame to the end, I take a slow, deep inhale, like I watched on the video.

Instead of the controlled, easy exhale, it's a jagged, fire-filled, hack.

"There," I say, between coughs, holding the lit joint out to her. "And stop using your expiration date to bully me into things."

She laughs, struggling to pinch her fingers around the joint.

"I'll hold it." I lift it to her mouth.

She takes a short, gentle inhale, followed by a cough, waving her hand through the smoke in front of her.

"How do we know if it's working?" she asks.

"We get bronchitis," I deadpan.

"The guy on your phone said we need to take a few hits." She ignores me, looking at the joint in my hand. "Maybe we need to smoke the whole thing or something?"

I don't know enough about it, nor do I have it in me to argue with her.

"Fine."

I take another drag, which stings like poison ivy being shoved down my throat, before holding it up to her lips again.

"What will you do when Mandy comes back?" she asks through her next cough.

I nearly drop the joint from shock and my jaw goes slack at the mention of Bo's wife.

"Well?" she demands, voice stern.

"I don't know, I haven't thought about it." My vague *I don't want to talk about this* response isn't good enough because she raises her eyebrows at me, letting me know we *are* talking about it. "I guess I would let him figure it out. She is Lucy's mom. His wife. I'm nothing, not really." My mind wanders to everything we've done and how opposite of nothing it really feels. I know he loves me; I believe him every time he says it, but I don't know if he loves me because he does or because Mandy isn't here.

"And if you get cancer?" she asks while I take another drag.

My eyebrows pinch through my next smoke-filled cough. "Where is this coming from?"

"What are you going to do with Bo if you get cancer?" she repeats, this time punctuating each word.

In the skunk-scented haze, I'm quiet. Thinking. Imagining the likely scenario that I have a million times: me getting cancer. Dying. But now, there's Bo. And Lucy. And hopefully Huck.

"I'd let him be there with me until I couldn't," I say. When I pause, she nods, just slightly. "Like you, I wouldn't want him to see me at the worst—any of them. If he was with me, I'd figure out a way to go, I think. To force him to remember me differently."

I expect to see a look of understanding on her face, but instead it's something else. Annoyance, almost.

"You'd die alone?"

I scoff. "Aren't you?" When I raise my eyebrows it earns me a withering glare that pulls a laugh out of me.

She huffs—frustrated—and waves her hand in the air, as if dismissing my words. "Well don't take all day, Birdie," she snaps. "Let me try smoking this thing again and see if I get it right this time."

I shake my head in disbelief, like we weren't just having the strangest conversation, and once again lift the joint to her lips.

Veda and I, two women who have never smoked pot, smoke nearly an entire joint while sitting in her sunroom pottery studio at three o'clock on a Thursday afternoon.

I know we don't smoke an entire joint, because when Bo finds us, sitting in smoke and repeatedly asking each other if the other feels anything, he takes the remainder of the joint out of my hand, dumbfounded.

"Are you two high?" he asks, eyes wide.

"No!" I say, lying. I know I'm stoned. My teeth and fingertips tingle like they've fallen asleep while my eyelids cut through my line of sight.

He chuckles, takes one hit as his eyes stay hooked on mine, and says, "Wow," tightly out of the side of his mouth. His exhale is smooth and controlled, like a villain on TV would do, with a slight cough that he makes look cool. Like I just watched his mouth make love to that joint.

As someone who never went through a bad-girl phase or did anything remotely considered dangerous, somehow, Bo smoking pot is the most beautiful thing I've ever witnessed.

"If I ever get cancer, I'm doing this every day," I say dreamily, staring at him.

Veda takes a sharp inhale next to me, and Bo's eyes narrow as he takes another smooth hit before smashing it out in a piece of Veda's pottery.

I open my mouth, weed-lubricated enough to confess everything, but Veda intercepts with a clipped, "Don't be so dramatic, Birdie!" She pins me with an angry stoned look. "You know all it takes is arthritis to get you high."

"They gave you this for arthritis?" Bo asks incredulously with a small laugh.

My nervous eyes tunnel to her narrowed ones for a split second. Then, as if she doesn't have secret cancer, a loud cackle steals the moment. *Her* cackle. She laughs so long and loud it turns quiet, wheezy, and tear-filled.

"Get it, Birdie?" she says, giggling.

I don't get it at all, which is apparently hilarious, because whatever I start to say next comes out like a snort. I laugh so hard my stomach aches like I spent three hours doing crunches. I bend over in my chair, wheezing, tears dripping down my face.

"Bo, I—Bo, I—B—" I can't complete a sentence through my cackle-filled gasps. What I want to say to him, I have no clue, but even his name is too funny to finish.

He shakes his head, amused look on his handsome face as his hair falls to the front of his ears.

I want to touch him.

My laughing turns abruptly to silent staring. He's wearing a thick flannel today and he looks like a cozy fireplace on a chilly night that I'd like to jump inside of.

Then I wonder.

What if...

What if the reason that everything happened in my life, and all the Birdie Roses before me, was because I was meant to know Bo now? A plan that had been set into motion generations before. Maybe with the first people.

What if the universe did this in collusion with the moon and sun and sta—

"Birdie?"

I shake my head, Bo kneeling in front of me with a smirk on his lips.

"Sorry." I push my heavy eyes open wider. "I didn't hear you."

He chuckles, tucking loose strands of hair behind my ears. "How far away did you fly?"

I hum out a laugh. Because far.

He rubs a palm on the side of my face, and I lean into it. His hand is my favorite pillow.

"You okay?"

"I accidentally got high with Gran." I close my eyes, rubbing my cheek against his callused palm.

His chest rumbles with a laugh as he leans forward, whispering, "I love you," in my ear.

I don't know if it's the weed or his words, but my heart becomes a warm fountain spreading heat through my entire body.

His warmth is contagious.

I look at him, his lips, and lick my own.

He's just so perf—

"Birdie, stop licking your chops over my grandson." Veda's sharp voice interrupts my thoughts as she pats my knee before standing up.

I forgot she was here.

Bo laughs, and I narrow my eyes. "I'm not licking my chops," I say defensively.

Twisted hand in the air, "Whatever you want to call it then, stop doing it," she says sharply. "We have a *cock* to get ready for the kiln."

Then, like she wasn't just being stern, she laughs again.

So do I.

And so does Bo.

An hour later, the three of us make chocolate chip cookies in Gran's kitchen with organic flour that I snuck into her pantry.

For the rest of the day I forget—Veda has cancer.

Thirty-nine

It's HARD TO BELIEVE on such a perfect October day—clear blue sky, bright yellow leaves, crisp blowing air—I become a total basket case.

I've cleaned three times, labeled and relabeled everything, and printed out every possible document the social worker might ask for.

Financial statements.

College transcripts.

Letters of recommendation.

Medical records stapled to my updated will listing Bo as a willing and able custodian.

Bo's financial statements.

And, after convincing Bo it was absolutely necessary for my sanity, his own medical records and college transcripts.

We're on my porch—me shaking, Bo telling me to relax too many times to be helpful, and George Strait whimpering and thumping his tail against the wooden boards. A familiar car parks in the driveway.

Sharon.

The same social worker I chased down the road with obscenities in hysterics.

Bo recognizes her, waves as she gets out of the car, and whispers, "Relax," before taking my hand in his and walking toward her.

"Birdie," she says, with a curt nod when we meet in the middle of the yard. "Good to see you again."

I force a weak smile with Bo's hand squeezing mine. "Sharon."

Inside, we sit in the living room where I have all the papers ready for her.

I rub my endlessly wet palms on my jeans. "I don't know how these things usually go," I admit as she sits across from me, clipboard on her lap, pinched with papers. "But I've prepared some material for you."

I swallow, then offer her a stack of papers.

She takes it, adjusting the glasses on her face, thumbing through them. She pauses once to flick her eyes to Bo before continuing.

"Mr. Monroe," she finally says, taking her glasses off. "Will you be residing in the same house as Huck?" she asks.

He clears his throat. "I don't live here if that's what you mean," he responds, dropping his elbows to his knees as he looks at her.

"I see," she says, pausing, studying us both. "But you are listed in the will to get custody of him should Ms. Hawkins pass. Which, I'll be honest, I've never been given something quite so"—she clicks her tongue, eyes lingering on me—"*thorough.*"

Bo laughs softly beside me. "I am," he says. "Birdie here likes to be *thorough*. I told her if it would make her more comfortable to adopt him knowing he had somewhere to go should something ever happen to her, I'd be happy to do it."

"Ah," she says, nodding, looking back at her papers. "And you have a child of your own?"

He nods. "I do. A daughter, Lucy. She's seven."

"And you're not married to the mother?" she asks, looking at him over the lenses of her glasses and through the tops of her eyes.

My body stills.

Because yes, Bo is married.

"I am," he responds, jaw clenching, not looking at me.

With palpable tension, I scoot a fraction of an inch away from him, Sharon watching the movement.

"I see," she says, taking her glasses off, setting the packet of papers down.

"I have the BRCA1 genetic mutation," I blurt like a confession, not wanting her to *see* whatever it is she thinks she sees. "It's more likely I'll get cancer than most people. I didn't want to put Huck in a situation, should I get cancer and die, where he would have to go back into foster care. I know I'm at a disadvantage because I'm not married, but I trust Bo to take care of him." I swallow the panic that's crawling up my throat, and then add, "He knows how to see people."

Bo sears the side of my face with his gaze, but my eyes stay locked on Sharon.

She puts the stack of papers on the table, flipping through the ones on her clipboard instead.

Clearing her throat, glasses perched back on her nose, she says, "Everything on your application looked good, but at one question, you crossed out 'Why do you want to adopt a child?' and wrote, 'Why do you want to adopt Huck?' Care to explain? Not to be harsh, but with his...condition, we typically don't see this kind of conviction."

I smile, relieved it's an easy question at least.

"I know what it's like to want to do things a certain way and be ridiculed for it," I say easily. "My hardwiring for cancer has made me cautious. Huck doesn't like certain foods for how they make him feel, I don't like certain foods because of what they might do to my body. Huck doesn't like to ask questions a normal way, I like lists." I shrug. "To most people these might not seem like anything, but to us—they matter. Finding someone who can see that is a monumentally difficult task. I don't know how to be a mom—yet—but I know how to sit with him. Sometimes, I think that might be more important."

Bo's hand finds mine and squeezes tightly. A tethering.

Emotion drips through my body, but my shoulders stay square, voice strong, and eyes locked on Sharon.

She nods, taking her glasses off again. When she sighs, for the first time, she softens.

"Let's see the house then," she says, standing up.

As I lead the tour, I relax as I talk her through every room. The bedroom that will be Huck's I've painted green and decorated with insect posters. There's also an accurately scaled map of the house showing an emergency exit route in bright markers, laminated, hanging by the light switch.

I show her the three fire extinguishers I purchased—above and beyond the one that's required—for different locations of the house, ignoring how Bo stifles a laugh at this revelation.

In the bathroom I show her the ingredients on the toothpaste, all non-toxic and free of artificial dyes.

I show her the non-slip mats I put under my rugs, so Huck won't fall.

I explain that George Strait is hypoallergenic.

I point out the air purifier that keeps the air free of dust particles and mold spores.

In the kitchen I don't have any medication, but I have my magnesium supplements in a locked container for safety.

Again, Bo poorly hides his amusement as Sharon—eyes wide—repeatedly says, "How thorough."

Standing on the porch again, she looks at me for a long time. As desperately as I want to run inside and slam the door on her, I hold her gaze.

"I'm sorry for how I acted the first time we met," I say. "When you took him from Miss Alice."

For the first time, she smiles genuinely.

"Don't be. He's lucky to have someone like you willing to chase after him." Her tone isn't quite warm, yet it's not frigidly cold either. "Any kid would be."

Astonished, I nod as she starts walking away.

"Now what?" I call toward her retreating back.

She turns, smiles again, and says, "I'll see you in court when you get your son."

Then, as if she didn't just announce that my life was changing, she's in her car, driving away, and Bo picks me up with a joy-filled laugh.

Forty

"WHAT THE HELL IS this pose supposed to do?" Libby hisses in a whisper from her yoga mat next to mine. Balancing on one leg, arms flapping in the air, she's so wobbly it's a miracle she isn't on the floor.

I stifle a laugh as a woman from the row ahead of us levels her with a frustrated glare, which Libby ignores, but I respond to with a mouthed silent, *sorry*.

Our first time taking a yoga class together and I can say for a fact I've never laughed so much while in downward facing dog. Like her husband, she has absolutely no filter. It's incredible.

After class, out of the studio and as we walk into the restaurant next door, every step she takes toward the table she does with a sort of squat in between. "Christ, Birdie. I can't feel my ass. And who the hell needs open hips anyway?"

Sliding into the booth, I laugh. "It wasn't *that* bad."

"How many times a week do you do that?" she asks, sucking down her water as soon as the waitress hands it to her.

"Usually three," I tell her, sipping from my own glass.

"It's so hot in there!" Her eyes go so wide it makes me bark out a laugh. "I'm serious, Birdie. Was it, like, a million degrees in that room?!" She lifts her empty glass toward the waitress across the room, signaling the need for a refill.

"Ninety-three, but close," I tell her over the menu I already know by heart.

We're at Mountain Farm, the healthiest restaurant in Laurel Hills. I don't eat out often, but when I do, this is my favorite place to come because something on their menu always works for me.

"Have y'all had a chance to look over the menu?" a perky waitress with blonde curly hair and purple fingernails asks.

"Do you know what the oil base of the new salad dressing is?" I ask.

She scrunches her nose. "Sorry, I don't think so. I can ask...? I know the ranch dressing is house made..."

"Do you know who's on the grill tonight? When Buddy is here, he makes my chicken in butter instead of oil."

Her mouth twists to one side. "Umm..."

"You know what?" I hand her my menu. "I'm feeling crazy, let's not worry about it. I'll have the grilled chicken salad, no bacon, no salad dressing"—I reach into my purse and pull out my emergency bottle and wiggle it in the air with a smile—"with the vegetable soup. No croutons or crackers. Instead, I'll have one slice of sourdough, but using the real butter please, not the margarine."

I smile, but her expression is frantic as she scribbles in her note-book. When she's finished, she looks at Libby, almost nervous as she waits for her order.

Libby smiles. "Yeah, so I'll make it easy on you—I want the cheeseburger cooked medium with fries and a local beer. I just went to hot yoga, I need to replenish whatever I lost in that torture chamber disguised as fitness."

The waitress laughs under her breath, relieved, and writes the order down before leaving our table.

"Okay," Libby says folding her hands on the table. "Your order was the most exhausting experience of my life. Explain this to me."

I chuckle at her honesty.

"The genetic mutation I have puts me at higher risk for cancer. Me closely watching my diet makes me feel more in control of what little bit I can control." I shrug with a smile. "I know it seems crazy, it's just second nature to me now."

"So—and I'm not attacking you here, I'm trying to understand this—you think if you order a basket of fries instead of your salad with your purse salad dressing stash, you'll get cancer?" she asks, taking a sip of her beer after the waitress drops it off.

"Not one basket of fries, no. But it's a slippery slope of habits and anxiety for me, so it's easier to always stay on, so to speak. I plan my meals, where I eat when I eat out..." I pause, trying to think of how I can explain it in a more understandable way. "When I lay down in bed at night, I know that I still might get cancer tomorrow, but at least I'll know I tried everything within my power not to today. I know your fries will be delicious, but so will my salad. At some point, that has to just be enough for me."

Her usual bright red lips, now faded from yoga and her drink, smile. "You're kind of a badass," she says, tilting her glass slightly toward me.

I laugh too loudly, organizing my silverware on the table. "Badass, I am not."

"I'm serious!" she cries. "You have a chest covered with ink, the balls to manage your risk of cancer the way you do and were the most flexible person in that yoga class. And that last one?" She clicks her tongue. "I'm sure Bo *really* appreciates." She cocks an eyebrow as a wicked grin cuts across her face.

When my cheeks heat, she cackles.

"I knew it!" she yells, smacking her hand down on the table, causing people from nearby tables to turn and look.

And, for the first time since I was in college and not forced by work, I have dinner with a friend.

She tells me about how she opened a bar: "I thought, why the hell not, I hate working in a bank!"

How her and John met: "I told him if he let me off with a warning, I'd have a beer with him."

By the time she's finished telling stories, my cheeks hurt from laughing.

Standing by our parked vehicles, she gives me one of her hugs that I think she should be famous for. She's thin, lean, and gorgeous, but she hugs like a boa constrictor. If I were thirty years younger, I'd tell her she was my best friend and rush home to make us matching bracelets.

"I hated yoga," she says, opening her car door and dropping into the driver's seat. "But let's do this again next week."

I almost can't wait.

Forty-one

OCTOBER IS THE EQUIVALENT of living in a dream.

An alignment of the stars.

A natural phenomenon that few people get to witness, but for some reason, I do.

Bo has fully imbedded himself into my life. We go to church on Sundays. We have dinner with Lucy most nights and play board games. And after Lucy goes to sleep, *we* sneak off to *his* bed.

All I keep thinking is, Bo loves *me*. It's as though nothing has ever made sense in my life until this truth.

On Tuesdays, I go to yoga and have dinner with Libby.

On Wednesdays, I pick up Huck. Most weeks, we spend the entire time sitting at the edge of the property where Bo's building a cabin and drink dyed-red hot chocolate while we watch them work. Stacking logs and fastening them together, Huck loudly narrating the whole thing. One week, my dad even joins us so he can meet his future grandson, something that clogs my throat when I say it out loud for the first time.

"Birdie ate an earthworm when she was seven," my dad tells him as they watch Bo and the crew move a log into position. Huck finds this to be both hilarious and appalling.

The realization that Huck is going to be my legal child knocks the wind out of me daily. When I get the notice a court date has been set for mid-November, I'm equal parts happy and terrified.

In a life where I never dreamed I'd have children, in my own way, I will. Huck will be someone I introduce as my son.

Sam tells me a normal number of times how disappointed he is with my chest and Mabel greets me every Friday morning with, "Now that's the glow of a happily screwed woman."

Veda is the outlier of perfection. The fall tree that doesn't burst with color but drops its brown leaves with a single gust.

In all appearances to anyone who isn't looking, she seems fine. She smiles at the right times, narrows her eyes like a hawk without mercy, and pins her hair back into her bun as her mismatched beaded earrings hang from her ears. But there's a swift undercurrent of exhaustion too. A weakening.

All the while, Bo keeps asking how she is and I keep giving him the vague answer of, "A pain in my ass." Not a lie, but miles and miles away from the truth.

After arriving at my usual time of eight o'clock and finding her sleeping two mornings in a row, I start coming at nine, making her breakfast at nine-thirty. She guides me through working the clay, but instead of sitting next to me with her own hands doing the work, she sits in the wicker chair with the blanket over her lap. As I mold clay into the petals of flowers, Veda sits quietly, often with her eyes closed.

I help her smoke pot—learning one joint is overkill from our first experiment—and fill her freezer with soups that she tells me are, *"Better than every other healthy thing I force down her dying throat."*

With every worsening I notice, no matter how subtle, the sharp thorns of guilt dig deeper into me. Bo is watching his grandmother die without knowing.

Some days when I think about it, I know I'm doing him a favor by not letting him see what's happening right in front of his face. Some days, I know I'm robbing him of something by not telling him. But mostly, when I think about it, the emotions are so heavy I have to lie down until the feeling passes. A tangled ball of guilt that's so complicated, I don't know how I'll ever undo it.

It's at her eightieth birthday party dinner at Bo's house in the first week of November where I know I can't keep this secret any longer. I have to tell him.

We're all there, Bo even invites my dad, and Huck joins us because it falls during our usual Wednesday evening time together.

My dad and Bo stand talking about the infamous counter-top—again. At some point, I expect they'll tire of this conversation. Not yet. Huck and Lucy run up and down the stairs playing wildly, and Veda sits in a chair, smiling. It's with both resignation and admiration she watches everyone gather to celebrate her.

She coughs into a napkin. It's slight—not a hack—but when she pulls the napkin away, I see three bright red drops of blood staining the material.

"You okay?" I ask her softly.

She scoffs, annoyed look in her sharp eyes. "I'm still dying of cancer, if that's what you mean."

"And a pain in the ass," I say without heat, crossing my arms over my chest.

She laughs, putting the napkin in her pocket, then looks at Bo. "You don't stop loving him, Birdie. Or letting him love you."

I pull my chin back, taken aback. "Why would I?" I ask, following her gaze to him.

She's quiet. Then, "You'll want to."

Looking at him, I can't imagine a life where me loving Bo, Bo loving me, isn't like the sun rising or setting. Just is.

Then I remember—Veda has cancer.

My eyes drop to her. She's in a floral shirt and black pants, hair pulled back showcasing all of who she is. "We have to tell him, Veda."

Her breath comes out in a puff, but she nods, watching him laugh at something with my dad across the room as they each sip on a beer. "Just not today."

Around the table, we sing "Happy Birthday" to Veda with a cake filled with eighty candles. Pointed hat on her head, face lit up by all the light representing her years on earth. A beautiful kind of sadness punches at my ribs.

She blows them all out, with the help of the kids, and smiles. Veda has suffered loss yet has lived a good life; I see it all over her timelessly lovely face.

Bo raises his glass, beaming at her. "To Gran, for keeping the world on its toes for eighty whole years!"

While we clap, she waves her hands around and stands up.

"Now I want to say something," she says, her tone somehow both stern and joy filled. As always, the room falls obediently silent in her wake. "You don't get to be eighty without learning a few things, and I want to say them. Bo"—she pauses, looking at him—"I love you. I was devastated when we lost your dad—a parent burying a child..." Her voice trails off until she shakes her head. "But you coming to be with your grandad and I?" She smiles wide enough her face fills with lines. "Your dad would have loved your cabins," she says, voice cracking just slightly. "But he would have been most proud of the way you love without end." Her eyes bounce to Lucy, then me, then back to him.

Bo reaches his big strong hand toward her twisted weak one, giving it a squeeze.

"Lucy," she says, smiling at her, voice playful. "You are sunshine, you always remember that."

Lucy giggles and blows her a kiss.

"Greg." She looks at my dad. "You raised one hell of a woman."

My eyes go from my dad—slowly—to hers. I know what this is instantly. This isn't a birthday speech; Veda is saying goodbye.

"I told you she loves you," Bo whispers into my ear. Ignorant of what's happening.

I ignore him, eyes staying glued on Veda, as she turns to Huck and says, "Huck, Birdie is going to be your mom, and I want you to try really hard not to let her feed you only healthy food."

Everyone laughs, even Huck, except me. Because a tear rolls down my cheek that my body refuses to hold on to.

"She's going to be a good mom, Huck," she says, and Huck gives me a blocky smile, swelling my heart as it shreds.

"Birdie," she says, Bo squeezing my hand under the table. "You are a better friend than one person deserves in a lifetime."

I open my mouth—to say what, I don't know—but her twisted hands cut me off, clapping. With a grin, she declares, "Now enough of the mushy stuff, let's eat cake!" earning a loud enough cheer from the kids and Bo.

With the attention off me, I slip away from the table, secret tears dripping down my face.

My eyes catch my dad's before I go to the bathroom. He nods. He sees the same lie I do.

Bo and Veda never stop smiling as they share a big piece of cake.

I say good night to my dad as he gets in his truck and Veda and Huck settle into the minivan so I can drive them both home.

When Bo hugs and kisses me good night, guilt stings. Everywhere. I hate myself as much as I hate the cancer in Veda's body.

She's silent the entire drive.

"I wonder if Huck had fun tonight," I say, numb, setting Huck off on a too-loud monologue about all the reasons he had fun, filling the quiet of the ride until I drop him off.

When I get Veda inside her house, I flip on her lights and glare at her, unable to decide if I want to scream or cry. "Want to tell me what that little speech was about?" I demand, hands on my hips.

She narrows her eyes at me. "Can't a woman give a speech at her birthday dinner? I'm eighty for God's sake!"

I huff out a breath. "I'm not playing this game, Veda. I want to tell Bo. Tomorrow. I can't do this. The lying—it's killing me!"

She looks at me, lips pursed, until she sighs. "Fine. We'll tell him tomorrow."

"Thank you," I say, softening, wrapping a hand around her arm. "I'll be with you; I'm on your side."

She smiles, just slightly, and nods.

"I meant what I said, Birdie. You've been a great friend to me."

I look at her, trying to understand what she's not saying, but I can't.

Instead, I hug her. Tightly. "You've been a great friend to me too. We can figure everything else out tomorrow." I pull back slightly, still looking at her, and add, "Just so you know, Veda, I'll never stop loving him."

She looks at me like she wants to say more, but she doesn't. She's quiet.

"Birdie?" I stop, turning to face her from the doorway. "You're not horrible with the clay."

I chuckle, hand on the doorknob. "Careful, Veda. Eighty might be the year you become tolerable."

Her smile makes mine widen, then I lift my chin, pull the door closed behind me, and I step outside.

Driving home, the only thing I can think is—Bo's finally going to know Veda has cancer.

Forty-two

I don't sleep.

I stare at the ceiling—all night—thinking about Veda.

Bo.

Veda and Bo.

When the clock next to me says 4:12 A.M., I get out of bed and start researching holistic ways to make these next months more comfortable for her. There has to be something other than copious amounts of marijuana and painkillers.

I print out twenty pages on self-massaging techniques, stretches, and some kind of mega green smoothie recipe that all claim to help. Organized, stapled, and in a folder on my passenger seat, my body buzzes with anticipation over how Bo is going to react as I drive to Veda's.

I'm ready for the sadness, but I don't know how mad he will be at me for not telling him right away. The sour taste of guilt yo-yos from the tip of my tongue to the pit of my stomach.

I'm at the door, it's still locked, and I pull the key out of my purse—as I have been more and more. I push it open, giving my usual, "Knock! Knock!" as I walk in, kick off my shoes, and hang my jacket on the hook. It's just after nine, but the house is dark. She's still sleeping, no doubt worn out from her later than usual birthday dinner.

I walk down the hall, reaching in my bag for the papers I'd printed, seeing I forgot the file on the passenger seat of my van. I pause, debate turning around, but decide to get them after breakfast.

"Morning, Veda!" I call, walking again toward her bedroom.

I knock gently, pushing open her door. "Hey, sleepyhead. Not that you care, but I printed out so—"

I freeze, unsaid words disappearing in my mouth, stepping fully into her bedroom.

She's in bed, sleeping.

Still.

Too still.

My heart slams against my chest. My throat.

"No!" I yell, dropping my purse and hurrying to the bed, putting the back of my hand on her forehead. Then cheek. Her skin is cold. Ice.

My hands on her shoulders, I shake her gently.

"Veda," I say, struggling to get her name out of my mouth. "Veda!" I repeat louder—a shout—to be sure I've actually said it.

I shake harder—nothing.

I fumble my trembling hands across her neck to find a pulse—none.

Hand over her mouth, she's not breathing.

Adrenaline and desperation propel me onto the bed, kneeling over her, interlacing my fingers and finding the point in the middle of her chest I've been trained to with the heel of my hand. Elbows locked, I start compressions. Driving into her chest, fast and hard.

One.

Two.

Three.

Four.

Five.

Six.

"Veda!" I cry, winded as I push into her chest quickly, changing nothing, repeating the motions anyway. When droplets of water land on the backs of my hands, I realize I'm crying. "Dammit, Veda. No!" I choke out.

Nineteen.

Twenty.

Twenty-one.

Twenty-two.

I keep compressing, changing nothing. Crying more with every pump of my fists into her chest.

Her normally tidy hair is splayed across the pillow wildly as I work in frantic desperation to bring her back.

"Veda!" Her name is garbled now. Barely understandable even to my own ears.

Minutes pass.

I stop. Breathless from compressions and sobs.

She's gone.

My gaze catches on the nightstand. There's a bottle of medication, empty, and two envelopes. My name scribbled across the one on top.

A brand-new realization hits as the next sob escapes my mouth: she did this.

I know without ever opening the envelope. The bottle, her farewell speech disguised as a birthday toast, the letters. What I couldn't see last night was something I never imagined: Veda was saying goodbye because Veda was going to end it.

She knew, and the sheer weight of that combined with the fact that she's gone crushes my chest like a semitruck driving straight into me in the middle of a highway.

"Goddamn you, Veda!" I sob, clutching her cold, twisted hand in mine and falling over so I'm lying next to her on the bed.

I need to call for help, but I know nobody can help. I just want more time. So I take it. Selfishly, I lay with her for a few minutes before I do anything. Letting my sobs pour out until they subside, holding her cold hand in mine.

Finally, I fumble for my phone. The 9-1-1 operator answers, and my voice is a detached sound. "My friend is gone," I hear myself say, before giving the address and hanging up on the lady who's in the middle of telling me to please stay on the line.

I have to call Bo, and that takes me to the floor next to the bed.

By the time he answers, I've gone from calm and detached to hysterical. Crying words that make no sense into his ear until I finally choke out, "It's Gran, Bo. Come now." I hang up on him the same as I did the operator.

Alone with my tears and Veda's lifeless body as I sit on her bedroom floor and look at the nightstand.

The bottle.

The envelopes.

I sniff, wipe my nose with the sleeve of my sweater, and take a deep breath through a series of shallow ones. The envelopes—I pick them up. Panic, fear, and something worse than sadness burns my hands as I hold them. My name scribbled on one, Bo's on the other.

Veda took the pills to end it, that's crystal clear. But the envelopes, whatever they are, are too much to process now. Would the police take them? Would Bo read his before I can explain?

No.

He's going to be devastated when he gets here. I can't let him find out this way.

I don't know if it's adrenaline, sadness, guilt, or all three, but I take the letters, crawl across the floor to the doorway, and shove them in my purse. I want to read them—with Bo—not here. Not when I'm swinging between feeling everything and nothing with every minute that passes.

The quiet that follows is deep. A sad serenity. I crawl up and sit on the edge of Veda's bed again, face soaked with tears and throat swollen with sorrow. I take her hand again in mine, handling it as though it is something delicate—like a too thin piece of pottery that might not survive a firing in the kiln. The only sound is the slow beat of my own heart in my ears.

I stare at her, sleeping but not, on her own terms. "You were a good friend, Veda," I whisper, broken. "And I'll never stop loving Bo."

As if Veda timed it all, as soon as the words are out, paramedics are pounding at the door and rushing into the room, shuffling me out, gurney in tow.

"Ma'am, can you tell us what happened?" one of them asks.

It's a blur of flashing lights, uniformed men, and me repeating the longest minutes of my life.

Now Bo is here. Grabbing me. Terrified look on his face.

I say something jumbled. Wet. Useless.

He fights to get by a paramedic and sees Veda—Gran—and drops to his knees next to the bed, her hand in his, and he leans his cheek against it.

Bo's cries for the woman who was both Gran and Mom hurt my knees and bring me down to them.

As they clear the room and prepare her body, we end up on the couch, leaning into each other as she's taken away. A voice says, "Bo, looks like she made a mistake with her pain meds."

I look up. It's John. *The police are here?* I missed that happen.

"Pain meds?" Bo asks, red eyed. "For the arthritis?"

John shifts his weight, eyes moving to me, no doubt trying to piece together what he knows. What he doesn't.

"Bo..." He pauses, swallows, and clears his throat. "The paramedics found medication in the bathroom...paperwork in the kitchen—Veda had cancer." Another pause, another glance my way, then, "Everywhere."

I squeeze my eyes shut as Bo sags back into the couch beside me. When I open them, he's rubbing a hand down the side of his face that's now carved with deep lines of sadness.

"I didn't know," he says to John with a weak nod. "Thanks, man." John gives a tight smile before walking out of the room with another officer.

Bo looks at me. "You okay?"

I almost laugh at the absurdity of the question. "Peachy," I say morosely, forcing a small smile.

"Gran had cancer," he says, more to himself than me. "She had it before, I don't know if she told you." He looks at me. "The treatment was hardly anything, but she told me she wouldn't do it again if it ever came back. Here we are." He laughs softly, unamused, and presses his palms in his eyes. He sighs, tone hardening. "Dammit, Birdie, I could have helped her if she would have told me. Anything!"

He shakes his head, hands clenched in fists.

His eyes are somehow both overflowing with devastation and completely empty.

I lean into him, wrapping my arms around him.

"You don't know that, Bo," I whisper against his shoulder. "Knowing her, she had her reasons."

Forty-three

"I'll drive," I offer, locking the front door.

"I won't argue." Bo walks down the porch steps to the minivan, shoulders slumped, not looking at me.

After a couple hours with people in the house, once everyone left, once Veda was gone, we cleaned. Quietly. The only sounds were one of us randomly sniffling and our footsteps across the wood floor. By the time we finished, it looked like Veda's house. Without her.

Walking across the yard, I'm so tired I want to curl up in a ball and sleep for a month.

I'm one step off the porch when everything starts to slip through my fingers like water in a fast-moving creek.

As if in slow motion, Bo opens the passenger door to the van and picks up the file on the seat. He lifts his eyes to mine—a split second—then lowers them back to the papers in his hands.

Opening.

Thumbing.

Dropping.

Papers about managing pain in terminal cancer float in the balmy November air and flitter across the yard.

A confetti of unspoken confessions. Grenades of guilt, silently detonating.

"You knew?" he asks, stunned.

My body reacts to his words first, weakening, muscles turning to heavy bags of concrete around my bones.

It's hard to move. Hard to breathe.

"Bo," I say, trembling, forcing myself forward. I reach for his arm; he pulls away.

"Did you know?" Anger and confusion overtake his usually unbothered face, and it twists my stomach.

"Yes," I whisper hoarsely. "But she made me promise not to tell you."

"Made you promise?" he shouts, shocked, bloodshot eyes wide. "Are you fucking kidding me right now, Birdie?"

"Bo, listen!" I plead, reaching again for him only to have him pull away. "She begged me! She didn't want you to s—"

"Bullshit!" he shouts. "That's bullshit and you know it!"

The cold way he looks at me burns like acid in my eyes.

"It's not bullshit!" I spit at him, tears starting to fall again. "She was protecting you. We both were."

Again, I reach for him, again, he pulls away, now walking—storming—toward his Jeep.

"Bo, please. Just let me explain," I cry to his retreating back. "I could tell something was wrong. She was sleeping more. And I found the medication. Then the doctor's appointment—I don't know. She asked, and then my dad said—"

He spins around, eyes wide. "Your dad?!"

When I open my mouth to explain, it's only to find I cannot breathe, much less speak.

He doesn't yell. This time his voice is flat. Cold. "You told your dad Gran was dying, but not me."

"Bo, it's not just that I promised her, legally, I'm bound t—"

"Legally?" He holds his hands up in outrage, heat back in his voice. "Gran was dying and you're clinging to goddamn rules?"

"I love you. Please..." My voice comes out strangled as I vibrate with too many emotions. Emotions that pour down my face, pinch at my throat, hollow out my insides, and make my hands tremble.

"You love me?" he scoffs. "Birdie, you lied to me. *Lied*. Not about your name, about the closest woman I had in this world to a mother dying."

He looks at me, and with every second that passes, I see him hate me more. And worse than the hate that's forming, it's the unloving that's simultaneously happening.

Bo is slipping away from me as he stands right in front of my face.

Never stop loving him, Birdie.

"I'm sorry," I say.

I reach for him.

Again.

He pulls away.

Again.

"When?" he demands.

"Bo, I wanted—"

"Dammit, Birdie, when?"

I hesitate, make a futile attempt to take a deep breath, then say, "The first night I stayed with you."

Fists clenched by his sides, color races up his neck. He drops his head back and lets out an angry, *Ahhhh!* as he smacks a hand against the side of his Jeep. There's a bulging vein in his neck that looks like it's on the brink of bursting through his skin.

Because of me. Because of Veda.

I can't think of a single thing to say to help him understand. Anything I tell him is moot.

"Bo, we were going to tell you today. She told me we could," I say, doing my damnedest to stay upright and not just lie down in the middle of the driveway like I want to.

"Birdie, let me make one thing perfectly clear—as you seem to have missed it in all of your research and color-coded lists. When you love someone, you don't lie to them. You tell them everything, then deal with the fallout. *Together.*"

It is a well-delivered blow that socks me right in the gut.

The sky, as if it's a mood ring decoding my crippled heart, opens up and starts to rain. Rain that cuts like winter soaks through my clothes, freezing my bones.

Water drips down Bo's face; he doesn't bother trying to wipe it as he stares at me. His outrage palpable.

"Did you know she was going to do this?"

My stomach drops. "Are you kidding me? No, B—"

"I'm not an idiot, Birdie, this wasn't an accident. You had an abortion—this isn't that much different."

A sharp knife in my weakest point.

"It's like you want to be alone!" he shouts, twisting the knife, blade destroying me deeper.

"You have no idea how to let anyone in and be part of your life."

Another twist.

"You think because your mom died of cancer you know what's best for everyone else."

He scoffs, glaring at me both with the heat of his rage and something colder than the rain.

Twist.

He opens the door to his Jeep, rain dripping down his face. "You did this, Birdie." *No.* He can't mean that. "She would be alive right now if you would have told me."

"She was my friend, Bo. I—"

"Your friend?" His laugh is full of disdain, cutting me off before raising his voice. "She was paying you, Birdie; she wasn't your goddamn friend."

I know he's angry, I know he doesn't mean it, but still—it's another slow, cruel twist of the blade that's already buried deep in my chest.

As he slams the door of the Jeep, I drop to my knees, gravel of the driveway digging into my jeans. The start of the engine and crunch of his tires over the gravel become blurred red blobs of his taillights disappearing.

I sit, cold and wet, and fall apart with cries and screams that are drowned by the falling rain.

He doesn't mean it; he can't.

But then I remember, Bo never says things that he doesn't mean.

Bo is gone.

Because Veda had cancer, killed herself before it could, and he blames me.

And a very real part of me thinks he's right.

Forty-four

"I DIDN'T KNOW WHERE else to go."

It's all I can say when Libby opens her front door and finds me standing there, drenched and broken, before pulling me into a tight hug.

When I finally forced myself into the minivan—wet, cold, and devastated—I thought of going to my dad. But his calm and easy, "It will all work out, Little Bird," isn't what I need. I need all the thread to unravel before I try to put it back on the spool. I need someone to let me be hysterical.

Libby gives me dry clothes to change into and a fake beer, shrugging. A silent, *I don't have a damn clue how to help you.*

Somehow, I laugh through my tears as I take it, and take a sip. Wishing it was real alcohol. Or marijuana. The thought sends a fresh batch of tears pouring out of my eyes.

Because I smoked marijuana with Veda.

Veda is dead.

Bo blames me.

I mentally recite the simple sentences over and over like a children's book that's filled with all the wrong words. A story no kid wants to read.

Finally, I'm dry enough to sit on her furniture, calm enough to tell her everything, and I do.

The sleeping. The medicine. The doctor's appointment. The blood in the napkin.

When I finish, I drop my head back on the cushion, stare at the ceiling, and blow out a shaky breath.

"Okay, first of all, this is not your fault," she says with genuine assurance. "Veda put you in an impossible position."

Fresh tears burn the back of my eyes and I blink to keep them at bay.

"And I know it doesn't seem like it, but Bo knows that." I can't tell if she believes what she says or not. Either way, I nod weakly.

She leans into me on the couch, head on my shoulder, and takes my hand in hers. "He'll come around; he just needs time."

"He was so mad, Libby. I've never seen him like that. The things he said..." Echoes of everything he yelled and a ghost of his rain-soaked face flash before me as my voice trails off.

We sit in silence, neither awkward nor comfortable. It's just quiet other than the sound of the rain on the roof, the windows. Finally, she says, "I'm sorry about Veda."

A tear runs down my face. "Me too."

Sitting on the couch, steeping in my misery, it feels like some kind of cosmic joke. I spent my whole life planning and working to never be the cause of this kind of heartache. The life-changing devastation of loss. Yet here it is. Happening. Because of me, even though it wasn't my cancer.

When John comes home, same police uniform on from when I saw him this morning, he finds me dumped like roadkill on his couch.

He smiles the same way Libby did when she offered me the fake beer. Like I'm something fragile they don't know how to handle and are terrified of breaking.

"You look like shit," he says.

"That's the look I was going for," I say flatly.

He chuckles.

"You talk to Bo?" I hear myself ask.

He nods, eyes on his shoes, telling me everything I need to know.

Trying to stop more tears from welling, I jam my thumbs into my eyes until I see stars. It doesn't work. I start to cry anyway.

"What would George Strait sing in a situation like this?" John asks, hooking his thumbs into the belt where a gun is holstered.

I make a noise that can neither be deciphered as a laugh or cry, wipe my eyes, and feel slightly macabre as I say, "'Easy Come, Easy Go.'"

He rumbles with a laugh.

Libby walks over to him, pecks him on the cheek. "Take it easy on her, John." She pats his chest with her palm. "I'll start dinner." She turns to me. "Birdie, you staying?"

I shake my head. "I should go." I force myself to both stand and smile. "Thank you for hosting my meltdown." I laugh a weak, watery sound.

She walks over, squeezes me in a genuine Libby hug. "Anytime, Pam Beesly."

When she pulls back, there's a slight smile ghosting her lips. "Anything you need, I mean that. We were Bo's first, but we're yours now too."

She means it. It would make me cry again if I wasn't so tired.

On my way to the door, wet clothes in a trash bag, John grabs me for a big hug. "You had months to accept it was coming, he's only had hours. Give him time." I nod against his chest. Then, "He's a stubborn asshole anyway."

He doesn't mean it, but I laugh anyway.

I cancel dinner with my dad; he shows up on my steps with food anyway.

While Veda is dead and Bo blames me, my dad cooks steaks in my kitchen and listens to me sob out the whole awful story. Again.

"Losing Bo hurts more than Veda dying, does that make me horrible?" I ask my dad as we do the dishes.

He makes a deep, *hmm* sound, then pauses the way he does. "Veda lived a good life. She told us that last night," he starts.

Last night.

Right. Because twenty-four hours ago, we were laughing in Bo's house eating cake, and Veda was still alive, and Bo still loved me.

"She had a life filled with love. Loss? Sure, but it's clear the love was stronger. Hers is a complete story. She did what she came here to do. Lived fully, died on her own terms after a lot of years." He puts a plate in the dishwasher. "But Bo?" He gives me a sideways glance. "It's a story that's ended in the middle. That never leaves anyone happy."

I swallow once. Twice. Three times. However many times I have to until I'm able to talk without breaking down.

"I hate that Bo hates me, but I hate myself more for knowing I wouldn't have done anything differently." The confession sounds like it comes out of someone else's mouth. Like I'm outside of my body, watching my own life from the sky.

"I know, Little Bird," he says. "I know."

Sitting on my couch long after my dad leaves, I stare at my purse on the coffee table. The envelopes—long forgotten in the pain of the day—poke out of the top.

I pull them out.

Bo scribbled on one, Birdie the other. Veda's shaky, slanted writing as familiar as my own.

My hands trembling, heart pounding, I open the envelope left for me.

Dear Birdie,

If you're reading this, I have no doubt you're feeling everything there is to feel toward me. Maybe you even hate me. Knowing how you feel about Bo, I'm most certain you must hate me at least a little right now. For that, I'm forever sorry. Just like I couldn't let Bo see me suffer, I couldn't let Bo find me gone. It had to be you. Part of me believes you already understand it.

You asked me once if the reason I hired you was because of the cancer—I told you that was only part of it. It was also because of Bo. The way he looked at you that first day on my porch was the way his grandfather looked at me in our college ceramics class. A look that was a poem without a name—so full of reverie.

I meant it when I said you were a good friend to me, Birdie. You made my last months special. Sacred. Gave me a reason to keep fighting, even on the days I didn't want to. I put my hands in the clay and laughed loudly because you kept showing up. I didn't know it, but I needed you in my life. Maybe even your food.

So does Bo.

If you can forgive me, he will most certainly forgive you.

Love him, Birdie. Let him love you.

Love always,

Veda

PS: I left you the cabin. Never stop making flowers out of clay—you have a gift I never told you about because I didn't want it to go to your head. Oh, and I put all the marijuana in the blue vase in the living room. I find you less annoying after you smoke some.

I read it so many times I memorize it, then I break down all over again.

Forty-five

MABEL FROWNS AS I drop onto her plastic-covered couch.

"You and the lumberjack get in some kind of fight?" she asks, scrunching her nose at me. Today she's wearing tiger-striped leggings and a shirt so pink it attacks my retinas when I look at it.

After Veda's letter, I cried until I fell asleep on the couch. When I woke up in the middle of the night, I dragged myself into bed but never slept again.

The short glance I gave myself in the mirror before leaving this morning was long enough for me to know I look like I've survived a trip through a wood chipper.

My eyes are swollen and bloodshot, hair in a ragged braid, and I'm still wearing Libby's clothes, which include sweatpants.

This time, when I tell the story of what's happened, I don't cry. Voice sluggish, I tell how I knew Veda was dying and did nothing to stop it.

When I'm done, she's quiet, but there's a calculating look on her face.

"Well, it was bound to happen," she says, matter-of-factly, pushing on the fluffy bottom of her wine-colored hair with her palm like she's some kind of beauty pageant contestant.

I scoff. "What does that even mean?"

"Birdie!" she says, hands up in the air with an exasperated huff. "Years of us reading these books and you didn't see this coming?"

"Sorry, no," I say dryly. "I've been too focused on the *fellatio* you shove down my throat."

She *tsks* me before continuing. "In all our stories there's the big blowout—right after all the good stuff—and *boom!*" Her voice raises with a loud clap of her hands, startling me. "A shitstorm! Hearts devastated!" She's almost proud.

My eyes narrow at her. My life is falling apart and she's breaking down the technicalities of storytelling. I'm too weak to argue.

"There's a lesson to be learned in all this," she says, pulling out a stupid notebook from her waistband, flipping through the pages.

"Yeah, life sucks," I mutter.

She scoffs, clicking her pen. "Of course, that's not the lesson! Haven't you been paying attention?!" She's stunned. Perplexed. Absolutely baffled that, after years of reading smut, all I noticed was the smut.

"Take Aaron," she presses, bringing up the last character I want to be talking about right now. "They have a few passionate weeks in his cabin—away from the noise of the modern world while she tries to sort out her father's will—but then Olivia is forced to choose between this life of solitude in the woods or going back to her career in the city. She's torn, not knowing what to do, and he reads her turmoil as him not being good enough for her compared to the opportunities of the modern world. They both fight internal wars, leading to a lack of communication, and a breakup that *we* know is stupid, but they can't see."

This time, I scoff. "Mabel, I didn't tell him his grandmother was dying, this isn't a silly misunderstanding about city lights versus going to the bathroom in an outhouse for the rest of my life."

"Semantics!" she cries, dismissing my argument.

I should have called in sick.

"Birdie, what have you learned?"

I sigh, looking at her ridiculous hair, bright lips, and gaudy jewelry. She's not going to show me mercy; I see that in all her maniacal brightness.

"I love Bo," I say with a sigh.

"What else? Love isn't enough, or we wouldn't be in this situation."

"He doesn't love me."

She *tsks* that away with her hand and gives me a look that says, *Try again.*

"I don't know," I snap, raising my voice, feeling my blood flow faster in my veins. "I learned that no matter how hard I try, people die and hearts break. I learned that life with someone is better than life with no one, yet somehow, hurts worse. I learned one more person in my life can make my world so much bigger but ultimately leave me feeling crushed and small. I learned that, after a lifetime of wishing I had a different life, it turns out a different life is just the same damn bullshit."

Then I'm quiet, loud ringing in my ears, and she scowls—annoyed with my response—before standing up.

"What are you doing now?" I ask, not moving from my spot on the plastic couch.

"Birdie, you've got a long way to go as a main character. I'm having a gin and tonic."

If I wasn't half dead, I would have told her it was only nine in the morning.

When she's back with a drink in hand, lipstick already on the rim, she sits next to me on the couch.

"What did you do after you left the convent?" I ask her, in an attempt to change the subject. "And I'm not talking about the men, I mean professionally. You must have worked."

A smile splits her face, revealing a faint yet familiar smudge of red on her front tooth. "I thought you'd never ask, Birdie dear," she says with a theatrical pause, taking a sip of her breakfast cocktail before adding, "I was a writer, of course."

My chin pulls back, eyes wide. "A writer?!" I look around her living room, bookshelves lining two walls. "What did you write?"

She's quiet, but not hesitating. From the knowing look on her face, Mabel is building the drama.

"Romance, of course." Another smile, another sip.

"Romance," I whisper, a missing piece of a puzzle slipping into place as I look around at the shelves again. It's as if I'm seeing her, and her home, for the first time. The constant questions, writing in her notebook, analysis of everything around her...Mabel is a writer.

My head snaps back toward her. "Have we read anything you've written?"

Another smile, another sip, then an easy nod. "Every single one, dollface."

I let this sink in. Mabel had Paul for however brief a time then spent her life writing love stories. Maybe even *their* love story. "So what happens now? After the *shitstorm*, I mean. How would you write this?"

"Ah!" she says, setting her drink down. "Well, let's see now. We, the readers, know that you think you've learned *a* lesson—not that we agree with you of course." She pauses, raising her eyebrows before continuing. "But we don't know about Bo. This is a single point of view story. So, unfortunately, we wait. We have to see—will you both be able to learn your own lessons from this heaping pile of hot garbage and want to work it out, or are you destined to live separate lives, only knowing each other in this tiny blip of time?"

I groan. She laughs.

"Then what happens?" I ask.

"Then there's a big gesture, letting you know that the lessons have been learned."

"And if we don't?"

She *tsks* me, scrunching her nose in disgust as she lifts her glass. "Then it's not a romance story, it's women's fiction, and nobody wants to read that horseshit."

I laugh. I have no idea what women's fiction is, but based on her definition, I don't want that. But also...

"Maybe I'm not destined for a romance story, Mabel. Are there stories with happy endings without love?" I ask.

She balks. "For God's sake, Birdie! I hope you never write a book with that kind of nonsense floating around your brain."

When she shakes her head in disgust, I chuckle.

By the end of the day, even though nothing has changed and I'm still in a million pieces, somehow, I leave the slightest bit better.

Forty-six

"No Bo tonight, Birdie?" Monica asks as I set my groceries on the conveyor belt of her register Friday night.

I keep my eyes down. "Not tonight."

When the belt stops, I don't look away from my cart. Part of me doesn't even care if I buy the food anyway.

Without warning, two arms wrap around me and squeeze me in a hug, making me grunt. Monica, with her dreadlocks, neon hair band, and Good Grocers name tag, pulls me into her so tightly I wonder if I'll ever be able to breathe again.

Under any other circumstances, I'd peel her off me, but tonight, my head in her hair that smells like coconuts, I start to cry.

"Wanna talk about it?" she asks, handing me a tissue from her pocket when we finally pull apart.

I shrug, wiping my nose, as she circles back around her register. "I fell in love with someone when I knew I shouldn't and kept a secret I knew would crush him."

"Hmm. That sounds tough, but you'll figure it out," she says with too much displaced optimism, once again dragging groceries by the scanner, causing a beep noise with each item. "I saw the way you two were together. Y'all have the good stuff."

She grins, and I force a smile.

If it were only that easy.

On Sunday, I go to church. Alone.

I consider calling Bo, texting him, something. But I don't. I can't. After everything that happened, everything he's said and I've done, there's just no point.

I pick one of the trails we'd been to—his hat on my head—and spend the entire walk crying tears that the November wind scrapes off my skin with gusts that cut like ice. The beautiful fall leaves are long gone; the bare trees that remain are as alone as I am.

With all the years I've spent alone in my life, I never would have imagined this change would be such a shock to my system. Yet, alone before Bo and alone after him are two very different places to exist. One manageable, the other a black hole.

I sit at my kitchen table and stare at the thick envelope with his name scribbled across it, the paper and ink taunting me.

My phone vibrates with a text from Libby. *Hey girl, I'm sending over the service schedule for Veda. Let me know if you need anything. Yoga next week? xo*

A picture of a paper with Veda's face next to times, dates, and locations comes through.

Veda's services. Because she died. And Bo blames me.

Setting my phone down, I don't respond. There's nothing to say.

Eyes back on the envelope, my phone vibrates again. This time, it's Bo's name I see. *Can we talk?*

The tightness in my throat those three words cause sends my hand to my own neck.

One breath. Two.

Instead of immediately responding, I reach for a notebook from a basket and take out a pen. I need a plan. A strategy. Some way to manage this situation that isn't driven by emotions and grief and the emptiness that fills me.

On one side I write, *reasons to talk to him*, on the other, *reasons not to*.

I can't be with him, I know that. This exemplifies everything I've spent my whole life believing: love has no place in my life. Some people might call it depressing, Mabel would call it *women's fiction horseshit*, either way, this is too messy. Whether I get cancer or not, I'm not equipped to be with someone else.

Under reasons to talk, I write: *closure, maybe friendship?, Huck might need him in the future, I have a letter for him from Veda,* ~~*I love him.*~~ I scratch the last one off. I do love him, but that can't be a reason. If I see him, it can't be because I love him.

Under reasons not to talk, I write: *he blames me for Veda dying, he said terrible things, I love him.* Somehow, keeping the fact I love him under reasons not to talk to him makes more sense.

Eyes pinging between the two lists, weighing my options, I pick up my phone. *Okay.*

His response is immediate. *Okay. Lots of family coming in tonight. Tomorrow before the visitation? Libby told me she sent you the times.*

A million things I want to say tingle at my fingertips, but all I write is *See you then.*

I park in front of Bo's house and grab Veda's letter for Bo from my purse. Not surprising, there are nearly a dozen vehicles parked in his yard and driveway.

Veda asked me to never stop loving him, and I won't. Last night, lying in bed, I decided that even though Mabel is hell-bent on love meaning love story, I know love can look different. Maybe I loved him like a lover before, but now our love will be something else. Friendship. Like we said it was supposed to be from the beginning.

Or like a brother.

I drop my head side to side, stretching my neck at the thought. I don't need to have siblings to know that after the things I've done with Bo, I'll *never* be able to look at him like a sibling.

Either way, this is my chance to explain everything. To clear the air and give us a clean slate.

Shoving my fear and anxiety down as deep as I can, I tighten the belt on my coat as I walk. Across his yard, up the steps, to knock on the door that, only days ago, I would have just pushed open.

When Libby's the one who opens the door, I'm flooded with relief. A friendly face. *Thank God.*

"Libby! Hi!" I say with an exhale.

She smiles but it seems forced. Nervous.

My eyes slightly narrow, but a high pitched, "Birdie!" interrupts my thoughts. Lucy pushes by Libby through the cracked door and wraps her arms around me. I kneel next to her and give her a hug, inhaling her sweet scent of strawberries.

"Lucy, I think you've grown since I saw you last week," I tell her.

She laughs, then her little face turns serious, blue eyes wide. "Gran died."

My stomach drops. "I know," I whisper, running my fingers through her hair. "I'm so sorry. She was the best Gran."

She smiles and hugs me again, whispering, "Daddy's sad." The words slice into my chest like a saw blade.

"Birdie, listen..." Libby says, her tense, hushed tone pulling me from the hug. "You should know th—"

Whatever she's going to say next is hijacked by the door opening wider. There, a woman stands who looks like a slightly younger Libby. Beautiful in a long black dress with long dark hair and bright blue eyes, she reaches for Lucy.

"Who's this, sweetheart?" she asks, eyes locked with mine.

I don't have to ask; without introduction, I know it's her. In the simple stare, another line gets added to the others that perpetually play through my mind.

Veda died.

Bo blames me.

Mandy is here.

"This is Birdie," Lucy says, stepping back next to Mandy—her mother that I now see she looks a lot like.

She nods, her eyes moving along me in a way that's assessing. "I see."

I can't say anything. My throat is so pinched, I know any attempt at a word will come out a choke.

Libby can't comfort me. I can't fall apart in front of Lucy—unfortunately a concept I now understand. I need to go.

Pulling the envelope from my pocket, my hand is shaking, moving so slowly toward Libby it's like the actual air is made of clay, and it takes all my effort.

"I—I—"

Libby's gaze clashes with mine; my own misery reflecting back to me.

"Lucy?" The familiar voice that calls from inside cripples me. *Bo.* There's not enough time for me to run. He's already there, in the doorway, next to his *wife*, child, and sister-in-law.

When our eyes meet, it's a sort of self-inflicted torture. As though the thickness of the air has been shoved down my throat.

My mouth opens and closes silently.

The letter slips from my fingers and drops to the porch with a soft *thud.*

I turn around as the first tear falls.

In a daze, I hurry across the yard.

"Birdie!" It's Bo's voice that calls my name, but I don't stop. *He invited me here to see his wife?*

Somehow, I'm in the minivan, turning the key, shifting the gear. Reverse to drive.

Forcing one breath, then two.

When I look in the rearview mirror, he's standing in the middle of his driveway, hands by his sides, shrinking as I drive away.

A mile down the road, I pull over, fall out of the door onto my hands and knees, and vomit.

I don't go to the visitation. After seeing Bo—Mandy—it felt like too much.

I swirl my hand around the warm water of the bathtub. Veda's funeral is in two hours, and as much as I can't fathom seeing them all again, I have to go. For Veda.

Just like I refused to let Bo stop me from taking the job with her in the first place, I refuse to let him stop me from saying goodbye.

I slide under the water, hoping for the dozenth time it will make me feel better. For the dozenth time, it doesn't.

Bo called me four times last night. Four times, I didn't answer. His text of *please call me, it's not what you think,* almost made me laugh from the irony. The same words he said the day I found out about his wife in Veda's living room. If it wasn't happening to me, I'd laugh and wonder if Veda planned this too...*just to see my reaction.*

How I'm supposed to love him in any capacity after that seems both improbable and impossible.

I can accept he's mad at me. I can even accept he blames me for how Veda ended her life. But to just let me walk up to *that?*

It's a kind of punishment I didn't think him capable of.

It takes every ounce of energy to get dressed. Black fitted pants, black turtleneck, black peacoat. I put makeup on, trying to make the bags under my eyes less obvious, but everything feels like a lie.

At the church, Bo is waiting at the top of the steps outside the door, greeting everyone who walks in. I watch him through my windshield. He's in a suit, handsome with his hair pushed back, beard trimmed short. People shake his hand, no doubt giving canned condolences, and he smiles kindly at them.

A smile he's given me so many times but never will again.

I imagine what I'd say to him if this were a different life. I'd be standing next to him, holding his hand, squeezing it every time someone said, "She was a great woman, Bo." A message would travel between our connected palms that would be as much about our love for each other as the woman we were saying goodbye to.

But that life is a foolish fantasy stolen by a secret I kept and a wife he has.

When the last people enter, I get out of my van and blow a steadying breath. As if he senses me, his gaze lifts across the parking lot and zeroes in on me. The door opens next to him. Mandy appears, tapping him on the shoulder, saying something, and gesturing inside.

He nods toward her, looks back to me—unmoving across the parking lot—before going inside.

I let out the breath I've been holding, ignore how the scene just sent a million splinters into my gut, and walk to the church.

The service inside and then by the grave happen around me. The words float in one ear, out the other, with only a few catching.

The people tell stories of versions of Veda I didn't know. They aren't the woman who yelled at me to wedge clay or forced me to hold a joint to her lips. They aren't the woman who blew out a candle because I was scared of the toxins or watched me fall hopelessly in love with her grandson. They are, however, Veda just the same. The pieces I do catch, make me smile. Because yes, Veda was who she was with me, but she was also someone else before that too.

In the church, Bo sits in the front row, Mandy on one side, Lucy on the other.

At the grave, Bo stands in the front row, Mandy on one side, Lucy on the other.

In both places, I stay in the back. Alone.

In both places, as if we can't not, our eyes find each other's more than once.

Every time, I look away first, feeling my own pain metastasize within me.

Because: Veda is dead, Bo blames me.

And when I see his wife standing next to him, I remember the next line—Mandy came back.

"Birdie?"

I'm unlocking the door of my minivan when I hear a woman say my name. I pause, turning to look. *Mandy.*

Instinctively, my eyes dart around for any sign of Bo, but she's alone. Beautiful in black with long, silky dark hair. I never asked what kind of music she sings, but she looks like a country music singer as she stands in front of me.

I force a tight smile. "Hi," I say, which sounds lame on my lips.

"You know who I am," she says, hands shoved in her black coat pockets.

I nod. "I do."

"And you slept with my husband anyway." She raises her eyebrows.

Really? This is what she wants to do?

"And you left him anyway," I say, deciding not to shy away from whatever *this* is.

Her laugh is almost an unsaid touché.

"Do you love him?" she asks.

"Do you?" I hurl back at her.

"Do you love Lucy?"

The question makes me stand taller. "Do you?"

Her eyes narrow, slightly, as she stares at me before she drops her head back. Perfect chin pointing up as she blows out a breath that sends a grey puff into the cold air.

When her gaze meets mine again, she surprises me by asking, "Do you ever feel like you're trapped in your life?"

I don't know what I expected the woman who left Bo and Lucy and never looked back to be like, but the question is one I am not prepared for. I have no idea how much she knows about me, but yes, I absolutely feel like I'm trapped in my life.

"Daily." I've shocked her because her eyes widen instantly. "But never with Bo."

Lips pressed together, her tongue moves around the inside of her mouth, as though she's batting her unsaid words between her cheeks.

When the heavy silence hangs between us too long, I break it. "Would you have done anything differently?"

"Is it ever that simple?" she volleys back.

This time, it's me who almost-laughs. Because no, it's never that simple.

I imagined once that if I ever met Mandy, my disdain for her would be black and white. But standing here with her between all the words we are and aren't saying, I realize it isn't. I can't imagine leaving everyone the way she had, yet I understand why Veda did it. Why I've never let myself get close to anyone.

A thought smashes into me, sticking. Mandy and I aren't that different.

Veda asked me once what I would do when she came back—she knew she would. For this. I told her I'd let him decide. I meant that. But when I imagined the scenario, she was still here guiding me, and Bo and I still loved each other easily.

As sure as Mandy is standing in front of my face, Bo and I are over.

Yet when I open my mouth to talk, "I love him," is what I hear myself say. Ache building in my chest like single bricks with every word. "I love him the way wildflowers love the warmth of the summer sun and the way Veda loved having her hands in the clay. I love him with Lucy and how he has a casual intensity on his face when he's stacking logs on top of one another. I love that he hikes on Sundays and spends Saturdays with your sister laughing in her kitchen." At the mention of Libby she winces, but I don't stop. "I love the way he sees other people and knows how to hold me upright when the world feels too heavy on my shoulders. I love how he loves. How he laughs. How his goodness is a deep well that gives and gives and gives."

Her eyes squint, like she's trying to see me, and her lips tug to one side, almost a smirk. Something between amusement and admiration flitters across her face. As if the whole reason she walked over here was to hear me say that.

"And I know you think those same things, at least some of them, or you wouldn't have come back." The final words that come out of my mouth burn my tongue as I say them. "I love him but we're over. I won't interfere."

She nods—slightly.

Then we're looking at each other—staring. The woman who gets to love him at the woman who can't anymore.

"Mandy," a voice calls, making us both turn at once.

It's Libby, beautiful in black like her sister. Her red lips force into a tight smile toward me when our eyes meet. A silent, *Everything okay?* telegraphs from her to me. I smile and give her a nod, my, *Yes*.

"I'll be right there," Mandy calls, making cold clouds float around her face from her breath. Then she turns back to me. "I'm glad I met you."

"Me too." Oddly, I mean it.

Then she's gone, walking toward Libby, where they meet John—looking shockingly tame in his suit when he lifts his chin toward me with a small smile—and walk across the parking lot together. I wish I was walking with them.

When Bo walks across the parking lot, my fingers lift in a slight wave as our eyes meet. He stops, just briefly, and we look at each other through the people dressed in black that walk all around us like a colony of ants.

Looking at him look at me sends a deluge of thoughts rushing through me. I love him; I hate him. I want to hug him; I want to slap him.

When someone calls his name, he turns, shakes a hand, and I take the opportunity to slip into my minivan. My eyes meet his through the windshield as I'm driving away.

The next tears that fall on my drive home aren't for Veda—every single one is for Bo.

Forty-seven

"Huck wonders where we are going today," Huck shouts from the back seat.

"I was thinking we could go to the library," I tell him. "They have an insect exhibit."

"Huck wonders if we could go see Bo at the cabin instead."

I blow out a long breath.

"You know, we can drive by, but he's really busy, so I don't think we can stop."

Reluctantly, I drive to the site I know all too well.

The cabin is nearly finished now; today they are installing windows. I roll the back window down for Huck to watch a few minutes while my gaze is steadfast out the windshield—anywhere but the cabin.

"There's Bo!" Huck shouts.

I don't turn to look.

"Awesome. You should wave to him because we have to go now if we want to get to the library before it closes."

"He's walking over here now. Maybe we can stay." I hate how excited he sounds.

I hate my response even more.

Rolling up his window with the button on my door, I start to drive away. "Maybe next time."

After the library, dropping off Huck, and dinner, I will myself to look at my phone and all the messages I've been ignoring.

From Libby, *You know, if I was the kind of girl that read into things, I'd think you're ignoring me. What's up, Pam Beesly? Call me. I miss watching you eat healthy food.*

I read it, smiling so I don't cry. I've put her in a terrible position that I had no right to. Her sister married Bo; she can never be my friend. Not really. Not now. Not with Mandy here. The nicest thing I can do to her is shut her out so she doesn't have to feel guilty for having to do the same to me.

Then, Bo.

Is your plan to ignore me forever?

Birdie, we need to talk about this.

Is this going to require a list?

I roll my eyes. Because what does he think? I'm just going to go over there and hang out with him and his *wife*? He can't be that delusional.

Part of me wants to tell him to piss off, and part of me wants to beg him to come over and fix it. The two extremes tell me the best response is none.

The week after Veda's funeral, I force myself to go to her cabin on a morning like I would be if she was still alive. When I walk inside, it's unchanged. Same earthy, wet smell. Same colorful blankets and gauzy curtains. Like any minute she's going to walk out of her room, hair pinned back in a tight bun, and order me to go wedge some clay.

It's empty. Quiet. Her echo.

When I get to the sunroom, I feel her. Hear her.

My eyes land on two bowls on a shelf—the last ones she made months ago. They have been sitting wrapped tightly in plastic bags, still too wet for the kiln. I pick one up and I'm instantly flooded with emotion. Vibrating with it.

I miss her and I'm mad at her, both with a rawness I've never known.

Using my arm like a bat, I swing it at one of the bowls—still in the bag—and send it off the shelf to the ground with a cry. Without thinking, I do the same thing to the other one. This time, with a louder *Ahhh!* and tears that fill my eyes.

When all that's left is silence, I realize instantly what I've done—destroyed her final pieces like a fool—and pick them up.

I open the bags; each pot sits in five to a dozen jagged pieces. My heart sinks as fresh tears well.

I've ruined yet another precious thing.

Then I think of my dad. Of his busted cookie slab and the Japanese method of *kintsugi*. I think of broken things becoming beautiful again. The cracks becoming the coveted.

With a long exhale, I vow to put them back together, somehow, though I have no idea how it's possible.

Pulling a big plastic tub out from under the table called a damp box that helps keep unfinished pieces wet or rehydrate dry pieces, I add water and put all the broken pieces inside, snapping the lid on and praying for a miracle.

I debate going home, but I hate the idea more than I hate being here without her, so I open a fresh bag of clay. I cut a hunk off with a piece of wire, and wedge it, Veda's commanding instructions whispering in my ear.

At the table, I roll out a slab, long and flat, before wrapping it into an asymmetrical cylindrical vase. The seam is obvious, a scar, but I leave it, lining it with flowers.

I work for five hours, only stopping to cry or use the bathroom, before it's finished.

It's beautiful—different—even in wet clay. I know it's the best thing I've made.

I put a plastic bag over it so it doesn't dry out, clean up my space with a wet sponge, and lock the front door. When I leave, it's as if I was never there at all.

Forty-eight

THE BROKEN PIECES OF the bowls I smashed are rehydrated enough to be pliable again, and I carefully spread them across the worktable the next day.

I don't have gold like they used in traditional *kintsugi*, and the epoxy my dad uses with his slabs of wood won't work, but I do have slip, *clay glue* as Veda always called it.

Scooping some of it into a bowl, I mix in some underglaze—a special slip-based glaze that can be used before the piece has been fired. I pick a shade of pink, mixing enough into the slip that it turns from muddy grey to a lush rose that reminds me of the flower bushes that bloomed in Veda's yard in the summer.

With a radio playing all my favorite country songs in the background, I start to piece the bowls back together like a puzzle, pink slip bulging out of the cracks. I fall into a rhythm, singing along with the lyrics I know by heart, trying to make the broken beautiful. It doesn't make sense, but hands in the clay, I'm compelled to create the sadness right out of me.

Luke Combs starts singing "Fast Car," and I turn the music up—loud enough to drown out my thoughts—and sing along loudly, losing myself in the lyrics and how I piece the pot together.

One piece turns to two, turns to—

"Birdie?"

My own name makes me jump, jerking to face the doorway.

Wearing blue jeans, a canvas Carhartt jacket, and a green beanie pulled over his ears with his hair curling out from the bottom, Bo walks into the sunroom.

"Jesus!" I gasp, bringing a clay-covered hand to my pounding heart, breathless. Because he's just scared the hell out of me, because he's here, and because he looks like *that*.

"I'm sorry, I didn't know..." I turn down the music, suddenly self-conscious in clay-covered black leggings, oversized blue sweater that's sliding off one shoulder, and hair in a messy bun on the top of my head.

He walks across the room, stopping before he's all the way to me.

He looks at the broken pieces on the table. "You've been busy," he says, with the slightest hint of amusement as a toothpick bobbles on his lips.

I tug my sweater onto my shoulder. "Yeah, just playing." My sweater slips again as I talk. "What are you doing here?"

He shrugs. "I've been checking on the place after work, today we stopped early."

"Ah," I say. "Well, I can leave. I was just going to finish but..."

No.

I'm not leaving.

My chin lifts.

"I mean, Veda told me in her note to keep coming here. I guess she wants me to have it." I pause, wait for him to argue. When he doesn't, I add, "I'm going to finish what I'm working on."

His lips twitch, and I can't tell if he's hiding a smile or something else, but he doesn't leave either. Instead, he sits in the wicker chair, elbows on his knees, watching me as I work.

Finally, after the silence that's as suffocating as the first day I walked in this house, I speak.

"I watched my mom die—wither away—Gran didn't want that for you." I don't look at him as I stick a jagged piece of the bowl into a line of slip. "And she also knew if she told you what was happening, you'd beg her to get treatment she didn't want. So—and I know you don't understand my rule following personality—but the fact she asked me, specifically saying, 'don't tell Bo,' and because I understood deeply how she felt, I did as she asked. Even if I wasn't legally obligated to keep her secret, I would have."

I've put one bowl completely back together. It's mangled, yet somehow whole, with lines of slip covering it, cracks visible. On display, even.

I move on to the pieces of the next one, this time mixing black underglaze into the slip. All the while, Bo stays quiet, which is exactly what I need him to do, so I keep going.

"When I remember my mom, I remember her dancing in the kitchen *and* slipping away to nothingness. I'd give anything to only have one of those. I don't know if I did the right thing, but that's why I did it. Veda asked me, and I said yes. Because she loved you."

When I've said it, I'm relieved. I stick another piece to the bowl without turning to look at him.

"You don't have to forgive me, I've come to terms with that, but I want you to know that I loved her, I cared what happened. I did it for her *and* you. But mostly her."

Without looking, I hear him stand, his footsteps moving across the room, and it's his familiar Bo Mountain Breeze when he's standing next to me.

"What are you working on?" he asks, close enough to touch me but not.

I blow out an amused exhale as I look at the pieces. "I broke something, and I'm trying to fix it."

I lift my eyes to his and his lips pull to a small smirk, toothpick dancing. "Here," I tell him. "Hold these two pieces together so I can add another one on."

He pinches the pieces firmly in place as I add slip to another one and slide them together.

"I don't remember Gran doing this." His skeptical tone makes me chuckle.

"She didn't." I grin. "I got the idea from my dad with his cookie slab table. He drew inspiration from a Japanese technique called *kintsugi*. Figured I'd try it here." I shrug, our fingers still holding the pieces together.

"I'm sorry for what I said to you. The day she died," he says, looking at the broken pieces in our hands. "I didn't mean it, Birdie, any of it. I want you to know that."

Every word he threw at me that day hurt. I never expected him to apologize, but now that he has, I know I needed it.

"You know, it was the part about the color-coded lists that really got me," I say, lightening the mood just enough to make him laugh under his breath.

Then, we work in silence, finding a kind of cadence with one another like we do when we hike—putting the pieces together, holding them in place long enough for them to set, before moving on to the next one. And the next. Until all the pieces are back together, lined with wet black slip.

"So you and Mandy, huh?" I ask, wrapping the broken-but-not-broken pieces in plastic bags. "I'll admit I was surprised..." *that you invited me over to see her and kept texting me after.*

He jerks around from where he's standing at the sink. "What?" He grabs a towel to dry his hands, dropping it on the table before walking across the room to me, plucking the toothpick from his mouth. "Is that what you think, Birdie? I'm with *Mandy*?"

He reaches a hand toward me but pauses midair, like he isn't sure if he should go any farther, before dropping it back by his side.

My cheeks fill with air before deflating with a whoosh. "I mean, she was in your house, next to you at the funeral, and accusing me of sleeping with her husband. So...yes?"

"Birdie, no. *No!*" He shakes his head, rubbing a hand across his forehead. "Is that why you've been avoiding me? Because of Mandy?"

I wring a sponge over a bucket of clean water. "Bo, you told me to come over, and she walked onto your front porch." I glance at him. "How would you interpret that?"

"She just showed up!" he cries. "I didn't know she was coming, definitely didn't invite her bu—"

"You don't owe me an explanation, Bo," I say, trying to maintain an air of confidence over what I'm saying. Trying to ignore the fact that him not being with Mandy is making the strangest feelings plant in me like a seed and shoot roots and blooms in a million directions within me. Trying to ignore how everything I'm saying is the exact opposite of what I actually want. "And, you know, you married her, so I wouldn't blame you if you were with her. It would probably be good for Lucy."

He nods silently, jaw clenching in the way it does when he's grinding out words he's trying not to say.

"And"—I clear my throat, dropping my eyes to the table I'm wiping—"I think it's best if we're just friends anyway." I ignore the way the words burn the entire inside of my mouth like I've just filled it with acid. "I have my routines, and Huck will be in the mix next week. And I'm six months into thirty-seven, which means I have six more months to go. I'm not sure what the statistics look like for me if I make it to thirty-eight, but either way, it's for the best if I figure it out alone, you know. Not drag a bunch of people down with me. Or distract me. Or whatever."

I reach across the table to give it a final wipe. He leans against the edge, jaw tight, hand scrubbing across his beard.

"And," I say, the ache in my throat making it hard to say the next words. "My dad said he'd take Huck if I…if you changed your mind."

His eyes widen. "No, Birdie. I didn't change my mind. Not about Huck…about any of it."

I nod; we're silent. All the words and events of the last weeks and months hanging in the familiar earthy-scented air. He moves first, grabbing the tools we were using and rinsing them in the sink. Music is the only sound other than our movements.

At the rack, I lift the bag slightly off the vase I made with flowers earlier in the week, spinning it carefully to see how it's drying.

I stop. On the smooth side, *Bo loves Birdie* is scribbled into the clay.

How?

I look over my shoulder, gaze catching with Bo's across the room. When his eyebrows lift slightly, mine do the same. It's all the confirmation I need: he did this.

I look back at the piece, his name and mine, ignoring the confusing knots that my insides are tying with each other, then cover it with the bag.

I glance back at him, not moving from my spot at the rack.

"I like that one," he says, leaning against the doorway, arms folded over his chest.

I'm quiet, looking back to the bag that now covers his words.

"I need you to know how sorry I am, Birdie," he says to my back. Neither of us moving. "If you don't want to be with me, I'll learn to deal with that, but I need you to know I don't blame you. If anything, I should be thanking you…for being with her when she couldn't trust me to be. To see what she needed when I couldn't." His voice cracks, just barely but I hear it, and I swipe my tears before they reach my cheek.

I clear my throat and nod, unable to look at him.

Then, a deep breath.

Finally, I face him. "Okay."

He smirks, familiar. "Okay."

Turning off the radio and the lights, we walk to the front door together. Close enough to touch but not.

"Did Mandy sign the papers?" I ask, lifting my chin to face him when I step onto the front porch.

"I thought it didn't matter," he says, teasing. "But yes. After she spoke to you." He raises his eyebrows but doesn't say anything else.

I laugh under my breath, backing up toward the railing, looking over my shoulder before walking down the porch steps. "You're kind of an asshole, I don't blame her for divorcing you."

He grins but doesn't make a move toward me. "If you say so, Birdie."

His voice—words—sound easy. *So* easy.

"Hey," I call from the middle of the yard.

He lifts his chin.

"Lock up, will ya? Apparently, this is my house now."

He nods, lips pulling to a small smile.

We look at each other longer than makes sense before I get in my minivan, and he turns to lock the door then jogs to his Jeep.

I let out a breath—one that I've possibly been holding for weeks—and try to make sense of what he's said.

Mandy is gone. Bo is divorced. He doesn't blame me.

Three simple truths that flip my reality.

I take out my phone, pull up Libby's name, and write, *Hey, sorry for the vanishing act. Yoga soon?*

Her response is instant. *Thank God you wrote, I was going to send John over to your house to do a wellness check soon. Tell me when and I'll be there. Xo*

For the first time since Veda died, I realize I'm smiling.

Forty-nine

"I WONDER IF HUCK'S nervous," I whisper, looking down at him before pushing open the heavy doors of the courthouse.

He shakes his head. "Huck can't wait to live with you and George Strait," he shouts. Even though I'm nervous as hell, I laugh as I squeeze his hand.

With Huck in his red bow tie and me in a pair of navy dress pants and a bright red shirt, with my hair pinned back, hand in hand, we step into the courtroom at 8:50 A.M..

When the doors open, I freeze.

The room is full. Grabbing the handle of the door, I crane my neck to double-check the number on the outside. This is it, but it can't be right. The only people we're expecting are my dad and Sharon. Do strangers sit in on these things? Seems, well, strange.

"Birdie, look at all the people!" Huck shouts, turning all the heads to face us.

And that's when I see—they aren't strangers. The courtroom is filled with people I know.

Monica—*Monica?*—sees me first and jumps from her seat. "Today is your day, girl!" She hugs me. "This is my husband, Roger, and our three kids, Natalia, Indigo, and Raven."

I shake their hands, staring at her, stunned. "How did you even know about this?"

She chuckles with a playful slap on my arm. "Birdie, how do you think?" Her eyes drop to Huck. "And you must be Huck!"

His eyes widen as he steps behind me, gripping my hand tight.

She smiles at him, gives me a wink, then takes her seat next to her family.

I keep walking.

Then Sam—*with one of his sons?* "Sam?" I ask, shaking his son's hand whom I haven't seen since I started working for him.

"Bah." He swats a hand through the air. "Don't get full of yourself, you still ain't got no tits, Bonnie." When I laugh, he smiles, and I don't miss the fact that he has his hearing aids in.

Next, Mabel appears, with a wink and a red-toothed grin, giving Huck a high five. "Something book-worthy is happening," she sings, pulling her notepad out of her waistband—giraffe print today—and taps the cover with her pen.

I snort a laugh, glancing over her shoulder at a white-haired gentleman in a grey suit.

"Who's this?" I ask.

"My current muse, Birdie dear," she says with a shimmy of her hips and coy smile before taking her seat.

I keep walking. *Is that Buddy the cook from Mountain Farm?* When he smiles and waves, I realize it is. Next to him—my yoga teacher?

What on earth...

There's Libby, John, and both their boys. Libby gives me a boa constrictor hug and John hooks his arm around my neck with a gruff, "What would George Strait have to say on a day like this, Birdie?"

I hug him back, but over his shoulder, I only see the familiar shades of brown looking back at me. *Bo.*

"'It Just Comes Natural,'" I say, not pulling my eyes off Bo even as John laughs loudly in my ear.

Huck tugs my hand as we approach the front of the courtroom. On one side, it's my dad and Sharon. On the other, Bo and Lucy.

"Hi, Huck!" Lucy squeaks. "I wonder what you think about Birdie being your mom today."

"Huck can't wait," Huck shouts. "Hi, Bo! I wanted you to be here. Birdie said you'd probably have to work."

He kneels down next to him. "Sometimes I keep secrets like this from Birdie," he says with a grin. "I wouldn't miss this for the world."

Then, like I'm not on the brink of bursting from the overwhelming beauty of what's happening, Huck hugs Bo, and the first tear slides down my cheek.

"Huck," I pat his back. "We have to take our spot. The judge will be in soon."

Grabbing his hand again, I pause, eyes on Bo. "Did you do this?" I ask, knowing the answer he'll never say.

He shrugs, looks around the full room, then says, "These people aren't here for me, Birdie, they're here for you. For someone who wants to figure it out alone, you have a lot of people by your side. Who love you." With a click of his tongue, he takes a seat.

This whole scene I've walked into is barely registering in my brain. I'm adopting a kid, and a room full of people showed up for me to do it—because Bo invited them. When Huck tugs my hand, I force the enormity of that out of my mind.

Before taking our spots, I give my dad a hug, who gives me a knowing smile, then shake Sharon's hand.

"You made it," she says.

I smile. "That we did."

When the judge walks in, an older woman with greyish-black hair pulled back, Huck and I stand in front of the court. She smiles as she takes a seat. "Hello there, Huck. That's a sharp looking bow tie, young man."

He looks at her and shrinks behind me, which makes her chuckle. "You have a room full of people here for you today too. You're a lucky kid."

When she gives her attention to the papers stacked in front of her, I glance over my shoulder to Bo. *He's a lucky kid because Bo did this.*

A question from the judge pulls my attention away from him.

After signing too many papers and reciting the required legal statements, the judge looks at Huck and gives him another warm smile.

"You're getting a family today, young man," she says. "Judging by the number of people here, a big one." A few chuckles come from behind us.

"Birdie's going to be my mom!" he shouts at her.

I look down at him, stunned. I knew that's what was happening, but to hear my name linked to the word *mom* holds a power I wasn't prepared for. Then he adds, "Huck wonders what it's going to be like!"

She laughs, eyes lifting to mine with the same warm expression on her face. "It's going to be wonderful."

Huck moves his legs in place next to me like there's too much energy in them, and I don't hide my laugh or the watery line that fills my eyes.

I can't change that Veda died or how Bo and I couldn't make it work, but standing here, next to a little boy who can't wait to come home with me, with a room full of people that want to see that happen, things feel less grim. Like life, a constant changing of seasons, knows just how to give what needs to come next.

"Sometimes, kids like to bang the gavel to make it official," she says to Huck, holding the wooden hammer in the air toward him.

He looks up at me and I nod, which is all he needs to run to where she's sitting. He takes the gavel from her and bangs it down loudly.

"I'm going to call Birdie Mom now!" he yells.

She laughs while everyone else claps, not a dry eye in the room, as he runs back to me.

"I love you, Huck," I tell him, crouching down to hug him.

"I love you, Mom!" he shouts back, nearly making me collapse with the breathtaking beauty of the sound.

Then we're outside, the usually elusive November sun shining brightly, warming us in the cool air.

It's another round of hugs and *thank yous* to everyone that showed up for us. Happy tears never stop falling down my cheeks for the people I didn't know to dream of wanting to be here for me.

At the very end, Bo's waiting, leaning against a column—looking way too good in a button-down white shirt, blue jeans, and blazer with his hair pushed back—and Huck instantly runs over to him, giving him a high five.

"Birdie's my mom," he says loudly. "We've been watching you build your cabin. It's almost done!"

Bo laughs. "Close, but there's still that pipe that needs a toilet," he says, tapping his chin, making Huck bark out one of his laughs.

My eyes are glued to Bo. Once again, *He's here!* clashes with *He's. Here.*

My dad walks up, extending his hand out toward him. "Good to see you again, Bo."

"Greg," Bo says, shaking his hand. "Big day for this guy." He tilts his head toward Huck.

My dad smiles, looking at the beaming eight-year-old. "It is." He looks at me, then, "Huck, Lucy's at the fountain over there and you can make wishes with pennies. I think we should try that out. Maybe wish for Birdie to take us to get some ice cream."

That's all it takes, and they're both gone, Huck running at full speed.

Then it's staring: me at Bo, Bo at me.

"Thank you for coming," I finally manage to say. "And for whatever source of wizardry this was." I gesture to the people around us.

He laughs under his breath. "No wizardry. Turns out, people want to show up if you let them."

I look around, all the people that I know and love that I never considered as feeling the same about me. Here. Loving me right back.

And Bo.

As much as I don't want it to be true, as much as I want to protect him from all the ugly that my life might contain, I love him. Endlessly. Looking at him look at me, I know it. Regardless of my genes and what that may or may not mean for the rest of my life.

I love him the way Veda hoped I would.

"B—"

"Daddy! I'm starving! Can we go eat?" Lucy's voice makes my own vanish as she runs up to us.

Bo's gaze drops to hers before lifting to mine. "Lunch sounds great, Lucy Goosey. Tell Huck and Birdie bye."

It's hugs, high-fives, and my unspoken words a whisper in the wind.

"Mabel," I call across the parking lot as my dad helps Huck settle in his seat in the minivan. She looks at me, smiles, and waves. I hold up one finger to her jogging to the car where she and *her muse* are standing.

"I'm thinking maybe I made a mistake or something," I tell her, shoving my hands in my coat pockets.

She raises her eyebrows, curious look on her face. "Really? How so?"

"With Bo..." I shake my head, not sure what I'm trying to say. "When I said maybe my story is one that doesn't end with love, I'm wondering if I got that wrong."

"Of course you got it wrong!" she says, both hands in the air.

"So now what? What should I do? Go tell him?" My eyes scan the parking lot until they land on the cherry-red Jeep and him helping Lucy into the back seat.

She chuckles. "Show, Birdie dear, don't tell."

I close my eyes, trying to understand what she means. How do I show Bo anything like what he just did for me in this courthouse? In the last six months of my life?

My eyes fly open. "Mabel, I have an idea."

Fifty

Libby loves Christmas; it's something I never would have guessed if it wasn't for the scene in front of me. Standing in the parking lot of her bar that's now completely covered in strings of lights the Friday before Thanksgiving, I laugh when she steps next to me.

"Christmas lights already?" I ask, squinting from how bright they all are. There are so many bulbs on the roof, Libby's Outpost is probably visible from space.

"If I didn't think it would hurt business, I'd keep them up all year," she says with a wide, red-lipped smile. "Huck with your dad?"

"Yep—first sleepover with Grandpa." My heart warms as I say it. Huck was so excited when I dropped him and George Strait off with a casserole dish of meatballs.

"You ready for this?" she asks, tilting her head toward the bar as we start to walk to the door. "You look hot as hell, by the way."

I snort a laugh at her compliment, tugging at the sleeves of the black sweater I'm wearing. I wore my best jeans, fitted and flared, black heels, and enough mascara for an entire fleet of models at a fashion show. My hair is up, because though it's cold, I'm so nervous I'm sweating.

"Does nervous as hell count as ready?"

She laughs as we stop at the door. "Always."

I bite my lip, rubbing my palms on my jeans. "Is everything ready? Is he here yet?"

"It is and he is," she says, squeezing my arms. "And Mabel," she adds, raising amused eyebrows.

She hugs me before slipping inside.

I take one final deep breath. "Here we go, Veda."

When I started my thirty-seventh year, I knew that the best thing for me was to keep my head down and cling to routines and lists. Alone. I thought living meant having a body that didn't have cancer. When I met Bo, I realized I had grossly misunderstood what I knew. About everything.

After adopting Huck in a room full of people, I knew I never wanted to be alone again. I want to spend the rest of my days—however many I get—with people that make me feel alive. I know why Veda ended her own pain and prevented Bo from seeing it, but my heart aches every time I think of her last breaths being taken without him. Or anyone.

When I talked to Mabel in the parking lot, she smiled when I asked, *Does the story always end with the man engineering the big gesture?*

She let out a thrilled, *That's what I'm talking about!* and we got to work—with Libby's help.

Now, as I stand hiding behind a Christmas tree that's stuffed in a corner behind the bar watching Bo—who's sitting on a barstool scrolling his phone with a toothpick rolling across his lips—I want to call the whole thing off and just go to him.

But I don't.

I wait.

"Whatcha doin'?" Libby asks him, leaning on the bar with a sinister smile that almost makes me laugh.

He drops his phone on the bar with an unamused sigh. "Nothing." He pauses as the DJ announces the next karaoke singer, earning a small applause, then, "Why am I here?"

She scoffs. "Rude," she says over the atrocious rendition of Willie Nelson. "But you've been a hermit, and John pissed me off." She wipes the bar in front of him with a rag. "Him having an extra kid seems fair."

Bo laughs, lifting his beer to his lips. "Christmas lights?"

"He wouldn't know holiday cheer if it bit him in the ass!" she defends.

I bite back my own laugh—because I can imagine the whole scenario between the two of them.

"Seriously, Bo. You laugh, but you kn—"

A man taps Bo on his shoulder, pulling him from Libby's rant.

"You Bo?" he asks.

"That's me," Bo responds, lifting his beer toward him.

"Dropped this." The man hands him a blue sticky note then walks away.

Bo's eyes drop to it, eyebrows pinched. I can't see it, but I know what it says.

On a scale of 1-10, 10

"What's that?" Libby asks, leaning over the bar to read.

He looks around the room—almost confused—then back to the note.

"I don't know," he says, showing her before sticking it on the bar.

"Bo?" Another tap on his shoulder, a woman this time. "I think you dropped this."

He takes the next blue sticky note, which I know says *Personality, 10.*

Tap.

"Bo, this is for you."

Single? Yes.

Another.

Lives alone? No, but kid is cute and can sleep through <u>anything.</u>

With every tap on his shoulder, he looks around the crowded bar, slow-to-grow smile widening, and I have to put my own hand over my mouth to physically stop myself from calling for him as I watch from behind the tree.

Tap.

"Some girl told me to give this to you, hot stuff," a woman says. Not just any woman.

He snorts a disbelieving, "Mabel?" then looks down at the note, grinning wide.

Puts Mabel's smut to shame.

"You've got main male character energy, Bo. Romp her socks off," she says with a tawdry wink before dancing away from him with hands over her head, one holding a gin and tonic, the other a notebook, cheetah-print covered hips rocking to the music.

When Bo told me he loved me in the grocery store, he told me he'd give me a hundred reasons why if I wanted him to. I know he was just saying that, but I really did. I easily came up with one hundred reasons why Bo makes my life better and I never want to let him go. So I wrote them down, passed them out, and they are now being hand delivered to him by the people around Libby's.

"If it doesn't work out with her, I'm single," I hear the dark-haired woman say, biting her lip, handing him one that makes him laugh loudly, which I know must say, *Does dirty things to my ear.*

They keep coming, one after the other, in perfect order.

His eyes are up, scanning. He stands. A line of people around him, arranging themselves numerically by comparing notes. I laugh at the chaos of it all.

"Where is she?" he asks the woman who's reaching the next sticky note toward him.

She shakes her head adamantly. "We aren't allowed to tell you. We were told to give these directly to you in order."

"Wha—" His eyes catch on Libby, leaning behind the bar, Cheshire grin on her face.

"Sit down, Bo. Pam Beesly is about to rock your world."

He looks around again, I swear seeing me—feeling me—but does as she says, ridiculously handsome smile on his face.

He takes the notes, reading every single one. The ones I don't need to see because I know what they say.

You dance to George Strait.

You learned to talk to Huck.

I'm happier when I'm with you.

Your cabins feel like castles.

You know how to see people.

You love me with my scars.

Repeatedly, his eyes lift, scan the room, and he laughs.

Then come the final few:

Bo, I love you.

You showed me a life I didn't know I could have.

I'm sorry for not seeing it.

But what I'm not sorry about...

Is what you're about to do...

Because you love me too.

One hundred sticky notes cover the bar, and between his smile and the way I see him looking for me—with joyful desperation—it's the most amazing thing I've ever witnessed. More amazing than a summit that overlooks the mountains I've grown up in or a field set ablaze by an unexpected late season bloom of wildflowers.

Then right on schedule: "Alright, folks, next up we have Bo Monroe. Bo, come on up," the DJ says, tonight wearing a blue polyester shirt with his hair pulled back in a low ponytail.

Bo shoots Libby with a leveling glare, but she's enjoying it too much to care. Hands cupping her mouth, her long, loud, "Wooo!" whips the bar up into a frenzy, and I laugh—louder this time.

I hate you, he mouths to her, taking off his coat and dropping it on the back of his stool.

When she laughs harder, he waves his middle finger at her.

"That's my wife, asshole!" a familiar voice jokes. *John.*

"Who's watching our kids?" I hear Bo ask, again looking around the room, no doubt for Lucy this time.

"My mom," John says. "You think I'm missing out on this mushy bullshit, you pussy-whipped bastard?" He slaps Bo's back and gives him a final shove toward the small stage.

With that, I slip out from my hiding spot behind the tree, shoot Libby a grin, and move toward the crowd.

Fifty-one

BEHIND THE MIC, BO squints toward the crowd with a half-amused, half-annoyed smirk pulling at his lips. I can tell he can't see me, but it feels like he's looking right at me.

"I'm only singing if Birdie comes out," he says into the mic.

Instantly, the room erupts in a loud *boo!*, and I don't bother hiding my amusement from the chair I'm sitting in that's hidden by the crowd.

"No can do, Bo my boy," the DJ says smugly. "Birdie gave us very strict rules. She will come out when she thinks you mean it."

With his words, the crowd howls.

Bo waves a palm toward them like a white flag, gripping the mic in the other.

Ready or not, the music starts. The familiar opening chords to George Strait's "Check Yes or No" begin playing.

I know he recognizes it because his head drops back with a loud laugh.

Then another when he sees I've changed the lyrics that he starts to sing along to.

"It started way back in summer,

I sat at a bar beside Pa-a-am Beesly.

A blue dress, wild hair, and a sticky note,

She kissed me in her minivan, but then she went away,"

He stumbles through it, laughing, and with the last choppy line, the crowd howls. Again, his eyes dart around the room.

New words pop onto the screen, but before he can try to sing them, it's my voice through the speakers. "I don't know, everyone; does Bo sound sincere about this? And is it even singing if you have a toothpick in your mouth?" I say into my own microphone I've been holding from where I sit, still out of his line of sight.

Another wave of boos comes in response.

"I can't be sincere if I can't see you," he says into his mic, smile wide as he plucks the toothpick out of his mouth.

"Keep singing, Bo," I tell him.

So he does.

He butchers the chorus, but the audience is nice enough to sing along and help him through it.

He's nearing the end, singing the final "Check Yes or No" when I step out of the crowd, standing in front of him.

"Yes or no, Bo? What's it going to be?" I ask with a grin into my mic, staring at him, staring at me, heart pounding in my chest.

He doesn't hesitate. He drops the mic, literally, and takes one step off the stage, one more to me, and wraps his arms around my waist.

"Yes, Birdie."

As everyone in Libby's Outpost roars, a smile splits my face in half, and he presses his mouth to mine. With two fistfuls of his shirt, I pull him to me, kissing him through the cheers of the bar. The taste and feel of him bringing every piece of me home.

When the DJ calls the next singer, I lean close and whisper, "Tell me something you like."

"You loving me," he says, tucking a stray strand of hair behind my ear. "You?"

"You singing bad karaoke." I smile; he kisses me again. Then I take his hand. "I have another surprise for you."

I blow a kiss to Libby across the bar and catch the wink that Mabel gives me as I lead us out the door.

We barely make it outside before his mouth is on mine again, making us stumble across the parking lot. Then we're at my mini-van—parked in a quiet corner of the parking lot—and I smile.

"That was amazing," he says, grazing my jaw with his knuckles before giving me a light kiss.

"Veda told me to let you love me," I tell him.

He laughs, something flashing in his eyes, and says, "Of course she did."

Looking at him is like the first night we met, except not. I'm not a nervous Pam Beesly, I'm an unguarded Birdie. He's not a stranger in a bar, he's the man I fell in love with.

I kiss him again, hoping it feels like one hundred love notes to him, because it certainly does to me.

"You bring me out here to make out in the freezing cold?" he asks, smiling against my skin as he peppers a trail of kisses across my jaw.

"Actually," I say, pulling the back door of the minivan open. "I brought blankets and a heater that plugs into the dash this time," I announce proudly.

He looks inside. All the back seats have been stowed and there are blankets—and pillows—covering the floor. A little heater glows a faint red between the front seats.

He laughs, scrubbing a hand across his handsome face. "You trying to take advantage of me, Pam Beesly?"

"Mabel says phenomenal makeup sex is part of every good story," I tell him, biting my lip.

"Well, if Mabel says so..." he says, fingers flexing to my hips, smile never leaving his lips.

"And according to my little black book of data," I begin, voice low, my final stokes to the flames already burning, "we don't even need a condom tonight."

His response to this is a needy growl against my skin followed by his mouth moving to my...earlobe.

Then, like we were never even never us at all, he pulls me into the blanket-filled minivan and closes the door.

Fifty-two

"Daddy! It's snowing!" Lucy's high-pitched voice cuts through the quiet morning. "And Santa came!"

"Mom!" Huck shouts. "Mom, it's Christmas!"

I force my eyes open as Bo groans next to me.

Head on my pillow, I smile at him. "Merry Christmas."

He kisses me on the forehead to the tune of another shrill, "C'mon, Daddy! It's snowing!" that pulls us both out of bed.

For the first time since I was a kid, Christmas is actual magic. The lights shine brighter and the songs sound sweeter because of the people I have around me.

Staring out the window of Bo's cabin, everything around us is bright white.

Huck in lizard-covered pajamas, and Lucy in her reindeer night-gown, run outside screaming with George Strait.

"Mom, it's snowing!" Huck yells. And like it does every time, the title makes a million flowers bloom beneath my ribs. Because no, I didn't grow Huck in my body or nurse him from my breasts, but he's mine just the same.

I step onto the porch next to Bo and he drapes a blanket around my shoulders as we watch the pajama-clad kids run and scream. "In case they didn't mention it in your adoption papers, every Christmas for the next decade of your life will include sleep deprivation," he says with a sleepy smile, sipping his coffee.

I snort out a laugh. "They forgot to mention it, but I think it's worth it."

When I lean against him, I notice the slightest tinge of a headache forming and rub my temples.

"You okay?" he asks.

I smile, forcing the mental dominoes that want to fall regarding all the reasons why I might have a headache to stay put. "Fine, just a headache. My body needs coffee."

He hands me his mug—of course he does—and wraps an arm around me as I take a sip.

My dad pulls up in his truck. Opening his door, he gives us a wave before bending over, rolling a ball with the little bit of snow, and lobbing it at the kids with a loud roar.

I laugh.

For a single white Christmas morning, I have everything. Noise I didn't know my quiet was missing, chaos I didn't know my order needed. The marvelous unpredictability of bringing more beating hearts into the rhythm of my own.

Palm to palm, fingers intertwined on one hand and his coffee in the other, Bo and I stand watching our lives happen in front of us.

The moments that will fill frames and become our stories should we be lucky enough to get so old we retell them too many times.

My dad reaches into the passenger side of his truck and pulls out boxes wrapped in reds and greens, making the kids shriek and file into the house—snow-dusted boots form a trail to the Christmas tree.

"Merry Christmas, Little Bird," my dad says giving me a hug around the presents as he steps onto the porch.

"Merry Christmas, Dad."

Then it's piles of presents and mounds of shredded wrapping paper while I make breakfast—pancakes with organic flour, raw milk from a local dairy, and North Carolina tapped maple syrup.

It's as beautiful as one of Mabel's books, Sam's stories of Vietnam, and Veda's clay pots. As I flip a pancake in the pan, the fact I've spent so much time fighting this makes me ache for all I might have missed out on.

"Merry Christmas," Bo says, slipping his arms around me as I stand at the stove, still in sweatpants and a T-shirt, kissing me lightly on the temple.

I hum with contentment, leaning against him.

His hand grazes the length of my left arm down to my hand where he traces my fingers that rest on the counter, fumbling with something before wrapping my hand in his. I look down at our interlaced fingers, seeing what he's done: on my finger is a ring. Not big and bold, but an oval opal on a gold band. I put the spatula down and turn to face him, my mouth hanging open.

"It was Gran's," he tells me, using his fingers to spin the ring around my own finger. "She wanted you to have it...when you were ready."

"For what?" I ask, knowing but not.

"To love me forever," he says easily, pulling my hand to his mouth and kissing my palm. "To let me love *you* forever. In sickness and health," he says, with another kiss to my palm. Then another.

My eyes burn. "You want to marry me?"

He laughs. "Yes, Birdie. I want to marry you. I know it hasn't been long, but it's been long enough for me to know I don't want any more time to pass without us and I—"

I cut him off with a loud squeal, sliding my arms around his neck, jumping into his arms with my legs wrapped around his waist, my mouth slamming into his. "Yes, Bo," I say between kisses. "Yesyesyes."

Because yes, I don't want to live in a life where I'm not Bo's and he's not mine for as long as our forever gets to be.

Tangled in each other in a kitchen Bo built, it's a, "Get a room, perverts," that pulls us apart in a laugh. John stands looking like Santa's outcast cousin in the doorway followed by Libby who fits easily into his side.

"You give it to her?" she asks.

"I did," Bo says, taking a casual sip of his coffee.

"Welcome to the family, Pam Beesly!" she shrieks, running across the kitchen to wrap me in a hug.

Laughter turns to the happiest of tears the instant she's next to me.

When the food is finally ready, it's a roaring sound of everyone talking over everyone else as we take our seats.

"Cool table," Libby says, putting a platter of pancakes in the center of it.

At her words, both Bo and my dad smile knowingly, raising their mimosas in a silent cheers to one another.

"It is, isn't it?" I say, looking at the work of art we are gathering around that was once a busted cookie slab in my dad's shop. The way Bo tells it, the second he saw the table he knew he had to have it. The way my dad tells it, the second he saw me with Bo, he knew where the table belonged.

With any luck, it's a debate I'll get to listen to for years to come.

"And these bowls." Libby lifts up the bowl of fruit in her hand, tilting her neck slightly to see the bottom. "Did Veda make these, Bo?"

This time, it's me who smiles. The bowl in her hand is whole yet cracked, held together with colors that showcase the broken instead of concealing it.

"You could say that," he says, squeezing my knee under the table.

It's a Christmas meal filled with screaming kids and unfiltered laughs and a man's ring on my finger.

For the rest of the day, I barely notice the headache I can't shake.

Fifty-three

Eyes open, the room is bright. Almost blindingly so.

I glance at the clock—*it's after ten?*

The bedroom door swings open, and Bo stands with a cup of coffee and a grin, dimples carved into his cheeks.

"Hey, sleepyhead," he says with a chuckle. "Christmas wore you out more than the kids."

I smile, rubbing my head and the slight headache that's lingered nearly a week.

"It's so late," I say, sitting up. "I don't know what's going on with me, I'm so tired."

He sits on the bed as he hands me a mug of coffee, kissing the side of my head. "Of course you're tired. John was an asshole and got the kids a keyboard for Christmas—we'll never sleep again."

I laugh softly, mentally trying to force myself to believe him, as I bring the mug to my lips.

As the days pass and nothing changes, I keep telling myself the same things. Lies on repeat.

I tell myself it's the stress of the holidays.

The stress of the last months.

The sound of the keyboard.

Just a cold.

But I know better. I know my body better.

Something is wrong.

When the first day of January comes, not only does the dull headache continue, but there's also a nausea that prevents me from keeping anything substantial down.

After I wake up three mornings in a row with a bloody nose, I can't ignore it anymore.

All the hours at the gym, organic ingredients, and preventative surgeries haven't saved me. As ready as I thought I'd be for it, I'm not.

"Bo, I'm sick," I tell him as we lie in his bed one morning. "I'm going to the doctor tomorrow."

He interlaces his fingers in mine, brown eyes seeing all of me. "I'm going with you."

Both relief and devastation sweep through me with his words. Because I need him with me as much as I hate the thought of him seeing.

The falling apart.

The decline that's coming.

But I don't argue.

Hand in hand, we sit in the exam room, waiting for the worst.

After blood is drawn, urine samples taken, and all vital signs checked, the doctor comes in.

"Birdie, it's good to see you," she says, smiling.

As much as I want to say, "You too," I stay quiet.

It does nothing to prepare me for what she says next—nothing can.

She shows me my chart, pointing to indicators and numbers, and the world stops spinning.

I hear, "It's early," and, "You're young and healthy."

But it's a scream that comes out of my mouth anyway and a sob-filled, "No!" that bounces off the sterile walls.

Because how? How the hell did this happen?

I sag in my seat, the gravity of the moment pulling me to the floor. Bo grips onto me and holds me both upright and together. Arms wrapped around me, he hushes me through my sobs.

"Birdie, I'll be right here with you the whole time," he whispers into my hair as he rubs my back. "We got this."

And as devastatingly hopeless as that feels, I know he will. Because he always is. Because Bo is a goodness I didn't know to look for, and I know will stay, for better or worse.

He'll love me, and I'll let him.

Epilogue

Bo, One Year Later

I'VE NEVER BEEN MUCH for visiting graves—of course not. Someone that hikes in the woods and calls it church wouldn't cling to something so traditional. The truth is, it never had anything to do with being traditional or not, it just never made sense before now.

Staring at the familiar name on the headstone, I know my life would have been so different without her. Lacking. Maybe even meaningless.

Now, I just wish she was here to see it all. *Them.* Just once. She would have loved us. She already did.

It was as if that day we got the news in that doctor's office was what she had been preparing me—us—for all along.

"You were right," I say with a slight laugh, kneeling down on the near frozen January ground. I put a hand on the stone, cool and smooth. "About everything."

Then, like she's there, a wind blows by, shaking the sticks on the bare trees. A rustle of hello or goodbye or both. Or, knowing her, neither.

When I stand, two little hands fit into each of mine—Lucy and Huck stand by my side, smiling.

"Huck wonders if you miss her," he says in his loud voice.

I nod, squeezing his hand, looking at his now nine-year-old face and smiling. "Every day." I mean it. Every day I miss her, wishing we would have had just a little more time together.

"Me too," Lucy says, dropping my hand to wrap my leg in a hug. "Can we go home now, Daddy? It's freezing out here."

I chuckle as I look at them—not bound by blood, but siblings through and through.

"We just got out here!" I tease, earning a unified groan from both of them.

"Hey, don't leave before I get to say hi," a voice calls from behind.

Both kids giggle as Birdie slips her hand around my waist.

I look at her, honey-colored hair glowing in the morning light, puffs of cold air from her warm breath framing her beautiful face.

"Little Veda wants to say hi too," she says, bouncing the baby—our daughter—wrapped in a blanket on her hip.

I take the baby from her, pressing my lips to the soft hair on her forehead.

Birdie looks at Huck and Lucy. "Van is running and warm if you two want to go get in."

With their familiar yells and giggles, they leave us behind, zigzagging through the cemetery.

Birdie smiles, looking at the headstone. "She have anything good to say today?"

"You know Gran—she made me promise not to tell," I say, laughing under my breath, palm running along little Veda's cheek.

"I know how that goes." Her brown eyes dance as she looks from me to the baby before leaning her head on my shoulder as we start to walk toward the van. She looks like an angel; they both do. So perfect it's hard to believe they're real. Hard to breathe. Hard to look away.

Yet—here they are.

When we got the news she was pregnant, she spiraled fast.

First, she had to figure out how this happened. When I playfully explained to her how babies were made, she didn't laugh. Actually, she cried.

The explanation she eventually came to was simple: she read the numbers wrong the same day she told me I didn't have to wear a condom.

Then came the part when she really came unglued. She printed out every statistic and study she could find on why having this child with her genetic mutation, at her age, was going to be the worst thing she could do to another person. She repeated the phrase *a death sentence* on a loop. Sometimes through tears, other times gritted teeth. I've never seen someone stretch their neck as much as she did in those weeks.

I let her spiral. I listened and never argued.

Then, one day, when she was still sleeping, I took the one hundred sticky notes she had given me and put them on her nightstand in a stack with a note that said, *Without your death sentence, I wouldn't have these.*

That day, she drove to my office, swung my door open, and said, "Let's have a baby."

So we had a baby.

Veda Rose Monroe was born in September in the middle of the night.

In some kind of weird pool.

"It's a less shocking entry for the baby, Bo!" she argued.

I couldn't wrap my brain around it, but once Birdie got something in her mind, there was no talking her out of it. With her in the water and me holding onto her shoulders from outside of it, she brought our daughter into the world.

Over the course of the year, Birdie's days have changed. Sam moved in with one of his sons, and Mabel died one night from a heart attack...in bed next to her current muse. Birdie was sad, but she also said it was the only way for her to go.

She left Birdie two never-published manuscripts: one about a woman with too many rules who falls in love with a man who builds cabins, the other about a nun who fell in love with a groundskeeper.

In the quiet moments when she thinks nobody is watching, I see her reading them, smiling to herself. About me. Us. Love she never thought to believe in, a different life she didn't know could be real.

With her clients gone, Birdie decided it was time to leave the career she had chosen based on her belief of never living to old age. "Time to focus on today, Bo," she had said with a smile.

She turned Gran's house into a classroom studio where she teaches all the lessons Gran taught her to anyone that wants to put their hands in the clay. She does especially well with kids and the elderly, a surprise to no one.

"Tell me something you like," she says, smiling before leaning against me.

"Hmm..." I tap my chin, as if I don't say the same thing every time she asks. "You." I run my fingers through her blonde hair that looks like it's glowing in the sun, adding, "Here with me."

She smiles—somehow wider—like she always does.

"You?"

"Going home with you," she tells me easily, meaning it completely, before pulling away from me and dropping into her seat in the minivan.

She doesn't need me to tell her that I like that too—she already knows. Us spending our days in a cabin I built will always be the thing I like most.

We'll get married this fall at church—just her and me—in a field of wildflowers that nobody expects to see bloom. Turns out, all the rumors on the internet were wrong—it seems a man had planted the field in memory of his late wife who left him and his daughter too soon. The man, I learned over a busted cookie slab table one evening, said he felt her with him when wildflowers bloom.

Every time I look at Birdie, I know exactly how he feels.

I bet you are angry enough to spit fire.

You have every right to be, and I'm sorry.

I know what I've done to you. You might feel a bit robbed, like there could have been more of something. I'm here to tell you, there wouldn't have been. It was ending, and ultimately, I saved us both a lot of pain and a long goodbye.

I couldn't let you talk me out of it as much as I couldn't let you see me. You might not agree with my choices, but they were mine alone.

You will forgive me, and when you do, you will forgive Birdie.

She loves you, Bo, but what comes next will be a struggle for her. She might blame herself, might pull away. You'll have to keep showing up. Be as big a pain in the ass to her as she was to me.

Show her you love her. Show her that if she gets the kind of sick she expects she will, you'll be there.

I realize the irony of what I'm telling you—me shutting you out while telling you not to let someone else do it. But I'm an old woman and she's the love of your life. You'll have to trust I know these things.

When the time comes, I've included my ring for you to give her. It's not fancy, but neither is she. I can't control your life, but if you slide the ring on another woman's hand, I'll haunt you. I have no idea the logistics of that, but I'll figure it out. I managed to raise you through your teenage years, haunting is probably a cakewalk.

I want her to have the cabin. She belongs in the studio making beautiful things.

You were a light of my life, Bo.

She was too.

Love always,
Gran

Acknowledgments

A FEW YEARS AGO, a friend of mine from college was diagnosed with breast cancer. I watched her through pictures on social media and our occasional text messages as she endured treatments, shared struggles, and celebrated triumphs. She fought fiercely, always with a smile and piece of scripture. She called me one night, panicked because her daughter nearly knocked out a tooth. I remember thinking after we hung up, *How can you worry about a baby tooth when your body is attacking itself?* As someone who's prone to anxiety over something as simple as showing up to my kid's soccer game on time, I admired her ability to keep living. To worry about baby teeth and bedtime routines when there were such scarier things happening in her life.

In 2023, she passed away at the age of thirty-seven.

When Birdie became a person in my brain, I knew I wanted her anxious to the point of not living as loudly as she could, but figuring out the reason why came later. Finally, I thought of my friend. How she handled her diagnosis with so much more grace than I ever could have. Birdie Rose Hawkins came to life as her polar opposite—someone so focused on not dying there was no space for baby teeth or random phone calls with old friends.

To my first readers: thank you for falling in love with Bo, empathizing with Birdie, laughing at Mabel, and mourning Veda with me. Sonia, Tayler, Whitney, Sunnye, Jacki, and Morgann...I couldn't have written this without you.

To my beta readers and ARC team: YOU ARE THE REAL MVPs!

To my editing team: Victoria, thank you for helping me find the story in all my rambling, Ciara, for helping me find the words to tell it, and Kaitlin, for making sure it was ready for the world.

To my cover artist and friend Elise: thank you for your artistic heroism and making this story look like art.

To Kevin and the kids for dealing with me. When I'm lost in writing, when I'm stressed about riding in the Jeep with the doors off, when I google symptoms and diagnose us all with death. Thank you for spending every Sunday at church with me.

To Spotify and George Strait for playing the music that helped me write all these pages and my pottery teacher, Rick, who barely freaked out when I said, "Let's break some shit."

To all my readers: thanks for the time you give my words. I'll never quite believe I deserve to write things that people read. Thank you is too small, but it's all I have.

Lastly, to the internet and its infinite wisdom for connecting me with a stranger named Kate, who gave me insight into the BRCA genetic mutations while I was in the thick of writing. Additional information on breast cancer and the BRCA mutations was found at www.bebrcaware.com, www.breastcancer.org, and mayoclinic .org.

About the author

Ashley Manley is current writer and former just about everything else. When she isn't stringing words together on her computer, you can find her chasing her kids, reheating her coffee, or dreaming of her next grand adventure under tall trees. While she's lived a little bit of everywhere, North Carolina will always feel like home. To connect with Ashley, visit ashleymanleywrites.com or find her on Instagram @ashleymanleywrites.

<u>Other books by Ashley</u>
Every Beautiful Mile